D1104944

TIME WAS

TIME WAS

John Foster West

RANDOM HOUSE NEW YORK

FIRST PRINTING

 Published in New York by Random House, Inc., and simultaneously in Toronto, Canada, by Random House of Canada Limited.

Library of Congress Catalog Card Number: 65-10458

MANUFACTURED IN THE UNITED STATES OF AMERICA BY

The Book Press, Brattleboro, Vt.

DESIGN BY TERE LOPRETE

In memory of my mother and father,

JOHN WILSON WEST AND ELVIRA FOSTER WEST

Part One

TIME IS

JOHN MATLOCK WARD

I

THE LANKY YOUNG MAN crossed the sagging floor of what had been the kitchen and stepped into the middle room, where he had first seen the light of day. His arms below the sleeves of his sport shirt were tanned and muscular, contrasting with his uncalloused hands. The prominent nose and firm chin of his father blended with the high cheekbones and wide mouth inherited from his mother. He stopped, staring at the narrow little fireplace, wondering how it could possibly have kept anyone warm, much less two adults and a house full of younguns. Raising his eyes to the pine ceiling, parchment-brown with age, he studied the black disk above the mantel—the *farboard,* his father had called it—a disk where smoke from kerosene lamps, shedding their wan glow over more than ten thousand nights, had left their soot.

Turning, John Matlock Ward stared at the corner to the left of the window where his parents' bed had sat, where he had been conceived on a thin straw tick in early March of 1918 and from which he had been cast forth into a December world during the great flu epidemic by a mother who should have died but would not, for his sake. There in that corner old Doc Ellis and his mother had conspired against death until her fever-dried breasts could feed him.

John Ward remembered the old doctor's face as it had looked when he visited him at Northboro almost twenty years before. John had been close to twenty then, and Doc Ellis, still county superintendent of public health, was in his late seventies. The old man had been quite precise when he spoke of that particular birth, his blue eyes staring backward into another time. Now, standing there in the quiet room, John tried to visualize what it had been like that winter afternoon—his mother delirious, her fever over a hundred five, laboring by will power to bear him in time, the old doctor working to save them both; and Will Ward, his father, stooped and tired at fifty-three, standing by useless, staring through the window at West Mountain and refusing to look at his wife give birth.

John could visualize Doc Ellis in the sallow lamplight holding the gleaming baby by his heels, the crimson cord of life trailing backward and downward—and his mother, briefly alert, inquiring if it was a boy or girl child. That was how Doc Ellis had described it to John Matlock Ward, who had hitchhiked to Northboro on impulse to find out. John Ward's eyes shifted back to the window, and he stared down across the fallow slope at the carcass of the dead Juneapple tree, where Will Ward had stood in the cold drizzle of a winter twilight and buried the afterbirth in the muddy hillside, while inside, Doc Ellis still worked over his mother, the new baby now safe and warm beside her.

John thought of his mother's words almost a week later, or what the old doctor had said her words were. "It ain't right for the pore little thing to die, just cause it had to be borned at the bottom of the ladder." That was after her milk had dried up, after they had learned the only wet nurse left alive was dying, after they had been unable to find any such contraption as a bottle and nipple at Northboro. But Doc Ellis had solved the problem—the only solution left in a world of winter, war-shortage, and epidemic. Will Ward had whittled him a nipple out of a fishing cane, and Doc Ellis had covered it with several layers of cloth. The contrived nipple had been thrust into a quart liquor bottle half full of fresh milk, and John Ward had lived.

The air in the room was stale and dry. John Ward inhaled a chestful, but it seemed too thin. It did not satisfy his need, and his vague uneasiness would not go away. He felt like an intruder here in this locust-shell of a house. He knew he belonged at least briefly, yet he did not belong. The boy who had once lived here until he was ten, ages and ages ago, was someone else. He could not have come from this place, from Will Ward's loins, and worked his way up in the world as John Ward had. Not from here.

He turned his head quickly and looked behind him, but there was nothing there. No faded denim jacket and battered black hat on the rusty nail above where wood for the fireplace would have been piled. No dogeared hymnal and tunefork on the end of the mantel. No shadow of substance. Only flyspecked silence and a cobweb high up in one corner where a black spider appeared to watch him judicially.

He turned back, shifted his stare to the spot where the sewing machine had stood, then beyond, through the dirty panes to the narrow valley between this ridge and West Mountain. Seven generations have gazed across this Carolina hollow, this little horse's ass of a valley, at that forest, he thought. The first four John Wards for a lifetime, Dad for most of his life, me for only the first ten years. And now, today, I have brought my only begotten son to see it—to see it and to escape it, all in less than an hour. He started to look behind him again, but arrested the urge, instead running his fingers through thinning blond hair, still pensive. John Ward the first, back in the 1760s, followed by John Thomas Ward, et cetera, et cetera. Today the Roman and his troubles are ashes under Uricon, you-all. *Ubi sunt qui ante nos fuerunt.* Kindly translate, Professor Ward, for the illiterate bugs and spiders present. Gladly, sir. Where are they who were before us? And who gives a damn in this age of happy pills and sad tourists?

He crossed the floor and entered the unceiled room they had called the Big House. John Ward's mother stood in the middle of the floor holding the hand of three-year-old John Kelly—John Ward the seventh. She was looking at the hole in the wall, torn by a shotgun blast accidentally fired by Lynn, her oldest son, a long time ago. John looked at Vi Ward. Her white hair was cut short and wavy now, not bound in the neat bun he remembered from those days when her head was black as a crow's wing and her back just beginning to give way. Now she was so stooped the hump of her shoulders appeared at first glance to be a deformity. The fingers holding Kelly's pudgy hand were pied claws. Her face was wrinkled, like crumpled brown wrapping paper. The folds of pain in her forehead were plain to see, and could not be eased by a vinegar-soaked strip of brown paper bound in place with a white rag. The pain was too deep. It welled up, extending its tentacles through her body, from the cancer eating away deep inside her.

John frowned and looked away from her. "This room's bigger than I remember it," he said in the direction of one dark wall. "It's large enough for two rooms. I wonder why Dad built one room so large."

His mother turned toward him. "He aimed to build another wall along there, stretchin from the front door to the back one. Wanted to have him a hallway and two glass doors, like Cousin Bill had. But he never got around to it."

"He never got around to a lot of things," John said.

Vi Ward looked up at him, her blue eyes troubled. "No, he never got around to some things. They was a lot of things he never got around to. He was too busy workin."

John started to answer. He could not think of a reply, offhand, but his mother's remark acted as a catalyst to his jumbled thoughts. He acknowledged suddenly his real reason for returning here today, out of all the years left him. Until this moment he had evaded the problem, skirting the edge of purpose as though it were a guilty conscience. But now he knew why he had changed his plans at the last minute, had driven miles out of the way to pick up his mother and bring her along. More than once over the years he had thought of coming back, but he had rebelled against the urge, knowing all the while his road must loop back sooner or later and pass again through this valley where he had lived as a child. The answer to an old nagging question could be found only here, if at all. And suddenly time had run out. It had to be today, or never. Fall semester started in three days, and next year would be too late. Alvira Ward's doctor had made that point quite explicit, with his clipped antiseptic English and his bastard Latin.

No, Will Ward had never gotten around to a lot of things. Like talking to his namesake, explaining things to him so he did not have to find everything out after a bloody nose or stumped toe. And what could the old man have explained, for Christ's sake, without distorting it with superstition and folklore? When John Ward remembered his contempt as a smartassed teenager, his frequent scorn for what he had thought of as the ignorant old bastard who fathered him, he felt a flush of guilt along his neck. Even back then he had known, ignoring the knowledge, that there was more to his father than that. But he had been too busy planning his escape from Will Ward's harness to see anything but what he wanted to see.

Although the association was vague, his memory shifted to the time he had stood beside his father's grave in 1946 feeling no grief, not even regret, other than that his own son would perhaps stand beside his open grave someday. He had gritted his teeth and gazed at the bronze vault. But nothing had come out. He had groped in his pocket as he looked furtively about to see if his brothers or sisters, half-brothers or half-sisters, to see whether grandchildren or great-grandchildren were watching him. Then he had dropped a stub of pencil, all he could find in his pocket, into the grave. It had struck the vault, falling away beside it. The soft little *ping* had been hardly audible, had been hollow, as though the expensive metallic shell had not held all that was mortal of what had been a man. And still John Ward had felt nothing. Not then.

Turning away from Alvira Ward, he walked out onto the front porch. He tiptoed down the rickety steps and stood in the clay yard, mottled now with clumps of crabgrass and nettles. The pear tree just below the bank where the yard dropped off was dead from the top halfway down, the Juneapple tree farther down the slope, a skeleton of warped grey limbs. From the yard all the way to Stud Branch, the field where his father had once tilled corn was overgrown with field pines and sassafras bushes. The pasture along the lower side of West Mountain was pine forest now, and higher up, the poplars and hickories and sourwood bushes were dappled with fall color.

His mind came back to Will Ward, rejecting his efforts to concentrate on the landscape, to resist dwelling on his reason for being here on this fallow hillside. Jesus, how he had despised the old tyrant! How he had hated the goddamned senseless hoeing and the goddamned incessant plowing from dawn till dark, day in and day out! He had fought it as much as he could. At first he hid a book or a magazine in the bushes at the end of the corn rows and slipped behind a tree to read while Will was at the far end of the field. And at first Will kicked his rump or swatted him with a calloused paw, when he could slip up close enough. But later, after John reached a fleetfooted twelve, the old man only glowered at him dourly and muttered beneath his breath. And John had grinned back, openly, at the stupid old clodhopper.

Alert suddenly, John Ward hurried over to the porch to help his mother and Kelly down the steps. The boy stumbled, and John grabbed for him. He turned around when Becky, Lesa, and his wife came around the corner of the house, Ann mincing in her white pumps, careful not to soil them. John looked from his mother to Ann—erect, pretty, protected from the world by the thin navy-blue suit, her short auburn hair aglow in the light of the descending sun. He glanced at Becky, lithe, proud, and fourteen. He looked at five-year-old Lesa, redheaded and so freckled all the oak-stump water in Arabia could not rid her of the damned russet spots. John grinned when he remembered Jim's cure for removing freckles, a cure that had never worked, that had left his brother, Major Jim Ward, almost as freckled as the day he first used stump water.

"You see that dead tree standing above those loblolly pines yonder?" he asked, pointing. "That's a persimmon tree. Our only cow was killed under it once. Lightning struck the tree."

"Daddy, we've heard that story a thousand times," Becky interrupted.

"I remember I didn't have any milk that night for supper," John continued. "I cried, and Mamma sent Vern to Cousin Bill's to borrow some."

"It seems I've heard that song before—" Becky sang. She spread her feet and played on an imaginary violin.

John stared at her, glanced at his mother. There was a puzzled, hurt look about Vi Ward's eyes. "Becky! go back to the car!" John ordered.

"But, Daddy—"

"Don't argue! Go back to the car! "

"Okay, Professor Ward!"

She whirled and pranced around the house, Lesa trailing her. John stepped past the corner and watched them. Becky strode up the slope toward the white Buick parked where the woodshed had stood. Lesa followed, mocking her. He shook his head. Becky was a good kid. Her only trouble was her age. He turned back into the front yard and looked across the narrow valley which had once seemed so vast that almost half the world lay between East Ridge and West Mountain. Now the valley and hills appeared shrunken, like a landscape in a child's sandbox.

He looked quickly toward Kelly, stooping between him and the edge of the bank to pick up a redbird feather. For a moment he was afraid for the child. His education was assured, his future open in any direction the boy chose to take, but something was missing. There was something the seventh John Ward needed which his father did not have to give, something no Ward could give again any time soon. Time was, he thought, when it filled the world like fresh air and toil and hunger and pain and Mamma's remedies, but now—

And what was that something? Where had it come from? Had all of it, or most of it, come from Alvira Ward? Or had some really come from the surly old man he had once called his father? Again John felt that urge to steal a quick glance over his shoulder when he remembered the conflict between him and Will Ward, the conflict and his own animosity. That past was all there in his head somewhere, lost in little flecks of memory, forgotten thoughts, words spoken long ago.

2

THE FIRST THING HE REMEMBERED were the little shapes he learned to recognize and sounds like *Mal* and *Lynn* and *Vern* that went with them. And there was a white-topped giant shadow that growled and thundered when it floated close and frightened him at first. But he learned the growls were the giant's way of being friendly, and he was no longer afraid. And he discovered soon that he was like the little shapes called Venna and Ora, except smaller.

Then the white-topped giant would take him on his knee and bounce him and chant:

"Ole Granny Rattletrap
Settin on a log,
Finger on the trigger
And eye on a hawg."

And he learned to laugh because he knew that was what the giant expected of him. Then the giant would twist each of his five toes, beginning with the big one and moving toward the little one and say, starting in a bass voice, "This ole sow say,

'Les go steal wheat.' This little pig say"—his voice rising with each pig—" 'Where we gonna git hit at?' This little pig say, 'Massa's barn.' This little pig say, 'I tell Massa.' This little pig say"—he would twist the smallest toe and speak in a shrill voice—" 'Wee! Wee! Wee! I can't git over the doorsill.' "

Then he learned his name was John, and when he heard the sound *John*, he answered as best he could, by laughing or squealing or wriggling. The large shape with the mother smell and the filling warmth talked to him and called him John. He liked the sound. *John* was the most important sound he ever heard.

The mother would place John on his back in something and rock him, and the big roaring giant would roar:

"Whatcha gonna do with the baby?
Whatcha gonna do with the baby?
Wrop it up in the tablecloth
And throw it up in the stable loft.
Whatcha gonna do with the baby?

Baby laugh and baby cry,
Stuck my finger in the baby's eye,
Whatcha gonna do with the baby?
Whatcha gonna do with the baby?"

Then the light would go out, and John would float away somewhere and stay awhile, before coming back. And when he came back, sometimes the one called Vern would lean over his cradle and laugh and say:

"Wake up old man,
You slept too late.
The crawfish is done
And passed your gate."

Time passed and John walked. The mother smell moved back a ways, and the inflowing warmth stopped when he began to eat solid food. Then he learned to laugh for the one called Venna, who sometimes treated him gently and sometimes squeezed him half to death and at other times pulled his ear just to hear him squeal. When he saw her ear-pulling spell coming on, showing up dark in her green eyes, he scooted away to Vern or to the big one called Mamma.

The one called Daddy was gone away a lot, but when he came back to where they lived called *house,* he played with John more than he did Ora, the next little one. He bounced John on his knees and taught him things to say that must have been important but made no sense to him, who was what everybody called *three.* Daddy taught him to say, "Seen anything of a high, tall, rawboned boy about the size of a man? Run away from Bussley Bungs day after tomorr. Rid a steer heifer with a straw bridle and a hay saddle. See anything of this man, I'll give'ye three pints of pigeon milk churned by the scratch of a duck."

And he taught John to say, "Nottle, nottle, forty fingers, hoot! Start a-power, kizzley coot, coot a-kasy—Francis Schizzledick—mobbledick—pibbledick—null." And John remembered the sayings better than words that talked, and never forgot them and planned someday to find out from Daddy what they meant.

About this time another one came along, smaller than John, and took over his cradle and robbed him of Mamma, most of the time. They called this one Jim, and Daddy moved away from John too and started talking to Jim and telling him all the things he used to tell John, but Jim did not learn them fast enough. One day John was outside and Jim was inside and Daddy was outside too and they walked in the meadow close by the spring. John thought he would fool the one called Jim and bring Daddy back close again, so he looked around him for something to talk about besides "Nottle, nottle, forty fingers, hoot!" which still did not make any sense to him. His bare feet found something to talk about.

"Daddy!" he called. "Oh-h-h! Daddy!"

Daddy turned and looked way beyond John. "What'ye a-yellin about, youngun?"

"Daddy," John called, moving close and looking up at him. "Why for the grass be green?"

Then Daddy looked straight at him like he was some new kind of big he had never set eyes on before. His face frowned.

"Cause Godamighty made hit green, that's why, you danged idjet."

Then Daddy walked away from him and never came close again, not the way it was, like it was with the new one called Jim, and like it was to be later after Jack was born. Something was over with and something else was just beginning, but John had not figured either one out yet.

3

John Ward's mother coughed suddenly beside him. He turned and looked at her, at her stooped shoulders and set face as she stared across the valley toward West Mountain, but it did not interrupt his train of thought. He skipped over the time Lynn ran away from home at fifteen and went to Texas, where he served several months at Fort Clark, in the Cavalry, until Will and Vi Ward got him out. He skipped over the games, like Aintney Over and Blindfold, he had played with Vern and Venna and Ora. He skipped his futile fights with swarthy Anton Harrison, Bart's boy, and the times he played with Greer Harrison's boys, Alvin and Walter, and sometimes with Ben Dugan, old Doll's last one. He skipped the molasses boilings and chestnut hunts, blackberry-picking, and Pink Dugan playing and singing the ballads he loved to hear. He was groping for Will Ward's face, for Will Ward and himself, back there in the limbo of childhood.

He remembered how he had bragged to Alvin and Walter Harrison about how his daddy had stood up to Lem Dyer when he caught Lem making liquor on his land, and how he had shot Tom Dugan full of squirrel shot for poisoning the butter left to cool in the spring tail. John smiled when he recalled the first and last time Will had driven a car. The Model-T would not "gee!" when he wanted to turn right coming up the Ridge Road, and it would not "Whoa! goddamn hit!" when he yelled for it to stop, but cut a swath through an ivy thicket.

Such nostalgia had always been canceled out, however, overshadowed in his mind by the harsher times, especially those long, long days in the cornfield, where Will Ward ruled with an iron tongue.

He remembered that first summer, when playing ended most of the time, at least during corn-hoeing season. John went with them to the field in the bottom along the branch and stood watching Mamma chop weeds and rake dirt tenderly around the two green shoots. Later, one of them would be pulled up, thinning the corn so the one left would grow better. Daddy came up behind John, spun him around, and shoved a bobtailed hoe into his hands. It had been used so long, the corners were worn off the blade, leaving an oval shape.

"You're big enough to start cuttin weeds, boy," Daddy said. "A weed is anything that ain't corn that's growin and don't jump when you chop at it. Git in front of your ma and start diggin. You cut any corn and I'll skin'ye ass like a shedded adder."

John took the hoe and tried it out on a ragweed. It was light and handled easy. He chopped down a nettle. Then he made his first and last mistake in a cornfield—he chopped down a hill of corn. The next instant he was flat on his back looking up at the white thunderstorm looming over him. He had not known Daddy was that close behind him.

"Goddamn it, boy," Daddy roared, "you want to chop somethin besides weeds, chop off'ye damned foot. But don't you chop down no more corn. That's what you're here for. Without corn, they wouldn't be nothin. Now git up off'n your ass and start hoein. In a few years I'll larn'ye how to plow." He shuffled back to the cultivator, where old Beck stood, neck bent back, watching him to see how long he would be gone.

By the time John had chopped his way along the row, he was tired of hoes, weeds, and corn. When he reached the end, he dropped beneath the shade of a wild cherry tree and stretched out, while his ribs slowed down. Venna finished next, then Mamma, then Vern. Ora was with Jim and the baby. Mamma came over and stood beside John. All he could see was her dusty ankles and ragged shoes.

"Are'ye tard, honey?" she asked from high above him.

John turned his head and looked at her brown calves. "A little tard," he said.

"Well, you just lay there and rest this round," she said. "They's plenty of time for you to larn to hoe corn."

Venna took off down a new row of corn chopping like she was fighting fire. Vern followed, slower, wasting no stroke of her hoe. Mamma started back. John turned onto his back and stared at the blue sky through the leaves of the cherry tree. His ribs moved easy. His arms felt like ropes attached to his shoulders and stretched too far.

"Hey, Van! Dan! Mal!" Daddy yelled from twenty rows over.

John whirled to his knees, staring. Daddy had stopped his plow, glowering at him, and Beck dropped her head and closed her eyes.

"Mal! Lynn!" Daddy went on, still mixed up. "Which ever the hell one you are! Git back a-choppin them weeds before I kick'ye ass till'ye nose bleeds."

"But Mamma said—"

"But Mamma hell and damnation! I'm bossin this here outfit. Now git!"

John got. He got up and started chopping. And he learned fast. He learned that the slower he chopped, the less tiresome it was, the easier it was on his hands. Even so, by dinnertime, which took years to come, both hands were red and white with fat blisters.

When he showed them to Daddy at the table, Daddy laughed and slapped him on the back, making his teeth click. "They're good for'ye, boy," he said. "They'll bust and grow hard and first thing you know, you can hoe and plow from here to Cubie and never raise a blister."

Before three weeks had passed, the blisters were gone and

callouses had taken their place. Only the bottoms of his feet were tougher. By the time corn was laid by that year, he felt as though he had been chopping weeds for a hundred years. It was hard for him to remember when he did not have a hoe in his hands. And he looked forward to the time when he could plow instead. He could not see how plowing could be as hard as hoeing.

These were the things that John Matlock Ward remembered most vividly about his father, keeping them like grudges against an enemy he was ashamed to confront. The Wards had left the little valley in John's tenth year. A few months after Will had made the last payment on his land, he sold it, and they moved to Carson County, becoming landless tenant farmers, moving from farm to farm, from shack to shack, and working day in and day out, with no end in sight.

Finally, when he could stand the fields no longer, John had left. In his fourteenth year, while Will was at the other end of the corn row he plowed, John Matlock Ward did, with malice aforethought, tie his mule to a sassafras bush and get the hell out. He rolled an extra pair of pants, a shirt, and a sweater in a bandana, hobo-fashion, took the dollar and sixty-five cents he had saved, and not a cent more, and headed west to be a cowboy, leaving Will with two days of plowing before the corn would have been laid by, and Jim not old enough to help. After ten days of hopping freights—he was in Shreveport, Louisiana, heading for Texas–he realized he had to get back and help the old man finish plowing the corn.

His return took only three days. But when he reached home, he found that Will had finished the plowing by himself. He met John in the back yard, studied his smoke-blackened face briefly with ice-grey though not ungentle eyes. "Howdy, boy," he said. "You look like hell. Better rest up a spell." He turned away and plodded toward the barn.

John Ward's mind skipped five years, a span no wider than a razor slash across his memory. The next time he left, it was for good. By the time he graduated from high shool, two years late because of the damned farm work, only John, Jim, and

Jack were left to work (Tad was still too young). That day, Vi and the other two boys were hoeing corn in the big meadow on High Creek, on Emmitt Hanson's farm. John and Will, loading alfalfa on the hillside above, were rushing to beat a thunderstorm which loomed over them from the west. John was tired and hungry. The dead hay clung to his bare, sweaty back, sticking and irritating him.

"Hurry up, damn hit to hell!" Will heaved out, along with a forkful of hay, tossed onto the load. "That storm's a-gallopin up on us faster'n a wild hoss with his tail on far."

"Hurry up for what, for God's sake?" John snapped. And suddenly he was fed up. He plunged his fork into old Hanson's good earth and strode away, left for good, and Will Ward did not even call after him. He did not order, even ask him to come back and help. John had turned one ear away from the wind, listening, but the old man had not called. He kept right on loading the wagon all by himself, the muleheaded old fool, and rain already starting to fall.

In the fall sunshine there on the side of East Ridge, John Matlock Ward, thirty-seven years old and in perfect health, was not satisfied with what he remembered. He frowned. There was more to Will Ward than the things he himself remembered. There were the vital statistics, of course, but what else had there been, across the years between the dates of birth and death? Cousin Bill had tried to tell him more than once, in his roundabout way of getting his point across. His mother had explained a great deal to him, at different times, often to refute one of his many snide remarks made behind Will Ward's back. Yes, he thought, he would have to go back long before his own time really to know his father. After all, Will Ward had lived an average lifetime before he himself was born. A lot could happen to a man during the first fifty-three years of his life.

Part Two

TIME WAS

JOHN WILLIAM WARD

I

John William Ward was born May 5, 1865, in a log cabin chinked with clay, at the head of Stud Branch in the eastern foothills of the Carolina Appalachians. In his long lifetime, he never read a book, never wrote more than his name and a few additional words, never rode on a train or flew in a plane, never saw the ocean, never left his home state. Born at the close of the Civil War, he lived through the Spanish-American War and two world wars, and never wore a uniform. After two wives, thirteen children, thirty-three grandchildren, fourteen great-grandchildren, eighty years and eleven months, and sixty-three crops of corn—Will Ward died in a log house chinked with cement and painted green, less than forty miles from his birthplace, in the adjacent county.

As a boy he had only a few months of schooling because the "goddamn Carpetbaggers, scallawags, and blackassed Republicans made schools well-nigh impossible." In the fall of 1882, he married for the first time. He was seventeen and Bell Marlow was twenty-six. She brought with her as dowry a yearling work steer, five patchwork quilts, a skillet, a single-bitted ax, and a rusty froe used for splitting shingles. They moved into the cabin with Will's father, John Witherspoon Ward, then in his late forties. Mark had already married and moved three miles away. The newlyweds and the father shared the one-room cabin for three years.

At the end of the first year, Van, their first child, was born. Almost two years later Tillie was born. Foreseeing the inevitable, John Witherspoon Ward moved into the smokehouse, the back end of which he had converted into a cabinet shop. He lived there twenty-nine years, until he died a pauper in 1914. Anna Ward was born to Will and Bell in 1887, followed by a long dry spell. By that time Will owned the cabin and three acres of the old home place his father had lost within three years after he had inherited it from his father, John Baylus Ward.

In the spring of 1892, Will Ward sent the children out to pick blackberries while a midwife delivered Dan, his fourth child. In the next thirteen years only corn incubated at the head of the little valley through which Stud Branch trickled—that is, corn plus the few vegetables planted in the little garden back of the smokehouse where Grandpa John lived.

The old century died and a new one was born. By now Will Ward was thirty-seven years old, or soon would be; Bell was forty-six and appeared closer to sixty. By that time Will had bought two more acres from old man Lake Harrison and now owned five acres of the old Ward place. Unfortunately, it was mostly upland, rich only in niggerpines and blackberry briers.

Early one spring morning Will Ward, now approaching thirty-nine, crawled out of bed and stooped, squeezing his thighs to rid them of sudden cramp. Rheumatism had been growing on him in recent years, and the occasional draught of corn liquor gave little more than temporary relief. He wore long cotton underwear and a faded blue cotton shirt, the tail of which came almost to his knees. Bell Ward had fashioned the shirt, using scissors, needle, and thread, and had learned during the first six months of their marriage not to make his shirttails balls-and-pecker short.

Will plodded across the rough floor on his bare feet. Lifting the wooden latch, he opened the front door and collided with a clear wall of brisk April air. He sucked his lungs full, squinted at the sunstreaks above the green crest of East Ridge, then padded over to the end of the porch and leaned his right shoulder against a post. Seizing his penis as firmly as a plow handle, he began to piss into the small clump of grass fighting for roothold in the packed-clay yard. His sparse auburn hair stood up around the white dome of his head like an uneven picket fence, matching in color his bushy mustache.

He grunted his relief as his bladder was depleted and studied the eastern horizon critically. The red and yellow streaks fanning skyward signified a clear day, a good day to plant corn. A good day to plant corn or to plow or hoe corn was the kind of day Will Ward was born for, and he felt good inside. He felt warm and full except for his stomach and bladder.

He re-entered the cabin, slamming the door behind him. Plodding over to the huge stone fireplace, he leaned down to stir the banked coals with a hickory-stick poker. When he stooped, sudden pressure built up in his bowels. He broke wind with a loud, bass, sustained blast that roared across the silence of the sleeping cabin. Bell Ward reared up in bed suddenly, throwing back the quilts and rubbing her eyes. The two girls in the bed five feet distant, across the room from Bell, stirred, groaned, and turned over. Up in the half-loft above the two beds, Van Ward sat up on his half of the pallet, careful not to wake Dan. Will glanced toward him from the fireplace, knowing he would be there and would be sitting up on signal.

"Time to git up, Pap?" he called down to Will.

Will turned back to the fireplace, not bothering to answer. Van knew damned well what the signal had meant. Everyone was awake or half awake now except Dan, the youngest, who stung like a yellowjacket early in the morning. Besides, Dan was not completely conditioned to Will Ward's communication system of sounds, gestures, and facial contortions.

Will began to pile wood on the coals, not because the cabin was cold (unless it was freezing it was a waste of wood), but because breakfast had to be cooked. Bell scooted over to the front edge of the bed on the thin straw tick, plopped her feet to the floor, and began to button on her high-topped shoes. Her long hair had burst loose from its bun during the night, and fell about her shoulders in stringy grey clumps. As she leaned over her shoes, her breasts swung forward like brown, elongated bladders, filling the neck of the petticoat she slept in. She was a stocky woman, plump and big-bellied from childbearing and a healthy appetite.

Fire began to leap up through the sticks of wood. Will crossed the cabin and removed his overalls from a wooden peg set in the log wall. He kicked his way into them, fastened the galluses, and returned to the bed to put on his shoes. As he sat down on the edge of the bed and stooped for them, Bell, on the other end of the invisible seesaw, bobbed up, took her long Mother Hubbard from a peg, and pulled it over her head. This was a routine morning, a typical daybreak at the head of Stud Branch Valley.

Bell Ward shoved her grey hair off her breast and shoulders until she could have time to re-do it into a bun. She limped over to the wall between the two beds, unhooked the rawhide thong, and shoved open the wooden shutters covering the window. Will watched her, not seeing her. The raw morning air billowed into the cabin, sharp and clear. Bell moved across to the end of the house beside the fireplace and opened the shutters covering that window. She could have lit the new kerosene lamp for light, but Will Ward would have stopped such waste, with day breaking outside.

Will sat on the bed another half minute, relaxed. He fished a half plug of Brown's Mule tobacco from his hip pocket and tore a chunk from one corner with yellow-stained teeth. Then he studied Bell as she shuffled routinely about the square cooking table, beyond the Lazy Susan, preparing breakfast. He watched her pour coffee beans into the hopper of the wooden coffee mill, watched her turn the crank, pull out the little drawer and dump the mound of ground coffee into the blackened coffee pot. She filled the pot with water from the bucket on the table, carried it to the fireplace, took the shovel and raked out a bed of coals to boil it on.

Will watched every move critically, as though she were passing her housekeeping test for the day. But he saw only her motions. He was thinking, "I got to get this corn in. Then they'll be several weeks to first corn-hoein time. I might can work at the sawmill for old tight-ass Harrison for a spell. Maybe I can pay for another acre of land by October. Goddamn the luck, I need a team of mules. I could make ten times as much haulin lumber for the old turd. Them slowassed steers couldn't git a load of lumber from Stoney Fork to Coleman's Ford before doomsday."

Van walked backward down the ladder from the loft. He jumped the last four rungs, striking the floor so hard he rattled the dishes and pans on Bell's cooking table. She turned and frowned at him. Will started to swear at him but changed his mind. Van Ward, going on twenty, was a stocky young man, taking after his mother. He had the same dark eyes and round face, but the ruddy complexion of his father, whom he outweighed by fifty pounds. And, like Will, he wore a faded blue shirt and patched overalls.

He stretched, groaning and grinning, and stamped his feet against the floor. "Lord ha'mercy!" he grinned, "I could have slept till next week. I'm still tard. Pap, I'm bound to have me some more straw in that pallet tick on that hard floor or some cornshucks or somethin, even if hit's jest leaves."

Will pushed himself to his feet, slow, as though learning to stand. He watched Bell slice sidemeat from the salty slab on the cooking table. "Go wake'ye grandpa for breakfast," he ordered.

Van stamped toward the back door, opened it, and left it open. Will followed close behind him, into the packed-clay yard. Twenty feet from the back door a small outbuilding squatted against the gently rising slope, one gabled end facing the cabin. It was built of vertical slabs, the rounded bark sides turned outward, but the dry bark had sloughed, or was in the process of sloughing, away from the boards. Van Ward walked directly to the closed door, pulled the thong dangling from a small hole and treaded a shaft of daylight into the dark interior.

Will circled the smokehouse and climbed past the corncrib toward the rail fence on the hillside above. Two dappled steers and a Jersey cow stood with necks poked through the bars, waiting patiently for his arrival. Shuffling to one of the three fodder stacks nearby, Will pulled two bundles of corn-tops from one side of the stack and dragged them over to the fence. He broke the bonds and scattered the feed in three piles beyond the rails, careful to keep them out of the accumulated dung near the bars. He stood for a minute watching the steers bite into their portions. He paid no attention to the cow. She was Bell's affair, and he had little truck with women's business. In the hog lot, his three shoats grunted and squealed, demanding their morning slop, which would not arrive until after breakfast. "Goddamn hawgs never larn how to wait tell the day they die," Will thought.

He turned away from the feeding cattle and faced the sunrise. The whole eastern sky was a fanwork of crimson and yellow and gold, converging with a yellow glow still below East Ridge. "Damnation, look at that sky!" he muttered. "Red as measles on a Injun squaw's ass. Gonna be a good day for plantin. Gonna be one of my finest days."

East Ridge and West Mountain did not come entirely together here at their convergence. The north end of West Mountain appeared to be mortised into the south slope of Fox Mountain, which extended over a mile eastward at right angles to it and East Ridge. Actually, a narrow valley almost concealed by the forest separated the two mountains. East Ridge beveled off a quarter of a mile short of Fox Mountain, creating another valley along the mountain base from east to west. From where Will Ward stood, he could see the pole shacks spreading slowly like canker sores along the bare slope of Fox Mountain, the first one only three hundred yards away. This was Coottown, where the Catletts multipled through common-law marriage like the fleas on their mangy hounds.

Will watched Matt Catlett in her Mother Hubbard come out of the shack carrying a bucket. She headed toward the spring, farther down the slope.

Will spat at a cowpile and turned toward the house. "Goddamn trash," he muttered. "I ort to git me some Ku Kluxers together and burn them shacks down some night. Wonder why old Harrison don't run'em off his land, nohow. Cause one or two of'em still work at his sawmills, I reckon."

When he came even with the smokehouse, Van shouldered his way through the door, followed by his grandfather. Van plunged over to the edge of the yard and stopped, facing the blackberry briers, his back to the older men. Old John Ward rounded the smokehouse, fumbling at his fly with his good hand. Finally, he found himself and squatted slightly, wetting the side of the building he worked and lived in. He wore baggy black woolen trousers, patched and re-patched in different colors and held up by rope suspenders. His butternut outing shirt was faded and patched, and both shoes gaped open at the toes.

He was a little man alongside Will, stooped as though much older than his sixty-odd years. He wore a ragged white beard and tiny brass-rimmed spectacles. His right arm hugged his side like the injured wing of a bird, the warped fingers reaching no lower than his trouser pocket. His arm had been paralyzed since childhood, when he had fallen from his grandfather's horse. John Thomas Ward, then in his eighties, had lost his grip on the child when his mount shied at a rattlesnake. This information shuttled through Will Ward's mind for the thousandth time as he waited for his father to relieve himself.

"Looks like hit's gonna be a good day for plantin," John Ward offered, glancing toward the east. "That sky looks like hit was purtied up for a frolic."

"I 'lowed to myself back up there a minute ago when I was a-feedin the stock that it looked like measles on a Injun squaw's ass," Will said.

John Ward finished up in amber squirts, then buttoned his fly with dexterous fingers. "I ain't never seed too much of Injun squaws' asses," he answered, his grin erupting a red hole in his white beard, "but I can bear witness that sky's red."

He followed Will back into the cabin. Bell was fishing fist-sized biscuits from the skillet and placing them on the Lazy

Susan table. Around the outer rim, plates had already been set. They sat down in the split-bottomed chairs John Ward had made, the two girls, still in their petticoats, joining them.

Sitting around the rim of the round table-waiter were the biscuits, a dish filled with the fried sidemeat, and a huge bowl full of cream gravy. There was also a fruit jar full of molasses and a mound of butter on a plate. The gravy had been made by frying flour in pork grease for body, then stirring in milk while the gravy thickened. Each member of the Ward family took a biscuit—turning the table-waiter in turn—opened it and covered it with the lumpy gravy. Bell poured the mugs full of black coffee, returned the pot to the small bed of coals on the hearth, and then at last sat down.

Will Ward dug into his biscuit and shoved a third of the top half, dripping with gravy, into his mouth, as he ducked to meet it. Globs of gravy matted the edges of his mustache. He closed his eyes and chewed hungrily, then took a swallow of black coffee, feeling it scald the trough of his tongue. It was the identical food he had eaten for breakfast for most of his life, but he never grew tired of it. Occasionally they had fritters, wide as his hatbrim, and later in the summer, day following day of stewed corn. But the sidemeat and gravy-covered biscuits suited him fine for year-in, year-out eating.

"Bell, you're the best damned gravymaker this side of Goshen," he muttered between bites.

Bell Ward lifted her round face, glancing away from her plate. She smiled so briefly no one saw it because no one was looking directly at her. "Anybidy that's had as much practice doin a job as I've had makin sawmill gravy is bound to be a expert or crazy as a bedbug."

"That's a fact!" Tillie swore, stirring at her plate. "It's good, better'n I could ever do, but it'd be a blessin to eat somethin different now and again."

Will glowered at her, grey eyes narrowed. At eighteen, she was a pleasant-featured girl, plump and big-boned like her mother, with a round face and big mouth. Her long brown hair lay in two plaits down her back. She looked quickly away from Will's stare, yielding to silence.

Anna Ward, now sixteen, looked from her sister squarely at her father. Her hair was black, and her hazel eyes were narrow slits as she opened her mouth, apparently in Tillie's behalf, then changed her mind and continued eating. She was tall and large-boned, but with good feminine lines. Her features were even as she matured toward womanhood and certain beauty.

"You can't hardly beat this kind of eatin," old John Ward nodded, pouring molasses over half a biscuit. "I been eatin it for nigh on to sixty-two year, and look at me."

The two girls looked at the stooped old man, brittle as a winter cricket, then at each other. Anna grinned and looked back at her plate. Will Ward caught the exchanged looks, the derisive grin, but said nothing, since his father had missed it. He stamped Anna's bare foot under the table and let it go at that.

Before seven-thirty Will was following the laying-off plow along the hillside, tottering to adjust his pace to that of the slow, swaying steer. The narrow tongue of the plow gouged a shallow trench in the harrowed field, straight as a gun barrel except for an occasional bobble where a rock deflected the point. The furrows were laid off about three feet apart. Several rows behind Will, Bell paced steadily down one of the furrows, Van another, each dropping two grains of seed corn about two feet apart. Tillie followed Bell and Anna followed Van, hoeing dirt over the corn grains. Young Dan kept Van and his mother supplied with seed corn. This was the way Will Ward had planted corn all his life, the way John Ward had planted corn before him. There was no other way to do it, and anybody who tried to figure out a short cut was a damned fool.

They knocked off when the shadow of Will's head had shortened to his extended foot and ate their noon meal, called dinner. In the afternoon they returned to the field, Will plowing the other steer. He was tired of gripping the bobbing plow handles, tired of stumbling over clods and rocks. He would have let

Van lay off the rows awhile, but for one problem. There was nobody, not Van, not anyone else, who could lay off corn rows as straight as Will Ward could. And corn rows deserved to be laid as straight as human skill could plow them, as straight as a man lived and thought.

Will finished his job around mid-afternoon and returned the steer to the small pasture. He stood, the bars half up, staring. The Jersey cow trotted along the fence, head up and eyes flared wide. When she reached Tom, the steer he had just released, she reared up on his rump and began to ride him like a rutting bull.

"So that's what you're a-needin!" Will growled. "Bell's been claimin you was holdin up on'ye milk. Damned old bitch, always bullin. She'll go dry as a powder house in hell tell she gets pronged and gits another calf. We're gonna miss her milk and butter tell she comes fresh. Goddamn the luck, nohow."

He yanked a rope from off the steer's harness and straddled back over the lowered bars. Old Jersey was too busy to notice when he looped the line around her horns. When he had her fast, he balled his fist and punched her once, in the ribs. The cow gasped for breath, slid her front hooves to the ground, and staggered in a half circle, her mouth open. Will examined his fist and grinned, then spat tobacco juice between his feet.

When he passed the field, leading the cow, Will stopped. Bell, Van, and the two girls halted and watched him. Dan was at the far end of the corn rows, splashing rocks into Stud Branch.

"This damned old cow's bullin," Will called. "That's why she's been holdin up on her milk. I'm aimin to take her over to Hill Anderson's and stand her."

"Well-l-l!" Bell Ward called back, nodding. She glanced at the two girls nearby. "You jest might as well git it over with. She ain't gonna give down no milk worth nothin tell she calfs. Git back soon's you can."

Will Ward led the rutting cow on down Stud Branch, following the path which paralleled its right bank. He passed through the bottleneck where West Mountain and East Ridge elbowed inward toward each other, then passed into the wider meadow beyond. Here, he swerved to the right, toward the base of the mountain, where a clump of alder bushes and weathered granite created an oasis against the grassy slope. When he reached the spot, he dropped to his hands and knees and drank, animal-fashion, from the cold spring filling the basin of rock.

"Got to fetch me a gord down here," he thought. "Gettin too old to drink like a goddamn mule."

When his guts were gorged, Will climbed to his feet and turned his back on the spring, squinting across the meadow and up the bare flank of East Ridge, where he planned, by God, someday to build his house. He stared a long time at the spot where the house would be, a weatherboarded mansion with at least six rooms, two chimneys, four fireplaces, and ceiled throughout. He mentally located the huge barn, the smokehouse, the crib, the woodshed, and the backhouse. Yes, by God, he aimed to have him a fancy backhouse and stop hanging his rump across bent sassafras saplings. He wiped his eyes and sighed and ignored the reminder coursing through his brain that he had stood here off and on over twenty years now, planning his house and outbuildings on land he had little prospect of ever owning.

He looked beyond the fallow slope, at the woods flung like a green saddle blanket across the spine of the ridge. He stared at one spot in the woods, stared as though he could penetrate the foliage, could see the earth beneath, as though he could penetrate the green foliage of time and see the huge log house that once had stood there. And even if he could have penetrated the leaves, he knew he would see nothing, no chimneys, no foundation, only a mound in the woods covered by huckleberry bushes and briers. Will Ward sighed again, or groaned, and turned away, leading the cow on down the branch toward the Big Road.

The bare south spur of West Mountain tapered off fifty yards short of where Stud Branch joined Tadpole Branch, which followed the valley formed by West Mountain and Anderson Ridge. After paralleling the mountain on the west, Anderson Ridge veered southeastward, and would have cut across the south spur of East Ridge, except that it also tapered off, a quarter of a mile short of Anderson Ridge, leaving a rolling plain which extended southeastward for almost a mile to where Stud Branch flowed into Bare Creek. Hill Anderson's house towered above the crest of Anderson Ridge, visible for miles in all directions.

Will Ward reached the Big Road and bore to the right, around the spur of West Mountain, heading for the side road on Anderson Ridge which branched off to Hill Anderson's place. He stopped once in the dusty, rutted road and stared back at the grassy spur of the mountain where it dropped off at the embankment flanking the road. Now, talk about a house spot—if he could have his druthers, this would win out over New Jerusalem. Level the top of the spur and that would be one of the best goddamn house spots in Wilton County. Back up the branch a short ways, a barn could be built, and a fancy backhouse on stilts out over Stud Branch. He wondered what Old Man Harrison would ask for the land like he wondered how much West Mountain weighed. Too goddamn much, like it had been Harrison land since Adam, and not Ward land clear back to the first settlement. Damned good house spot, but he had about as much chance building there as a hailstone in hell.

He turned and went on, plodding along the rutted road. He stepped across Tadpole Branch and bore to the left, following the S-curve up the slope of Anderson Ridge. At the top he turned left, leading the cow, along the side road which followed the crest of the ridge. Barbed-wire fences paralleled each side of the road, reaching away to enclose both grassy slopes of Anderson Ridge. On the south side, more than a quarter of a mile of lowland was included. More than thirty head of mongrel cattle grazed in the two pastures, part of the wealth Hill Anderson had inherited from his father or had accumulated since.

A hundred yards short of the Anderson house, Will Ward stopped as he always did and studied the lay of the land in all directions, eyes narrowed. He could see up Stud Branch all the way to Fox Mountain. To the west, he could see the distant chain of the Blue Ridge. He could see from the open fields, west of Anderson Ridge, which curved away to the north, across West Mountain, on across East Ridge, to the rolling fields of Cousin Bill Ward's farm. Beyond, on the rim of the world, he could discern the grey steeple of Mount Hope Church. And all that land, those hills and valleys and rolling fields clear back to the ridge he stood on, had once been Ward land. He turned and looked southward, to Clay Messick's woods, beyond Bare Creek. Even beyond this ridge, all the way to the creek, Ward land.

From Bare Creek "as fur as eye can see north'ards from the Ridge," which was to the crest of Fox Mountain, "from the public road west of the Ridge to Turkey Branch," halfway to Mount Hope Church, where Cousin Bill's land ended, John Ward I, II, and III had owned. But now gone, long gone. And this ridge, this high ridge overlooking the holdings of the first three John Wards was the last to go. The last meager folkstead of Will's own father, John Witherspoon Ward, lost through mortgage foreclosure so young Hill Anderson could build his shithouse castle on the highest ridge south of West Mountain. Will thought briefly that Fox Mountain formed a headstone and Anderson Ridge a footstone to the original Ward holdings.

The cow tugged suddenly at the rope, trying to drag him down the road toward where she sensed a bull waited to serve her. Will slapped her with an open palm, staggering her. He turned back and stared again up Stud Branch at the rusty, angular pile of logs on the clay hillside, waiting for his return. His grey eyes were slitted. Finally he inhaled a deep draught of air, spat tobacco juice at a fence post, and continued on, holding back on the trotting cow.

As he approached Hill Anderson's house, he cast a squint up along its side, refusing to look at it squarely. It towered three stories, with arched windows, bastard columned porches, and gingerbread decorations. Above the steeply pitched roof, a cupola towered even higher than the massive central chimney. It resembled a turret on a castle, except for its embracing glass windows from which one could see for miles in all directions.

"I reckon that's Hill's poontang lookout," Will muttered. "I reckon he sets up there on his broad ass and watches for womernfolk and gals in all directions, so's he can waylay'em and talk'em out of a lay in the hay."

When he came even with the front porch, Hill's wife, Matilda, came to the front door, glowered out at him, spat black bile over the porch banisters without touching them, then disappeared, swallowed by the shadowy hallway behind her. She was a gaunt woman, older than Hill, without breasts, hips, or buttocks. Will had seen her face glowering from a door or window on several occasions, but he had never spoken to her since before she married, seven or eight years earlier.

"Wonder what in God's name that horny bastard seen in her," Will mused. "Old Matt Dugan's oldest bastard, ugly as a mud fence daubed with chinquapins. And she ain't ebem got him a miscarriage up to now."

They passed the house and turned left, toward the barn. The cow began to low, tugging at the rope and heading toward the pasture fence off to the right, beyond which a huge Jersey bull grazed placidly. Will punched her in the ribs with a quick fist, and she groaned, submitting to his yank. They continued on down the slope and entered the shadowy barn driveway.

Will stopped and threw up his head, listening. He stared at the bank of closed stall doors on his left. From beyond the central door, leading into the cutting-room, he heard noises. He heard a squeak like a high voice, and he heard grunting and rustling. He heard something like a palm beating on a bare thigh. Will relaxed. "Probly old Hill gettin evenin feed ready," he thought. "Probly measurin out some cottonmeal for the stock or chop for the hawgs."

"Hey, Hill!" he called. "Let's go in there. I need a tad of stud service out here."

The noise in the cutting-room dwindled and stilled. There came a silence. Then a muffled voice called, "Hold'ye tater. I'll be out d'rectly."

It was three minutes before Hill Anderson slipped from the cutting-room, closing the door after him. He blinked rapidly, as though the dim light of the driveway bothered his pale-blue, almost white, eyes. He was a huge man of around thirty, broad and short, with a tangle of kinky red hair covering his head almost to his bushy red eyebrows, where two red wens, like sprouting horns, divided hairline from brows. Neat khaki trousers and a white linen shirt were stretched tight over his two hundred thirty pounds, a shoestring tie at his throat. His rump protruded, his legs curved backward, and his toes pointed inward, reminding Will of the rump end of a massive goat.

He frowned at Will Ward, flashing a mouth half filled with gold teeth. "What manner of stud service you got in mind?" he growled. "I got stud hosses, stud boars, stud goats, stud bulls, stud roosters, and I do a little studdin myself."

Will's eyes narrowed, the grey changing to pale ice. "This here's a cow I got behind me. What sort of stud service *would* I need? Less'n you figure you could do a better job than your bull."

"You wouldn't be makin out I was up to somethin in the cuttin-room?" he demanded.

"I wasn't makin out nothin. All I'm ater is my bullin cow stood. I got the fee if you got the bull. If I broke up'ye prayer meetin, I didn't aim to."

Hill Anderson's eyes clashed with Will's for several more seconds. Then he threw back his head and roared with laughter. His laughter boomed throughout the barn and rolled down across the hillside. His gold teeth gleamed in the dim light. His eyes disappeared back of his shaggy brows. Will stood there watching him, his fists mauls of cartilage and bone by his sides. He itched to bury his right fist up to his elbow in Hill Anderson's quaking paunch.

Hill cut off his laughter like a severed limb. One moment his face was contorted with laughter, the next it was calm. "I wasn't mad, Will," he grinned. "I was jest testin your vinegar."

"I reckon you didn't find it likin none," Will answered.

Will felt around inside himself. He found nothing new. He despised Hill Anderson deep down in his bloodstream. He did not know why. He could not have figured it out in a coon's age. But everything about Hill, all he represented, all he had, the way he sat on top of Anderson Ridge and looked down on the world riled him through and through. He felt it in his corns and rheumatism, sensed it in his blood, carried the knowledge low in his heavy testicles—yet did not fight it. A man had to deal with whom he had to deal with, and Hill Anderson had the best damned stock animals for miles around. Furthermore, he could castrate a pig or a steer calf neater than Bell could make a buttonhole.

Hill waddled over to Will and cuffed him on the shoulder, staggering him. "You know me better'n to git riled at what I say, Cousin Will," he chuckled. "Come on, let's git this here cow pronged good and proper."

He moved away and opened the gate at the far end of the barn, leading into the pasture. Will followed him, holding back on the cow, now tugging at the rope in her efforts to reach the bull a few seconds quicker.

Hill watched, holding the gate wider, until the man and the cow were through it. "Jest look at'er," he grinned. "Can't bide tell old Buck pokes it in her. They're all alike—cows and womernfolk. When the heat hits'em, they're gonna find pecker service or bust a halter."

Will Ward looked at him but did not answer. He wanted to tell Hill he knew a few women that were not like cows in heat, but let it pass. Hill would argue with him, and he did not feel like arguing with the sonofabitch. He wanted to get the cow stood and get the hell back off Anderson Ridge as quick as he could without seeming to be in a hurry.

Will slipped the rope off the cow's horns. She threw up her head, her mouth wide, stringing saliva, as her mating bellow broke the silence of the hillside. Toward the foot of the slope, a herd of cows stared toward the barn, then continued grazing. The cow plunged forward, rounding the barn at a gallop. Will Ward and Hill followed her. They stopped beyond the corner of the barn, where they could watch. The bull had heard her bellow and was already on his way to meet the cow–head high, eyes ringed with white, ring in nose bouncing, heavy scrotum beating his hocks like a bladder stuffed with river rocks.

The bull and cow came together head on. Will stiffened, waiting for them to collide. At the last second the bull swerved, coming up behind the cow, now with her legs braced, waiting. The bull thrust his head high in the air, his upper lip curled back, his yellow teeth and gums bare. Then he hit her. Briefly, the cow staggered under the bull's bulk. She caught herself, spreading her stance.

Will heard a gasp close beside him. He turned. Hill Anderson's eyes were almost closed, his lips were drawn back exposing his gold teeth, and saliva drooled from the corners of his mouth. His right hand was thrust deep in his pocket, his legs widespread. The wens on his forehead pulsed red. His pale-blue eyes were dazed as he watched the bull thrust deep.

Will frowned and looked away from him, spitting at a nearby rock. He caught a flash of movement out of the corners of his eyes and shifted his stare. A young woman was running across the pasture away from the end of the barn. Just before she reached the fence on the slope below, she threw her face around and looked back over her shoulder. Will squinted, recognized the face and auburn hair. It was Doll Dugan, Matilda Anderson's youngest sister. She reached the fence, hoisted her skirt, and straddled through it. Will caught a glimpse of white flesh and red fleece. Then she was gone, into the niggerpines beyond the fence.

He turned back, in time to see the bull rear up for a second plunge.

"Look at that Buck go," Hill Anderson said, his voice tight. "Ain't he some bull? Sometime I'd like to trade what I got for what he's got. I bet he could crawl ever cow from here to Goshen."

"I bet he'd be a tard-peckered bull if'n he did," Will grumbled.

After a third leap, the bull lost interest in the cow and began to graze. She kept rearing up on the bull, and Will had little trouble looping the rope back over her horns. But it took him and Hill both to drag the cow away, back into the driveway of the barn. Will paid Hill and was just leaving the barn when a wagon pulled into the drive from the road. It was drawn by two huge draft horses. He led the cow to one side and waited until the wagon braked to a stop in front of him.

Two men in their twenties sat in the spring seat, one stocky, the other tall and skinny. They were Old Man Harrison's boys.

"Howdy, Bart." Will nodded to the tall one. "How-do, Greer."

The Harrison brothers nodded to Will, then turned their attention to Hill Anderson, who had emerged from the driveway of the barn. Like Hill, Bart and Greer Harrison were dressed in store-bought clothes—but they wore corduroy trousers and muslin shirts.

"Howdy, Hill," Bart called. "We fetched'ye that fertilize from Northboro you ast for."

Hill waddled on out to the wagon. "Well, thank'ye, fellers. Let's yank them bags out'n the wagon-bed and set'em in the barn."

He moved to the tailgate of the wagon. Greer Harrison got up and straddled across the seat, then stepped over the three bags until he reached the back of the wagon. He slid the tailgate out and leaned it against the side of the bed. Greer was a handsome young man, dark-haired and dark-eyed, but there was a plumpness to his face and a weakness about his chin.

Will Ward spat and started on up the drive, turning his back on the three. He did not give a good goddamn whether they paid him any attention or not. Fertilize! Might just as well piss on his soybeans. Nothing like old-fashioned manure to make crops grow.

"Will!" Greer Harrison called. "What you doin over on Anderson Ridge, it corn-plantin time?"

Will Ward stopped and turned back. "I brung my cow over here to see the Blue Ridge Mountain," Will called back. "Old Jersey ain't never seen the Blue Ridge Mountain before."

Greer Harrison stared at Will, mouth open, still half stooped above the tailgate. Hill Anderson threw back his head and roared with laughter.

"Cousin Will's jest joshin'ye, Greer," Hill guffawed. "He claimed he come up here to git his cow stood, but he jest come to look over the land his grandpa used to own."

A fist knotted in Will Ward's guts. Hill's use of Cousin made it worse. Will was first cousin to Greer and Bart Harrison, whose mother was his Aunt Susan, but he played hell being any cousin to Hill Anderson. Hill's father, old Jed, had married Will's Aunt

Rhoda, but she had died leaving no children. Hill was the only get of Jed Anderson and his second wife, Lucy Adkins. Will knew damned well what Hill had meant by calling him Cousin Will.

"I wanted to git Anderson Ridge back in the fambly," Will grinned, eyes narrow, "so's I could bring my cow up here and stand her to goat-ass Hill. But he was holdin prayer meetin in the cuttin-room with his redheaded, red-groined kinfolks, so I turned her to his bull."

Hill Anderson shuffled several steps closer to Will, feet wide, fists clinched. "You wouldn't be lookin for a fight, would'ye, Cousin Will?"

"You better not mess with Will," Bart Harrison called from the wagon seat. His frown was worried. "I seen him knock a mule out'n his tracks once with his bare fists. Done it on a bet."

"I'm not lookin for no fight, Hill," Will Ward said. "I'm nigh on to forty year old. A man's a damned fool if'n he looks for a fight. If'n he's got to fight, he's a bigger fool if he don't end hit the quickest way he can."

Hill licked his lips, shuffled two steps closer to Will. Will Ward stood in the road, loosejointed, shoulders slumped, holding the cow's rope in his left fist. Only his jaw was tense, beneath the brim of the floppety old black hat.

"Why don't you and Will throw these here fertilizer sacks at one another, Hill?" Greer Harrison grinned. "Two hundred pounds apiece ort to slow you both down."

Hill looked behind him, then back at Will, quick as a snake striking. "You might knock a mule out'n his tracks, but I bet you can't shoulder no bag of fertilize from the level ground."

"Sounds like tomfoolery to me," Will growled. "How the hell do I know where I can shoulder one or not. I've allus had more sense than to try, up to now."

"I bet I can lift one and shoulder it," Hill Anderson said. "And I bet I can do it with my feet flat in a bushel measure. And I bet you can't."

"I don't give a good goddamn if'ye can lift hit with your ass in a tub," Will muttered.

"You ain't aimin to let Hill show'ye up, Will?" Greer Harrison laughed.

Will shuffled a few steps closer to the wagon, the cow following him. "I ain't set myself up as no champeen lifter," he argued. "Hill outweighs me fifty pound. He's had more practice totin that ass of his'n around than me."

The grin left Hill Anderson's face. He turned away from Will. "Will can plow and chop and haul cowshit, but he knows damn well he can't outlift me. He ain't aimin to take no chances."

Will Ward chuckled, his eyes narrow. "Go git your bushel measure. I'll shoulder as much standin in hit as you will, *Cousin* Hill."

"How about fetchin that bushel measure out'n the cuttin-room for me, Greer," Hill said. "We'll git this here contest over with so's Will can git back to Coottown."

"Watch out you don't slip up on his pecker tracks in there," Will called.

Greer jumped from the wagon and trotted toward the barn. Hill waddled to the wagon, grasped the ears of one of the fertilizer bags, and yanked it to the ground. It struck like a boulder, jerking Hill off balance. Bart Harrison tied the lines around the brake pole and jumped down, taking the cow's rope when Will handed it to him. In half a minute Greer was back, and set the bushel basket on the ground close by the bag of fertilizer.

Hill Anderson stepped into the basket and faced the three men, showing his gold teeth in a grin. He unbuttoned his shirt sleeves, spat on his hands, and stooped. Clutching one ear of the tow sack in his left hand, he got a handhold on a bottom corner with his right and lifed the bag onto its narrow side. Then with knees close together in a half-sitting position, he pulled the bag onto his knees and slid it slowly upward until it rested across the top of his thighs. He held it there, breathing hard, the two short horns on his forehead flushed with blood.

After a short rest, Hill squatted a little more, released his hold with his right hand, and encircled the top of the bag. His left arm moved beneath the bag, until he was embracing it.

Then slowly, inch by slow inch, he lifted the bag toward his right shoulder, tilting it parallel with his body at the same time. Will Ward watched him, his own muscles flexed. Slowly, slowly the top of the bag moved above the level of Hill's right shoulder.

The veins stood out on Hill Anderson's neck. Sweat gleamed on his narrow forehead. His jaw muscles bulged as he bit hard with the strain. The bag was four inches above his shoulder level now. Slowly it inched upward, slowly. It was almost ready to tilt backward onto his shoulder. Hill hesitated, panting, his face flushed. Suddenly the bag pitched forward to the ground, yanking Hill with it. He rode the bag down and landed across it on hands and knees, sucking for breath, the overturned basket still on his feet.

"Well good! good!" Greer Harrison sang, dancing around Hill. "You didn't quite make it, Hill, but you might nigh did."

"Yeah, but you didn't shoulder it," Bart argued, looking at Will. "Looks like you and Will's even. Ain't neither one of'ye shouldered a bag of fertilize with your feet in a bushel measure. Not yet, you-all ain't."

Hill climbed to his feet, shaking his head. "Not by a damn sight we ain't ebem," he panted. "I might nigh had her. Will ain't come that clost by a damn sight."

"Bullshit!" Will swore. "Far as I can see, they ain't no difference betwixt *might nigh* shoulderin hit and not budgin hit."

"That's one way to give up," Hill grumbled.

"Jesus Christ! I got to git home before midnight." Will shuffled over to the bag and kicked the basket close beside it.

Will Ward stepped into the basket, spread his feet as far as he could. Stooping, he grasped the fertilizer bag by its ears and lifted it to a sitting position. Then slowly he worked the bag upward until, half squatting, thighs together, he had the bag on his knees, balanced there on a fulcrum, his body as a counterweight. Holding the bag balanced upright, Will bent his body, working his right shoulder down the side of the bag.

When he decided he had reached the middle, he paused to rest. After a minute, he worked his arms down around the bag of fertilizer, grasped it tightly, and began to straighten up, inch by inch. He could feel the bulge of his biceps, the pull on his back muscles. He could feel the swell of his neck, the bulge of his cheeks, and the strain, the inhuman strain, on his belly. Gradually, painfully he straightened upward. He could glimpse the taut faces of the Harrison brothers out of the sides of his squinting eyes. He could see Hill Anderson's face, mouth half open, shoulders hunched, as he strained and pulled, working against the weight of the bag, which bore down to overpower him. The acid stink of the fertilizer choked him. Grey blobs floated before his eyes.

Will was almost erect now. The back muscles were easing off, but the strain on his belly was living pain. Just a few inches more. Just inches, and he would be erect, the bag across his shoulder, the bet won—the goddamned fool bet pitting his manhood against Hill Anderson's manhood. Four more inches, three more. Will shuddered suddenly, almost losing his grip. A slash of pain shot down his sides, low on his belly. A knife slash—that was how it felt. It flashed and then was gone. But his belly quivered like a catgut string, a bass-fiddle string, plucked gently.

He stood there, confused, clutching the bag, his guts vibrating. The pain was a dull throb down both groins.

"That's where Hill got to with it," Greer Harrison laughed. "You might jest as well drop it, Will."

Suddenly Will was angry. Goddamn Hill Anderson and his horny prick. Goddamn his stud animals. Goddamn his shithouse castle, his barren wife, and the ridge they lived on.

With a final heave, he stood erect, the bag balanced across his right shoulder. He could feel the sweat, pasting his shirt to his back. He could feel the throb in both groins. He could feel the breeze cooling his wet forehead.

"Hey! how about that!" Bart Harrison yelled. "He done whooped'ye, Hill."

"Aw, who gives a damn?" Hill Anderson kicked the ground. "He's had more practice than me pushin them steers back'ards and for'ards across that pore upland he tends."

Will Ward stared at Hill Anderson. Then he dropped the fertilizer, heaving it as far as he could. It struck the ground, and the bag split, spreading the grey powder in a ten-foot fan. "Now you can pick hit up, Hill," he growled. "Git'ye a tablespoon and pick hit up a little tad at a time—and shove a spoonful up your fat ass ever now and again."

He took the rope from Bart Harrison's hand and plodded off up the drive, leading the passive cow. And the pain went with him, the dull, quivering pain low in his groins. A short distance beyond Hill's house, he stopped again and stared across West Mountain and across the valley where Stud Branch ran and across East Ridge as far as Mount Hope Church, then back to the base of Fox Mountain, now lost in shadows, where his cabin sat. And as he looked, he reached his right hand, like a scared mouse creeping, down inside his overalls and unbuttoned the front of his long underwear. Still furtive, his calloused fingers crept across the hairy dome of his belly, paused, then prodded the nodule bulging into the hollow of his right groin. Will yanked his hand back as though he had touched human excrement. He stopped, listening inside himself. Then he felt again, more daring. He moved his hand across his quivering belly and touched the twin nodule in the opposite groin. His pubis was wet with sweat. His groins were throbbing with flashes of heat.

Will Ward slumped. All of a sudden he felt very, very old. At thirty-eight years and eleven months of age, the weariness of five generations of hard labor seemed to settle about his shoulders, and he slumped perceptibly, his head thrusting forward to accommodate his tilted face, his staring eyes. As he fingered first one groin and then the other, he felt a part of his manhood ooze into those obscene lumps, seeping away from him like the sweat at his pubis. He felt half-leg deep in earth, and sensed the long years ahead when he would periodically carry his guts in each hand, like broken tendons leading to his heels. Yet this knowledge only flickered along the surface of perception. Deep down where his reason burned, he denied the knowledge his groping fingers imparted to his mind.

And because he denied it, he made a sudden decision in the direction of hope. He turned away from his view of the past and headed on up the ridge. When he reached the Big Road, instead of turning back to the right, the way he had come, he continued westward, the cow, her glandular needs satisfied, following him passively.

The Big Road veered away from the crest of Anderson Ridge, channeling along its western slope. A short distance from Hill Anderson's road, he came even with old man Lake Harrison's place. It was a large two-story house built so recently of raw lumber it had hardly darkened from the weather. Off to the right was a massive mansard-roofed barn, where old Lake kept his draft horses and logging mules and steers. To the left of the house, a conical black monument to Lake Harrison's enterprise towered in the open field. It was the sawdust pile where his first sawmill had buzzed, before all the timber adjacent to the area had been cut, from virgin oaks and pines to leg-sized saplings.

Goddamn greedy bastard. Will Ward glowered at the house and barn. Be sawin up cornstalks and alder bushes next, after he strips all the trees and saplings off of God's green earth. My folks jest kept money in the bank for'em tell he come along and married Aunt Susan and hogged all the Ward land 'ceptin what Cousin Bill and that fartblossom Hill's got and my little mite. Will squinted at the lowering sun and plodded onward.

A little way beyond Lake Harrison's place, the Big Road bore sharply to the left, heading down the slope of the ridge and disappearing between two lesser hills. Will continued along the slope, following a tributary road which branched off to the right at the curve. He moved slowly with a peasant plod, the cow dragging her feet in the dirt behind him. Now and then Will slowed to finger first one groin, then the other, to see if his strange new appendages had gone away, to see if he had imagined them. They had not gone away. If anything, they gradually swelled as he stamped along the rutted road, but the pain remained constant.

He crossed over a low spur thrust out from Anderson Ridge and passed down the other side. At the foot of the slope, he stopped in front of the big vertically planked building which had recently been built on the right side of the road. Already, snuff and castor oil advertisements were papering its new pine sides like measles. A sign over the door read, "Doc Ellis's General Store and Rowdy Branch Post Office."

Bessie Ellis came out on the porch, grinning at Will. She was a huge woman, tall and big-boned, with black hair and a sparse black mustache. Will Ward swore she could yank a tooth faster than it had time to hurt. She could also lance a boil or stone bruise or set a broken bone if she had to.

"Howdy, Will," she said. "You out of Brown Mule tobacco? You spect me to wait on you and your cow out here in the public road?"

Will grinned briefly. "Nope. I ain't never run out of tobacker. I buy some before that ever happens. I was wonderin is Doc out at the house."

"You ain't aimin to take your cow for Doc to doctor, are you, Will?" Bessie chuckled.

"Nope," Will said. "She's had her share of doctorin for one day. I wanted to see Doc concernin another matter."

"Yep, he was at home a little bit back," Bessie nodded. "One of Lake Harrison's offbearers sawed his hand and had to get it fixed. But no tellin when he'll go ridin off again."

"Well—I'd better mosey on out there if I spect to catch up with'im today," Will said. He turned away, leaving Bessie Ellis on the porch, her eyes narrowed in puzzlement. "Old busybidy," Will chuckled, "she'll have it figured out what ails me before I ever set eyes on Doc."

Doc Ellis had one of the few white houses for miles around. It was a two-story box-like structure with a one-story wing at the back, where the kitchen and Doc's Doctorin Room were located. Will led the cow up the driveway to the back of the house and stopped, watching Doc Ellis as he came out of the kitchen door carrying his black bag. His horse was tied to a nearby post.

When the doctor saw Will, he stopped, grinning. He looked tired. "Howdy, Will. How're you today?"

"So's to be about, Doc. How're you makin out?"

"Fair to middlin," Doc Ellis said.

The doctor studied Will silently, his brow furrowed. Will knew why Doc was puzzled. He knew nothing short of a broken leg or a ruptured artery would send Will Ward to the doctor, and he knew Will was not leading a cow around late in the afternoon during corn-planting time for fun. Will wanted to grin when he stopped to think what was going through Doc Ellis's mind.

"I got a birthin up at the Fork, Will," Doc Ellis said. "Could I help'ye any before I ride."

Will shuffled his brogan shoes in the dirt of the driveway, looking away toward the Blue Ridge. "Doc," he muttered, not looking at him, "I think I got me some trouble."

"What sort of trouble, Will?"

"I think I strained myself, Doc," Will said. "Usually I don't mess with nothing that piddlin. But I's over this way and I 'lowed I might as well let you take a look. But if you're too busy—" He turned back down the lane, the cow wheeling to follow.

"Will!" Doc Ellis called. "Damn it, come back here. You got me curious. Besides, you know I'm not too busy to check you."

Will stopped, shuffled back around. "Awright, Doc, if you say so. But I despise to take up'ye time for nothin."

Will tied the cow to a fence post and followed Doc Ellis across the spacious kitchen, past the dining table to a smaller room the doctor called his Clinic, whatever the hell that meant. The doctor turned on him.

"Now, Will, what's ailin you that you're ashamed to talk about?" Doc Ellis demanded. "You ain't gone and got you a dose of clap from one of them Hackett gals?"

"Hell, no!" Will snorted. "You know I wouldn't tech them with a pine root. Nope, I went and lifted too much and—and I strained my guts."

Doc Ellis's eyes narrowed back of his silver-rimmed glasses. "Drop your overalls, Will, and unbutton your drawers."

Will fumbled with his galluses, unbuttoned them, and dropped his overalls about his shoes. Then he unbuttoned his underwear from his navel down. Doc Ellis dropped into a chair, dragged it close to Will, and held open his underwear, squinting at Will's belly. He felt along Will's left groin, then his right. He was very brief. He stood up and met Will's level stare.

"You've gone and got yourself double hernias, Will," Doc Ellis said. "They're reducible though, for what that's worth."

Will gripped Doc's slender arm, squeezing until the doctor flinched. "What in hell is a hernia, Doc?" he demanded. "God-damn you, don't you browbeat me with your doctor talk."

"Will, you know what I mean." Doc Ellis wrenched his arm from Will's grasp. "You have a rupture in both sides."

Will's arm dropped away to his side. "Yeah," he nodded, "I knowd it. I knowd it was a rupture, and I knowd that's what *hernia* meant. But *rupture* sounds more like the ugly truth—like *clap,* maybe."

"Well, you are ruptured. And that's the ugly truth, Will. And you've got to do somethin about it. You can't just walk around with your guts bumpin against your knees."

"What, Doc?" Will pleaded. "What in hell can I do?"

"You could go down to Reynolds and get operated on. But it might not help. And you wouldn't go anyway. In the first place, you've not got the money. In the second, you wouldn't because you're too damned hard-headed. It won't kill you, so you'll go ahead and live with it, and probably till a hundred and four, if you're like your grandpa, which you are."

"Then they's nothin left but a truss, is there, Doc?"

"That's all there was to start with," Doc Ellis said. "It's your only choice, Will. And trusses are fairly satisfactory. How in hell did you get yourself in this fix? You had to strain yourself mighty hard, tough as you are." A grin flickered across his thin lips. "You've not been totin that cow around to save milk, have you?"

"Hit was that goddamn Hill Anderson, Doc," Will complained. "Hit was that goddamn Hill Anderson. Damn his soul, hit was him."

"How in heaven's name did Hill rupture you?" Doc Ellis looked puzzled. "He didn't hit you, Will? You could poke your fist clean through Hill's paunch."

"No, he didn't hit me," Will said. "I wisht he had. He'd be

eatin through his nose right now. No, the bastard shamed me into a liftin match in front of them Harrison boys."

"Liftin? What in the world did you-all lift?" Doc Ellis frowned. "Sawlogs?"

"Hit was a bag of fertilize," Will explained. "He bet me he could shoulder a two-hundred-pound bag of fertilize with his feet in a bushel measure and I couldn't."

"And did he?"

"Hell, no! He didn't, and I did."

"And you got ruptured, and he didn't."

"Yeah," Will muttered, looking at the Blue Ridge through the west window. "A man ain't never too old to be a damned fool."

"Well, let's get a truss on you," Doc Ellis said. "I'll show you how to push your entrails back in without hurtin yourself—"

"Doc!"

Doc Ellis paused. "Yeah, Will?"

"Wouldn't it help some to scrape the inner lining off of white-oak bark and spread it underneath the trusses?"

"About as much good as to spread chicken turds, Will. Where did you get that remedy from?"

"Bell's pa done that. He had one of the *Beach's Fambly Physician* books. Swore by it. Pa's got one, too."

"Will, that book came out more'n sixty years ago. This is the twentieth century. No, you'll have to face it. If it don't grow back by itself, it won't grow back without surgery."

"Well, if that's the way it's got to be," Will Ward said, "I reckon, by God, I'll jest have to put up with it."

"I figured you would," Doc Ellis said. "I didn't think anything else. If you lost your head, you'd learn to put up with it."

Will led the cow up the path leading from Doc Ellis's house and crossed Anderson Ridge, then West Mountain in forest darkness. He came out of the woods above his cabin, into the dusky-dark of twilight. He could see Bell moving around beyond the open window as he plodded down the slope. It gave him a comfortable feeling to see Bell at her endless work. There was something changeless about it. But when he concentrated on the strange yokes embracing his hips, pressing into his groins, he felt a touch of sickness. Things changed, all right, and usually for the worst. Even Bell would not be there at her work forever. He wondered if he would ever get used to the trusses, as he had to shoes when he was younger.

A blue crayon line of smoke led straight up from the chimney into the still air, merging with the indigo sky. Windows like sparks dotted the mountainside up where Coottown cabins hid in darkness. Matt Catlett's voice rolled out over the valley, echoing back from West Mountain, then bounding down Stud Branch, calling Jake to supper. Lower than her voice, riding the surface of twilight sounds, Will could hear the plunking of old Grandpa Eli Catlett's banjo. These were noises as unchanging as sunset and growing dark.

But something was different about them tonight. Something was goddamn changed all to hell and back. He was changed. Will Ward was not the same Will Ward who had got up early that morning and greeted the new day with his matin fart. Part of his manhood had been dropped like an afterbirth on Anderson Ridge.

"Got to git this cow up and fed," he muttered. "Got to feed my steers. Gonna be darker'n midnight in a witch's womb before a feller can say scat."

2

On Sunday mornings Will Ward, Bell, and some of the children went to meeting at Holkirk Church. Usually it was Tillie and Dan. Van was growing too old, and was already too big to order around when not working, and Will did not argue with his tomcatting as long as he did a good day's work. And Anna was too stubborn to go when she decided she would stay at home. Will figured she was a whole hell of a lot like him, so contrary that she scratched her butt when her head itched. Dan was still young enough to boss, although he showed growing signs of going his own way.

They always walked down Stud Branch in file, Will in front, followed by Bell. They always stopped at the spring and drank, whether they were thirsty or not. Then they continued on down the branch, after Will paused to point out to them where he intended to build his house on the ridge above. But on the Sunday following his rupture, Will did not stop at the spring. He did not even glance at the hillside above the branch. Bell and Tillie exchanged glances, brows arched, but said nothing.

Cousin Bill was waiting in his wagon as usual, at the Big Road. Rosa would be sitting beside him, a plump, rosy-cheeked little woman, the top of her hat coming just above her husband's shoulder. Two empty split-bottomed chairs, for Will and Bell, sat behind the wagon seat. In the back of the wagon-bed, quilts would be spread over wheat straw, on which the young folks rode, lying or sitting or sprawled like crippled birds, their teeth clicking from the jolting wagon.

This day, Bell climbed the spokes of the rear wheel like a ladder, and Will steadied her. She stepped into the bed and waddled over to the left-hand chair, letting herself down into it. Will followed her, biting back his new pain. Tillie and Dan climbed into the back and slouched down with Cousin Bill's two youngest children. His older son and daughter were already married and both attended Mount Hope Church, nearer where they lived.

Jan Ward was a skinny boy Dan's age. He lived through long spells of quiet like a dam backing up water. Then suddenly, when someone would wrench a word out of him, it was like lifting a floodgate. His word-hoard poured out in a torrent until his reservoir was empty. His sister Delia was a fat little vixen of six. She chattered like a mockingbird, every tune and mood she had heard, and, like a mockingbird, she became so much a part of the background sounds she was rarely ever heard.

The Sunday trip was ritual, from the moment Will Ward and his family left the house until they returned. The mule-drawn wagon was a prayer wheel—or four of them—rattling along the Big Road from landmark to landmark. In between there was the casual talk, but a part of the ritual demanded intervals of silence. Will and Bell and the children were to nod, but not to speak until they were loaded and seated. It was a part of their humility while accepting a favor from Cousin Bill, who had inherited a great deal more through his father from a grandfather he shared in common with Will Ward. Not that Cousin Bill demanded, or even desired, any consideration. He was too generous for that. It was the debt Will exacted from himself and his family because they required the ride to church, and his steers were too goddamn slow to pull a canemill. Someday he aimed to have him a two-hoss buggy to ride to church in, like old

Lake Harrison. By God, he might even put some pedals on it and leave the team at home. The singing leader at Holkirk Church ought not to have to depend on riding in another man's wagon, even with his own kinfolks.

This Sunday Will Ward spat tobacco juice over the edge of the wagon-bed, as Bill clicked his tongue for the mules to "get up!" "Well," he began, "I hear tell Preacher May is hell when he gits wound up. I spect we'll hear a good'un today."

"Yep," Cousin Bill nodded, "if you recollect, he converted seventeen last Sunday up on Hog Elk Creek. Preacher May's got fire, but he makes a whole heap of sense, too."

"I hear so," Will agreed.

"—and I see this big bird," Delia was chattering back in the wagon-bed, "an it ketcht a big worm right out in the yard, by its neck—an it pulled and pulled—and you know what, Cousin Tillie? That worm pulled back–and the bird pulled, and the worm stuck his tail in the ground and took a holt—and dontcha know, that worm pulled back—and the bird pulled still harder—and you know what, Cousin Tillie? That big, fat redworm yanked his neck out of the bird's mouth and flopped back out of sight, and you know what? That bird jumped up in a apple tree and set there cussin that worm, mad as a ole wet hen. And you know what—"

Tillie Ward smiled and nodded to Delia, but she did not look as though she was hearing a word.

Dan sat with his back braced against the tailgate, staring off up the road past his father, his jaw set. Every now and then he glanced at Jan, who sat at right angles to him, his back to the wagon-bed. When Will turned around and glanced at them, he could tell from the expression on Dan's face what was going on inside his head. He was probably thinking, "I'll see ye in hell before I start ye talkin, Cousin Jan. You jest set there like a knot on a log, if ye want to." Will grinned and looked back at the mules' bobbing rumps.

The wagon followed along the west slope of West Mountain, turned left, fording Tadpole Branch, lumbered around the S-curve, climbing, and crossed over Anderson Ridge. Will glanced toward Lake Harrison's house as they passed. Lake was loading up the two-seated surrey in the yard, two black horses hitched to it. Hoggish old sonofabitch—Will caught himself. Today was Sunday, and he was getting close to church. Selfish old hawg—cuttin all the timber in creation and stuffin the money in his pocketbook for them sorry boys.

"There's Old Man Lake and his folks gettin ready," Bill Ward said, as casually as though he had remarked that the sun was coming up, as usual. It was a regular thing for the wagon to rattle down the rutted road just as the Harrisons were loading up, and just as regular for them to arrive late at church. Will could never figure out how the hell a man could manage to drive a two-seated buggy drawn by horses slower than a mule-drawn wagon.

Bell Ward and Rosa had been talking steadily for several minutes about early beans, careful not to raise their voices enough to interfere with their men's more important conversation. Back in the wagon-bed, Delia was telling Tillie about their new calf that tried to eat its mamma, starting at her belly, pretending she did not know better. Dan and Jan still looked straight ahead, their stares intercepting at right angles.

They continued on down the Big Road, past Finley Swanson's millpond on the left, and forded Bare Creek. Beyond, they climbed the long, straight incline along Allen Ridge, then turned back to the right, over the crest, passing Allen's Blacksmith Shop and his house on the left. They followed the gashed spine of the ridge southwestward, oak forest on the right—except for a little scab of open earth where Allen's Shop Schoolhouse squatted—pine woods on the left. A half mile beyond Allen's Shop, the road forked, the left branch curling down the steep slope toward the Yadkin River valley, the right continuing straight ahead along the ridge. Bill Ward's wagon took the right fork and pulled into Holkirk churchyard a quarter of a mile beyond.

Meeting was already taking up, and the last talkers were straggling through the front door of the little weatherboarded church with the wooden fish on its steeple. Cousin Bill wheeled the wagon into the spot custom had reserved for him, and they unloaded. Jan had begun to talk about the new calf a half mile back down the road and was still talking, Dan Ward nodding now and then to show he was not deaf, a fixed grin on his face. Delia chattered on in the background, like a mockingbird in a treetop.

Cousin Bill helped first Rosa, then Bell down out of the wagon and began to unhitch the team. Will helped him. They tied the mules by their lead straps, one to each rear wheel, then shuffled away toward the front steps. The little church was almost gorged, from front to back. The rough plank benches were bulging with men, women, children, and grandchildren by the dozens. Bell and Rosa Ward found seats toward the back after herding the four children toward the middle, ahead of them. Bill and Will paced on up the aisle toward the pulpit, speaking to those along the ends of the benches as they squirmed around to watch.

The pulpit sat on a raised platform at the rear center. On Will's right as he approached, at an angle to the pulpit and congregation, four rows of benches were filled, chiefly with elderly laymen. This was the Amen Corner. In a similar position on the other side of the pulpit was located the choir, made up of men and women of all ages, and even children and grandparents. Cousin Bill, by right of inheritance, took his father's old position in the front row of the Amen Corner. Will walked across in front of the pulpit, nodded to the preacher, and approached the choir.

"Damn old baggy-assed suit," he thought. "I aim to have me a real fancy store-bought suit someday, like them Harrison boys. The singin leader ort to be dressed as good as the preacher, looks like."

Preacher May was a big man, looking more like a sawmill hand than a minister. His head looked square, his face looked square, and his big square hands covered his open Bible like hairy five-pronged hams.

"I take it you be Brother Ward, our singin leader," he smiled down at Will from the right hand of God. "I'm powerful glad you got here. I had jest reached that point where I decided to go on without your part in this here service."

Will Ward grinned and nodded to him, then turned to face the choir. Preacher May sat down behind his lectern like a thundercloud withdrawing below the skyline. Will motioned, and the choir stood up, individually—the younger ones popping up like jumping jacks, the middle-aged ones together, the older men and heavy women grunting to their feet, reminding Will of disturbed cattle. Removing a tunefork from his back pocket, Will struck it against a bench, held it to his ear, and listened to the ringing instrument, in key.

"Do! Do!" he chanted. "Do, re, mi, fa, sol, la, te, do!" Then he waved his hands and the choir followed:

"At the cross, at the cross
Where I fust saw the light
And the burden of my heart rolled a-way—"

After two more selections by the choir, Brother Lake Harrison, who had come in late as usual, opened service with a fifteen-minute prayer. He thanked God for the blessings of a bountiful world and exhorted the stingy and hypocritical and those who coveted their neighbor's worldly goods, to be saved today or burn forever and ever in the blazing furnaces of hellfire—hotter than any sawmill boiler ever stoked. Will Ward, listening carefully, kept thinking, "Amen! Amen!" but back of it meant, "And you too, Brother Lake. If I got any say-so with Old Scratch, I'll put in a word for'ye. Many sawmill bilers as you got now, they ort to make you head stoker down yander." All this was beneath the surface of his honest amens however, a level on which he went along with Brother Lake's prayer—even if he was a greedy sonofabitch cutting down every sapling in creation.

Will Ward's universe was a fairly simple organism without hidden complications. It consisted of the earth, which was square (or how else could the winds blow from the four corners like the Good Book says, by God?). The sun and moon and stars rose in the east and set in the west over a fixed geography, the center of which was Stud Branch and the outer perimeter of which dwindled out to vagueness beyond the distant place called Cubie. In addition to the earth, there was Heaven, just beyond the blue of the sky, where the stars, moon, and sun moved, and Hell, somewhere underground too deep to reach by digging. He had heard more than once when he was younger the devil cursing his wife when he had listened, ear close to a nail thrust into the ground after a thunderstorm.

Heaven was a city bigger than Northboro, with marble palaces twice as big as Hill Anderson's shithouse castle, separated by golden streets, and with pearly gates on the side where the Baptists entered. In the center of the town called Heaven, in the square, was a huge golden throne upon which God sat, a frown on his white-bearded face, bossing the whole works, on earth and in Heaven.

Hell was a huge cave where flames leaped and roared out of side furnaces like fifty thousand sawmill boilers ready to explode, forever and ever. Naked men and women, their peckers and pussies charred, rolled and squirmed on hot beds of coals and begged for water, while Old Scratch danced around them waving his pitchfork and tail and laughing his head off. In spite of the screaming damned, the cave of Hell was silent as the grave, except for the roaring flames.

God never came close to earth except sometimes in thunderstorms. Will was half convinced that God straddled thunderclouds now and then like black horses, and roared his displeasure at the sinful world. But Old Scratch walked about on earth almost every day and night. Will had glimpsed him time and again duck behind a big oak tree out in the woods. Being in the presence of Old Nick was a terrible thing to consider, yet Will watched for him without flinching. He was sure the old fart was trying to catch him sinning, and he, Will Ward, was going to be damned sure he did nothing bad enough to go to Hell for. Oh, he cursed pretty bad, but it was during the week, mostly. He always made up for it, leading the choir on Sundays at Holkirk Church. Weekdays did not count for cussin. Life was so goddamn hard for most folks they would go batty if they could not cuss a tad. Will was certain God was reasonable enough to understand that, even though he probably did not approve. Anyway, he was at his post on Sundays, and he made up his mind long ago to pass on on a Sunday so there would be no nay-saying when he answered roll call at the Pearly Gates where the good Baptists entered.

However, these ideas formed no consistent pattern, organized by meditation, in Will Ward's mind. Rather, they were isolated, formed in brief flashes of wonder, followed by solution.

Preacher May led off, slow and precise, outlining the sins of the immediate congregation and illustrating how it led to inevitable damnation. Then he exploded into blazing detail, describing that damnation. Will Ward sat back, the choir around him, a relaxed look on his face, feeling some pity for the fifty or more per cent he figured would go to Hell. He found himself wondering how fat-assed old Lou Goforth would look squirming on a bed of hot coals stark naked. Not that he bore her any ill will. It was just that he was curious. Preacher May aroused no dread in him. He was one of the elect; that was for damned sure. He had it all worked out in his mind, and arranged with God Almighty. Besides, many a gallon of water would pour over Finley Swanson's millpond before he had to answer roll call at the Pearly Gates. Grandpa John Baylus Ward had lived to be a hundred and four, and Will had the same blood.

After the last prayer, Will worked his way toward Preacher May, hemmed in by handshakers out in the churchyard. Cousin Bill was just in front of him, with big-assed Lou Goforth crowding him on the left and big-tittied Maud Dooley bearing in from the right.

"Preacher May, I'd be right proud for you to drop by and take Sunday dinner with us," Bill Ward offered.

"Well, now, I preciate that, Brother Ward." Preacher May's square face divided in a grin. "But Brother Lake Harrison done and axed me this past week. And I hear tell Miz Harrison cooks up a handsome mess of chicken and dumplins."

Will Ward turned away. "The greedy sonofabitch," he thought. "Hogs all the company to be had. I hope that hongry-lookin preacher gobbles him out of house and home."

He was not annoyed with Lake Harrison, because he had intended to invite the preacher to dinner himself. He knew he could not compete in hospitality with Cousin Bill or Lake Harrison or Hill Anderson. But, by God, someday when he got his new house built, he'd have preachers to Sunday dinner. It was just that Lake thought he was so goddamn—so dadburned highfalutin, when he wouldn't have a pot to piss in if he had not married Ward timberland.

As Will approached Cousin Bill's wagon, he saw someone duck behind it. He hurried around the bed. No one was in sight. He checked the leather lead straps holding the mules. They seemed to be intact. He turned away, then glimpsed something unusual about the brake line. His eyes narrowed. He ran his hand along the rope and found the gap. Someone had cut the brake line over half in two. Going down Allen Ridge or Anderson Ridge the rope would break and the wagon would run away, in spite of the mule's breast chains holding back against the wagon tongue.

Will stood there thinking. Who was the low-down bastard and where had he disappeared to? Suddenly he squatted. His eyes were only two feet from the face of Tom Dugan, who squatted under the wagon staring back at him. Will reached for him, grasped him by the collar, and yanked him from beneath the wagon, onto all fours. Leaping to his feet, Will cocked one brogan, ready to send it into the side of Tom Dugan's head. Tom went rigid, his scowling face half turned, as he braced himself to move fast.

"You low-down hellion, why'd you cut that brake line?" Will growled.

"I didn't cut no brake line," Tom Dugan grumbled.

"Git up, you swarthy bastard."

Tom unhinged slowly and stood erect, watching Will with shifting black eyes. He was about twenty, handsome in a gawky way, dark-skinned, with straight black hair. Will had once described him as "lookin jest like a Injun that got his ass kicked out'n his tribe for lookin too much like Tom Dugan." Will glimpsed his right hand as it slipped into a pocket.

"If I see your arm twitch like your paw's comin out of that pocket holdin that frog-sticker," Will said, so low only Tom could hear him, "I'm gonna tear your black head a-loose from your turkey neck with one lick." He balled his bony fist to prove it.

"I didn't cut your damn old brake line," Tom Dugan muttered. "You can't prove nothin."

"I reckon you's jest squattin down under that wagon-bed to piss, Tom Dugan?" Will said.

"I was tard. I was squattin in the shade. You can't prove nothin."

"I can stomp hell out'n you jest cause you're a smart-ass," Will said.

"What would your preacher say?" Tom Dugan's tongue flicked out, licking his thin lips.

Will cut a glance toward Preacher May, who was talking to Bell and Rosa Ward. "You git the hell out of here, 'fore I change my mind," Will said. "You ever mess with me or my folks again and I'll fix your clock, you Injun-lookin young hoss's ass."

Tom Dugan wheeled. The next moment he was thirty yards away, among the wagons. Will watched his bobbing head, then grinned and turned away. He began to tie a knot in the brake line. He shook his head. "Some folks was jest borned mean as hell. What made that hellion go and do a mean trick like this for? And why'd he pick Cousin Bill's wagon? That jest goes to prove the devil goes to church with the rest of us."

3

In early April of 1905, Will Ward's fifth child, third son, was born, with Doc Ellis in attendance. Will was now forty years old, and Bell was forty-nine. The child was normal and strong and grew like new corn. Bell named him Melvin for some reason, but Will called him Mal. The short form stuck.

Late in the summer of that year, the Wards busied themselves laying in stores for winter. Irish potatoes and sweet potatoes were "holed" in beds of straw or leaves beneath mounds of dirt, kraut was chopped and set in brine, beans were strung from the rafters in thick clusters to dry, and later on, corn was cribbed. Hot peppers were also strung from the rafters and log walls. Onions were piled in one corner of the half-loft where Van and Dan slept. Here, it would be too cold for them to sprout during the cold winter months.

When she could find time from her many chores, Bell would direct Tillie, now twenty, and Anna, eighteen, in peeling and slicing apples to dry in the sun. Will's two oldest hogs were growing fat from slop, and there would be hog-killing time after the first frost. Everything was stored that could be found to store, as the Wards scurried about like ants before a storm—and the Catletts fiddled on the slope above. The loose ends of farming were taken care of, and Will had a few weeks on his hands with little to do.

Dan was still in school at Allen's Shop. The older children had nowhere to go, nothing to do but work around the house and small farm. Will, restless, just over the rush season, decided to try another circuit of teaching singing down the river toward Northboro, as he had done almost every fall for the last eight years. It had been his custom to leave for two weeks at a time, carrying his songbook and tunefork and an extra pair of socks. Other clothing presented no problem. He simply wore the underwear and suit he left in until he returned. Who in hell ever heard tell of a body changing long underwear any more often than once every two weeks or so in the fall and winter? A feller was liable to catch newmonie fever like that.

On these trips, Will would catch rides on passing wagons or buggies, or walk, and travel from church to church teaching on weekday nights, if folks were too busy to come by day, and almost all day on Sundays.

Board was no problem. Will Ward could walk up to almost any door in a forty-mile radius between Northboro and the Carson County line, identify himself—if he was not instantly recognized—and be welcomed for as many nights as he cared to stay. But like preachers and traveling drummers, Will knew where the best food was served, the best featherbeds were found, and the prettiest gals listened in silence to conversation among their elders; and such places as these were where he managed to spend his nights.

In the late afternoon of Sunday, October 7th, Will was holding a singing class at Quaker Falls Baptist Church, southwest of Northboro. He had worked his way down the river since the Sunday before, had served Cub Creek Church on Saturday, and was ready to circle back, following the Boone Trail. He stood before the upturned faces and explained the notes as proudly as though he had just invented them and fitted them to the hymns they were about to practice. He held his songbook in front of him, reading the notes from it. He squinted at the book through his brass-rimmed spectacles, pretending to read both notes and words, although he actually knew both by heart and could have done as well in a dark room. He could not read a single printed word without first spelling it out in a whisper and pronouncing it. Tillie read new songs to him until he memorized them.

Will could tell from the way his pupils looked at him that they admired his skill. It never occurred to them, he realized, that Will Ward was practically illiterate, as most of them really were, and for that matter, Will did not admit it to himself. The congregation, or school, ranged in age from about eight to seventy-eight, but most of them were between their late teens and forty. It was a special occasion, and important visitation, when a singing teacher visited their church to "larn" them new songs and to lead them in old ones. They were happy to be a part of singing their way to glory, especially if they had better-than-average voices. Some of the younger women, in their prim white or striped blouses, long skirts, and high-topped shoes, cut more than interested glances at the rugged teacher when they thought he would not notice such brass. But Will Ward noticed. It was not fittin and proper for a young woman, especially a single young woman, to look straight at a married man too often and too long.

On this fall afternoon, when the air reminded Will of cool spring water, he was as close to contentment as he would ever be on this earth. The dollar a day he received was nothing to the self-satisfaction he felt standing above the many watching eyes. He forced his sloping shoulders back and stood as erect as his musclebound frame and yoked loins would permit. His new suit, only eight months old now, was a little small for him, but as nice as any in the small church house. It was black serge with light stripes running vertically; if the trousers had ever held creases, they had long ago disappeared. He wore a celluloid collar with round tips and a dark tie. His shoes were brown, lacing two thirds of the way up and hooking the rest of the way. Will's bald dome was partially concealed beneath a coxcomb, created when he had combed his long hair on either side toward the middle and then backward, hair that matched the auburn handlebar mustache.

Will lowered his head, struck his tunefork against his raised heel, then placed it to his ear. He grinned encouragement at the youngest singers and wondered where the hell he would spend the night. He had already turned down two invitations where he suspected the fare would be no better than on Stud Branch. He had counted on old Mrs. Watson, who had the best goddamn darky cook in the county, but so far Mrs. Watson had not appeared among his students, and this was the last song. It would be a hell of an out, he figured, if he had to ask someone if he could spend the night, with more than forty people in the room.

He listened to the tunefork. Then led off with notes. "La, la, do, te, do, la, sol, mi; mi, sa; mi, sa; mi, sa—" Then he went back and picked up the words matching them with the notes, and the class followed.

> "Yes we'll gather at the riv-er,
> The beauti-ful, the beauti-ful riv-er,
> Gather with the saints at the river
> That—"

Will missed a word, staring to his left.

> "—by the throne of God."

What had caught his attention was the young woman on the second row, over to his left. Or rather, what had attracted his attention was the fact that a young woman sat there watching him and not singing. Everyone else in the room was trying hard. Mouths were gaped wide, all the way back to the last bench. But she sat there making no attempt to sing and watched him calmly, her face passive, as though she were only moderately interested in his waving hands. There was nothing brazen in her level stare, yet nothing shy about her wide blue eyes. He had seen the same frankness in the face of a curious ten-year-old.

Will Ward studied her with a second glance, noted that she had to be tall, was comely, and fairly young, though her youth was rendered indefinite by the neat bun of black hair at her nape, a style usually reserved for older women. All he could see of her clothing was the white blouse, a tight band of a collar about her neck. He also noticed, without thinking about it, that her head was held high and that she was full-bosomed and apparently large-boned and strong. Then his attention flickered back to the song, and he forgot her. He would not have noticed her, at least at the time, if she had been singing.

After the last song had dwindled into silence, Will stood in front of the pulpit and shook hands with those who came forward to thank him or exchange small talk.

"Mighty good singing, Brother Ward."

"You's the best teacher we ever had, Mr. Ward."

"Anybidy that can't larn from you is not cut out for singin no-how." This from a fat middle-aged woman speaking past a red gooseberry tumor on her lower lip.

"Thank'ye. Thank'ye, folks," Will Ward nodded to them, shaking their rough hands. "I preciate'ye kind words. Thank'ye, Brother Messick. Thank'ye, Sister Parsons." And never a goddamn— Never a dadburned word from Old Lady Watson. And where in hell would he stay the night? With some of the grubby poreasses, sure as Hell sizzled.

"Yes, sir, Sister Hamby. You right as rain on that matter."

And finally they had all melted away but three young men and the woman who had not sung. She stood in front of him, straight and tall, watching him level-eyed, waiting for her turn. Her jet-black hair was parted precisely in the middle and pulled back to the bun. Her nose was a bit prominent, but along with her high cheekbones and strong chin, it added the strength of symmetry to her face. Her complexion was darker, or more amber, than the blue eyes would seem to indicate, but could have resulted from working long hours in fields without a hat.

"Yes, sir, young lady," Will Ward grinned. "What could I do for'ye?"

"Ma Watson sent me," she announced. "She wants you to come and spend the night. She was feelin a little porely and reckoned she wouldn't come to the singin."

Will suddenly felt good. Relief flooded in on him, filling him with cheer and good will. He wanted to jump straight up and click his heels together twice before he hit the floor. He nodded to the girl, shook hands briefly with the young men, and followed her out of the church. She had said nothing else after the invitation, but had turned to leave, not even confirming whether he would accompany her.

Will came up with her in the churchyard, striding fast to overtake her. A chilly breeze buffeted him in the face, a breeze fleeing the mountains, ahead of fall. Will shivered. It would be a good night to sleep in one of Old Lady Watson's featherbeds instead of on a thin-assed straw tick sagging between bed slats, with bedbugs playing leapfrog across his pecker all night long.

"I don't reckon I know you," Will said, looking sideways at her. "I've stayed at Sister Watson's house time and time again, and I never seen you thereabouts. You some kind of kinfolks?"

She turned her face to look at him, walking fast to match his stride. Her eyes were still frank, her face passive. "I'm no manner of kin," she said. "I work about the house. Cook, help out with pore old Doc—like that."

"I thought she had a cook," Will argued. "I thought Mandy was her cook. She was last time I stopped at Sister Watson's."

"She's dead," the young woman said. "Dropsy, or somethin. Ma Watson hired me."

"I be damned!" Will swore. "That's too bad. That darky womern could shore cook. Best danged biscuits this side of Jericho. Big as cowtur—" Will caught himself, glanced toward her, but she looked quickly away. "Big as my double fists, but real light and meller."

"I bake biscuits," she said, straight ahead. "But they're not as big as you seem to fancy."

He looked at her, on his right, but she was staring westward, where the egg-yolk October sun slid toward the dark blade of the Blue Ridge. She had donned a light coat over the blouse and skirt, a faded blue coat that reached within an inch of the high-laced shoe tops. He noted again how sturdy and strong-looking she appeared, and found himself allowing that some feller would get him a damned useful wife. He thought of her and Van together and reckoned it would make a fine match. Van was twenty-one now, and she—whatever her name was—had to be about the same age.

"What are you called by?" Will asked.

She looked at him, and her face softened but did not smile. "You mean, what's my name?"

"That's what I axed'ye," Will said.

"My name's Alvira. Alvira Matlock. I've been with Ma Watson for some months now."

"Why wasn't you a-singin a while ago back there?" He motioned over his shoulder with his right thumb. "Don't you like singin?"

She looked away again toward the Blue Ridge, and her face tightened in thoughtfulness. And when she was thoughtful, her eyes narrowed, and she looked sad. "I can't sing," she said. "I don't waste no time tryin to do what I can't. I don't reckon they's any singin in me."

Lucinda Watson met them at the front door of the big white house—a box-like mansion facing on the highroad leading from Northboro to Carson County. Dressed in dark folds of fabric, she reminded Will of a small haystack dressed for a funeral, except for her head. The white headache band and round white face stood out like a waning moon above her darker mass.

"Howdy, Will," she greeted solemnly. "I didn't feel up to singin today. My alto pipe's rusty. I knowd you'd be spectin to visit as usual, so I sent Vi, here, to fetch'ye."

"Howdy, Sister Lucinda." Will shook her pudgy white hand with his horny paw. "I'd about give up visitin'ye tell'ye gal showed up after the singin."

Vi Matlock turned and stared at him, her eyes wide and cool. Then she turned her back on him and entered the front door.

"Hit was a God's pity about Mandy," Will said. "Looks like the best darkies always dies fust."

"It shore is a pity," Ma Watson nodded sadly. "She was a good'un. But that Vi Matlock ain't no slouch. She can outwork any two men I ever seed, and ain't a lazy bone in her bidy."

"She'll make a ketch for some hard-workin feller," Will said.

"I hope it won't be no time soon," Lucinda Watson vowed.

"I've growd to depend on'er. Come on, let's go to the kitchen and chew the fat a spell."

Will followed her into the front hallway and past the carved oak banisters which climbed the stairs into the gloom above. They passed the parlor on the right, shadowy from the dying afternoon light and the drawn drapes. The old organ, the overstuffed black sofa, and leather-covered chairs squatted in cave-gloom waiting for some propitious occasion when they would be used again—perhaps Dr. Watson's wake. Ma Watson floated, her skirt just above the carpet, and Will Ward stamped along the hall and into the kitchen, which occupied most of the rear area of the house.

The cooking was done at the back, on the huge range surrounded by cupboards, a cooking table, and a chest containing bins for flour, meal, and sugar. Toward the front of the room was an oval dining table with ten chairs around it, but set at present for only three. Two rocking chairs addressed each other over near the south window. Lucinda floated over and deflated her bulk until she rested in one of the rockers, filling it from armrest to armrest. Will Ward let himself down into the other, careful not to spill his viscera into his groins. Vi Matlock was bustling about the range, moving silently, her hands quick and sure above the pots and pans.

Will Ward studied her as she stopped to light a kerosene lamp on the cooking table. He liked the way she moved without fumbling or wasted motions. He liked her youth and strength, which she wore like a party frock. And there was something else about her that stirred him inside—something new and strange to him. He squinted at her, trying to concentrate, trying to determine what it was that made her so different from the young women he saw frequently and knew, back in the hills. Tillie for example. It was not that Vi Matlock was pretty. It was not that she was better dressed than many girls he had seen in their Sunday best. Perhaps it was the neatness of the garments, the way they fitted her, indicating the obvious care she had taken in making them and in preserving them. That was part of what made her different. But there was another difference Will Ward was not capable of recognizing because there was nothing in his experience for a comparison.

"I say—how's the wife and fambly makin out?" Lucinda Watson said for the second time, eying Will curiously.

Will shifted his stare away from Alvira, momentarily trapped. "Why, they're fine," he swore. "Fine as frog hair." Will grinned. "My younguns turned out so big and strong, I might jest raise me a dozen of'em for field hands—if Bell holds out."

"You rascal you!" Lucinda Watson reared her rocking chair backward and slapped her right thigh, laughing. "You better cut out that foolin around. Your pore womern ain't gonna hold out if you don't let up."

Will grinned, stroking his handlebar mustache. He glanced at Vi Matlock. She was busy turning ham slices. "The Good Book say to produce and replenish the earth."

"Yea, Will Ward, but it don't mean for you to hog the whole show."

Will rocked for half a minute, chuckling deep in his chest. He was at ease and comfortable. The peace of the cozy kitchen and the fragrance from the cooking food filled him with pleasant impatience. His glance flickered toward Vi Matlock again. Somehow he knew her cooking was going to be good.

He started to tell Lucinda about his new boy, then remembered that he had never told her how many children he had. She knew very little about his business, and he liked it like that. He figured the less these lowlanders knew about their singing teacher the better off he was.

"Yep," he repeated, "I got to raise me some more field hands. I'm gonna buy some more land to add to my farm, one of these fust days, and I got to have me some ready field help. I believe in big cornfields and in good hoein." He glanced again at Vi, but she seemed to be paying no attention to what he was saying.

"You'd better start grabbin that land," Lucinda Watson grinned, "less'n you spect to live tell doomsday."

Will's brow furrowed like plowed upland. He looked toward the range, then out the window at wool-grey dusk. "How's the Doc?" he asked. "Is Doc Watson restin well these days?"

Lucinda's face clouded. "As good as a bidy could spect. But he's gettin bad bedsores, and they bother him more and more. His mind's slippin more, too. I swear, paralysis don't have no mercy on a bidy, doctor or drummer. I find myself thinkin it would be a mercy if he jest slipped away easy-like to the Promised Land. I hope and pray that's the way I'll go."

"Pore Doc!" Will nodded. "It ain't fair to'im, after he spent his whole livelong life tendin to sick folks."

"I got so's I can't handle'im," Lucinda groaned. "If it wasn't for Vi, I'd have to have me a buck nigger jest to come in and move him around."

Vi Matlock carried the lamp to the dining table, her face copper-bright. "Time I get the dishes set on the table, it'll be time to eat, Ma Watson," she announced.

Lucinda looked at Will. "You want to go outside and wash up and sech-like before supper."

"I don't mind if I do." Will pushed himself to his feet, leaning away from his guts.

Opening the back door, Will walked to the end of the porch. He leaned his right shoulder against a post and idly unbuttoned his fly, as he stared down across the slope, now leading away into dusky dark. He reached inside his britches, then whirled toward the back door. Nobody was in sight.

"Whew-w-w!" He wiped his forehead with his hand. "That was closter than pissin in a coiled rattler's eye."

Swinging from the post, he let himself down from the porch and strode toward the white outhouse, two hundred feet away. When he came back out of it, he turned and studied the building, backing away and holding his head at different angles, like a curious bird.

"Damn nice'un," he muttered. "I aim to have me one that purty some of these here days."

He shivered and turned away. Some sonofabitch jest stepped on his grave spot. He glanced at the October sky, where more and more stars were exploding into flecks of light. To him, that was just what they were—flecks of light God Almighty had stuck up there for purposes that did not concern mankind.

"Gonna frost next week," he muttered. "Got to git home and git my barrels and rocks handy. Hog-killin is a-comin up." Then he thought of Bell, plump and warm in bed, and his right hand crept into his pocket.

On the back porch, he washed his hands in the washpan on the shelf, dried them on the towel swinging from a nail in a post, and entered the kitchen. Alvira Matlock had the table set, and she and Lucinda Watson were seated and waiting. Will looked first at the biscuits. There was a dish full, brown-crusted and smoking. Little old bitty things no bigger than his single fist. But he reckoned two such fancy biscuits could be as good as one the size of a cowpile, like Mandy used to make and like Bell's.

Will sat down. "Gittin chilly out. Gonna frost in another few days."

"Soon's the moon's wanin, we start hog-killin," Lucinda Watson added. "Pass the taters, Vi, honey."

Vi Matlock, on Will's right, handed him the dish of stewed potatoes, not speaking, not even looking directly at him. He glanced at her. Her face was still, her blue eyes wide, as though her mind were miles away. He looked toward the biscuits, hungry for them. Goddamn flat table! Folks couldn't never eat for reachin vittles around to one another. Why in hell everybody didn't own a round table with a turnin-waiter was more than he could understand.

Will piled potatoes onto his plate, selected two thick slabs of ham, then passed the dish on to Lucinda, on his left. He accepted the cabbage dish, served himself, following this with a helping of steaming turnips. Then he began to eat—after he had sniffed a dab of each vegetable to test it. He always did this with strange cooking or an unfamiliar dish. He cut a chunk of ham and shoved it into his mouth, following it with a bite of biscuit. He closed his eyes and stopped chewing, absorbing the taste. Jesus Christ, it was good. Damned good. He could not figure how a gal no older than Alvira Matlock could cook like that. He began to chew again, slowly, swallowing the tangy juices.

After he had swallowed the ham and biscuits, he reached for the potatoes. They were not as good, but they were potatoes. He never put two kinds of food in his mouth at once. It confused his taste. He would eat a bite of one, then dip into another. On Stud Branch, this was no problem since usually they had only one or two dishes on the table in addition to the bread. He could not understand how some folks he had watched eat could cram three or four kinds of eating into their mouths until they ended up with a mouth full of mixed-up mush. It did not make good sense to him.

Lucinda Watson ate hurriedly, forking up small bites and feeding the fires of her bulk as though she stoked a furnace through a door too small. Vi ate slowly, methodically, staring out the back window. But her head was cocked slightly as though she listened for something she dreaded to happen. There was a sadness about her eyes and shallow weariness not obvious from a distance of several feet. Will glanced at her over a loaded fork. She was a quiet woman. Will had never figured how to make out with a quiet woman. But a talking woman like Old Lady Watson he could hold his own with any day in the week.

"What you think of Roseyvelt now?" Lucinda delayed her eating long enough to look at Will.

Will Ward chewed rapidly, swallowed his cud, cleaned his teeth with a sweep of his red tongue. "I think he's in the wrong party. I think he's way yander nigher to bein a Democrat than a Publican. He's as different from old McKinley as night is from day."

"The trouble with Teddy is he ain't neither one," Lucinda said. "He jest makes out as he goes along, like a feller fightin a bresh far."

"I don't know about this here canal they're plannin down south a ways," Will affirmed. "I heard one smart feller say they's liable to cut North Amercie a-loose from the south part, and we's liable to float north'ards to the North Pole and freeze the United States stiffer'n a Eskymo's pec—" He caught himself, "—harder'n a Eskymo's farm," he finished.

Alvira Matlock glanced at him, the shadow of a smile about her wide mouth. Lucinda tossed her head erect.

"Now, I don't reckon they's any danger of that a-happenin. I'll allow the North Amercie part is too heavy to float furder'n a few mile. We got to be knockin noggins about matters more serious. If we don't come up with somebidy else sides Bryan, we liable to git licked again in nineteen-oh-eight, and the Publicans is liable to end up puttin a king on the throne up there in Washington. They been in so long now, with their land grabbin, we liable to end up ownin the whole world and we can't hardly feed ourselfs."

"I reckon you're right, there," Will nodded. "Why in hell they ever tuck that Cubie place is more'n I can figure. Hit's as fur away as the moon. Hit's so damn fur away, it ain't fit for nothin but to grow furreners on."

"That Teddy's gonna be a hard candidate to lick—"

A low wail cut across her speech, not loud but penetrating, seeming to fill the whole house and to originate at no particular point. Alvira Matlock sprang to her feet, shoving back her chair, her eyes narrowed in dread.

"Never mind, honey," Lucinda said. "He wants me. You set back down and keep Will company, and I'll go see what he wants." She braced her hands on the edge of the table and worked her way to her feet, a notch at a time.

Will Ward finished up his second round of helpings, gulped his black coffee, and shoved back his plate. He belched but trapped it in his mouth. He had heard tell that low-country gals did not take to gentlemen belching at table. He looked at Alvira. She sat with her elbows forking her empty plate, her chin in the cup of her hands, gazing out the dark window. There was a remoteness about her stare, but her half-tilted head indicated an awareness of the room where the cry had originated, of the house about her, even of Will Ward's scrutiny.

"How long you been with Sister Lucinda now?" Will asked, wiping his mouth on his sleeve.

She dropped her hands. Her head tilted to one side like an alert robin's. "How long?" She stared at him. "About eight months, I reckon."

"Where bouts you from?" Will demanded. "Where'ye folks live at? Northboro, I spect."

"No, I'm more of a country girl than that," she smiled. "Papa's name's Henry Matlock. Lives over about Ready River. Mamma was a Groot. Her folks own land along the river over there."

"Groot!" Will mused. "That's a quare name for a human bein. Must be them Dutch folk that settled in around there way back yander."

She looked straight at him. "They *was* Dutch folk. My great-great-grandfather, Stephen Groot, come over and settled that land before eighteen hundred sometime. They been citizens like you and me for a good many summers and winters now."

"I didn't go to be a-pokin shame cause they's Dutch," Will said. "Dutch is damned good workers. You know, my great-great-grandpa come over from low country in Scotland and done the same thing. Settled a whole passel of land up in the hills. I still own some of it."

"Is *Ward* a Scotch name?" Alvira Matlock asked, meeting his level stare.

"No, hit's a Merican name," Will grinned. "Jest like Groot is."

Vi smiled and dropped her eyes. "Now we're even," she said.

"This your fust job away from home?" Will asked, trying to keep her talking. He could not endure sitting in a room with someone and not talking. And something in the back of his mind kept goading him to learn all he could about this young woman. She was a fine looker, strong as a mule, it looked like. If he could just team Van up with her— But she probably wouldn't look twice at Van, her from the low country and all.

"No," she said, meeting his eyes again. "I've got six brothers and sisters, four of'em less than ten. Papa's a storekeeper. Not much of a store. I had to get out and help. I folded papers on the *Hornet* back a little over a year ago. Not much pay, but some."

Will Ward's brows arched in disbelief. "You mean your folks is blackass—" He caught himself again. "—is—Publicans?"

Vi laughed. "No, as good Democrats as a body could find in this Publican county."

"Well, then, what in God's name was you doin a-workin on

that blacka—" He caught himself as before. "—that black-lie Publican paper?"

"Cause I needed a job," Vi Matlock sighed, "and I wasn't very old, and the Democrat *Foolcatcher* didn't need another girl to fold papers."

"I reckon beggars can't be choosers," Will grumbled. "But I'd die and go to hell with my back broke before I'd be caught dead just techin one of them *Hornet* black-lie papers."

"I reckon I'm doin some better here," Vi said. "I got a fancy room and good board, and that takes a load off my folks. Then I send Papa the fifty cents a week extry I get, and that helps'em out too."

"Fifty cent!" Will's forehead wrinkled. "Looks like Sister Lucinda could spare you a mite more'n that, a big strong womern like you."

"Thank'ye," Vi Matlock smiled. "But I don't spect I can complain. She's not as well off as this house would make'ye think. And she's right good to me. Just like a mother, might near."

After supper, Lucinda Watson and Will rocked and talked politics while Alvira Matlock washed the dishes. When she was through, she carried a lamp and led them upstairs to their bedrooms. She stood in the door of Will's room and held the light while he lit his lamp, then she turned away, without speaking, and closed the door after her. Will dropped into a chair, frowned in pain, then began to unlace his shoes, one eye on the four-poster bed and its thick bedding of straw and goose-feathers.

Will had just blown out his lamp and stood by his bed in his long underwear when he heard Dr. Watson cry out again. He padded barefoot over to the door and eased it open, placing his eye to the crack. The hall was dark, but the door to the room across from him stood ajar and a shaft of light slashed through it. He started to turn away, when the door suddenly opened wider. Alvira Matlock stood in the doorway, peering down the hall toward Dr. Watson's room. Her hair was loose and reached her waist in a mass of gleaming black. She was dressed in only a thin petticoat. Will could not avoid seeing the full swell of her breasts and the outline of her long, tapering legs. For several seconds he lingered and stared, feeling a flush of excitement and guilt along his neck. Finally he eased the door shut and stood with his back to it, breathing hard and feeling something between guilt and satisfaction.

"Jesus Christ! but she's a fine-lookin gal," he thought. "Real sturdy and strong-lookin. If I was twenty year old and not hitched a-ready, I'd go a-courtin with that gal, shore as green simmerns set'ye teeth on edge."

The next morning Will ate breakfast with Lucinda Watson. Alvira Matlock was nowhere in sight, and Will guessed she was either with Dr. Watson or sleeping late after sitting up with him. He did not mention her name, and Lucinda did not bring it up. He left early and headed back up the river for Stud Branch, whistling as he walked, his coat slung over his shoulder in spite of the fall air nipping his earlobes, songbook and tunefork crammed into his back pocket. Folks up around Trap Hill would have to wait until his next circuit to larn singin; hog-killin came first, by God.

4

On Thursday, a week later, Will Ward killed his two fatted hogs, or rather Albert Essex knocked them in the head with the back of a single-bitted ax and stuck them through the neck into the heart. Will swore he had never learned how to bleed a hog right and was too damned old to learn. Albert was paid for his skill with a mess of fresh pork. Later the extra shoat, castrated in June, would be moved into the pen vacated by the butchered hogs and would be fatted for spring slaughter.

It was a busy morning for all the Wards. Bell and Tillie scraped fat from the hogs' entrails and worked busily at rendering it into lard over the open fireplace. Dan held the carcasses still while old John carved them into appropriate sections with his good left hand. Will and Van salted the sections down on the shelves in the front area of the smokehouse, where John lived in the back. Anna was in charge of the baby, who was fussy from cutting teeth, and took him for a stroll down Stud Branch late in the morning.

Will shuffled out of the smokehouse for a breath of fresh air and to rest his stooped back. Raw lean meat and salt filled his thinking. After working his entrails back inside his belly beneath the trusses, he braced his shoulders and squinted at the sun. Almost eleven-thirty. Soon time to eat. His guts burbled hungrily. That first meal of fresh lean pork was always a treat he looked forward to, and Bell could fix it up proper. He sniffed smoke from the chimney. It was a bright, clear day under the blue sweep of a cloudless sky. The frost had long ago evaporated, but the air was sharp to his taste, like a sip of pure mountain corn. West Mountain, the slope of Fox Mountain, and the north spur of East Ridge were changing from green to mottled red, yellow, and brown. Will thought of the patchwork quilt his ma and pa had once had their likenesses struck in front of as it swung from a tree limb, and then forgot it. He did not dwell on the fact that the blue sky and warm sun, the sharp air and fall colors combined to create a special kind of world about him. His hands were red and sticky with hog blood. But he knew he felt suddenly good, goddamn good. And if he had thought beyond his feelings, he would have sworn it was because he would soon be chompin on Bell's cookin.

"Godamighty! what a purty day for hog-killin!" he said aloud. "Godamighty! what a purty day for eatin and workin and lookin around!"

His right hand slipped into his pocket and fingered his loins. When Will felt good about things in general, his hand always gravitated downward and settled about his genitals. He thought furtively, "Might try hit tonight if me and Bell ain't too tard from workin all day long with hog meat."

A woman's scream angled across his musing, a shrill scream of terror and pain. It came from inside the house. He stood there, legs widespread, fists still clinched. Before he could move, a tall shaft of flames erupted through the back door, followed closely by Tillie, who wailed as she swam through the smoke-filled air. The torch writhed as it danced, and out of what seemed to be a head, now crowned with flames, Bell Ward's screaming leaped, to knife across the blue October silence and goad Will's indecision. Bell's long dress and petticoat burned like a stack of straw, concealing everything but her voice. She fled blindly up the slope, wearing her destruction as a brilliant cloak.

"Stop!" Will yelled. "You goddamn idjet, stop!" He leaped toward her, intercepted her. He shoved her to the ground, scorching the hair on his hands and wrists. The stench of burning fabric and hair choked him. He rolled her like a log, along the ground, reducing the flames. Her feet and hands groped out of the smoke.

Van dashed up beside Will. He tore off his denim jacket and beat at his mother. Tillie danced around them, slapping at the smoke with windmill strokes and sobbing. The flames died in grudging flickers after exhausting most of their fuel.

Bell Ward writhed against the packed clay, naked except for a fringe of blackened fabric about her shoulders. Her lumpy flesh—massive thighs, scorched loins, torso, pendant breasts—had turned a bright pink. In areas where she had scoured her flanks and limbs against the ground, raw flesh oozed lymph and blood. Her head was a blackened knob covered by a stubble of burnt hair. Will thought he smelled the fresh meat back in the smokehouse.

"Goddamn it! Pick'er up, Van!" Will Ward yelled. "She's gonna skin herself alive. You know I can't tote her, heavy as she is, and my guts spillin out."

Van Ward knelt and worked his huge arms beneath his mother. He struggled to his feet and carried her without effort toward the back door. She moaned gently in his arms. Will and Tillie followed, colliding with each other at every other step. Van stared straight ahead, as though his mother were something obscene that he could not bear observing. Tears ran down his cheeks and down his chin and dropped onto her raw flesh, but his mouth was straight as a knife slash.

As Van disappeared through the back door with his burden, Dan came charging up, followed by his grandfather. Old John stood, feet apart, sobbing for breath. Will whirled on him.

"Bell cotch her frock on far and burnt herself real bad!" he shouted, close in front of them. "Dan, you hightail it over acrosst the mountain and fetch Doc Ellis. Tell'im to ride like hell, for God's sake."

Dan, huge and white-faced, started to question him. Will swung at his head and Dan ducked. "Git, damn you!" he yelled. Dan whirled and charged up the slope of West Mountain toward the woods.

Will ran into the house, followed by John. Van had placed Bell Ward on her bed and stood staring out the open window.

Tillie wrung her dry hands and whimpered, her full-moon face warped with grief. Bell lay on her back and stared dully at the rafters, her breath coming in almost silent sobs. She seemed unaware of those about her. Now and then she would shiver violently, as though cold gusts of wind swept across her naked flesh.

Will stooped and covered her with a sheet. "What do we do?" he demanded of his father. "What in hell does a bidy do tell Doc Ellis gits here?"

"A poultice of arsh tater scrapings and milk is good for burns," old John whispered. His white beard quivered as he sucked in air through his pursed lips.

"Godamighty, Pap!" Will Ward stormed. "It'd take two bushels of taters and a peck of milk to cover all of her that's burnt. It'd take a day's work to git it ready."

"I know that," John Ward nodded solemnly. "Don't you reckon I seed how burnt she is. The main item is to ease her hurtin tell Doc gits here."

"Well, how in hell does a bidy do that?" Will argued. "That's what I been tryin to git'ye to say."

"The best thing is to wrop her with sheets wet in cold water," old John said. "That's what Doc Beach writ in his fambly medicine book."

Anna tottered through the front door, the baby in her arms. "What's goin on?" she yelled. "What's happened to Ma?" Her eyes were mostly white, her breast heaving for air.

"Your maw cotch her frock on far and burnt herself real bad," John Ward repeated. "Dan's gone to fetch Doc Ellis."

Anna slung the baby onto the other bed and rushed across the room to her mother. "Ma! Ma!" she shouted. "Ma! you old crazy fool, what did'ye go and catch'ye frock on fire for? Ain't you got a lick of sense?"

Will Ward struck her across the face with the back of his hand. She reeled backward and collapsed, sitting against the bed on which the baby wailed. "You didn't have to go and hit me. I dread her bein burnt as much as anybidy. What did she go and do a fool stunt like that for? Crazy as a bedbug, that's what she is."

They wet a folded sheet and worked it beneath Bell Ward.

Then they covered her with another and pressed it around her sides. She still lay on her back, breathing harshly, her stare fixed on the rafters overhead. She was like that when Doc Ellis's horse galloped up, outside.

Doc Ellis stalked into the cabin carrying his black bag and plowed his way between Will and his father, who stood by the bed studying the woman. The doctor pulled the wet sheet back carefully and almost casually examined the red flesh. Then he turned to Will.

"Will," he said, "you and your pa come outside. I want to talk to'ye a minute."

Will trailed the doctor, a knot tight as an erection in his guts between his hernias. Outside, near the well, Doc Ellis turned to them. He stood for a time staring over their heads toward the fall-draped slope of East Ridge, his thin, weather-brown face without expression.

"Will," he said finally, "I won't mince no words with you. Bell's done for. It's just a matter of a few days."

Will Ward threw up his hand to stop him, as though stopping his words would stop what he predicted. "But goddamn hit, Doc, can't you—"

"Nothin!" Doc Ellis said. "There's nothin I can do but try to ease her pain. She wouldn't survive a burn of half that area. You'd better get the younguns set for her dyin. It's got to come, sure as sunset."

Will turned and stared at his father, silently begging counsel. The old man chomped a few times, his white beard wagging. He gestured with his good left hand, then let it drop back to his side. "I'll go—" he began. "I'll go and start fixin her a coffin, son," he said. "I'll make her a fittin coffin to rest in."

In less than a week, Bell Ward was dead, her vital fluids having seeped from her raw flesh, dehydrating her like a squeezed sponge. And Will, despite his shock, ate well of the food donated by a startled community.

Old John had finished the poplar coffin with time to spare, and Bell was laid out in it, on a folded quilt covered by a tucked bedsheet. Her head was placed on a pillow. Bessie Ellis and Rosa Ward dressed her as neatly as they could in what had been one of Bessie's Sunday frocks, a red-and-blue-flowered print. Even then it had been necessary to bind her sticky torso and legs with strips of torn sheet before the oversized dress (the largest one to be found) could be slipped on. Bessie Ellis added a hat —actually half a hat—as an afterthought. Rosa's green straw hat was cut in half and placed over the front of Bell's head to conceal the blackened stubble of her scalp.

When they were through, the two women called Will, who sat on the front porch staring off down the valley. They stepped back, arms folded, and waited for Will's approval, as though the corpse were some kind of flower arrangement Will was to judge. The casket sat on two sawhorses to the left of the fireplace. Will squinted down at what had been his wife. She looked so uncomfortable and out of place, wedged into the narrow box —and that crazy hat, for Christ's sake—that Will wanted to grin at her and tell her to stop playing possum and get up off her dead ass and go to work.

But that was before the wake, before the folk ritual had run its course and the vicarious bereaved had withdrawn—before the knowledge settled on his stooped shoulders like a bag of fertilizer that Bell was not playing possum, that she would never get up and work again, that he would never rut between her massive thighs and thrust deep into her passive flesh again, that he was left all alone on Stud Branch with a family to manage. Of course there was a fetal ache at loss of his mate, an ache he could neither acknowledge nor express. But that was no problem. Aches gradually diminish, whether a body is able to weep or not. But problems arising from loss of a damned good helper can multiply day by day.

Anna took the baby and stayed at Cousin Bill's house during the Friday night, Saturday, and Saturday night wake. Bell lay in state without flower or wreath, and people came from miles around to see. Bell Ward was not just dead, not just a corpse. She had burned to death. She was a corpse well worth seeing —they hoped. Will sat at the back of the cabin beside Van when the Catlett clan filed in, in an almost endless chain, from bare-tailed toddler to stoop-assed old granny woman. They reminded Will of tumbleturds shuffling across a cowpile.

"Look at'em!" Will hissed to Van. "Ever goddamn Catlett, ever goddamn houndog, ever goddamn hoppytoad in Coottown must be a-stumblin past pore Bell a-gawkin down at her."

"It's a free show," Van said. "You can't cheat the bastards out of a free show. They ain't seen nothin this big since old Granny Lucy set down in a coon trap."

"When I die," Will said, "I want'ye to lay me out with my pecker pokin out of my britches and give'em somethin to gawk at." He grinned. "You do, and I bet old Matt'll cry all the way back to her shack grievin over what she missed in life."

Van turned his head aside, his massive shoulders quaking with silent laughter.

The Catletts came first and returned to their shacks, to sit and stare out across the valley and wait for an act of God to deliver their next meal. The other neighbors came a little later, in dumb sympathy, expressing what they could not say with gifts of food, or by sitting through the long nights while Will and Tillie and the two boys tossed and tumbled in their beds. The wake was a communal rite which arranged itself automatically and with little discussion.

Cousin Bill, Rosa, and Albert Essex and his wife, Mater, divided shifts and sat by the warm fireplace all night, keeping the corpse company, the corpse and the bereaved, and, incidentally, warding off evil spirits of the dead by their wakefulness, although they did not admit even to themselves that this was one of the main purposes for a wake. The Harrisons came on Saturday, came, looked, mumbled polite condolences, and departed. They seemed to think that no one expected them to leave the comfort of plump beds and sit all night in the miserable cabin, not even with kinfolks. And Will Ward, glowering from the back of the room, allowed he did not give a good goddamn. He would have felt ill at ease with them staying and him knowing they resented it.

Tom Dugan came, slinking and furtive, as though he expected someone to kick him out before he reached the casket.

He divided his shifting glances between Will and the corpse of Bell Ward, then sidled toward the door, one eye on those in the room, nervous as a whore, as Will put it later, who had stumbled into a prayer meeting. Hill Anderson was well-dressed, solemn, and proper, but he seemed more interested in the live women present than in the corpse. Will caught him watching Tillie with narrowed eyes. He did not appear even to glance down at the corpse but waddled toward the front door, his kinky red hair dull in the dim light. The last expression Will saw was a frown as Hill glanced about the cabin. No one had expected his wife to come. She never left the shadows of the big house on the ridge.

"Frown at my belongins, you horny sonofabitch," Will thought, looking away from Hill's back-thrust rump. "When hit comes your time to go, that fancy shithouse castle of your'n might jest as well be a corncrib or a hogpen."

The funeral at Mount Hope Church—where Bell had been baptized and had first worshiped—was altogether successful, from opening prayer until the last red clay clod had fallen on Bell's grave. Cousin Bill hauled the casket in his wagon, along with his own and Will's children. He permitted Will to drive his new buggy drawn by his recently acquired bay mare. Rosa rode in the buggy with Will. Even though they left home early, they found the church grounds already covered with wagons and buggies when they arrived, many of them from the Holkirk Church area. The duty of the pallbearers was more than honorary; they had to carry the heavy coffin over fifty yards to the church altar.

The crowd overflowed the building. Will and his offspring sat on the mourners' bench in full view of the congregation, while Preacher May, borrowed from Holkirk, declaimed on the virtues of the departed sister. The congregation watched Will Ward more than the preacher's waving arms, studied him openly or covertly to see if they could trap him with his emotions down, to see if he would show some sign of grief for his dead wife. Of course they glanced occasionally at Tillie, who sniffed silently, at grim-faced Anna, both girls in new black dresses made by Rosa from cloth donated by Bessie Ellis. And they glanced at Van and Dan, hulking giants in wrinkled blue serge suits long ago discarded by Doc Ellis.

But it was chiefly Will's day. And Will Ward was not about to show emotion, because he had little to show. He had been too busy to equate the corpse in the crazy-assed half-hat with Bell, good old Bell, who had taken him patiently to bed when he was seventeen and she was twenty-six, who had labored in the fields and in birthing his offspring, who had cooked for him, and who had spread her flaccid thighs to accept his hard, rutting body, all without protest and with little compensation. The shock was a drowsy awareness back of the ritualistic excitement he shared with those about him.

The shock was sudden. It hit him where changes always hit him hardest. He had healthy appetites, and catered to them as best he could with the means at hand, because sleep, sex, and food were the closest blessings to luxury he would ever experience. When he sat down to Tillie's supper on Sunday night after the funeral, he was ready to be filled. He took a bite of the skillet cornpone and immediately blew it all over the table, following the bite with a gulp of black coffee. He rinsed it around in his mouth and swallowed it with a frown.

Tillie stopped feeding the baby cream gravy and stared at him. "What ails'ye, Pa?" she asked, brows arched. "You act like'ye bit into a red pepper pod."

"This goddamn bread!" Will roared. "Hit's pure salt and mushy as a fresh cowturd. You jest might as well make corn mush mixed with salt."

Tillie started to speak, stared while he sampled the fried kraut. He spat that out too. "Godamighty, Till!" he thundered. "Why in hell didn't you jest put a pinch of kraut in'ye fried salt?"

Shoving the baby into Anna's arms, Tillie leaped to her feet, her face contorted. "Ma never larnt me how to cook nothin," she wailed. "How was I spected to larn? Ma didn't plan on bein livin one day and dead the next." She stumbled from the cabin into the night, hands pressed to face, her sobs trailing her in gobs of sound.

"She's actin mighty peevish here lately," Will grumbled toward the rest of the family. "I didn't aim to git her bowels in a uproar. But goddamn, when I set down to supper, I didn't come spectin to find no damn salt lick."

"The reason she was upset," Anna said evenly, "is that she might not a-tuck what you said to be braggin on her cookin—the way you meant it. Tillie's a little slow-witted like that."

Will glowered at her dark eyes. "If you mean them words to be smartalecky, you'd better watch out or I'll yank'ye ass out of jint."

Anna's breakfast the next morning was no better. The two girls alternated for the next several days, but neither of them seemed to gain much experience, at least so far as Will's taste buds could distinguish. He reached the point where he would sniff the food, then explode into a tirade, knowing the dish would taste worse than it smelled. Tillie labored frantically to improve, testing and retesting as she squatted by the fireplace. Anna shrugged his oaths off as though they were snowflakes, and went about her business. Finally, Will sent them to Rosa Ward for instruction.

Tillie arrived and listened carefully to her teacher, so Rosa told Will later. And it was a long time before he learned that Anna spent most of the day sleeping in a pile of dry leaves on the side of East Ridge. Both Anna and Tillie were careful to keep this secret. It was not that Will was consistently violent: he was as inconsistent in his tantrums as dynamite with a faulty fuse.

Around the first of November, one of Will's work steers broke out of the pasture. The boys were away, and Will followed the animal's tracks east along the valley toward Coottown, then south up the spur of East Ridge along the narrow wagon road. Once in the road, the tracks did not veer, but entered the woods and continued southward along the crest. They were easy to follow because the Catletts had no animal larger than a hound dog, and Will's steers had not traveled the ridge since the last rain. Each stride Will clomped down the long road tamped harder the powder of his ire. Once he stopped by a fresh dung pile and spat brown tobacco juice at it, as though the juice could defile the excrement and, indirectly, harm the steer.

He left the woods, crossed the fallow saddle, re-entered the tunnel of half-naked trees and green pines, which ended abruptly at the Big Road. There, the tracks turned left, becoming lost in the clutter of wagon ruts and hoofprints. Because there was nothing else to do, Will kept going, shoulders slumped as he searched the road for marks. A hundred yards east of the Ridge Road, he veered to the right, plodding the course of the steep S-curve along the side of the ridge; then he bore northward, to parallel the base of the slope and ford Ward Branch on the stepping stones. No one was in sight at Albert Essex's house, below the road and between the curve and the creek. He decided not to ask any of them if they had seen the goddamned dumb creature.

Beyond the stream, he discovered another pile of dung and several tracks on the right side of the road, where the steer had milled around, confused. A path led down the left side of Ward Branch, and the animal had started to take it, but had changed its mind. Will yanked his hat off and scratched the marble dome of his head. Then he figured it out. He had bought the steer when it was a yearling from Cam Essex, who lived a half mile down the branch. For some strange reason in the muddled animal brain, the steer had decided to return to its original home. It had found its way until it reached the path, where its instincts had deserted it, leaving it lost and confused.

Across the road on the left, he found another pattern of tracks. Then they led in a straight line along the right bank of Ward Branch, which washed the eastern base of East Ridge. The field had been recently plowed and harrowed, making the tracks easy to follow. Cousin Bill Ward's big house sprawled in the fork between Ward Branch and the Big Road. It was on Will's right in a random grove of apple trees, as he made his way diagonally across the plowed field. When he reached the path which led from the house, across the bald area of East Ridge toward West Mountain, he stopped to rest and work his entrails back behind his trusses.

"Howdy, Will," Rosa Ward called from beneath a loaded Virginia Beauty tree between him and the house.

Will yanked his hands out of his overalls and stood erect. "How-do, Rosie. You dang nigh scart me out of a year's growth. I didn't know they was anybidy about."

"You follerin' your steer's tracks, I reckon," she stated.

"I shore am. Dang fool jest broke out'n the pasture and left without no leave. Come down the Ridge Road and back around the Big Road. I reckon he was a-headin for Cubie, or some other furren seaport."

Rosa smiled at him, an amused but friendly smile. Her prim little head sat on her prim little shoulders as erect as a kewpie doll's, despite her grey hair and premature wrinkles. Her white, delicate hands concealed the callouses in the palms. Her clothing was neat and clean. She had often told Bell Ward that she dreaded to drop dead all of a sudden and have folks discover she wore dirty undergarments. But if long hours and hard work and good management were a gauge of health, Will did not figure Rosa would drop dead any time soon.

Will looked from her neat figure to the big frame building with its one-story wings, then on to the huge barn beside the Big Road. He let his eyes roll covertly in their moist sockets and take in the fertile lowland surrounding the house and barn, and he strained, trying to despise Rosa Ward. He wanted to hate her and Cousin Bill for inheriting and for occupying the cream of the original Ward land. He wanted to, but he could not. Even with his special talent for despising people who offended him, he could not. Bill and Rosa Ward labored sixteen hours a day the year round to be good neighbors and good kinfolks, labored, not selfishly, but the way Will tended corn, for the sake of a good crop of neighbors and kinfolks. Even so, as often as Will grew scrub corn out of red clay soil, despite five plowings and three hoeings, Will and Rosa produced scrubby neighbors. But it was the fault of seed and soil, not of the husbandry. In Will Ward's case, however, their efforts bore fruit.

"Well, he headed on up the creek there," Rosa called. "I thought you might like to know for sure."

"Thank'ye," Will called back. "I reckon he's headin back in

towards the east end of Coottown. I reckon some of the Catletts'll git off their butts long enough to head him home, if they don't take a notion to eat him blood-raw."

Rosa Ward laughed, her teeth white in the sunlight. "Are Tillie and Annie doin any better with their cookin?"

"Lord, no!" Will exploded. "I'm so hongry for decent vittles, I'm a mind to go back on the singin road and git my guts back in practice."

Rosa smiled. "Well, don't give up on'em. I've not got much hope for Annie. She's got her notions set on things way beyond the Blue Ridge. But Tillie's tryin hard. It'll come to her sudden one of these days, and you'll eat so much you'll founder."

"The day that happens," Will grumbled, "I'll sell my house and buy a gold-plated cookstove and live under a white-pine tree."

"You're not all that famished," Rosa Ward laughed, and turned toward the house.

Will continued on up the branch, following the tracks. He chuckled. "Goddamn crazy womern!" he muttered. "Wanted to tell me my steer passed by, like I couldn't foller a one-legged goose's tracks acrosst this plowed field."

When he reached home, Tom, the wayward steer, stood patiently before the bars chewing his cud and waiting to be let back into the pasture, his odyssey petering out. Will stalked him, fist knotted to punch him angrily in the ribs. The steer swiveled his neck and stared dully at his master. Will's fist dropped back to his side. "Look at the crazy bastard," he growled. "Jest tuck a trip halfway around the world, and ain't got enough sense to remember hit."

He was tired from the long walk, but somehow he felt better as he plodded down the slope to the house. He glanced toward the cold sun, sliding toward a straight-edged rack of clouds closing over the sky like an eyelid. Somehow Will Ward felt better, felt as though he had solved some problem more important than regaining the lost steer. But when he sat down to supper and discovered Tillie had put too much baking soda in the corn bread, he slumped deep into his chair, his grey eyes hidden beneath almost closed lids.

5

As November and December shuttled slowly over the valley from east to west, Will Ward's frustration grew. Van had taken to staying away from home for days at a time and would not tell where he had been. Sometimes Dan would go with him. All Will's ranting and swearing slipped off them like the cold winter rain, leaving them grinning and undisturbed. They had long ago learned that Will's oaths exceeded his reach. Anna, whose duty it was to care for the baby, ignored him most of the time, leaving him to Tillie, who already had more than she could do. The house went uncleaned, clothes went unwashed and unpatched, and the meals became worse, if possible. To increase the tension, Tillie had suffered a personality change—from overwork, Will reckoned—and would explode into frantic weeping at the first word of criticism. Anna enjoyed provoking her. It got to the point where Will dreaded to ask her the time of day.

About halfway through December, a plan began to germinate deep in Will Ward's mind. Actually, it was not a plan, because he never would consciously admit what he hoped might happen. But if he made certain arrangements by being at the right place at the right time—and held his mouth just right—something might happen in his favor. After all, a body never knew what God Almighty had up his sleeve, provided a body arranged things so the old fellow did not have to reach too far.

What jarred his vague plan out of its notch of mere speculation and onto the track of time was not decision. It was another supper. On Friday night, December 29th, Will came in tired and wet after a long walk in the rain across West Mountain from Doc Ellis's store. He had run out of Brown's Mule tobacco earlier in the day and had stopped chopping wood to go get some. Van and Dan had been gone since early morning, some goddamn where, or he would have sent Dan. He stood with his back to the fireplace and absorbed the heat, while the steam curled up from his overalls and denim jacket. His muscles ached from rheumatism and from the cold, and his wet feet were miserable in the slippery brogans.

He stood for a while with his eyes closed, rocking on his feet while warmth permeated his back in countless needles of pleasure. He shuddered, because he was still chilled in front. He reached inside his overalls and adjusted his heavy scrotum inside his long underwear, then caressed himself briefly, pleasantly. Finally he opened his eyes. The baby crawled across the floor a few yards away, trailing a wet streak behind its piss-baggy rag of a diaper. The thin cotton dress could have offered little warmth in the cold toward the rear of the cabin. Will's grey eyes narrowed and shifted. Anna lay sprawled on her back on Will's bed staring at the ceiling. Her dress had worked upward until it exposed her white thighs brazenly. Will stared at her a moment longer, ill at ease.

"Annie," he growled, "if'n you're gonna lay there on'ye dead ass tell doomsday, pull'ye goddamn frock down and stop showing your nakedness like a goddamn Catlett."

Anna plucked aimlessly at the hem of her dress. She tossed onto her stomach and rested her chin in her cupped hands, staring at the wall. Will turned his attention to Tillie. She was setting the table. As he watched, she carried a dish of steaming cabbage from the fireplace to the Lazy Susan.

"How many more heads we got from the late patch?" he asked as pleasantly as he could.

She glanced past him. "Bout six or sebem, I reckon. Looks like to me you ort to figure out some better way to store cabbages so's they'll last longer."

"I ort to figure out a short cut to the Pearly Gates, too," he grumbled. "But a roundabout road to Hell's easier to foller."

"Come on and set down and eat," Tillie said. "Annie, git the baby and git it to the table."

"Git the baby your ownself," Anna muttered.

"Git off'n your lazy ass and git the youngun!" Will growled.

Anna did not move. Will shuffled over to the round table and dropped into his chair. The round table-waiter stood about four inches above the table, which was two feet larger in diameter. In the center of the waiter was a small round stand holding a kerosene lamp. The plates were arranged around the rim of the table, and the dishes of food sat around the rim of the waiter. Will seized one of the series of small knobs projecting down from the edge of the table-waiter and turned it until the dish of cabbage came even with his plate. Grasping the spoon as though it were a spade handle, he served himself a huge pile of the hot vegetable. He shoved the spoon back and turned the waiter again, serving himself potatoes.

He glanced up as Tillie sat down across from him, the baby in her arms. He glanced at the child. Its face was crusted with dirt, the top of its dress wet with saliva, and gobs of murky mucous cut twin paths downward from each nostril and over the ridge of its lip.

"For God's sake clean hit's nose," Will complained. "And wash hits face sometime this month. Hit looks like hit had been pokin hits face in cowdung."

"*Hit* has," Anna said, as she sat down on Will's left. "I seen it when it done it."

Will glowered at her. Then he turned his attention back to the table-waiter. He turned it until the bread plate came even with him, and reached for a chunk of cornpone. "Godamighty!" he yelled. He yanked his hand back as though he had touched a firecoal. "Godamighty, Till, what in thunder are'ye doin a-cookin biscuits for supper?"

Tillie tilted her white face and looked at him. "We run out of meal," she said. "I didn't know it till I started to cook supper."

"Why in God's name didn't you notice it at dinnertime, when you fixed dinner?"

"Cause Annie fixed dinner," Tillie said. "I did mention yesterday we was a-gettin low."

Will turned on Anna. "Why didn't you tell me we was out of meal, so's I could go to the mill?"

Anna's dark eyes clashed with Will's. "Cause I heard you mention you was out of tobacker," she smiled, "and I knowd your tobacker come before everthing but breathin."

Will looked from the biscuits to the cabbage. "Who in hell ever heard tell of cabbage and biscuits together?" he groaned. "I'd as leave eat hoss manure pie." He reached for a biscuit again, hesitated. "I got to make me some changes in my cookin arrangements. I can't put up with this dreadin to come to table. Hit's like dreadin you'll fart when'ye sneeze in church."

Tillie jumped up, shoved the baby onto Anna's lap, and ran through the back door, her hands pressed to her face. Will stared at the closed door. "I be dammed! She's narvous as a pregnant fox in a forest far, here lately."

"She's sufferin from overweight," Anna smiled. "This here cookin you can't stand is agreein with her fine and dandy."

Will got up early Saturday morning and walked down the Ridge Road, turning left down the path to Cousin Bill's house. Bill was at the barn greasing the buggy wheels when Will found him. Jan was helping, silent, his eyes on the ground. The hub nut was off the right rear wheel, and the tip of the axle was resting just inside the hub, held steady by Jan, who gripped the wheel rim as though he held back a falling tree. Cousin Bill was swabbing gobs of black axle grease onto the axle.

"Howdy," Will said, as he came to a stop a few feet away.

"Howdy, Will," Cousin Bill said. "Broke out of your pasture early this mornin, didn't you?"

"No earlier'n needs be." Will spat a stream of tobacco juice to one side. He squinted at the cold blue sky, watching a bird rowing by high overhead. "See you's greasin your fine-lookin buggy's wheels," he observed. "Ort to make hit a whole heap easier to pull."

Bill Ward glanced at him, the trace of a smile on his face. "Yep, that's what I'm doin. I'm a-greasin my buggy wheels."

Will worked his Barlowe knife out of his pocket. Opening the blade he hunkered down on his tiptoes and reached for a stick close by. He sliced at the stick, and a shaving curled along the keen edge of the blade. "A hoss and buggy is a fine thing to own if a feller needs a hoss and buggy," Will said, slicing at the stick.

"They shore are," Cousin Bill nodded. "If you need to travel you can't hardly beat a hoss and buggy. Or like in my case, a mare and buggy."

He took hold of the rim of the wheel and shoved the wheel back onto the axle. "Now you fasten the nut back on far as you can with your fingers," he said to Jan. He carried the wrench around to the other side and began to loosen the left rear wheel.

Will Ward clutched his thighs, pushed himself to his feet, and shuffled around close to Cousin Bill. He squatted down again. He hewed at the stick for a minute in silence. Bill worked the wheel off, and Jan held it in place as he had before. Will aimed down his hewing stick at Cousin Bill, one eye closed, then hewed again.

"I could shore as hell make use of a hoss and buggy for about a week," he finally muttered, to the stick.

"You plannin on takin a trip, Will?" Cousin Bill asked, dabbing on the axle grease.

"Thought I might go on a little singin circuit," Will said. "But I jest ain't up to trompin all over hell and half of Georgie with my rheumatism in the winter rain and cold."

"When did you have in mind to set out?" Bill Ward seemed as though he talked to accommodate Will.

"I 'lowed I might mosey down around Goshen or maybe as far as Quaker Falls. It jest crossed my mind. I ain't got no idee I'll go through with it, far as it is."

"You reckon the folks down that way wouldn't be glad to see'ye if you showed up?" Bill asked, shoving the wheel back on the axle.

Will Ward chuckled. "I don't have no idee but what they'd be proud to see me. But like I say, I don't feel up to trompin up and down hill and valley in the winter weather punishin my feet and legs."

"It's not good for a man your age," Cousin Bill agreed, "trompin around in the winter cold, you with rheumatism to boot."

"I ain't but forty-one," Will argued, throwing up his head to stare at the other man. "Won't be forty-two tell May."

Cousin Bill turned away, but Will glimpsed his grin. "It ain't good for any man to do it," he said. "Where he's forty-two or sixty."

"That's the God's truth," Will nodded solemnly. "That's why I ain't aimin to go on this trip, much as I'd like the chance."

Cousin Bill turned and looked at Will Ward. "I'm not spectin to be needin my mare and buggy for the next week, Will. Why don't you use them?"

Will went stiff, caught off guard before he was ready. Reaching up, he yanked his floppety black hat low over his face so Cousin Bill could not see the sudden pleasure he was unable to control. "I couldn't rob'ye of your hoss and buggy, Bill," he argued.

"It could be a business matter, Will," Bill Ward said. "You could pay me what it's worth to'ye."

Jan raised his head and stared at his father, a grieved look on his face. "You told me I could drive Rhody to meetin tomorr," he grumbled.

"You got years to drive her in," Bill Ward said. "You can drive her two Sundays in a row. If Will needs her bad, we can't stand in the way of our kinfolks, can we?"

Jan started to speak. His shoulders slumped, and he trudged off toward the barn, head down. Will turned and watched him, eyes narrowed. Then he turned back to Bill.

"I git a dollar a day," he said. "I'd give'ye half of it. Rhody would git good feedin, too."

"That'll be fine and dandy," Bill Ward nodded. "When you aimin to leave?"

"I 'lowed I'd leave after dinnertime," Will said. "Give me a chance to git down there and make arrange-ments for the singin."

That was how Will Ward happened to be driving Cousin Bill's bay mare down the Yadkin River late that afternoon. He had made his brief arrangements with the family, chiefly with Tillie, and then left, later than he had planned. Rosa had promised to check on the girls every day or so until Will returned, which, he had assured her, would not be ten minutes more than a week. He glanced back over his left shoulder and squinted at the sun, slipping like a flat red cardboard disk toward the paper-edge skyline.

"Well, at least hit's gonna be fair for a few days," he muttered. "At least I ain't bound to put up with rain or snow or sleet or hail or God knows what for a few days—like it'd be if I was walkin."

The buggy climbed the winding grade south of the river as twilight sifted down, layer after thin layer, over the winter world. When Will reached the highroad at the crest of the ridge, he turned left toward Quaker Falls and Northboro beyond. Once he blinked his eyes and it was night. The cold of deepening darkness began to press in on him from all sides, beginning with his feet and creeping upward along his calves like a heavy liquid filling a barrel. He wore nothing heavier than his cotton longhandles and serge suit, in fact owned nothing heavier to wear. A life spent in daily labor in the fire of summer and in the ice of winter had tempered him and inured his flesh to long periods of cold, but inactivity was not a part of his resistance. Stamping his feet against the floorboards was not enough.

He sat up straighter when he saw a window light up ahead, when he recognized the massive outline of the old mansion against the steel blue of the sky. He sucked in breath, and the cold air slashed down his warm throat as sharp as a barbed icicle. When he reached the drive he turned Rhody into it, then reared suddenly back on the lines, dragging the mare against the singletree. She tossed up her head, startled, stamping the hard ground and jangling her harness.

"Whoa!" Will called quietly. "Whoa, gal! Whoa, Rhody."

The mare calmed down. Will sat there staring at the bulk of the big house. He could not see the kitchen window from where he was, but the dim light still burned upstairs, probably in Dr. Watson's room.

"The old feller ain't passed on yit," Will told the mare. He slapped himself sharply on the thigh, feeling better. "He's still hangin on and a-needin tendin to."

He sat there for a long time staring at the house. Twice he lifted the lines and started to slap them down across the mare's rump. Both times he dropped them deferring action. Suddenly he shuddered. The cold liquid of night air gushed in around him as though a dam had broken, filling the world deeper than his head. His feet were becoming chunks of cold flesh somewhere in the blackness miles below the dashboard. He tugged backward on the lines, and the mare reared against the shafts and backed the buggy into the road. A few minutes later he passed the dark hulk of the church on the left, and headed toward Northboro, the mare trotting stiffly along the hard, rutted road.

Will spent the night with One-eye Wilson, a hunter and trapper and fisherman who lived in a one-room cabin a mile beyond the church. Will had selected One-eye because he had an extra bed and no children and because the hunter and his wife thought Will Ward was just inches below God Almighty.

The congregation at Quaker Falls Church was glad to see him again. They rushed up to shake his hand before services began. Preacher Messick invited him to stay for a few days and teach singing. Will leaped for the bait like a swooping chicken hawk, and the deal was closed in half a minute. Ike Shoemake turned the singing for the Sunday service over to him, a courtesy Will accepted for more than one reason, the most important one being that he could look the congregation over without craning his neck.

Will was leading the last song after the sermon before he became uneasy. As he sang, his face beaming, of a land beyond the river, deep down a dread persisted that he would be sleeping with some pissy younguns that night. He looked the gaping faces over for the twentieth time, but could not see her. She was just

—damn the luck to hell—not there. Neither was Sister Lucinda.

He was trapped, cut off. It was either accept the invitation to spend another night with some poreass, or go to Lucinda Watson's house with hat in hand and make like he was just stopping a spell to say howdy. And just before dinner on a Sunday, the old gal would be too smart to believe him. Of course she would not let on; he would be asked in and would be welcomed. But deep down she would know he had come begging her hospitality, and he would know that she knew it. He could not endure going to anyone's house like a dog slobbering for a bone, even if he did have a good reason. Will Ward did not beg from no goddamn bidy.

Then he saw her. Just as the last line of the chorus was stretching out toward its end, he spotted her. Lucinda Watson sat on the very back row, only the top of her grey head peeping above the heavy left shoulder of Jake Morley. She usually sat on the front row, where she could spread out. She had come in late, Will reckoned, and had taken the back row rather than waddle all the way up the aisle with folks staring at her haystack proportions.

After the pastoral prayer, Lucinda plowed her way through those gathered around Will as if wading through a field of wheat. When they saw the sudden pressure forcing them apart was old Doc Watson's woman, they yielded, but grudgingly. Even the old women gave ground—with an impatient frown, perhaps, but without argument. Will watched her progress with one cocked eye, while he chatted with those wedged close in front of him.

"Howdy, Will." She thrust out her hand, her pumpkin-size bosom heaving as she gaped for air. "You was in fine voice this mornin, as usual."

"How-do, Sister Watson." He grasped her pudgy hand, looking surprised to see her. "I had jest about give up on you bein here."

"Well, to tell'ye the truth, I near about didn't come. The Doc seems like he's gettin worse and worse. Jude Mathley come along and said he heard you was here, so I rid down here with him to hear'ye."

"Reckon Doc'll last tell you git back?" Will Ward cocked his head to hear her better, his horny hands gripped at his sides.

"Vi said she could make out till I come from the meetin," Lucinda panted.

Will's shoulders relaxed. He exhaled a burst of air. His grip loosened and he grinned. "If that Vi Matlock is there," he said, "Doc'll be tuck care of proper tell you git back."

"We're spectin you for dinner," Lucinda said. "I told Vi to make more dumplins to go with the chicken. I recollect how good you liked chicken and dumplins."

Will licked his lips, his eyes shining. "You can't hardly beat chicken and dumplins for Sunday dinner," he said. "I don't reckon kings could fare better."

Will helped Lucinda Watson into the buggy, not out of courtesy but out of necessity. She could never have climbed the short distance from ground to seat without his added strength. When she dropped into the seat, the vehicle creaked and tilted far over to her side on the thin leaf springs. Will rounded the rear end and climbed into the seat on her left. He noticed several groups standing around in the churchyard staring at the mare and buggy. He sat high in his seat, squared his shoulders and waved his whip at the onlookers.

"This here's a mighty fine mare and rig," Lucinda said, as he pulled into the highroad. "You must be doin tolable well on your farm to afford them both."

"I'm doin some better'n I was," Will grinned. "But nothin like I'm aimin to do." A little lie would not hurt, he reckoned.

"I was grieved to hear tell your wife passed on," Lucinda said. "Sometimes I think it's harder for menfolk to lose their women than t'other way around."

"Hit was sudden as the heartburns." Will brought the lines down against the mare's sleek rump. "If she'd died of a sickness, I could a-got used to her passin before she had went."

"Vi and me was talkin about it," Lucinda nodded. "She was sore troubled for you—Vi was."

Will turned and stared at her. "You don't say so? What did she say?"

"She mentioned it must be hard on'ye with them four younguns to raise all by yourself."

"Four—" Will caught himself. "I be danged!" He grinned and clucked at the mare. "I never thought she hardly looked at me that night I stayed all night there."

Lucinda Watson's laugh shook her belly and the buggy. "Alvira Matlock sees a whole lot more'n you'll ever get her to say."

"I be danged!" Will chuckled.

They pulled into the barnyard, and Will helped Lucinda out of the buggy, dreading to see her slip and crush him like a piss ant. "Go ahead and put'ye mare in the first stall on the left," she said. "Oats is in the cuttin-room and some fodder in the loft. I'll wait for'ye on the apple-tree bench close by the outhouse."

After he had watered the mare and fed her, Will left the barn and Lucinda Watson joined him on the path to the house, waddling fast to intercept him. She rocked from side to side as she walked, like an overfed duck, her huge breasts swinging in rhythm beneath her dress.

"If I get much bigger," she puffed, "I'm gonna have to get rid of Vi and go on starvation rations for two or three year."

"I wisht I was in your shoes," Will groaned. "My oldest gal couldn't bile water without scorchin it."

Lucinda grasped a post and heaved herself onto the back porch. As they entered the kitchen, Will stared around him, sniffing. The room was flooded with aroma, the aroma of a meal already cooked and ready to serve. The pots were on the range. The table was set. But Alvira Matlock was nowhere in sight. Will licked his lips, and his guts burbled hungrily in the silence. He suddenly felt good—goddamn good. He wanted to leap high in the air and click his heels together two or three times. Instead, he thrust his right hand into his pocket and automatically adjusted his genitals.

"You go ahead and wash up, Will," Lucinda said. "By that time Vi ort to be ready to jine us. She's more'n likely gone upstairs to check on Doc."

Will washed his hands on the back porch and returned to the kitchen just as Alvira Matlock entered from the hall. She stopped and stared at him. Will stared back at her. Lucinda Watson turned from the range.

"You recollect Mr. Ward, don't you, Vi?" Lucinda asked. "He stayed here a night—when was it? Last fall, I reckon."

"Howdy, Mr. Ward," Alvira Matlock said, her face unsmiling. "Yes, I recollect Mr. Ward—quite well."

Will swallowed. It burbled in the silence. Alvira Matlock had changed. She looked older. Perhaps it was because she looked so weary. Her eyes were dark and sunken, her cheeks gaunt. She looked as though she had not slept in days. Her faded print dress was clean, but wrinkled, as though she had slept in it.

"How-do, Vi," Will nodded. "I shore recollect your fine cookin, too."

A smile flickered about Vi Matlock's full lips. "I remember you was worrried about North America floating away when they cut the canal through."

Will chuckled. "That was a crazy idee, wasn't it?"

"Vi, was Doc settled down?" Lucinda asked, waddling toward the table.

"Yes, he seemed to be. He was dozin when I left. That bed-sore keeps plaguin him."

"Well, let's try to get some eatin done." Lucinda pulled her chair back from the head of the table and dropped into it. "Maybe we can get through before he needs tendin again."

Lucinda Watson and Vi sat at their places eating quietly. Will Ward wolfed the chicken and dumplings down, but mostly the dumplings. They were the lightest, fluffiest, tastiest damn dumplings he ever ate, along with the best gravy sauce. The thick white dumpling sauce matted the bottom edge of his mustache and dribbled onto his chin, but that did not bother him at the moment. He ate his third helping and served him-self a fourth, paying little attention to the stewed meat and other food on the table. This was vittles a governor or sheriff could put up with. With dumplings and gravy like that, he would not be ashamed to ask any preacher that came along to his house for Sunday dinner—even that damnable shack up on Stud Branch.

Finally, Will shoved back his plate and reared backward, stuffing his hands inside the waistband of his trousers. He grunted to hold it back but belched in spite of himself. "Vi," he said, "I vow I got to speak up. That's the best dadblasted dumplins I've eat in a coon's age. I don't reckon I ever eat anything as good before."

A smile flickered across Alvira's face again. "I thank'ye, Mr. Ward. A body likes to have her cookin thought good about."

Lucinda chuckled. "You ain't never heard tell of me fussin about your cookin, honey."

"No," Alvira agreed. "But I don't believe I'm good for'ye, Ma Watson. I do declare, you keep gettin heavier and heavier from my cookin. If we don't be careful, you'll get so big you can't feed yourself, and then you'll starve, sure-nuff."

"It ain't your cookin, Vi, that's a-makin me fatter and fatter," Lucinda groaned. "I got the sort of carcass that would gain on bread and water. So I don't see no reason in me sufferin by not eatin, if I'm bound to gain anyways."

"I don't gain none," Will said. "I eat like a hoss, and it comes and goes. I guess I work it all out."

Alvira looked at him, and her eyes were sad again. "I was sorry to hear tell you lost your wife a while back, Mr. Ward," she said.

"Thank'ye kindly for them words." Will was silent for a moment, arranging his thoughts end to end. "It's a hard blow to a feller with a fambly to raise."

"You got four younguns, I recollect," Alvira said. "Can't your oldest help out well enough with the little'uns to tide'ye over?"

Will threw up his head and eyed her. "They can make out, I reckon. But they sore do miss a real ma."

"I spect they's nothing like a ma for growin younguns," Vi mused, staring through the window. Then she looked straight at him again. "Mr. Ward, why don't you—"

"Why don't you jest call me Will?" he interrupted. "I'm not the oldest feller on earth and you ain't no chile."

"All right—Will." Alvira hesitated, looking at her plate.

Lucinda was staring at Will Ward. "Vi's a whole heap closter to bein a chile than she is a middle-aged womern."

Will shifted his stare to Lucinda, then back to Alvira. "What was you fixin to say, jest now when you said, 'Why don't you'?"

Vi stared at him. Then she smiled. "You know, I've got no idee. Whatever it was, it was important, but I got no idee what it was."

After dinner, Lucinda Watson and Will sat and rocked in the big kitchen and talked while Alvira washed the dishes. Will kept glancing at Vi, but she paid no attention to him that he could see. It plagued him for her to ignore him. Every time he turned his face directly toward her to speak, Lucinda would ask him a question and recapture his attention. Like, "How long you aim to stay this trip, Will?"

Will reared back and scratched the side of his head, careful not to disarrange the hair combed across his bald dome. "Well, I don't rightly know for certain. I made arrange-ments to stay about a week. It all depends on how good folks take to my singin classes this go-round."

Lucinda rocked for half a minute in silence. "We shore do miss menfolk to talk to, Vi and me," she sighed. "With Doc not able to talk. Why don't you stay here, Will? You'd be company for us two dreary women."

Will stopped rocking, his head alert, his eyes narrow. "I could stay with you-all a day or so, Sister Lucinda," he said finally. "But a whole week would git way t'other side of jest visitin."

"Now, Will, you know I wouldn't ask'ye unless you was welcome as sunshine."

"I know that." He glanced at Vi, who stood, hands in dishwater by the cooking table, head cocked as though listening. "If you'd let me pay a little tad, I might could."

Lucinda pivoted her head and looked at him, her round face serious. "Would it make'ye feel better if you paid some?"

"I'd feel honor-bound not to stay more'n three days if I didn't," Will swore.

"All right, then, Will." Lucinda slapped her fat knee through her black dress, and it sounded like wet dough. "You pay me fifty cent a day for you and your mare the last three days, and you can stay through next Saturday. Is that a bargain?"

"It's a bargain!" Will grinned. "Signed and swore to."

Alvira Matlock had turned to look at them, her hands still in the dishpan. Her blue eyes were narrowed, her face relaxed. Will tilted his head and looked at her. Their eyes clashed, and Will felt a jolt, like missing the bottom rung of a ladder. She was not just looking toward him, as she had up until now. She was seeing him. He felt her eyes looking *at* him.

Will grinned at her. "Vi, you look a mite tard. Don't you need a little rest on a purty day like this here'un is?"

Vi Matlock looked from Will, quickly to Lucinda. Her face was an impassive mask. Lucinda was studying Will. He could feel it.

"I am a mite tard," she nodded. "But I'm not sufferin any. I'll make out."

"What did you have on'ye mind, Will?" Lucinda Watson asked.

Will looked at her. Her eyes, deep in their fat white sockets, were moist crescents. He felt as if he'd been kicked in the groin. He wanted to clutch himself for security. He knew Lucinda was a sly old fox, good but sly. And he could not guess what direction she would take. Vi had turned back to the dishpan.

"I thought when she got the dishes warshed, Vi might want to go for a little ride in my new buggy," he said.

Alvira whirled from the pan, her hands dripping water on the floor. Her face was flushed, her blue eyes flared wide.

"I reckon it's plain to see what Miss Alvira Matlock thinks of your proposition," Lucinda stated. "It would be a burden on me if I had to take care of Doc all by myself."

Alvira's face snapped back to its former impassiveness like a rubber mask twisted and then released. Only her eyes were troubled. Her shoulders slumped. "It's all right, Ma. I thought it would do me good to get out of the house a little spell. But I won't put you to no trouble."

Lucinda Watson rocked her bulk for half a minute in silence, studying empty space. Will glanced at her, needing to speak. Finally Lucinda stopped rocking and looked at Vi.

"Why'f course you can go for a ride, Vi, honey," she smiled. "I've got to where I use you too much. You're tard. You need a little while out of this sad old house. To be sure, you can go for a little ride with Will, here."

Alvira barely smiled, but her eyes brightened. "I thank'ye, ma'am. We won't stay gone too long." She looked at Will. "I'll finish the dishes and then I'll go upstairs and put another frock on and then I'll be ready to go."

"Take'ye time! Take'ye time!" Will leaned back in his rocker, feeling good, feeling like Will Ward, the owner of the best mare and buggy in Quaker Falls. "Plenty of daylight left. We got worlds of time."

They rode out the highroad toward Northboro in the early afternoon sunlight. The sky was blue as a spring violet and brittle as the inner surface of a robin-egg shell. Snow lay along the spine of the far-off Blue Ridge. Chill breezes spurted past the buggy, but between them, the air was dry and sharp. The quilted lap robe protected their feet and legs. Alvira's faded blue coat appeared to be all she needed to keep her warm above the robe.

Will glanced at her as he clucked at the mare, already prancing along the road at a fast trot. Vi Matlock sat very straight, her calloused hands curled in her lap. Her face was fixed straight ahead, but her blue eyes were darting, shining, missing no one or no object they passed. She wore a half smile on her full lips. Suddenly, as Will watched, her bosom heaved upward as she inhaled the cold air in an excited gasp. Will grinned, feeling proud. He sat straighter himself, squaring his shoulders, and waved his buggy whip at Preacher Messick, who stood in his yard staring at them. The minister's face hardened, and he forgot to wave back.

Will laughed deep in his chest and slapped his thigh with his left hand. Vi tilted her head and stared at him. Will motioned back over his shoulder with his thumb. "Preacher Messick, back there, wasn't spectin to see me sparkin a good-lookin young gal like you. He near about lost his teeth gawkin at us."

Alvira smiled and looked back to the front. "I been shut up in that house so long tendin to Doc Watson, he likely didn't even know who I was."

"Well, now it's time you got out for a little fresh air." He was silent for more than a minute, watching Rhody's flashing hocks. "If I had my say-so about it, they'd see a-plenty of you for the next week."

She looked at him sharply, her forehead pinched into a frown, but said nothing. Will started to follow up, breathed his lungs full of unmade words, then held his breath briefly and exhaled slowly. Somehow he felt he had said enough for the time being.

The mare reared back against the shafts as they wound down the ridge toward the river between the faded brick buildings of Old Town. They crossed the river between two forests of dead cornstalks and clattered onto the bridge. Beyond the river, Will turned right and headed into Northboro. The wheels jostled over the brick-cobbled street, jarring Will and Alvira and chattering their teeth together. He slowed the mare to a walk. As they drove down the main street, he pointed out different stores where he had traded, as though she had not been to town dozens of times to his one, not even asking her whether she knew the stores, whether she had ever set foot inside them. Alvira Matlock listened and stared and smiled. Her blue eyes sparkled. Her brown cheeks were flushed, but it could have been the cold air.

The buggy climbed at an angle along the slope. Near the crest of the ridge, Will turned right and headed down a steep, rutted side street toward the railyard in the bottomlands along the river. He turned right again at the foot of the hill, taking a rutted road along the edge of the lumberyard.

"See all that stacked lumber?" Will pointed his whip at the lumberhacks lining the spur track to their left. "They's shipping that out down the river to Reynolds. Big building boom in Reynolds. Big backer factory there keeps hiring folks to make snuff and backer and sech, and folks keep pilin in there and needin houses."

"That looks like a heap of lumber," Alvira observed. "Looks

like you could build a many a house with that much lumber."

Will Ward laughed. His laugh boomed out across the Sabbath silence. "Lord ha'mercy! you ain't seen lumber yit. Old Man Harrison has had it stacked for a hundred mile dryin out."

She looked at him curiously, a half smile on her lips. "That is a heap of lumber. Am I supposed to know who Old Man Harrison is?"

Will clucked at the mare. "Nope, I reckon my tongue got ahead of my brains. He's my uncle by marriage and my neighbor. Owns a passel of sawmills. Saws ever damn bush and sprout he can git logged to the mills."

Alvira pointed. "Them planks look too broad to be sawed out of bushes and sprouts."

He looked at her. "They ain't started haulin the sprout lumber down here yit." He clicked automatically at the mare, his tongue curled around the sharp sounds. "I hope haul lumber down here a year or two back. Hauled it nigh twenty mile from my place with mules and wagon."

"With a mare and buggy like this, I wouldn't suppose you'd need to be a-haulin lumber with mules and wagon." It did not sound like an argument. It sounded more like an observation.

Will stiffened, his grey eyes narrow. "That was before I come by the mare and buggy," he said. "That was before I got holt of my last parcel of land." He felt as if he had got caught stealing eggs.

They were silent for some time, as the buggy crunched along the rutted street. Suddenly Alvira turned her head. "That old tannery," she said, sniffing. "I declare, it smells to high heaven."

"Yep," Will nodded, "hit shore stinks like cowsh–" He pointed with his whip. "That's hit over there. See all that stacked brown stuff underneath them sheds. That's chestnut-oak bark. Hit's called tanbark. I used to help haul some of it–before I come by the mare and my last parcel of land."

"What goes with the trees that's left over when you skin the bark off?"

"They saw'em up," Will said. "Sometimes they make crossties out of'em."

They turned again into the main street beyond the railyard and headed back across the river. It was after four when Will halted the mare in the barnyard. A tarnished silver dollar of a sun dropped toward the snow-spined Blue Ridge, far to the west. Will rounded the buggy and helped Alvira to the ground, not out of courtesy but because it was difficult to get down alone.

"I thank'ye," she said, meeting his look squarely.

"You're more'n welcome," Will said. "It wasn't no trouble. Why, I've shouldered a two-hundred-pound bag of fertilize in my time."

Alvira Matlock smiled, a rare bright smile that crinkled her eyes and spread her full lips apart. "I hope you hold me in higher regard than a bag of fertilizer."

Will let his stare pass down her trim, mature figure, high-breasted and narrow-waisted. He felt that sudden lurch in his guts. "Nope," he said in a husky voice, "you ain't nothin like no bag of fertilize."

She laughed again, but it cut off as though she had tripped. They stared at each other a moment, in the barnyard beside the buggy. Will scratched the back of his red, latticed neck. The mare turned her head and stared back at them to see what was going on, then stamped her feet and switched her tail. A cold breeze slapped them in the face, and Will shivered.

"Well," he said, "you go on to the house, and I'll put the mare up and feed'er and come on in d'rectly."

Alvira hesitated, turned away, walked a few paces and stopped with her back to him. Will watched her, waiting. She pivoted slowly and looked at his feet, planted wide apart in the dried dung of the barnyard.

"Why don't I help'ye?" she asked. "Then you could get finished that much quicker and go on to the house with me."

Will Ward's heart lurched once, like a leaping trout, then quieted. His fists uncoiled by his sides. "That's a good idee," he nodded solemnly. "Four hands is allus better'n two."

She stood and watched him while he unhitched the mare, and walked beside him into the shadowy driveway of the barn. He could feel her there beside him, although he did not look at her directly, could feel her almost like the glow from the hidden sun on a cloudy summer day. There was something he wanted to say to her, he flexed his throat to say, but words would not come. He sensed that whatever he tried to say in a serious manner would sound like bullshit to a low-country gal, a town gal, almost. He feared he would mess things up with her, and he half believed she was beginning to take to him just a little. But he ought to say something sensible to her or she would think he was a damned fool.

He stopped beside Rhody's stall and turned to face Alvira. She watched him, meeting his eyes. He opened his mouth to speak, then clamped it shut. "I'll unharness her," he said finally. "How about measurin her out some oats in the cuttin-room and fetch them to'er."

"All right," she said. "I won't be a minute."

When she brought him the oats in a peck bucket, Will dumped them into the mare's trough. He passed Vi, moving back toward the cutting-room. "I got to go up in the loft and get a couple bundles of fodder," he explained. "You can wait here, if you like."

He entered the shadowy cutting-room, which held old harness, bridles, a saddle, all on wooden pegs along one wall, stacks of feed along the opposite. Since Doc Watson's stroke, Lucinda had sold his horses, and the huge barn stood empty of stock, going to ruin. The bags of unused oats, the barnloft half full of hay and corn fodder was a wealth Will Ward coveted, a vast wealth. He stood there for a moment in the close twilight staring about him and inhaling the warm, suffocating atmosphere of decadent affluence. He felt sudden sickness inside, the sick bile of frustration and envy. Life was sure a goddamn strange fallow field to plow in. Here this barn stood, empty and going to hell with a bellyful of feed, while he had no barn at all, not even a stable to turn his steers into, out of the cold and rain. Something was wrong, goddamn wrong, somewhere in the plans of creation.

His mind circled and circled and stopped, pointing an accusing finger directly at himself, but he drove the guilty away. "If Pa hadn't lost this land!" he thought bitterly. "Goddamn it to hell, why did Pa have to go and lose his parcel of the land

and leave me without even a crawdad hole to piss in?"

He climbed the wooden steps slanting upward against the right-hand wall. At the top, he stepped into the old brittle hay and waded through an ocean of stuffy sweet air in the direction of the stacked fodder toward the front of the barn. He selected the bundles and turned back, then stopped, staring. Alvira Matlock stood ankle-deep in the hay near the stairwell holding her skirt almost to her knees. Will stared at her round calves above her high-topped shoes, then looked quickly away, waiting for her to scold him.

She looked at him, her blue eyes wide. "I happened to remember I've not got the eggs today," she said. "They's a hen's nest back here in the hay."

Will did not answer. He watched her turn and stoop her head below the slanting rafters and walk toward the side of the barnloft. He watched her sink to one knee and reach into the nest. She picked up the eggs one at a time, as though she were afraid to break their yolks, and placed them in her coat pockets. Will Ward licked his lips. He looked about him at the empty barnloft. He cocked his head and listened. Rhody stamped her hoofs and snorted in her stable below—then silence. The world was as silent as though only he and Alvira Matlock were left alone in it. And he had a sudden feeling that it was so. That only he and Vi were left and the barnloft covered the whole world, that the grey-bearded God who squinted down at the old world eternally frowning was gone, along with that world. The sweet dry air of the barnloft became as thick as honey, too thick to breathe. He threw back his head and swallowed, his throat burbling with saliva.

Whirling, he flung the fodder into the driveway below. Empty-handed, he waded toward her, cat-footed in hay, hands clutched at sides. He stared at her slanting body. He passed her silently and stumbled down the stairs, almost falling. In the driveway, he stopped and adjusted his hernias beneath the trusses, then carried the fodder to the mare's feed rack and dropped the bundles in. When he turned around, Alvira was stepping out of the cutting-room.

"Got seven," she smiled. "That enough for your breakfast?"

"More'n enough," Will nodded. "I don't eat more'n three or four at a setting. I ain't no wild bear."

For the second time that day her face lost its tension completely. The corners of her eyes crinkled, and her mouth parted in a smile. "You look more like a overgrown fox than a bear," she said. "Except foxes don't have nearly-red mustaches."

He studied her, eyes narrow, trying to see if she was laughing at him inside. He decided she was playing. His laugh boomed out, filling the shadowy barn to its high rafters. "We'd best git on back to the house, or Sister Lucinda'll turn out to be the bear."

She walked beside him toward the house, silent, her hands in her coat pockets, holding the eggs from jostling. Will kept glancing at her. And as they approached the house, he could see a change come over her. Gradually, her mouth became a grim line. It was a mask again, a mask carved to reflect weariness and fatigue, twisted into a smile, then slowly released and allowed to readjust to its natural lines. Will Ward relaxed. He did not reason out what was happening to her. His eyes squinted thoughtfully as he began to sense—on the level of muscle and blood and nerve fiber—what was troubling Alvira Matlock. He had felt the same way himself during the long hard days of planting and during harvesting season. The difference was, there was no harvest for Alvira, it looked like to him.

Because so many of the congregation at Quaker Falls Church were working, many of them in the tannery and lumberyard at Northboro, it was decided that Will would conduct his singing school only in the evenings. The potbellied stove could warm little more than the front area of the nave. In spite of the cold which filled the back area of the church, a cold thick enough to swim in, the pews were almost full every night. But the singers wore three coats and knitted sweaters and whatever else they could find to ward off winter. Some of the women even clutched quilts about their shoulders and sang lustily, heads balanced on the crest of stacked autumn leaves, it looked like to Will. And sometimes they became so heated with their spirit of singing, they threw off their covers and became women again, heavy, swaying bodies supporting their own heads with wide mouths and almost-closed eyes and contorted faces, almost hypnotized faces—until the song ended and the cold gushed in around them and the cold floor reappeared from Zion to press against the soles of their cold feet and the fat little kerosene lamps sputtered in their brackets high on the walls.

Evening classes made it possible for Will to do as he pleased during the day. In the mornings he practiced singing, all alone at the church, but the afternoons were something else. He had broken the ice, and Lucinda Watson could find no resistance after giving in to Alvira's ride on Sunday. It was a simple matter to take her for another buggy ride on Monday. And on Tuesday. And on Wednesday. By Wednesday, the schedule had become so routine that Lucinda Watson was ready, even volunteered, to wash the dishes. And on Wednesday, Alvira, apparently having seen enough of the lumberyard and tannery, suggested a new direction. They rode far down the river road toward Reynolds and returned late, after sunset, in a yellow-gold twilight.

On Thursday they rode back along the ridge toward Carson County, but took the side road to Quaker Falls. They sat silent in the buggy and watched Quaker Creek pour over a granite-stepped bluff and squirm away toward the Yadkin River. Will Ward kept his mouth shut, not because it was his nature to be quiet, but because he sensed that Alvira Matlock seemed to want it that way, and he did not want to disturb her. It was too near the end of the week for him to chance talking too much. They sat in the little park among the walnut trees where young folk picnicked in the summertime and waited for the lowering sun to signal their return. And they rode back mostly in silence. Alvira hurried to the house as soon as Will had helped her from the buggy.

On Friday, they rode back to Northboro again. Will stopped at Panda's Grocery Store long enought to buy Alvira a box of peppermint-stick candy. She thanked him kindly, and they rode on up Main Street, down the slope, back by the lumberyard and tannery, munching the candy in silence. When they reached the Watson barnyard, Alvira for the second time that week offered to help feed the mare. While Will unharnessed Rhody and turned her into her stall, Vi measured out the oats. He left her standing in the driveway and climbed the stairs for the fodder.

When Will turned back, clutching a bundle of fodder in each hand, he stopped and stared. Alvira was again kneeling by the same hen's nest she had inspected on Sunday. Will watched her, legs apart, feet planted in the hay. He rocked unsteadily as his grey eyes narrowed. Almost automatically he tossed the fodder away from him, to the driveway below. Alvira peered into the shadowy nest, then reached down and groped around in it.

Will paced slowly toward her, his feet still spread. His belly muscles were knotted; his chest rose and fell, rose and fell as he sucked at the close sweet air. He stopped just behind her, his eyes slitted, his fists knots of bone and gristle by his sides.

"That plague-goned old chicken," Vi Matlock muttered. "Nothin here but the nest egg—" She pivoted on her knee, her eyes level with Will Ward's thighs.

She remained motionless, half kneeling, half turned, mouth open to complete the speech, but silent. Slowly she tilted her face as her wide blue eyes climbed his form from hips to hard face. She studied his face. Her mouth closed slowly. Her eyes narrowed. But there was a quiver of fear about the corners of her mouth.

He reached forward and seized her by her left arm, above her elbow. He felt his fingers bite into soft flesh. He watched her mouth open in pain, in pain and fear.

"Will!" she whispered. "Will Ward! What're you up to?"

"I been here nigh a week," Will growled through set teeth. "I'm bound to go home tomorr. I've rid all over hell and half of Georgie sparkin'ye. I ain't got no time left for messin around. Are'ye a-aiming to marry me or ain't'ye?"

Slowly the fear melted from her face. Her mouth slowly closed and her eyes softened. He could see her studying his face in the gloom of the barnloft as though seeing it for the first time. Alvira Matlock's eyes became narrow and thoughtful. Will could tell she was no longer seeing his face. He knew she was looking beyond it, her mind dissociated from the staring blue.

Then she was focusing again on his own squinting grey eyes. "I thank'ye for astin me, Will," she said. "I'll have to think about the matter."

"I got to go home tomorr," he argued. "I can't leave them younguns by theirselves no longer."

"I'll tell'ye before then." She smiled a fleeting smile, then climbed to her feet and waded toward the stairwell. She turned back, still close to him, and looked up into his face. "I'll let'ye know in plenty of time to set out."

Will and Alvira walked back to the house in silence. They ate supper that night saying little. Lucinda Watson worked hard at keeping quiet herself, glancing first at one of them and then the other as the meal progressed. Her eyes were thoughtful and furtive. She would look from her plate to Alvira's face, her white forehead pinched into a frown. Will left them early and clomped up the stairs, shoulders drooped, to his room.

He lay there in his underwear between the cold sheets and tried to figure matters out. His body was tense with trying to think. His jaws clamped together as he ground his teeth in the dark silence of the room. Somewhere he had made a mistake, but he could not figure where. Goddamn it to hell! these low-country, town-cured gals were different from the womenfolk he knew. There was some special way to court them he never heard tell of. Goddamn the luck to the middle streets of hellfire! a week wasted and all that money he had paid out for nothing. Goddamn! What had he done wrong?

The sheets began to warm about his hard body. His muscles relaxed like melting wax. His teeth dropped apart and he smiled in the darkness. She was some woman! Some woman! Purty and strong and big enough to get hold of. Some woman! God Almighty, it was a pity. She would make some lazy bastard a fine wife, a damned fine wife. Maybe even Van. He shook his head against the pillow, rolling it. God Almighty, what a fine figure of a woman! Young too. Years younger than Bell was.

The bed grew warmer and warmer. Will Ward's mind went round and round, chasing Alvira Matlock's face around the shadowy interior of a ten-acre barnloft. Gradually, she gained on him, outstripping him, and disappeared far ahead, darting into a dark corner. He followed her, and disappeared himself, into blacker sleep.

Sometime later on, a woman found him in the dark barnloft, and they joined in erotic throes. After they were through, her face glowed in the darkness and it was Doll Dugan. When Will spat in her eyes, she disappeared, leaving nothing.

Will Ward awakened suddenly. There was a warm snake on his face. He reared up in bed, his mouth gaped to yell before he opened his eyes. Then the snake coiled over his mouth. But snakes were not supposed to be warm. He opened his eyes.

Alvira Matlock stood beside his bed. She drew back her hand from his face. "Sh-h-h!" she hissed. "Be quiet or you'll wake the Doc."

He stared at her. Gradually, she materialized out of the shadows, washed by dawnlight from the nearby window. She wore her winter coat clutched tight in front of her. Her black hair flowed down across her shoulders, below her waist, black as the night still crammed into the corners of the room. She leaned slightly toward him, her eyes wide and dark in the gloom. Her face was twisted into a serious frown.

"What are you up to?" Will Ward hissed. "What you want, a-comin in my room in the nighttime like this?"

"I had to come," she whispered. "I had to come to'ye here. I hope'ye don't think hard of me for comin to'ye here in your room."

Will Ward waited, arms braced stiffly behind his slanting body, eyes narrow. He stared at her troubled face, at her young, young face, cameo-white against the black background of her flowing hair. She leaned closer, right hand braced on right knee, coat clutched with left. He studied her, his head cocked, his ears tuned for any sound outside the room. She was so close he could smell a sweet warm smell about her face and head and upper body, an odor that reminded him of new clover honey.

"What's on'ye mind?" he demanded hoarsely, through dry lips.

Part Three

TIME IS

JOHN MATLOCK WARD

I

GLANCING AT THE SLANTING SUN, John Ward shivered as a sudden fall breeze scurried past him. The day was ending. Summer was ending. Time was a rack of clouds moving to meet the sun. He looked at his mother, who watched her grandson with concern. She never had time to check on her own eight children or to worry about them, John thought. But now, with leisure time on her hands—the little time left her—she watched her grandson with troubled eyes as he stooped close to the bank, examining a red feather so small only a child would have noticed it.

In a flash John remembered that special day he had tumbled down the same bank and hurt himself. He had started to get up, whimpering, when he happened to see Will Ward coming up the path from the spring (it was after he had given up John for Jim, the new one). He fell back and lay still, yowling. His father's footsteps clomped up the slope and stopped beside him. He looked up at his old-man father.

"Boy, git up off your ass and stop bawling," he ordered. "If you bruised yourself, that spot ain't never gonna hurt no more. The furder you walk up that bank, the less you'll hurt and the gladder you'll be you found out what hurtin feels like." He turned and climbed the bank, leaving John there alone.

Mamma had tied potato scrappings on his bruise. In those days, she was physician and executioner with a peach-tree switch. The hills were full of hurts and full of cures for them, and Vi Ward seemed to know them all. John remembered the time he jumped and hit a rock, causing a stone bruise on his heel. His mother had tied a potato poultice about it and brought it to a head. Strips of fatback or wilted cabbage leaves were tied over boils, and crushed ground ivy was bound about sprained ankles.

He remembered she placed folded brown paper under the upper lip to stop nosebleeds, and he decided brown paper must be especially strong medicine. For weeks at a time, she had headaches that squinted up her eyes. She doctored them with brown paper soaked in vinegar, then folded into a band and wrapped about her head. She held these in place with folded rags, usually torn from an old sheet, and John got to where he was used to seeing the white signal. She never fussed about her headaches any more than she fussed about anything else she could not control. On rare occasions when John saw her without the white band about her head, he was surprised and had to stop and try to figure out what was wrong with her.

Will Ward never had time for sickness. John remembered the time he almost died with appendicitis. He had made Vi heat stovelids and wrap them in rags, then place them on his naked belly. This went on for almost a week. Doc Ellis got him to the hospital at Northboro just before his appendix ruptured.

And Will never had time to worry about schooling, either, because he, by God, had his land to pay for and his cornfields to till. John thought back to the fall he started school. Late that summer Mamma, Vern, and Venna tied up the dried white-pine bark they had skinned, and Daddy hauled it to Doc Ellis's store. With the money from the bark and from eggs she had already sold, Mamma struck out around the countryside, as she did every year, looking for second-hand school books. This time John went with her. They went by Bart Harrison's and Tom Allen's, where they bought books for the three girls.

Later, they came back by Greer Harrison's, and Mamma got Alvin's old primer for John. Reba, Alvin's mother, would not take any money, and Alvin looked at John with his white-blue eyes and laughed, and John knew why. Alvin laughed because he lived in a big white house protected by gold lightning rods and because his daddy owned several sawmills and because he and Walter, who was Jim's age, got a new roller-coaster wagon every Christmas and because they had a talking machine that played Uncle Josh records. Mamma left a quarter on Reba's kitchen table anyway.

Thirty years later John Ward, standing beside his mother, felt a lurch of regret because he knew he could never tell her why he remembered these things, even if he could have cast it into words she would understand. It would have made her ill at ease. He thought of her near death with flu when he was born, yet refusing to die. Turning farther in the weed-pocked yard to study her, John thought, What if she had not set her teeth against dying for my sake? The answer was obvious. There would have been no John Matlock Ward, who had risen so far from this Job's turkey valley and still planned to set the world on fire. And there would have been no smart-assed eighteen-year-old boy, aching with ambition, to walk away in the teeth of a storm, leaving the old man he had blamed for his poverty to labor alone.

And Will Ward was to blame, John had decided a long time ago. One special sperm had placed him here in this valley in his own time, instead of somewhere beyond the Bushy Mountains. A slight rearrangement, and he might at least have lived in the comfort and security of Greer Harrison's white house, since he and Alvin shared a common ancestor. But it had not happened like that. And if it had, someone besides John Matlock Ward would be standing here on the side of East Ridge on this day trying to come to terms with Will Ward and half wondering if the old man was worth the trouble.

John glanced at Ann, who shuffled her spike heels impatiently, wanting to leave (he knew her mood as certainly as though she had shouted it at West Mountain), impatient to get the hell out of this depressing little valley and away from this locust-shell of a house which meant nothing to her, which could mean nothing to her because she had grown up in comfort and leisure in a home four times as large beside a warm sea. No, this place meant nothing to her—yet more than she would ever come to realize. Because she had happened to attend a small college in the mountains, a last-moment choice, John Kelly Ward had been born. And because the valley was here, Will Ward had brought Alvira Matlock to it, and John Matlock Ward had been born. Perhaps it was because John had lived on Stud Branch the first ten years of his life that his son would be only one in thousands who someday would know who his forefathers were as far back as six generations, who would know or even give a damn.

His thoughts shuttled back to his mother, to Vi and Will Ward, suspended back there in memory like bees preserved in amber honey. He remembered the day Will had come stamping into the middle room, yanked off his overall jacket and hung it on its nail, slamming the old black hat on top of it. He backed up to the fire and stood for a long time warming his back, his hands curled like old leather gloves behind him, his eyes closed.

"Vi! Come in here!" he called, not turning his head.

Mamma came in, her hands gobbed with cornmeal dough. She waited, holding off surprise. Lynn stopped playing on the guitar he had recently brought back from the army in Hawaii. Everybody stared up at Daddy, their mouths open.

"I been doin a passel of thinkin," Daddy said that day. "These red clay hills won't hardly sprout a pea. I done decided to leave here and move to Frank Moses's place in Carson County, where I can grow me some real bottomland corn. Tom Allen has rented it for me. Albert Essex's boy has offered me six hundred dollars for my place, with ten year to pay it in." He whirled on Mamma. "What do you think about that?"

"I figure just about anywhere is better'n Stud Branch," Mamma said. "I can't see much to be gained from workin our hearts out here. I been waitin ever since I first come here for a chance to get out. I was scared to death I'd be buried here, after all was said and done."

And they moved away during the Christmas holidays that

year—1929, it was. They had gone to the farm in Carson County. John remembered stepping onto the rickety porch and staring at the Catlett-type house they were going to live in. He looked at the vertical black planks and the wide cracks. Mamma moved over to the plank door on tiptoes and pulled the leather thong. A wooden latch clacked up, inside, and John followed her into the kitchen. The floor sagged. Tattered newspapers and magazine pages covered the walls, the flour paste, yellow with age, showing through, grooved with the teethmarks of mice.

"Will is gonna be tard to death when he finally gets here tonight with the wagon and mules," Mamma muttered, close in front of him, "I dread for him to see this place. This wooden latch is bound to break his heart."

But the moving from farm to farm was long over; the hard labor and the skimpy crops, long past, though they had left their marks on the stooped shoulders and gnarled hands of Alvira Ward. John looked at her, and because his thoughts were often linked with imagery, he could almost see her as she appeared in her faded wedding picture, superimposed against the wasted shell of a woman. He could almost see the blue dress, the white Bertha collar, her violet-blue eyes, without pain. And she was only seventeen, before that one-way wedding journey to Stud Branch.

And beside her, he could visualize Will Ward, seated as was proper, his hair brushed into a coxcomb because he was too damned proud for posterity to see his balding head. He could see a middle-aged man seated, a young wife beside him, hand on shoulder, a wife younger than his three oldest children by another woman, but unaware of it yet. She was a comely strong wife, that ageless picture-bride who lived in comfort with Old Lady Watson. John Matlock Ward shook his head in puzzlement, after all those years. He could not understand how it could have happened. What had that gentle girl from the low country seen in the gruff mountain man? What circumstances had motivated her consent to marry Will Ward, and how had she been able to live with him afterward? Perhaps Vi Ward had known a man John had never discovered, or had refused to understand.

Part Four

TIME WAS

ALVIRA MATLOCK WARD

I

ALVIRA MATLOCK WAS BORN on March 10, 1888, in Ready River Township, five miles west of Northboro. On her mother's side she was fifth-generation Dutch. The first Stephen Groot came to America in the late 1700s, claimed over two thousand acres of bottom and hill land along Ready River, and with a broadax brought from Holland, hewed logs with which he built his huge house. He, with his wife Lydia, begot one son, born May 8, 1811, also called Stephen. This second Stephen died in 1901, aged ninety, leaving seven sons and three daughters. The original Groot land was divided among the ten children. With careful planning and frugality, the Groots were able to wrest a livelihood, each from his portion of soil; and some of them gradually prospered.

Stephen Alex Groot, the elder Stephen's fourth son, seventh child, was born in the original log house in April of 1846. A son and a daughter were born to Stephen Alex and Bell Groot, the daughter, Amanda, in June of 1868. Amanda married Henry Matlock on August 6, 1886, and Alvira, their first child, was born less than two years later.

The genesis of Henry Matlock is more obscure than that of the

Groots, who were a proud people and kept careful records. The most characteristic trait possessed by William Matlock, Henry's father, was reflected in the way he died. He was an independent man with an uncertain amount of Cherokee Indian blood flushing his stubborn flesh. He thought the Civil War was insane and none of his affair and he would have no part of the "war of politicians," as he called it. He refused to answer the local muster, refused to buy his freedom by hiring someone else to take his place, and was driven into the hills by a gang of ruffians calling themselves the Home Guard. Late in 1864, he was shot down in the forest like an outlaw, hauled on a sled to the front yard of his cabin, and tossed onto the porch like a butchered hog. His wife was of mettle too stern to lose the baby she carried, and Henry was born a little over two months later.

Without his black handlebar mustache, Henry Matlock could have passed as an Indian brave when he was a young man. He was towering, erect, with blue-black hair and dark, penetrating eyes. His complexion was dark, his nose aquiline, like that of the silhouette on a buffalo nickel. Amanda was pure Dutch—short, plump, and florid. Henry made a satisfactory living for a time tending a small farm and running a country grocery store. But by the time his sixth child arrived, in 1901, a new source of income was necessary to supplement the family needs. Alvira, who had helped take care of her brothers and sisters from her early childhood, was the logical supplement. Even so, she managed to finish the fifth grade in the one-room school three miles from her home.

At that time, two rival papers were published near Northboro. They were propaganda organs rather than newspapers, and propaganda is a mild term with which to identify them. The Democratic paper was the *Foolcatcher*, published by a self-educated poet who used words like incisive straight razors. The other was the *Hornet*, the Republican sheet, whose editor worked with adjectival clubs (Will Ward, a mountain farmer Alvira Matlock had never heard of, said that "anybidy ebem wipin his rear on the *Hornet* deserved to lose his insides through the fester").

Wilton County was one of the few counties in this area of the South where the Republicans were not greatly outnumbered, and the two papers full of invective were widely and gleefully read by the two parties. The sheets were printed on the flat-bed press powered by a waterwheel, and were folded by hand. Alvira Matlock's first job was folding copies of the *Hornet*, long hours for a few cents, after walking more than three miles to the plant. Fifteen at the time, Alvira accepted the job, despite the fact that her parents were both rabid Democrats, because the *Hornet* press was closer to her home.

After more than a year of folding papers a few days each month, Alvira Matlock accepted the job with Lucinda Watson. It not only paid her more money a month, which she could send home, but it eliminated one mouth for Henry Matlock to feed. By 1906 he had seven children, four daughters and three sons, of whom four where less than ten years old. And by the time Will Ward arrived on New Year's Eve to spend a week at Lucinda Watson's house, Alvira had almost exhausted herself, physically and emotionally, caring for what was left of Dr. Watson.

The night before, she had been awakened around two in the morning by his animal shriek of frustrated outrage. She leaped from bed still half asleep, squirmed into her coat to elude the aching cold pervading the old house, and plodded down the hall to Doc Watson's room. A kerosene lamp, turned low, sat on a chiffonier and washed the room in sallow, sick gloom. As she passed it, Alvira's shadow leaped at her out of the far corner, then shrank before the giantess she became as she left the lamp behind.

Doc Watson had worked the covers off himself with the short pendulum strokes of his right arm. The rest of his body was dead, so far as movement was concerned, except for his eyes, eyelids, and lips, and of course those hidden cords which created that one shrill note left him. Some tattered web of nerve remained half alive from brain to right shoulder, carrying enough impulses so that the upper arm moved a few inches forward, then back; forward, back, over and over. All his former strength and energy, all his frustration and trapped outrage were concentrated in these short movements and in his eyes.

Now he lay half sprawled on his left side, his mushroom flesh turning blue with cold. The powerful bulk of a two-hundred-pound man had wasted away to little more than ninety pounds of bone and skin and entrails. His lower legs and thighs joined at immense knobs, once well-proportioned knees. His elbows were smaller knobs; his knuckles, blue knots tied in white truncated thongs. His rib cage pressed outward against his white, hairy skin as though swelling to explode through its confinement. A serrated ridge bisected his back, and just below the shelves which were his shoulder blades, gleamed a crimson puddle.

Alvira never could look directly at the bedsore. She sprinkled it with powder without focusing her eyes and held her breath when she leaned close above it. There were other sores, but they were mere blemishes compared to the disk of blood and pus and seeping lymph which covered his spine. And there was little that could be done for the sores. A gown was impossible because the raw flesh would stick to the fabric and dry, then tear loose, causing a worse hemorrhage than before. For that reason the invalid was kept naked, an insult, Alvira sensed, he resented almost as much as his helplessness.

Alvira Matlock leaned over him, placing her hand gently on the swinging arm. Her eyes were heavy with lack of sleep and her brain filled her skull like a ball of cotton stuffed behind them. "Did you uncover yourself, dear?" she asked gently. "You ort to try and keep your arm still at night. The covers wouldn't work off, then."

His blue-green eyes moved in their hollow sockets and found her face. They blazed in outrage, in resentment so intense, so charged with the energy of hate, they might have burned holes in her if the brain behind them could have controlled some source of energy. Alvira was not offended. Without thinking she understood that the resentment was not directed toward her. Many times she had seen the gentle glow of appreciation, of love, in those same eyes when she tried to ease the hurt flesh which had once been a powerful man. She understood, as women know who are created with short cuts around reason, that his anger was against the circumstances which punished him. A rational and intelligent mind looked out of those glowering eyes, a mind imprisoned in a cage of bone and atrophied muscle. Doc Watson was like a man held captive in the arms of a giant gibbering idiot who slowly squeezed the life out of him.

For a moment longer Alvira's eyes clashed with Doc Watson's. Then she looked away, dilating her vision to include the Golgotha of skin stretched over bone with no padding between, a pale Golgotha with black, wavy hair. "Why can't he snap?" she thought desperately. "Oh, God in heaven, why can't he lose his mind till it's all over?"

She placed rolled quilts against his back, above the sore and below it, then tilted him gently backward until he lay at an angle facing the corner where the wall and ceiling converged. For a short while, she knew, he would rest, but it would be a short while. With her eyes still on his face, she reached down to draw the cover over his wasted body. She understood that deep in the shell of his humanity he still had pride, he resented his wasted manhood, resented his nakedness being exposed to her youthful eyes. She did not know it, but she understood it, saw it in his eyes, and was always careful to keep her gaze averted when she had to uncover him. And the softness in the blue-green eyes told her as well as words could have that he appreciated her consideration.

Clutching her coat about her, Alvira hurried from the room, ran down the hall, and entered her own bedroom. She paused before slamming the door. Beyond the closed panel across from her, Lucinda Watson's snores sounded like thunder, far away toward the Blue Ridge on a summer night. Alvira frowned, resenting her deep sleep. Then she cast the resentment away from her. Ma Watson was old, old and tired and burdened with fat. And this was what she was paid to do—the getting up, the tedious care, not the heartbreak and compassion she could not exhaust, could not even share with the stoical old lady who was Doc Watson's wife.

Closing the door quietly, she crossed the cold floor, threw off her coat, and crawled into the still-warm cocoon her young-woman body had left between the feather tick and the piled quilts. She lay there warm and shivering and stared at the dark ceiling, while tears filled her eyes, brimmed over and ran down her cheeks and into her black hair. She did not sob, did not whimper. But her mind cried out for the old man she had never known except as an invalid. And she thought frantically, "Let him die, God. Oh, do let him die, before I lose my own mind just lookin after him."

After a long time, the shivering diminished and went away, and the deep-down source that fed the tears dried up and her eyes closed. Finally she was asleep, the deep, mindless sleep of exhaustion. But it was not for long. She was awakened twice more before the long night fused slowly with dawn. A typical night—one of the long, long nights that stretched out behind her almost as far back as she could remember, it seemed; that stretched out ahead of her without promise of release, almost forever.

So it was that when Will Ward asked her to go for a buggy ride that Sunday afternoon, her heart leaped into her throat like a startled wren. Could Will Ward have known this, he might not have waited until Friday to propose. But had he known her excitement had nothing at all to do with him personally, he might not have had the courage to ask her at all. The truth was that Alvira had been scheming for weeks in the secret channels of her mind, trying to find some excuse to escape the depressing house and her job for a few hours. It was not that Lucinda Watson was unreasonable and would have opposed her leaving. The corpulent old lady was so kind to her, so pleased with her work, and had grown to depend on her so completely that Alvira felt guilty at leaving her, at even considering leaving her alone for any length of time. She reached the point where she would not have dared ask for an hour's leave.

When Will Ward broached the subject, she spun from the dishpan, startled that he should suggest such a thing, fearful that Ma Watson would explode in anger—and hopeful, ever so hopeful, that the old lady might agree. Her heart pounded in her throat; her wet hands were clutched by her sides, dripping water on the floor. She watched Lucinda Watson's narrowed eyes, her thoughtful face. And when the old woman finally smiled and agreed, Alvira controlled the rush of compressed breath. Her shoulders squared, thrusting her breasts against the tight bodice of her dress.

She felt lighter as she turned back to the dishpan. She felt like singing, but she knew she did not sing well, so she rejected any attempt. She thought about whistling, then remembered that a whistling woman and a crowing hen always come to some bad end. She was happy, happy, and Will Ward was only a tiny fleck lost in the vast circle of her joy. She hummed softly above the clatter of the dishes the approximate tune of "Go and tell Aunt Rhody, the old grey goose is dead."

She sat high in the buggy, her head erect, and stared about her as they rode out the ridge toward Northboro. She watched the sleek coat of the bay mare ripple as her muscles flowed beneath. She gazed from left to right, at the neat black oilcloth of the buggy, at the red shafts and twinkling yellow wheels. She glanced left at the man beside her. He was handsome in a rugged, musculine way. He sat slightly slumped forward, facing straight ahead, left foot on dashboard, but he held the black whip like a scepter. His black serge suit was wrinkled, although it looked nice on him. His black felt hat pulled low over his eyes, his huge auburn mustache, his narrowed grey eyes, gave him a look of grimness, a look of cold aloofness that almost frightened her. But then he turned his head and grinned suddenly, his face warped with good humor, alive, channeled by deep grooves of joy, and the look of coldness flashed off like a flipped coin. How could she have thought for a moment that Will Ward looked cold? And on such a day, why should she trouble herself with how he looked? The answer was simple: She did not care one way or the other.

Alvira was just as relieved to go for the rides on Monday and Tuesday as she had been on Sunday. Even the fact that they covered the same route all three days did not disturb her. She was out of that house, and that was all that mattered. But on Wednesday she did suggest the alternate direction, down the river toward Reynolds, and was happy she did. The ride along the quiet country road, between the river and a vast bottomland of dead cornstalks was quieting to her nerves.

"You see," Will Ward explained patiently as they rode, "the notes is equal to different tones of voice. *Do* sounds like this here—" He sang *do* to prove his point. "When you sing any words with this sound—" He sang *cross*. "Now that's equal to *fa*. And so on through your notes." He sang the scale: "Do, re, mi, fa, sol, la, te, do." He grinned. "Now let's hear you try it."

"It don't mean nothin to me," Alvira smiled. "It's just sounds. I can't sing a lick. I can cook and sew and do a heap of necessary things, but sing? No, sir. It's a mystery to me, and I've got no voice for church singin. So I just listen and feel good."

"Ah! it's easy when you understand it." He cracked his whip over the trotting mare's back.

She glanced at him. "Who larned you the notes?"

"Didn't nobidy larn me," Will stated. "I took it up by myself. I guess you might say I was borned with hit in my noggin."

She looked back ahead, watching a wild duck lift above the river. "Only thing borned in my noggin was a headache," she said.

After she had dismounted in the barnyard when they returned, she stood in the yellow-gold twilight and gazed westward. She stared at the bars of gold and crimson stacked like fairy treasure above the Blue Ridge where the sun had gone down, and she shivered, drawing her coat tight about her. She shook her head. "It looks like a honest gateway to paradise," she thought. "A body would think you could go in that direction and find the Promised Land."

Alvira was so silent as they rode out the highroad on Thursday toward Carson County that Will Ward seemed subdued. He glanced at her several times, made several remarks, but when she did not respond, he lapsed into silence. Poverty Knob reared against the southern sky ahead to the left, almost conical. High up, rows of apple trees marched across its crown. Will reined the mare to the left, onto the narrow side road, and they headed in the direction of the knob.

Alvira could hear the roar of the falls long before they reached the creek. She tilted her head and listened. Her head was so filled with other sounds that she hardly heard the water. The buggy meandered along a narrow lane between fields of loblolly pines, finally exiting into a fairly large meadow. Walnut trees towered here and there, black and leafless. Someone had piled the black walnuts into scattered piles, where they lay in brittle shells, but had not returned to gather them. Will Ward coaxed the mare forward, over her head in sound, and stopped her facing the waterfall. Quaker Falls gushed over the giant steps of worn granite and churned up a fume in the pond below.

Will Ward turned and looked at Alvira out of the sides of his eyes. She could see him watching her, but she pretended not to notice. She stared at the falls and ached—ached with disappointment and something close to despair. Because she could not possibly leave Lucinda Watson without a replacement, because her nature was such that she knew she had to find someone to replace her if she ever left, someone dependable, she had wracked her brain over the past months. She had lain awake checking off names and had come up with Mary Phillips, Jesse Phillips's eldest girl. A note had brought Mary to the house. She had jumped at the chance to live at the Watson house and had agreed to keep the secret until Alvira had settled with her own father. She knew Mary would work out; she was a big, rawboned girl, not too much on brains but sturdy as a mule and almost as strong.

The arrangement had been made over a week before. Alvira had hurried a letter off to her parents explaining her misery and telling them about Mary. She had waited, waited with hope and dread. And the letter she had expected had arrived that morning, saying what she had dreaded.

Dere Dauter,

We be sorrie for your troubled mind. Sure its no happie job takin keer for a pore parlized man and see him sufer. But presntly we got no room for you here. May be if and when we move to Reynolds—

She sighed and Will Ward looked at her sharply. She was

hardly aware of his attention. The buggy seat was a remote pressure against her. The mare's head was an indistinct blur between her and the falls. The taste in her throat was bitter when she thought of returning to her work.

But by Friday, Alvira Matlock had adjusted to her disappointment, and she had tossed the plan of escape aside like a coat that would not fit, refusing even to think about it. She had work that had to be done, and she had worked as efficiently as ever, and with the helpless doctor, as tenderly as ever. When Will Ward stopped the buggy in front of Panda's Grocery Store, she watched him fish a worn sow's ear of a purse from his right front pocket and twist the latch, opening one of the compartments. She watched him squint into it and shake it, weighing the contents. He fished out a quarter, turned it tenderly, studied it, then returned it. She smiled when he selected two dimes and a nickel, his calloused fingers probing reluctantly, as though the purse were an open wound.

"Wait here for me," he said, climbing down from his seat.

She watched him as he stalked toward the store. "Like I'd take his buggy and ride off," she thought with a smile.

He was back in three minutes, carrying a small white pasteboard box. He tugged his way back into the buggy and thrust the box into her hands. "Here!" he muttered, not looking at her. He seized the lines and slapped them down across Rhody's rump.

Alvira stared from the box back to Will. "What's this?" she demanded.

"It ain't tobacker," Will grinned. Then he roared with laughter. "No, siree!" he guffawed, "it shore as hell ain't tobacker."

Alvira opened the box and looked down at the red-striped peppermint candy. She had worked around her father's store too much to be impressed by the simple gift, but she was touched by the gesture of this aging man from the hills. She looked at him, her face serious. Her blue eyes were wide and tender as she studied his rugged face.

"Thank you kindly, Will," she murmured. "It's the first present I've had since I don't know when."

"It ain't much," he said. He looked down at the candy, licking his lips. "Jest thought you might like a little sweetenin, bein our time is jest about to run out."

She handed the box toward him. "Here, take you a stick."

He hesitated, then grabbled in the box, coming out with one of the sticks. He grinned happily, thrust it into the side of his mouth and bit it in half. His molars, crunching the hard candy, sounded to Alvira like a horse chewing corn, but she did not let it disturb her.

It was when they returned to the barn that Will proposed to her as she knelt beside the hen's empty nest. Will Ward reached forward and seized her upper arm. His fingers dug into her soft flesh, hurting her. Her mouth opened in pain, pain and fear. Her mind whirled as she fought for control. "Will!" she whispered. "Will Ward! What're you up to?"

"I been here nigh a week," he growled through tight lips. "I've rid'ye all over hell and half of Georgie. I ain't got no time left fer messin around. Are'ye a-aimin to marry me or ain't'ye?"

Alvira felt her face relax as her fear melted. She closed her mouth and studied his rugged face through narrowed eyes. Her first impulse was to laugh out, laugh in hysterical relief and then at his awkward proposal. But as she studied him, saw his face close up for the first time, the impulse died. She studied the wrinkled brow below the black hat, the hooked nose, the big stubborn mouth, the hard-set chin with the trace of a cleft. Then she raised her stare again, past the mustache, which divided his face, and looked into the grey eyes. And back of the icy glint she saw a tenderness, she saw frustration, and she glimpsed the deeper glint of a quiet desperation akin to her own—a desperation he needed to explain to her, discuss with her, but could not, never would, because he did not know where to begin.

When she had feared him only moments before, he had crossed a threshold and had come close to her. He was no longer an abstraction casually tagged "Will Ward." The abstraction who had sat beside her and had taken her on buggy rides during the past six days had disappeared. Her mind bounded back and began to re-examine those rides, all in a rush of memories and sensations and recalled sounds, gestures, visions. He was a man named Will Ward—a simple mountain man but a man, an individual, the only Will Ward ever to walk the earth. And he had paid her the greatest compliment a woman can receive from any man, whether or not she felt him worthy of her. Alvira was touched by the compliment. No one had ever proposed to her before, bouquet in hand or any other way. She was touched and she was sincerely flattered that Will Ward, anyone, should choose her.

And in that moment of revelation, the possibility of her ever marrying him was as remote and improbable to her as the prospect of stretching out her arms and flying away. "I thank'ye for astin me, Will," she said softly. "I have to think about it."

And she thought about it. It was impossible to forget the proposal for a moment. She thought about it as she prepared supper, and she was burdened with the proposal during the almost silent meal. She could tell Will Ward was disturbed, was disappointed that she did not agree on the spot to marry him. That was the way mountain men thought. They did a woman a favor by asking her to marry them when the time was ripe, and the woman did not hesitate. At least that was the way she thought it worked back in the hills. She watched him with averted eyes as he got up and clomped toward the stairs, heading for his room. She shook her head. Somehow she felt she had done him an injustice.

She washed the dishes in silence, told Ma Watson good night, and climbed the stairs to her own cold room. Undressing down to her petticoat, she stood looking out the window until the cold drove her beneath the burden of quilts. She lay there for a long time, staring at the dark ceiling. She tried to re-experience the buggy rides with Will Ward. She visualized his strong face, his expression, his slightly stooped shoulders. She remembered his speech, his earthy mountain expressions. Then, after avoiding it as long as she could, she tried to imagine herself as his wife, in bed with him—and there her thinking stopped dead, in revolt. She could not go beyond a simple marriage ceremony.

Her imagination could not or would not span the gap between marriage vows and their consummation, in bed.

And as she thought, Alvira became aware that her neck was stiff from holding her head to one side, alert. As she mused, she listened. She always listened. Dread of sudden sound hung over her like a teetering boulder—the sudden sound of Doc Watson's cry of indignation and misery. The dread was a curse. She was damned by it, damned and trapped, with nowhere to go. Even her own family had no place for her. What a relief! What a blessed relief it would be if she could just find some place, some hiding place, where she knew that raw, bloody cry could not seek her out! Then she dozed off. Off and on while she was thinking about Doc Watson and then refusing to think, she dozed off and slept.

The cry came as always, sudden, loud, and indignant. Alvira swam upward from sleep, fought off the burden of quilts, and stood swaying in the cold air before she knew who she was or what to do. Groping, she found her coat, squirmed into it, and plodded barefoot down the hall to Doc Watson's room. Beneath her feet the floor was a cold path with no end, only a delay on the way to the morbid room ahead. After she had cared for the Doc, she returned to her room and slept again, fitfully. She was aroused again around three, and a third time a few minutes past five.

After the last call, she could not go back to sleep. She lay there filled with Doc Watson's hurt blue stare and contorted mouth. She was filled with the stink of his sores mixed with the acrid urine of diseased kidneys. She thought of the strong, old-young face of Will Ward, she thought of the bay mare, and the yellow-spoked buggy. She thought about gold bars above the Blue Ridge at sunset. She thought about Lucinda Watson, old and fat and dependent on her. She thought about big-boned Mary Phillips, dumb but dependable. And she stopped thinking at that point. She put further thought out of her mind and left direction to feeling, feeling and intuition.

Crawling from bed, she slipped into her coat and tiptoed

back down the hall to Will Ward's room. She opened the door carefully. Grey dawn was a rectangle set in the wall of night. Will was lost in sleep at first, somewhere beneath the bulk of bedclothes, but his snores rolled out and occupied the farthest corners of the room.

She closed the door softly behind her and plodded across the floor, stopping beside his bed, the window behind her. She leaned forward and placed her fingers on his face, shaking his head gently. She could feel the prickle of his beard, the warm jets of breath from his nostrils. He reared up suddenly, mouth open to yell. She snatched her hand back.

"Sh-h-h!" she hissed. "Be quiet. You'll wake the Doc."

"What're you up to?" Will whispered. "What you want, a-comin in my room in the middle of the night like this?"

"I had to come," she said. "I had to come to'ye here. I hope'ye don't think bad of me for comin to'ye in your own room."

He leaned back on braced arms, staring up at her through slitted lids. "What's on'ye mind?" he asked hoarsely.

She opened her mouth to speak, then closed it. She stood erect. She turned her head and looked through the grey windows. She turned back and leaned toward him. "I decided to marry'ye, if you're still of a mind to," she murmured.

Will Ward stared up at her face, his mouth open. Abruptly he flung back the quilts. "Well, godamighty! don't stand there freezin. If we aim to git married, let's get a-goin."

She looked down at him. He was a white blur in his long underwear. He glanced down along his torso and sprawled legs, and yanked the covers back over himself.

"I'll go and get ready," she said. "Give me bout twenty minutes. Be careful and not wake Ma Watson."

"I'll be ready in two shakes of a sheep's tail," Will grinned.

Squatting by her bedroom window, Alvira Matlock scribbled a farewell note, a note of regret to Lucinda Watson, on the back of the envelope she had received from her father. She placed it on her pillow. Then she picked up her battered Gladstone bag and lugged it downstairs. Will Ward was waiting for her in the kitchen, a lamp in his hand. He had shaved with the warm water left in the range reservoir, and a streak of blood angled across his right cheek. Alvira started to tell him, but changed her mind.

Will grinned at her. "Howdy, Vi," he greeted. "Bout ready to ride?"

Alvira held back the pressure building up in her. She refused to see beyond the moment, refused to see beyond his blood-streaked face. "Ready," she said. "Let's go, for goodness' sake, before Ma Watson wakes up."

Alvira found Mary Phillips milking in the cowshed behind the Phillips cabin. She squatted on her haunches, feet planted in soft, stinking dung, and exposed her red-fleeced loins to a sleeping world. With two hands, she milked pelting streaks of white into a peck bucket. In the cold morning air, she wore only a thin print dress and a ragged blue sweater. Her long red hair hung in tangled, curly strands about her face and shoulders.

"Mary!" Alvira called.

Mary Phillips leaped to her feet, almost upsetting the bucket of milk. She stared across the cow's back, then grinned, her freckled face wreathed in good humor.

"Vi!" she said. "You nigh scart the giblets out'n me."

"I didn't mean to scare'ye," Alvira said.

Mary looked beyond Alvira at the buggy waiting in the clay yard. "That Will Ward and his buggy yander a-waitin for'ye?"

"It's him. Me and him—" Alvira paused, licked her dry lips. She inhaled a deep drought of January air, and it gushed down her soft throat, filling her with cold. "Me and him are on our way to get married, Mary."

Mary Phillips' face exploded into another grin. "Glory be to God, Vi!" she moaned. "I wish'ye well. I do wish'ye well."

"Thank'ye, Mary." Alvira paused. "There's one problem, Mary. I can't get married if I can't get past it."

"What's it, honey?" Mary's brow furrowed in concern. "Can I do somethin?"

"If you can't take my place at Mrs. Watson's, I can't go. I can't just ride off and leave her without nobody to tend to the Doc."

"Glory be to God!" Mary sighed. "You know I'm purely achin for that job. You know I'm achin to git out of this cowdung and cabin full of snotty-nosed younguns. You do aim for me to live with Miz Watson, don't you—Vi?"

"If you will and can, Mary."

"If I will!" She ducked down and seized the bucket half full of milk. "Come on, honey. I'm done and on my way."

"Jedge" Blossom, the magistrate, was a little blackhead of a man in a black suit too large for him. He reminded Alvira Matlock of a crow that had lost so much weight its skin and feathers did not fit properly. Mrs. Blossom had absorbed the family excesses. She towered over Jedge Blossom in a black satin dress, florid and fat. Her official presence as witness bore heavily on her broad shoulders, twisting her face into a frown of concern. Will Ward and Alvira Matlock stood before them in silence. Alvira's emotions and thoughts lay flat against a blank wall she had thrown up across her mind. She stared at the J. P., she considered all of them, she sensed Will Ward, heavy and hard and solemn, beside her. She heard the Jedge and she knew what to say. Beyond that, she did not enter into the ceremony because she could not. Far back in her mind she was plagued by a growing fear that she had left something undone—like not making up her bed back at Lucinda Watson's, except that was not it.

"Your age?" Jedge Blossom repeated, squinting at Alvira.

"My—my age?" She rolled her lips together to moisten them. "Twenty-one," she said, almost like a question. "Yes, twenty-one."

"And you, John William Ward," Jedge Blossom asked, "what be your age?"

Alvira glimpsed Will Ward as he glanced toward her. He shuffled his feet on the hooked rug. "Thirty-eight!" he announced, as though daring Jedge Blossom or his wife or both to disagree.

But the Jedge did not deny it. He got on with his job. He filled out the marriage certificate and then ran through the simple ceremony. "And do you, Alvira Matlock, take this here feller fur your lawful wedded husban to cherish and to obey howsomever long either one of'ye happens to live?" Jedge Blossom demanded sternly.

Alvira opened her mouth. The wall across her mind sagged, leaped erect, sagged again. She closed her mouth. She glanced at Will Ward, who waited, face tense, his grey eyes gleaming. She could see his face muscles bulge as he ground his teeth silently.

"Well, do'ye or don't'ye?" Jedge Blossom asked shortly.

"I—I do," Alvira murmured.

Mrs. Blossom rushed forward and enfolded Alvira in her heavy arms. Vi had a sudden terror of being absorbed in her soft bulk. Mrs. Blossom sobbed as she clutched her.

"Oh, my dear! my dear!" she whispered. "I've witnessed at many a marryin, but you're about the purtiest bride I near about ever set my eyes on."

"Thank'ye," Vi muttered, her voice muffled by the heavy shoulder. "I thank'ye for sayin so."

Alvira stepped back, on guard, when she was released. Will took the worn leather purse out of his pocket, twisted the catch apart, and fingered around in its secret maws with calloused thumb and forefinger. Finally he fished out a fifty-cent coin. He held it up between him and a window and squinted at it. He caressed it tenderly. He clutched it tightly a moment longer, then thrust it into the ready palm of Jedge Blossom.

"Here'ye go, Jedge," Will grinned. "I thank'ye for your services."

"It was my bounden duty," Jedge Blossom announced, with a mortician's gloom. "Hit's what I come into the world fur."

When they left the magistrate's house, the sun was standing a half hour high above the Bushy Mountains. Alvira Matlock stopped suddenly in the yard and squinted at the sun. She lifted her blue eyes and stared at the sky, the same hue directly above her. There was not a cloud with her inside the embracing horizon. Suddenly the barrier across her mind bulged, and one small corner gave way. Emotions came pouring through the gap, overwhelming her. Dread swept away before them because it was still morning and a long time, a long ride, till nightfall. She had plenty of time to look and feel and not to think too much. And she had escaped Doc Watson's skeletal clutches.

She turned her head and looked up into the strong, eager face of Will Ward, and he met her stare. She inhaled a deep gasp of cold air. She reached out, then clutched his arm. He grinned and escorted her toward the buggy, her fingers still biting into his hard muscles. She felt a light-headed joy as she glanced again at the morning sun.

They stopped in Old Town at the house of Levi Goforth, a picture taker. He was a neat little man, hair parted neatly in the middle. His huge tripod camera was neat, and he had neat ideas about how the likeness of a new bride and groom should be struck. He arranged John William Ward and Alvira Matlock Ward the way he wanted them, outside in the sunlight, then began a ritual, ducking in and out beneath the black cape over the camera, squinting between his fingers and aiming across his thumb. He made Alvira think of a sparrow hopping around a black snake, trying to scare it off, except he was too happy for that.

Finally the picture was taken. The groom sat in a split-bottomed chair, legs crossed, left hand in lap, right hand on top of left. His coat hung open, his vest was buttoned, the dark blue tie slightly askew to the right, though not enough to crumple the white shirt collar. The photographer failed to see the small streak of blood on the groom's face.

The bride stood by the groom's left side, white-gloved hand resting on his shoulder. In her left hand she held a folded fan. The bride wore an ankle-length, light-blue taffeta dress, ruffled at the bottom with three tucks just above, and gathered at the waist beneath a narrow white belt. A huge white Bertha collar with Hamburg lace covered her shoulders and maiden breasts and matched the broad white cuffs about her wrists. On her head she wore a broad-brimmed white hat of ribbons and lace, turned up on the left side and held in place with hatpins. A silver pin like a leaf cluster, worn on her collar just above her right breast, completed her ensemble. In this manner the wedding day of John William and Alvira Matlock Ward was eternized.

2

THEY RODE BACK ALONG THE RIDGE through Quaker Falls, mostly silent as the sun climbed, gradually warming up the morning. Three miles beyond Lucinda Watson's house, they turned right, slanting down the slope to the west and crossing the river at Coleman's Ford. Beyond the river, they crossed the railroad track, a lumberyard on their left. Alvira peered curiously at several wagons backed up to the siding and at the men loading the boxcars with plank.

"This is where Old Man Harrison hauls his lumber to now," Will explained. "Didn't use to be no sidin here, and we hauled all the way to Northboro. But old Harrison got a sidin put in. Smart old bastard. Saves him sebem or eight mile of haulin."

"How far up the river does the track reach to?" Vi asked. She was not really interested. A tight little knot of dread had come back, low in the stomach, and the farther they drew away from Quaker Falls, the heavier and colder it became.

"Clear up into Carson County. Git a whole heap of lumber and tanbark out of up in there." He looked at her. "They got a trunk line that goes up Hog Elk Creek, most of it spiked to a trestle that's set square in the creek bed. If it ever comes a big freshet or cloudbust, it'll wash that track clean to Cubie, shore as hell."

Alvira smiled. "Maybe the folks could use a railroad in Cubie."

In the afternoon they crossed the Bare Creek Ridge and headed down the other side, past Ab Forester's store. It was an unpainted, weatherboarded building set on the left, much longer than wide. A green kerosene drum sat on the front porch. The sides of the building were plastered with tattered signs advertising Square Snuff, Brown's Mule Tobacco, Stud Hoss Smoking Tobacco, Peach Snuff, and Mother's Castoria. The door was closed, and smoke corkscrewed upward from a narrow flue.

"That's Ab Forester's store," Will announced, pointing with his whip. "We do some tradin here, but most of it at Doc Ellis's place cause it's closter to home and they got the post office there."

"Looks bigger'n Papa's store," Alvira said. "Does he take roots and yerbs?"

"Some. Caters to lobelia and star root and sech. But Bessie Ellis, she'll take anything from white-pine bark to mullen leaves. Got a whole upstairs loft in their store where they keep it dry."

"Well," Alvira paused, "that looks like a good way for pore folks that needs it to make a little extry cash."

She lifted her eyes toward the Blue Ridge. A long rack of clouds, straight as a furrow from north to south, rolled in from the west to threaten the sun—the leading wave for an ocean of dappled grey. A cold breeze buffeted her in the face like a slap, and the warmth of the day was swept away. She clutched the faded blue coat tightly about her, but the chill had penetrated too deep. It clung to her bones.

At the foot of the grade, they forded Bare Creek and turned left along the flank of another ridge, heading upstream.

A quarter of a mile beyond, the ridge tapered off, and a side road skirted its spur, leading up Stud Branch. Will turned the mare away from Bare Creek and headed up the branch road. Fifty yards from the intersection, an ancient log house sat in the fallow field to the left, between the road and Stud Branch. The weathered grey logs were chinked with mud, powdery yellow. The black shingles were curled and tattered. From the buggy, Alvira could glimpse holes in the roof where shingles were missing. A thin trickle of smoke curled upward from the river-rock chimney.

As the buggy approached, a young woman opened the plank door and poked her head around it. Her long auburn hair flowed down her back and about her shoulders. She squinted at the buggy, then came out into the yard, her right forearm shading her eyes, a half-eaten apple in her hand.

"Is that you, Will Ward?" she called, and paced toward the road, her hips swaying.

"Whoa!" Will tugged at the lines. "Whoa, Rhody. Howdy, Doll. How'ye doin today?"

Alvira studied the woman. She had a pretty face, even-featured and white as skimmed milk, powdery freckles about her nose and cheeks. She wore a thin print dress and hugged huge breasts into a double bundle in an effort to clothe herself from the chill air. Beyond her, Vi saw another woman, black-headed and swarthy and somewhat older. She came out of the house to stand in the yard, two little girls swinging onto her skirt tail. A young man thrust his head around the doorjamb, stared at them balefully, then ducked back out of sight.

"Who's that thar young womern you're a-haulin around, Will?" the auburn-haired girl asked, pointing the apple at Vi. She shivered, and her bosom quaked beneath the thin fabric.

Will Ward spat tobacco juice to one side, wiped his mouth with the back of his hand, then grinned. "I bet'ye couldn't guess in a month of Sundays, Doll."

Doll, shuffling closer, squinted up at Alvira, her face screwed into a frown of concentration. "I can't say that I've ever seed her before. Nope, I wouldn't venture a guess who in hell you're a-cartin around, Will."

Alvira bit her lips, annoyed. She felt like some kind of off-breed heifer Will was showing off.

"This here's my new wife," Will announced, rearing back. "Her name's Alvira Matlock. Her pa's a storekeeper down around Ready River."

"I do be double damned!" the young woman swore. "You old hoss, you gone and got hitched again."

"Shore as sunshine," Will grinned. "Alvira, this here is Doll Dugan. She lives down the branch a ways from my place."

"How-do." Alvira nodded formally, glancing at Doll's breasts, which looked about ready to explode through the faded dress.

"Howdy, Alvira," Doll grinned. "Welcome to Rowdy Branch Township." She looked back at Will. "She's a mighty fine-lookin gal. You aimin to take her up on Stud Branch to Coottown to live?"

"I have you know," Will Ward growled, eyes slitted, "that I don't live in no goddamn Coottown." Alvira turned to look at him. Will's jaw was bulging with muscles, and his chin was set. His chest heaved with a sudden intake of air.

"From where you're a-livin at, a bidy could fling a tomcat by his tail into Matt Catlett's winder," Doll smirked.

"You tend to'ye own prayer meetins in Hill Anderson's cuttin-room and leave my business be!" Will grumbled.

Doll opened her mouth to retort, clamped it shut, and spun about, stalking back across the yard, her round buttocks shifting beneath the dress. Will brought the lines down across Rhody's rump with a *whack* and the mare leaped into a canter.

"What in the world went wrong between you two neighbors?" Vi frowned at him in puzzlement.

Will spat out of the other side of the buggy, then stared straight ahead, his eyes squinted. He opened his mouth to speak, closed it, then opened it again. "Wasn't nothin wrong except that no-good bitch tried to git smart with me."

"What did she say so bad?" Vi persisted. "I didn't hear her say much."

"It wasn't *what* she said, it was *who* said it," Will explained. "She's no damned good. She and her two sisters and two brothers are the bastards of old Matt Dugan. She lived in that log house forty year and had fourteen younguns. All of'em died—starved, I reckon—sept five."

"That don't sound like it's Doll's fault," Alvira argued. "I don't see as you ort to take that out on Doll."

"She's jest like her ma was," Will snorted. "That was her sis Lil in the yard. She's done got two bastards. The oldest sis married Hill Anderson and ain't ebem bore him a miscarriage. That was that sneakin, low-down Tom stuck his head out the door. They's a younger boy named Pink that acts decent. Four of them live in old Matt's cabin back there, and don't nobidy know where Lil's two belongs to the brothers or to Hill Anderson or jest who. And Doll's startin out jest like Lil, sept she ain't got caught yit."

"Whew-w-w!" Alvira sighed. "What inter-restin folks you've got hereabouts."

She saw Will glance at her, mouth grim. Up ahead to the left, a high ridge rose against the sky. As they rounded its spur, a huge yellow building appeared on its crest, towering against the skyline. Alvira studied it. Her heart beat faster. Will had never mentioned the house he lived in, and Ma Watson knew nothing about it. She wondered if the three-story mansion could be his house—his and now her house. She kept looking at the building, the house and the barn below it, as the buggy moved on up the road, drawing abreast of them. There was a flutter in her stomach which increased as they approached the intersection with another road just ahead. When Will wheeled the mare away from the ridge on which the yellow house sat, the flutter crystallized into a cold lump.

The buggy skirted the spur of another ridge, tapering off on the left, and headed eastward, away from the branch road they had just left. The sun had already disappeared, washed under by the ocean of clouds. Alvira glanced upward at the grey rack, now directly overhead. She shivered. The warm week of sunshine was over, and the air steadily grew colder.

Vi stared straight ahead, lost in wonderment. She grabbed at the seat frame as the buggy wheeled suddenly to the left, up an incline, and into the woods. She looked ahead and to either side. The buggy followed a narrow clay road through the forest. Trees and saplings rose like walls on either side, gnarled oak claws reaching down here and there to scratch the buggy top. Alvira glanced nervously at Will Ward's face. He stared straight ahead, his cheeks bulging as he clamped down on his tobacco, his eyes narrow. The knuckles of the fist gripping the lines were white as pebbles. She started to break the silence, then thought better. Suddenly she was afraid to speak to him, afraid of what he would say and how he would say it. The man beside her was, in a heartbeat, a stranger hauling her through a strange forest toward a house she now dreaded to see.

She thought, "This is no through road. We'll foller it to a dead end. That's where Will Ward lives, I bet. At the end of this road."

The road, following the crest of the ridge, curved through an ivy thicket farther along and broke out into the open beyond another stretch of taller trees, mostly pines. The crest and flanks of the ridge were bare for about three hundred yards on the right, for a much greater distance along the lower half of the left. To the west, across a narrow valley, Alvira could see a wooded mountain running parallel to the ridge. To the south, the almost bare ridge with the yellow mansion on its spine stood higher against a sky still blue and unclouded. Far away, beyond the house, the blue ridge of the Bushy Mountains lay along the rim of the world. Vi knew they were the old familiar Bushes without being told. She turned her head and looked eastward. The ridge along which the mare paced dropped off into rolling fields that reached away into the distance, no other hill or ridge breaking their regularity. Just beyond the stream cutting along the base of the slope, a large farmhouse sprawled in a grove of apple trees, a huge barn and other outbuildings scattered in the fields beyond.

Vi studied the comfortable setting and sighed. "This would be a nice house spot," she thought. "The top of this ridge would. Not a house up here."

"That's my Cousin Bill's place," Will said gruffly, not looking at her. "Used to be part of the land my great-grandpa owned."

She looked at him, started to speak, but closed her mouth. "It's a nice-lookin farmhouse," she said, finally. "Looks like they're well-to-do down there."

They followed the ridge road back into the forest, and the mare slowed, steam jetting from her nostrils. Alvira glanced into the dark woods on either side of them. She shivered. She could see no sign of a clearing ahead or around her. The way it looked to her, the forest reached on and on clear to the end of the world. She had never thought there were so many trees left in the whole wide world. Vi would not have been surprised to see a black bear as big as a cow come lumbering out of a thicket, or an Indian leap from behind a tree with a stone ax. Of course she knew better, but she would not have been surprised. And it would have surprised her less if either bear or Indian had taken one look at Will Ward's grim face and turned to run.

The ridge tapered abruptly downward, and they coasted through a grove of field pines no taller than the mare's withers. Alvira stared across their tops, gripping her white-gloved hands in her lap. A mountain loomed up across the narrow valley below, running at right angles to the spur of the ridge, a mountain covered in forest except for the lower flank just ahead, which was bare—bare except for a village of shacks like dung-heaps flung against the fallow slope. From that distance she could see children and dogs working like ants about the clay yard, could see an occasional woman plodding from shack to woodpile or with a bucket toward a large oak tree, below which she guessed there was a spring. Pale ribbons of smoke fluttered upward from a few rock chimneys.

Alvira's mouth dropped open. The dread growing inside her became a little harder to bear. She could see that the road they followed ended somewhere along the base of the mountain. "Is—is *that* where you live at?" she asked, not looking at Will.

He turned his head and stared at her, his grey eyes flared open. "Jesus Christ, no, womern! That's Coottown. What do'ye think I am? Nothin but trash?"

Alvira sighed. She even smiled her relief. "That's a blessin to know," she said. "I could tell this road wasn't aimin to hold out much longer with that mountain rarin up in front of us."

The road curved suddenly to the left and crossed an open field. Alvira casually studied the log house which they were going to pass on their left. It looked somewhat better than the shacks of Coottown, but from the slope of the ridge, she had included it in the dismal little village. She identified a smokehouse, the narrow corncrib, and farther up the slope she could see a rail fence and several stacks of fodder. Whoever lived here was obviously more industrious than the people in the shacks Will had called Coottown, but it lacked a lot being the farmstead they had just passed belonging to Will's cousin. Vi craned her neck to see beyond the house, to discover where the road led. Apparently it followed the valley between the two converging mountains ahead, and Will lived somewhere up that valley hidden by trees.

Now they were even with the house. Will Ward tugged on the left line and pulled the buggy into the backyard close to the smokehouse. He yanked back on the mare, causing her to rear against the shafts and back the buggy several feet. They sat between the big log building and the smokehouse—where the road had run out. There was no road entering the valley up ahead. Only a fallow field stretched away beyond the smokehouse toward the pasture. Alvira stared about her, trapped. This was the end of the road, really—the dead end.

Will did not look at her. He backed down out of the buggy and looked at the top of the mountain beyond her head. "This here is where I live at," he stated. "This here is where you're gonna live, too." He turned away and shuffled to the rear of the buggy. Alvira could hear him removing her Gladstone bag from the package carrier.

She stared from the log cabin to the corncrib, then back at the smokehouse. She clutched her white-gloved hands in her lap and pressed them between her hard thighs, creating a barrier. She tasted a copper-coated sickness in her throat that would not rise. Her heart was an aching stone in her breast. She wanted to cry, wanted so much to burst out weeping, but no tears would come. Her eyes remained open and wide and blue. She felt wronged. She felt that someone had done her a terrible injustice. Some of it she blamed on Will Ward. But someone else was chiefly to blame. She wracked her mind and could not think who it was that had dealt with her so unjustly—or would not admit it.

Will came around the buggy and reached up for her. Stiffly she let him take her arm and help her down. When she touched the ground, he released her and she almost collapsed. Her legs were stiff from the long ride. She hobbled behind him toward the back door. He carried the bag, preceding her, not glancing back. He tugged at a leather thong dangling from a hole in the door and wood clacked against wood, inside. The door swung open on leather hinges. Alvira followed him inside as though he led her with halter and rope, and Will flung the door shut behind her. She spun toward the slam, turned back, staring about her.

Alvira's first impression was that she was in an immense cavern deep underground. But her eyes dilated rapidly, adjusting to the gloom. The windows were covered with rough wooden panels similar to the door, and some light seeped through the cracks in these shutters and through the cracks in the two doors. A fire flickered in the huge fireplace at the end of the house, to her right, illuminating what appeared to be the kitchen area. After her eyes had adjusted to the gloom, she could see at once the Lazy Susan and the cooking table, though she could not discover the cookstove. There was a close, dry smell to the room, flavored with smoke and fresh coffee, and an unpleasant odor which reminded her of unwashed bodies, old shoes, and fermenting hog slop, all mingling to suffocate her. When she became dizzy and reeled, she realized she had been holding her breath.

"Pa?" someone said from near the fireplace. "Pa, who's that you got with'ye there in the purty hat and frock showing below her purty blue coat?"

Alvira pivoted her attention back toward the sound of the voice. A young woman of around twenty sat in a split-bottomed chair to the left of the fireplace. As Vi discovered her, she stood up. She wore a faded purple-print dress ripped down the right side from the base of her breast to her hip. The petticoat beneath was ragged, showing splotches of chubby white flesh. She was barefooted, and her uncombed black hair swept down her back and about her shoulders. But the girl was only a background to what caught Alvira's attention. In her arms she clutched an infant less than a year old.

The baby dangled across her forearm with its eyes closed in

sleep. It wore a long smock made from an old flour sack. She could see printing on one side and part of a lion's picture. Its diaper was soaking wet and swung to its knees, stained through with excrement and soiled with dirt mopped up from the cabin floor. The young woman's lower belly and upper thighs were also wet, and clung to her heavy body in a translucent sheath. Alvira raised her eyes to look at the girl's face. It was round and full, but even and rather pretty. Her eyes were gentle and sad, and there was a pained expression about them as though she were embarrassed at being compared to the young woman who stood beside her father staring at her and the baby. Alvira felt a surge of sympathy for the girl, but deeper and stronger, a slow anger was beginning to burn.

"Vi, this here'un is my oldest gal, Tillie," Will Ward said. "Till, this here's your new ma I brung'ye. Her name's Alvira, but you and the other'uns is bound to call her *Ma.*"

A smile worked its way across Tillie's face and was gone. "Howdy—Ma." She looked at Will. "You shore enough went and got married, Pa?"

"Shore as Hell's hot!" Will Ward chuckled for the first time.

"Ain't you gonna speak to me, Ma?" Tillie asked wistfully, looking back at Alvira.

"Pleased to meet'ye, Tillie," Alvira said. She turned to Will. "Who does the baby belong to? Is it her'n?"

Tillie's face clouded. "I have you know I ain't married, ma'am," she snapped.

"Shet up, Till!" Will ordered. He looked straight at Alvira, and their eyes clashed. "The youngun's mine. It was borned a few months before Bell died."

"That's inter-restin," Vi said. "That's a little matter you forgot to let on about."

Will looked at the fire, shuffling his feet. "I don't see what matter one youngun more or less makes."

"No," Vi said, "I don't reckon you would."

Will dropped her Gladstone bag to one side. "Well, I ain't got time to stand here jawin all day. I got to git Cousin Bill's mare and buggy back to'im before dark."

"I might a-knowd," Alvira said, angry and hurt. "I might

a-knowd. Who does your store-bought suit belong to, Will Ward? Some of'ye neighbors on the hill up there in Coottown?"

Will turned on her, his eyes slitted. "I have'ye know, young lady, I don't wear no goddamn second-hand clothes. Hit's my own suit. Sides, they ain't a man buck in Coottown that owns a suit of clothes like I do."

"Glory hallelujah!" Alvira said softly. "Pity the pore menfolk of Coottown."

Will stared at her. He opened his mouth to speak, then closed it. "Make yourself at home," he growled. "I'll be back d'rectly." He left the house, slamming the door after him. Alvira, unmoving, heard the buggy turn and roll away, back up the road that had brought her the long journey to Stud Branch.

Vi paced closer to the fire and into a circle of warmth, unbuttoning her coat as she moved. "Where's your other sister and two brothers at, honey?" she asked.

Tillie relaxed and sat back down, the smile remaining on her face. "My sis is back there on the bed, sleepin as usual." She nodded toward the back of the cabin.

Alvira turned her back to the fire and shivered in the warmth from it. At the back of the room, two wooden beds sat in the opposite corners, about five feet separating them. The bed on the right was made up, a patchwork quilt with a maple-leaf pattern topmost. But the other bed was unmade. A girl of eighteen or nineteen lay sprawled on her back, her dress hem almost to her hips. She snored softly, her mouth wide, her hair piled about her head on the pillow. Vi could see she had a nice figure and shapely round thighs almost to their juncture. Her face was pretty too, but there was a hardness about it, different from Tillie's gentleness, a hardness even her sleep could not relax.

"That's Annie," Tillie said. "She's headstrong. She ain't much help." Tillie looked down at herself, then looked Alvira up and down. "That's a mighty purty frock you're a-wearin underneath that coat."

"Thank'ye," she said. "It's my weddin dress. A girl's due to have a purty weddin dress. I made it on Ma Watson's sewin machine."

"Annie!" Tillie called. "Annie, wake up! Somebidy's here."

Anna turned onto her side, then rolled back, stretched and yawned. She opened her eyes and stared upward at the rafters, then sat up and swung her bare feet to the floor. She reached under the bed for her shoes, changed her mind, and rested her elbows on her knees, her chin cupped in her hands.

"Guess who's here, Annie?" Tillie called to her.

Anna yawned. "Maybe the King of England," she muttered. "Who gives a damn?" She turned her head and blinked at Alvira. "Maybe the Queen of Cubie, I ort to a-said."

"This here is Pa's new wife, Annie," Tillie explained, standing up again. "Her name's Alvira, but we'uns is to call her Ma, Pa says."

Anna Ward sprang to her feet, frowning in interest. She paced slowly toward Alvira, like a stalking cat. Vi watched her come. She did not like her. She sensed trouble. Anna stood to one side and looked Vi up and down.

"Jesus of Nazareth!" she muttered. "She ain't much older'n me. How can I call her *Ma* and her no older'n me? Is Pa crazy, old as he is?"

"How old really is your pa, Anna?" Vi asked.

Anna stared at her. "Didn't he tell'ye, honey-chile?"

"He mentioned thirty-eight."

Anna Ward laughed, throwing her head far back. "He shoveled you a load of bull manure, honey. He's forty-two, come May."

Alvira inhaled, then let it out slow. "And how old might you be?" she asked softly.

Anna grinned, head to one side. "I might be twenty-five," she said, "but I ain't but eighteen. Till here is twenty. How old might you be, honey?"

Alvira ignored the question. "How old are the other two—the two boys?" she asked, clutching her hands by her sides.

"Van is twenty-one," Anna said. "Dan is just fifteen."

Alvira peered about the shadowy cabin. Her breasts rose and fell, rose and fell as she fought the growing storm inside her. "That's your bed, I reckon," she said. "The one you was layin down on?"

"That's our'n," Anna said. "Mine and Till's. And that's your'n and Pa's over there nigh to it." She smirked. "The baby, nachly, sleeps with you and Pa."

"And where do the boys sleep?" Vi asked. "With me and Will and the baby?"

Anna laughed, tossing her hair, her dark eyes flashing. "Wouldn't that be cozy, and Van probly older'n you? No, ma'am —Ma—your two oldest sons sleeps upstairs on a pallet."

She pointed toward the ladder over beside the left-hand wall, beyond the back door. Alvira studied it. She traced it upward to where it leaned against the edge of the half-loft, which extended past the beds beneath it. Upstairs consisted of rough planks, gaping cracks between them, placed on top of the rafters. Alvira thought fleetingly of her wedding night, the girls in the bed five feet away, the boys overhead. She felt that copper-coated sickness in her throat. She tried not to think that far ahead, but the taste in her throat persisted.

She turned to Tillie, who had sat back down. "Where's your stove?" she asked. "I don't see no cookstove, Tillie."

Tillie looked down at her feet. "We ain't got nairy'un," she muttered. "We cook in the farplace."

"This here ain't no fancy Northboro mansion," Anna laughed. "You're back in the hill country a ways, now—honey."

Vi turned on her, started to speak, then turned back. "And where are the boys?" she asked Tillie. "Where are Van and Dan now?"

Tillie looked away into the glowing coals in the fireplace. "I've not got no idee," she murmured. "Runnin around the mountainsides, some'ers."

"She does have some idee where bouts they're at," Anna smiled. "Pa don't know but she knows. And I know—"

"Annie!" Tillie snapped. "Shet up your big mouth or I'll slap it shet."

Anna paled. Her lips compressed into a firm line. "You jest try it, big sis," she snapped. "You jest try slappin my mouth shet."

"You'd better hold your tongue," Tillie said. "You'd jest better not go too far."

Alvira hardly heard them. She looked around the cabin. She

looked at the meager utensils piled on the cooking table. She looked at the two beds, then upward to the loft. She turned and looked at Tillie, at her ragged dress, the sleeping babe in her arms. She turned and looked at Anna, who met her stare with a grin and a toss of her head. And the copper-coated sickness filled her—the sickness that was despair and dread and resentment. It was not right! It was not right for her to be deceived as she had been. It was wrong. It was a downright sin. How could a marriage be sanctified when plighted in deceit? It was all wrong. She could not go through with it. To save her, she did not see how she could live up to their marriage. It was all wrong, all wrong. Will Ward had deceived her. Will Ward and someone else. At the moment she could not think who had deceived her other than Will.

She ran across the room and snatched up the Gladstone bag. She reached the door, raised the latch, and yanked the door open. The cold afternoon air gushed about her and she shivered, fumbling at her coat buttons.

"If you're a-runnin off, Ma," Anna called after her, "you're a-wastin your time. You're Pa's now. Pa don't give up what's already his'n."

Alvira slammed the door behind her.

3

Alvira Matlock Ward plodded down the Ridge Road she had recently traveled on her wedding journey, the heavy bag weighting her to one side. She had no clear idea where she was going, only that she was going. She came out of the woods halfway down the ridge and stared toward the west. Somewhere behind the grey clouds the sun was going down. Not much daylight left. She looked toward the big yellow house on the crest of the ridge to the south. Perhaps they would take her in, for the night at least. Or perhaps Will's cousin Bill and his wife—

She inhaled, and the ache of despair was a cold tumor below her heart. She shifted the bag to her left hand and thrust her head to the right to counterbalance it. She looked to the left, at the house in the grove of apple trees below the ridge. The house and grounds looked prosperous and peaceful. She saw a man in the barnyard, but it was not Will. "A good manager lives there," she thought. "A body can tell where a good manager lives. Everything stands up straight. I thought Will would live at a place like that."

She entered the woods again, heading toward the Big Road. She had no idea which way she would turn when she reached it.

Only one thing she was certain of—she had to leave. She was bound and compelled to leave, before Will Ward got back to her.

She circled the ivy thicket around which the road curved, and could glimpse light up ahead, at the end of the forest. She speeded up her steps. Somehow, she felt lighter, felt safe now. She had almost escaped. As soon as she reached the road, she would be free again, out of the forest. She could forget that miserable cabin and the miserable people who lived there and go back where she came from, where there was at least comfort with the misery. Ma Watson would be glad to take her back. That was where she would go! She would spend the night somewhere along the road and go back to Lucinda Watson's house and go on living with her. Watching the agony of Doc Watson's slow dying was way yonder better than spending her life at the end of the road in the middle of a forest that reached clear to kingdom come.

She threw up her head and smiled, her mind made up. She began to hum softly, "Go and tell Aunt Rhody, go and tell Aunt Rhody, go and tell Aunt Rhody, the old grey goose is dead—" Will Ward appeared suddenly from behind an oak tree. One blink of her eyes he was not there, the next, he filled the road in front of her.

"Jest where in hell do'ye reckon you're a-headin, young womern?" Will demanded. He stood before her, feet spread, shoulders and head hunched forward, arms hanging loosely by his sides.

Alvira's heart had leaped to choke her song, then plunged downward. Her breath stopped. She stared at him, glanced down at the Gladstone bag, looked beyond him toward the Big Road, which led to freedom. She sucked in air suddenly, her breasts heaved upward. The air was cold to the hot passage of her throat. She dropped the bag at her feet and squared her shoulders.

"I'm leavin you, Will Ward!" she announced. "You fooled me and lied to me. And I ain't aimin to spend one night with'ye and ruin my whole livelong life."

"How did I fool'ye?" he growled. "Jest how in hell did I fool'ye?"

"You come down there on purpose, courtin me with that fancy buggy and fancy mare," she cried. "Actin like a fancy farmer. Tryin your level best to make me think you was somebody."

"By God, I am somebidy!" Will thundered. Then he went on, his voice quieter. "My folks used to own this land as far as you can see from East Ridge. As for the mare and buggy, I never did say onct they was mine. Not one earthful time did I say so."

"You acted like it," she argued. "Everbody, even Ma Watson, thought so. That's how you made it look."

"I wanted to marry'ye," he said, looking away. "I had to do it like that. But I never said they was mine. And I never told'ye I lived in any fancy place, not onct."

Alvira clutched her hands and unclutched them, searching for words. Her mind was not working. She could not think, could not argue with him. She had everything on her side, and she could not tell him, did not know what to say to make him understand he could not have her, that he had betrayed her. "But—but you did lie," she argued. "You did lie to me."

"I didn't lie, neither," he said, shuffling closer. "What did I lie to you about?"

"You didn't tell me about the baby," she said. "That's a lie of o-mission, as the Good Book says. And you told me you wasn't but thirty-eight. Annie told me you're as good as forty-two."

He looked at his feet and lifted his gnarled hands, closing and unclosing them while examining them closely. "That ain't much of a lie," he muttered. "What's three or four year, more or less?"

She ran toward him, and he stepped back, throwing up his hand. For an instant alarm warped his face. Then be braced himself, his cold grey eyes squinting at her. "You know how old I am, Will Ward?" she cried. "I ain't but sebemteen. I'll be eighteen in March. Van is older'n me. Tillie's older'n me. Even that hateful Annie's older'n me. Dear God, how can I be your wife and a mother to three grown folks older'n I am?"

He studied her, mouth firm. "Who lied to who, missy?" he demanded. "Jest who in hell lied to who? You're the young lady that told me you was twenty-one year old. And you told the magistrate, too."

She stepped back, a white-gloved hand leaping to her mouth. He was right. Of course he was right. And now she had to admit who the other guilty party was, who had betrayed her along with Will Ward. Below her thinking she had known better, had told herself only what she wanted to believe. She was more to blame than Will because deep down she had known, step by step, that she was deceiving herself. The marriage was not good because most of her reasons for going into it had been wrong. Her escape had become a trap, a trap with no escape. She sensed it. She looked hopefully beyond him, toward the edge of the forest, at the Big Road, which led away toward Quaker Falls.

"Age ain't got nothin to do with it," Will Ward explained patiently. "When a gal marries, she's a wife. It don't make a damn if she's fourteen or forty. Wifes has got purposes. They got jobs to do. I was sebemteen when I married first. They's no turnin back for husbans and wifes. Age ain't got a damn thing to do with it now."

"It won't do," she begged softly. "It just won't do. I got to go back to Ma Watson's. I just can't put up with the way you-all live."

"I'll build another house," Will argued. "I'll buy some more land and build a plank house on the side of East Ridge. I got me a spot picked out. I'll build'ye a house."

He half reached toward her, his face soft and pleading. Alvira could see the weariness of years of hard labor and poverty in his face. She felt a surge of pity for him, but she steeled herself, believing she had him in retreat.

"It would take years," she continued. "You might not be able to do it anyway." She stooped and picked up the bag. "No, I'm goin. I'm not livin with you up there in that ungodly valley. Just one night would be too late."

Will Ward's eyes narrowed again. The softness left his face. His teeth snapped shut, startling her in the silent woods. "You made a bargain," he stated. "In front of that peace jestice you made a bargain before God and man. And you made a bargain with me. Sech bargains ain't to be tuck light."

"I didn't know where I was goin then," she said. "I didn't know all this about you then."

She advanced on him, started to pass him on his right. He seized her right arm, whirled her about, grasped her left arm, his fingers biting into her soft flesh. Before she could inhale, before she could even blink, before her heart could increase its pace, he was escorting her back up the Ridge Road, lifting her to her tiptoes, striding beside her, and she was running to keep up with him. The heavy bag banged against her legs, staggering her.

"What're you doin?" she raged, glaring up at his face. "What're you doin to me, Will Ward?" All she could see was his profile, the hooked nose, the compressed mouth, the stubborn chin. The edge of his right eye gleamed like melting ice.

"I'm taking'ye back home," he told her. "I'm takin'ye home, where a wife belongs at."

She twisted her arm, but the bone turned inside her flesh. The muscle tingled numbly beneath his grip. He stopped her once, reached around her and took the Gladstone bag in his left hand. She could walk easier then, and it was less difficult for him to hurry her along up the rutted road. She did not hold back any more. It would have done no good. She walked freely because she understood there was nothing else to do. So she went along without resistance, though he did not release his hold on her arm. He relaxed his grip, but she could feel its firmness. There was no escaping it.

When they were almost across the saddle of the ridge, Will Ward stopped. "You see that patch of alders down yander at the foot of West Mountain? That's a cold spring there. I aim to build my house right down there on the west side of this here ridge, bout halfway down."

Alvira did not want to talk. She did not know what to say. "There's nothin but slope there," she murmured. "I don't see no flat place for much of a house."

"You got to dig out a place," Will explained. "You got to make a step-like in the side of the ridge. Behind the house, I'll build me a smokehouse and out there a ways I'll build my barn, a nice big barn like Doc Watson's. My house'll have a hallway through it like Cousin Bill's and it'll have several rooms and glass doors."

Vi looked away, toward the big yellow house on the distant ridge, against the Bushy Mountains. "It sounds like dreamin," she said, disinterested. "It sounds like fancy dreamin to me."

He started to answer her but changed his mind. He escorted her on up the ridge, more slowly this time. Once he stopped and stared out through the trees to their left. Alvira, startled, turned her head to look at him. His face was thoughtful, even sad, she thought. His eyes squinted, a wistful expression about them.

"Yander's where the old Ward house used to stand," he murmured. "That was way back yander before my time."

She traced his line of vision. All she could see from the road was a clutter of vines and bushes and what looked like a huge mound, the grave of a giant. It looked like the very heart of the forest instead of some old house site.

"Now that's all that's left," Will said. "Them goddamn Catletts sledded off what rock they was to build their own chimbleys. Not hardly as much as a hole in the ground left to show where the Wards started out from."

Vi did not answer directly. She had nothing to say concerning the Wards of another time. Her own problem bore down on her, canceling out the problems of a family long gone. She stared out through the trees, her mind far away. "I don't see why you don't shave that old mustache off," she murmured. "I never did like them things."

Will started to answer, apparently, but decided not to. They turned together and continued the long walk back. The farther up the ridge they went, the more hopeless her escape seemed. And she sensed that when she finally reached the log house, when he got her inside and closed the door, it would be over. There would be no other course open for her but to exist as Will Ward's wife. She waited and glanced about her and hoped, but nothing happened. She thought about praying, then remembered how her prayer to escape Doc Watson had been answered. She left it up to God. But the white hand of

God refused to reach down from the domed sky, through the trees, and lift her away, placing her beyond the dark woods.

And twenty minutes later the cabin door banged shut behind her. Tillie still slouched by the fire holding the baby, now crying. Anna had returned to the bed, but leaped up when they entered. Will tossed Vi's bag against the wall. Vi stared straight ahead, not looking at any of them, refusing to examine the four walls and what they enclosed.

"I told'ye," Anna giggled. "Didn't I tell'ye he'd fetch'ye back? Pa wouldn't let nothin as purty and as strong as you git away from'im."

As she came within reach, Will Ward slapped her across the face. She reeled back, her mouth open in shock. But her dark eyes slitted in anger a moment later. "What'd you go and slap me for, Pa? I didn't do nothin."

"Keep'ye big mouth shet and don't pester her any furder," Will growled. "She's your ma now, and you'd better treat her with fitten respect. You don't, and I'll kick your rump tell'ye nose bleeds. You git that straight in'ye noggin, Annie Ward."

Anna retreated before him, her anger changing to fear and wonder. "I didn't mean nothin," she pouted. "I jest told'er she'd never make it. I jest told'er—"

"Jest shet up! Jest tell'er nothin from now on. She'll be a-tellin you from this day for'ards, and you don't give her none of your damned sass." He turned to Tillie. "Till," he said, "you take the youngun and Annie and go out for a while. Go set with'ye grandpa in the smokehouse. And if any of'ye pokes your heads back in here tell I come for'ye, I'll knock'em off square at your shoulders."

"But, Pa," Tillie whined, "I don't feel—"

"But hell!" Will stormed. "But damnation! Git out of here. Git! I've got a private matter to settle with my wife."

Alvira watched them go, dread heavy inside her. Hope was past. There was no more hope. There was nothing she could do. Nothing. He took her arm and led her to their bed. She followed passively, like a heifer led to her first mating with rope and halter. He placed her on the bed. She did not resist.

Her mind was far away, leaving her flesh in Will Ward's control. Her mind had deserted her and cringed somewhere behind the dark barrier across her mind. Only the most tenuous of nerve fibers led from her condemned body to where her mind hid.

Still, she was rational enough to realize that he tried to be gentle, to realize that he was as modest as he could be under the circumstances. Despite the pain, the dreadful, quick pain that found her mind along the tenuous nerve, she realized it could have been worse. And she sensed that he regretted what he was doing, the manner in which it had to be done. It was his way, the only way he knew, of settling the affair between them once and for all.

When the consummation was over, she lay on her back staring at the shadowy rafter. Her body pulsed with pain she hardly felt. Part of her mind came back to her slowly. She knew he sat on the edge of the bed, head clasped in hands, knew it without seeing him. The rafters grew darker as twilight fell outside the house. "I'm no longer a girl," she thought. "God help me, I'm a wife. I'm a ready-made mother. What'll I do? What'll I do first?"

"You hongry?" Will asked, somewhere outside the rim of her vision. "You ain't eat all day. You want a bite to eat? You want some supper now?"

She understood how his mind was working. She turned her back on him, not angry, and stared at the dark wall in front of her. She lay there for a long time trying not to think what she had to do first. After a long time, he reached over and placed his hand on her head, stroked it once as he might have a kitten, then stood up. He crossed the cabin and left through the back door, slamming it after him. Vi lay and stared at the wall, unmoving, while she throbbed with pain. She understood, knew beyond doubt, that here was where she must stay, at least awhile. But she could not make up her mind, to save her life, what to do first.

She lay for hour after hour in the same position, staring at the log wall in front of her. She felt as though her skin were stretched tight over empty void. She could not even feel her bones and flesh inside her, except where the bed barely touched her length and the pain. The slow drum of her heart was a remote pulse dissociated from the taut skin and the spark that was her mind. Voices came into the cabin, Will Ward's voice and the voices of the two girls. A light appeared, and she could see the shadow of her head in front of her. There was a fourth voice now, an old-man voice, at times peevish, at other times resonant with the worldly wisdom and self-confidence of the patriarch, as he told about the time he shot a Yankee soldier and buried him in the woods.

"Jest leave her be," Will Ward's voice commanded, once. "Jest goddamn leave her be. Forgit she's back there. She needs to be let alone jest now. She's got to puzzle her way through this all by herself."

"But looks like she could help out," Anna's voice argued. "Looks like—"

"Looks like you're astin for a bruised ass," Will said. "Now shet the hell up!"

Alvira barely heard them. The spark of her mind reached out to test her pain, now and then, and recoiled like a finger probing a hot coal. She heard the clatter of pans, the shuffle of plates, and circular voices around the Lazy Susan. She knew everything that happened behind her without seeing, without caring, without even thinking. The baby cried and the baby was changed and the baby was put to bed across the room from her. A long time later the old-man voice withdrew. Anna went to bed, followed by Tillie. Alvira lay on her left side staring at the wall, until it exploded into darkness when Will blew the lamp out.

She heard him go outside. Sometime later, he came back, crossed the floor and sat down on the edge of the bed. He began to take his shoes off. Vi did not think about it. She felt him lean back and kick out of his pants, then roll beneath the covers. She remained on top of the quilts, her back to him.

Time passed. How long? How could she know, when her mind glowed dimly like a dead firefly outside time? Only her tight skin knew time, and it was shivering. Her teeth were chattering. She knew she was cold, but she was not concerned. And if she had cared, she could not think how to remedy her problem. She lay for a long time and shivered. After a while she felt other movement. The quilts were worked from beneath her and placed over her. She felt the weight of them against her skin. Gradually, the cold withdrew, the shivering diminished. Gradually the spark of mind dimmed, as its source of power weakened. It flickered while the sound of snoring filled the narrow world of warmth around her. It flickered and went out, and she knew no more.

Alvira Matlock Ward awakened with a start. Her flesh and bones were back inside her, and her mind was clear. The cabin was gloomy with the dim light of morning seeping through the shutters and doors. A fire roared in the fireplace, lighting more brightly the front area. She twisted in bed. Will was gone. She lay alone beneath the covers, still wearing her wedding clothing. Across from her Tillie and Anna slept, the baby between them. He lay on his back playing with his fingers and laughing to see them squirm. Vi slipped quietly across the bed and placed her feet on the floor, amazed to discover she still wore her shoes. Standing up, she looked down at herself. The dress was a wrinkled mess. She brushed halfheartedly, then gave up.

She tiptoed across the floor, leaned over the bed, and smiled down at the baby. He looked up at her, his blue eyes wide in astonishment. Then he grinned, a four-toothed grin, and waved his fists at her. Vi leaned down and kissed his nose. He smelled like sour vomit, but it was not unpleasant. The odor saddened her, and she turned away, her face drawn, her hand on her belly.

She walked to the fireplace and stood before the blazing fire, feeling the heat lap at her from the knees upward. She held her hands to the heat, then stared at her gloves. They were no longer pure white. Somehow, somewhere on the journey to this moment, she had soiled them. They were splotched and sooty. She peeled them off slowly, first the left, then the right, and dropped them into the edge of the flames. She stared wide-eyed as they turned brown, like last year's locust husk, exploded into flames, curled into black ashes. She choked on the astringent odor but made no sound. Finally, she turned away, inhaling the cold air of the room just beyond the warm hearth, where the heat stopped.

In the kitchen area, she found the flour sack leaning against the cupboard, and she saw a wooden pail half filled with water on the cooking table. She found the mixing pan and the rolling pin and the lard bucket. Working quietly, she made biscuits and placed them in the skillet. She had seen her mother bake with a skillet on rare occasions and knew how to use it. She carried it to the fireplace, shoveled a bed of coals from beneath the logs, and placed the skillet on it. Then she covered the ringed lid with another bed of coals. After this, she ground coffee in the coffee mill, placed the grounds in the battered pot with water, and set it on the end of the logs, where the flames would not smoke it too much. She was guessing now, but she could see no other way to make coffee.

She was kneeling before the fireplace frying pork when she heard the back door open behind her. Her hands were clasped together about the iron handle of the pan. A halo of aroma surrounded her—coffee, sizzling meat, baking bread. She heard a shuffle of brogans, followed by a sharp intake of breath, then a stillness. It seemed like a long time to her, Will's period of amazement, but it could have been only a few seconds. She heard him sniffing, animal-like. He came on inside, closed the door, and approached her. He stood beside her, holding his hands out to the hot fire, warming them. Their veined backs looked red from cold.

"You feel all right?" he asked as softly as he could. He could not cancel out the natural gruffness.

She glanced at his dark overalled legs. "I'll do," she said. "I'll make out, I reckon."

She felt his bulk nearby, looming over her. She wanted to hate him for what he had done to her. She needed to hate him, but she could not. She could not hate him, neither could she feel anything like affection. What she did feel was confusion. It was sympathy and respect and understanding. It was mixed and confused. And because she was a woman, there was even appreciation for the fact that he had gone to so much trouble just to marry her. She was flattered. But she did not feel that she was truly his wife, his mate. Somewhere they had missed a necessary rite. And it was not the wedding ceremony. It was not even the consummation, crude as it was. But she sensed a dreadful void between what she felt and what she imagined a new wife should feel. However, she now knew what she had to do first. She had to prepare breakfast, and then, perhaps, look after the baby.

"I didn't figure you'd know how to cook on a farplace," he said. "You've got a purty good start there, looks like."

"It don't take much figurin." She turned the sizzling meat with a fork. "It don't look to me like there was but one way to do it right."

He shuffled his heavy feet close beside her, then chuckled deep in his chest. "Then Till must be a hell of a sight smarter'n you. She found fourteen ways to cook everthing, and all of'em wrong."

Her solemn face softened as a smile flickered by like a fast butterfly and was gone. "It takes time," she said. "I been cookin just about since I was ten. Mamma had her hands full with her younguns."

She glanced up at him, then stared. The long mustache was missing. He must have got up early and shaved it off with cold water. Her gaze shifted to the back door as it eased open. An old man shuffled through at a mincing gait and turned all the way around to close it after him. He required three or four steps to turn back around. His face was wizened and shrunken, though he had the same ice-grey eyes, the same hooked nose that Will Ward had. The chin was concealed somewhere beneath a scraggly grey beard, but Vi could trace its stubborn outline. She knew who he was before he had shuffled one step closer to her.

"This here's my Pa a-comin in," Will said to her. "He lives in the back end of the smokehouse."

Alvira set the frying pan off the fire onto the hearth and stood up. The old man finally reached them and stopped, peering into her face, his petulant lips trembling between concern and friendliness.

"This here is Vi, Pap," Will said, "my new wife."

John Ward hesitated, then extended a bony left hand, grinning and nodding. His right was a plucked wing hugging his side. Alvira took his grey fingers awkwardly with her own right hand. They were cool and dry as old leather. "Will outdone hisself," he grinned, nodding vigorously. "You're purty as a picher. I hope you make out with us up here in the hill country."

Alvira smiled, releasing his hand. "Pleased to meet'ye, Mr. Ward," she said. "Thank'ye for the kind words. I reckon I'll make out onct I get used to it. Will has promised to build a new house right soon." But she thought, I will be far away from here by then—far, far away from these hills.

The old man shuffled around and stared into Will Ward's face. He wiped his mouth, tugged at his white beard. Then he turned back. "If Will said hit, he'll build hit sooner or later. Us Wards ain't folks to go back on our word. And you can call me Grandpa like the younguns does."

"Van! Dan!" Will yelled toward the loft above, his head back. "Let's go, up there! Breakfast is a-cookin!" He turned to Vi. "My two boys come in late last night. You'd better make a passel of that sawmill gravy. They eat like hawgs."

Alvira looked at him. "I didn't hear them come—"

Will grinned. "They come in barefooted. They know better'n to wake me up in the middle of the night."

"Pa!" Tillie called from her bed. "Pa, is it gettin-up time aready?" She leaped to the floor and ran toward them in her petticoat. "Lordy ha'mercy, I overslept. I didn't aim to oversleep, Ma."

"Don't fret," Will said. "Go git'ye frock on. Hit's Sunday. Your new ma has got breakfast might nigh ready."

Tillie padded back across the floor. Vi turned back to Will. "Have'ye got any eggs I can fry?"

"Eggs?" Will chuckled. "Hen's eggs? Great godamighty, womern, we can't keep no hens up in here. The foxes and coons and weasels and wildcats and sech eats 'em as fast as they hatch."

She stooped, picked up the pan, and carried it over to the cooking table. Removing the sidemeat, she dipped a cup of flour from the sack, returned to the fire, and began to make gravy. She heard Tillie talking to the baby, changing it. She heard Anna sit up and yawn. She heard a shuffle of shoes from the loft above the beds. She could glimpse Will Ward's legs, close beside her, as he stood with his back to the fire. Grandpa John had pulled a chair up close to the hearth and sat patting one foot in time to some tune in his head. She could glimpse the patting foot out of the corners of her eyes. It sounded as though it were tapping out an apology in some kind of code she could not quite decipher.

"Van!" Will Ward yelled suddenly. "Git the hell back up that ladder and git some britches on!"

Alvira looked around, startled. A huge young man was backing down the ladder from the loft in shirttail and long underwear. He had stopped and was staring over his shoulder in puzzlement, one knee crooked in midstep. Vi thought of the giant backing down from the beanstalk.

"This here's your new ma down here, I went and married while you was gallivantin about," Will called. "She's a young womern, younger'n you. They'll be no more hossin around in your tailfeathers."

Van stared a moment longer, then scurried back up the ladder out of sight. A few minutes later he backed down again with his overalls on. A younger giant followed him. The two of them crossed the room shoulder to shoulder, as though yoked together, and stood staring owlishly at Vi, their long, uncombed hair as tangled as rag mops.

"This here little'un is my boy Dan," Will said. "And the big'un is Van. Boys, this here's your new ma, and I spect'ye to treat her proper."

"Howdy, boys," Alvira smiled. "They look the same size to me—big as skinned hosses."

Dan grinned and looked at Van to test him. "She don't look

like no ma I ever seen," Van laughed. "She looks more like a catalogue picher."

"She looks like to me she slept in her dress," Anna said, coming up behind Van.

Will turned to her, then stopped and turned back to the fire. "You boys git ready," Alvira said, "and I'll have breakfast on the table d'rectly."

They ate, circled around the Lazy Susan, intent on feeding themselves. It was no social occasion, and little breath was spent on words. When Van ran out of biscuit and molasses and meat, he turned the table-waiter and replenished his plate. Alvira ate slowly, aware of their hunger, conscious of the manner in which they wolfed their food down, but she tried not to reveal her awareness. Grandpa John mixed molasses and pork grease and ate it hungrily, matting areas of his white beard with it. The concoction gagged Vi, and she looked away. She tried not to prejudge them for their manners at the table, realizing she must adjust to it. She understood that this for them was normal behavior. Finishing first, she took the baby from Tillie and continued feeding it with the lumpy gravy and with milk.

After breakfast, Tillie took the wooden water pail from the cooking table. "I got to go milk now," she said to Vi. "You want to come and watch?"

"I may just as well," Vi agreed. "I'll probly need to sooner or later."

They left through the back door, and Tillie dumped the rest of the water onto the ground. "You mean you milk and use water out of the same bucket?" Vi asked. "That seems mighty troublesome."

"It's all the bucket we got," Tillie said. "We tie it to the well rope and draw water with it. Then we untie it and tote the water to the house. Then when it comes milkin time, we got to dump out the water and milk in the same bucket."

"I do declare," Vi muttered, "why don't Will get another bucket?"

Tillie turned her head and looked at her hard. "They's lots

of things we need. Some things as bad or worse'n another bucket."

Alvira did not answer. They passed the smokehouse in silence. "Where's the backhouse?" she asked, finally. "I've not seen no backhouse yet."

"You won't see no backhouse," Tillie scoffed. "Not this side of Cousin Bill's. If you got to pee, you can go on the other side of the smokehouse, there. For other matters, you got to go out in the bushes along the branch bank yander"—she pointed—"other side the well. In the summer that field between the well and branch is growd up in weeds and blackberry briers, and you can go there."

Alvira shook her head. "That arrange-ment is mighty bothersome. Looks like to me Will would build some kind of a little old backhouse."

"It's in his long-range plans," Tillie said sadly, "but his plans keep waitin and waitin. He claims he means to have him a backhouse someday. But he's near to forty-two and ain't never owned one yet. Could be he'll live to be a hundred and spend his whole lifetime settin acrosst a bent saplin."

Vi shook her head again. "That does sound like a mighty bothersome arrange-ment."

4

Alvira Matlock Ward's first full day on Stud Branch was a Sunday. Will, Alvira, and the two girls with the baby, walked down the branch to catch Cousin Bill's wagon at the Big Road. Tillie and Anna wore the somber dresses Rosa Ward had made them for mourning clothing when Bell was buried. They stopped at the spring and drank from the water gourd Will had placed there. He stood with his back to West Mountain, legs spread, pointing out to Alvira where he would build his house and its outbuildings. She was not impressed with the location but thought it better than the head of Stud Branch, with Coottown hanging on their flank like an ugly sore. Furthermore, away from the wild creatures of Fox Mountain, she might be able to raise some chicks and have some eggs to do with until she could get away for good.

"Who owns this land now?" Vi asked, looking across the bare slope of East Ridge, rising beyond the branch.

"Old Man Harrison," Will said. "The Publican sonofabitch cheated my pa out'n his share to cut the timber off of it."

"The sonofabitch he's a-talkin about," Anna said, "is his Uncle Lake Harrison."

Will pivoted on his heel. "He plays hell bein my uncle. He

married my Aunt Susan and got his start with her parcel of Ward land."

"What I was wonderin," Vi interrupted, "is Mr. Harrison willin to sell that land up there?"

"I don't know," Will said, shoulders slumping. "I ain't got around to astin him yit. The five acres I live on belonged to the north end of it. But all the trees is gone now."

Alvira felt sick. The land he planned to buy on which to build a house someday could very well turn out to be like the mare and buggy, like his house not being *in* Coottown. She turned away from East Ridge and stared at her foreshortened image in the spring, and saw beside it the foreshortened image of an aging man. And at that moment she would not have given a plug of Will's tobacco for the prospect of ever living in a new house on the side of the ridge above.

"Pa'll do it," Tillie swore, looking at Vi. "Don't you fret, Pa'll get this land sooner or later. I'd bet my life somethin'll happen so's Pa can get it. He's been waitin too long for it not to happen."

"Yeah," Anna nodded, her dark eyes flashing, "and it's bound to rain two-dollar bills, sooner or later. But they'll turn to hoss-turds before Pa can pick one up."

"Watch your tongue, young lady!" Alvira frowned at her.

"Hit's a damned good thing she's standin out of my reach," Will growled.

They filed on down the branch and waited for Cousin Bill beside the road. Will pointed to the spur of West Mountain. "Now if I had my druthers," he said to Vi, "I'd druther build me a house on the end of the ridge there so's I could see folks a-passin by on the Big Road. Everthing goes down the Big Road. But I ain't got the chance of a bumblebee in a baboon's belly gettin holt of that land."

Alvira looked at the house spot, and her heart leaped. It was a fine place, an ideal place to sit and watch time go by. She could imagine a white house sitting there in a step carved in the ridge, those young locust trees towering above it. "Why couldn't—" She paused, bracing for the disappointment. "Why couldn't you get that land?" What she really meant was, "Why couldn't you fail to get that land just as you've failed to get that on East Ridge?"

"Cause that damned tightwad Greer, Hill's boy, has got his eyes set on it. If he ever cotch holt of a cow's tit, he wouldn't turn a-loose without totin off her whole bag. I don't know why he wants it, when he ain't ebem got a wife yit."

"Why don't you try askin'im?" Vi asked. "It don't hurt nothin to ask."

"It don't hurt nothin to spit into the wind," Anna said, "septin you're apt to get splattered by'ye own spit."

"Pa, do ast him," Tillie begged. "It don't hurt to try for the best. Then you can back down."

"I'll think on it," Will promised. "I'll think it over. There comes Cousin Bill a-ready."

Alvira liked Cousin Bill immediately, and Rosa became her second mother almost as soon as she was seated in the rear spring seat. Rosa moved back beside her, while Will climbed into the front seat beside Bill. Vi held the baby as though it were her own, as though she had been holding babies most of her life, which she really had, until she had left home to stay with the Watsons. Tillie and Anna sat on a quilt in the back of the wagon-bed with Jan and Delia. Jan scowled out at the turning wheels, as though pretending he was all alone. Delia was chattering about the kewpie doll Santa Claus had brought her.

"Why don't you hush up?" Vi heard Anna snap. "They ain't no such a thing as Santa Claus any more'n they's a man in the moon."

"It sure was a surprise to us," Rosa said, smiling. "We didn't have no idea Will was borryin our buggy to go off and find'im a wife."

"Of course we knowd one another before he made this trip," Vi explained. "It wasn't like we—"

"Of course it wasn't, Vi," Rosa interrupted. "I didn't mean it like that. I just meant we didn't know Will was goin to fetch you, when he left."

Alvira laughed and looked at the baby, dozing in her arms. "It was a mite sudden, sure-nuff," she said.

"If there's anything—" Rosa Ward hushed as she appeared to

be thinking, choosing her words. "If I can help'ye get started off in any way, you feel free to call on me," she said. "They might be some things I could let'ye borry, till you get started."

Will Ward turned in his seat. "That's good of'ye, Rosie," he said firmly, "but we got everthing we need at home. Vi's goin to make out without troublin anybidy."

"It's no trouble, if I can help, Will," Rosa argued. "You know that."

"We'll let'ye know if you can," Will said.

"I thank'ye for offerin, Rosie," Alvira answered, not looking at Will. "I'll sure call on'ye if I need any manner of help."

"Mommy give me some red cloth," Delia was saying behind them, "and I'm gonna make my kewpie doll a new frock next week."

"Humph!" Anna snorted. "I can't sew. Tillie can't sew. How's a little old gal like you gonna sew?"

"Cause Mommy learned me how to sew," Delia retorted.

"No use'n talkin to her," Jan Ward said, not looking at Delia. "Annie Ward's too mad at herself to care about you and your old doll."

"I'm the only person I'm not mad at," Anna scoffed.

"That's what you say," Jan laughed.

"Looks like you-all could be cheerful on the way to meetin," Tillie broke in. "What if Jesus come back all of a sudden?"

"He'd turn around and go back," Anna said.

"I aim to go see Old Man Harrison, come Monday," Will was saying to Cousin Bill. "See will he sell me that parcel of land along Stud Branch—on some kind of time."

"Looks like he would," Cousin Bill said, snapping the whip over the mules. "He's done cut all the decent timber off it. You could haul for'im over the years and pay on it."

"That's what I aimed to offer," Will nodded. "He needs haulers and he shore as hell don't need that land without no big timber left on it."

After church, Alvira was assailed from all sides by older men and women trying to meet Will Ward's new wife. She found the hill folk friendly, sincere, eager to make friends and to see the best in a new neighbor. They were also as frank as ten-year-olds back in Northboro. The young men and women her own age, most of whom were unmarried, were reserved but curious. She was a member of the married set, and they accepted her as mature, as a woman of a household, as Will's mate, despite her obvious youth. The married ones chided Will playfully about robbing the cradle, and Will grinned back, but he was careful not to let slip Vi's actual age. As for herself, Vi was not eager for anyone to learn that she was only seventeen, with three stepchildren older than she was.

She stood beneath an ashen January sky, caught up in a whirlpool of grinning, friendly faces, and met those who could work their way close enough. Doc Ellis and his wife, Bessie; Uncle Lake Harrison, dry and gnarled as a dead chestnut; Greer and Bart, the Harrison brothers; Bart's wife, a pale young woman as plain as a faded gingham dress; a heavy goat-rumped man named Hill Anderson, who looked her up and down with pale, narrow eyes, mouth half agape. There was a dark angry-looking young man working his way about the outer edge of the crowd like a weasel stalking a flock of chickens (Will told her later he was a sneaking sonofabitch named Tom Dugan). There was a young man named Greely Milton, so fat he wore a belt made from an eight-foot lead strap. There were others, so many others she could not begin to remember all the names. But they were all so friendly, so eager to welcome her that some of the lingering ache of captivity was made more endurable.

"By gravy, Will, you went and brung back a prize, didn't 'ye?" one old-timer grinned.

"Doggone, she's a nice-looker," a younger man chortled.

"She's a sturdy-lookin gal, spite of bein good-lookin," a stooped old grandpa offered.

Alvira heard the compliments, not meant for her ears, honestly felt, as echoes behind the babble of closer voices swirling about her. She heard and was glad inside. For one brief moment, looking out at the cheerful Sunday faces, she had a feeling of belonging, of being home in the hills with nowhere else she needed to move to. But it lasted only a moment and fled, leaving her with the old sense of impermanence here, of being rootless in the clay soil. It was a fleeting need to belong, but she rejected it.

The next morning Will went to see Lake Harrison about buying the land along Stud Branch. Alvira made Tillie an everyday dress out of one of her own, by shortening the hem and letting out the waist to fit Tillie's thick girth. She tried to sew up the dress Tillie had worn the day before, the only everyday dress she owned, but the material, faded and rotten, came apart in her hands.

"I reckon it's done for." Tillie shook her head sadly. "It was a good'un in its time. Had it three year. I reckon it was so piss-soaked from the baby it jest nachly rotted."

"I reckon," Alvira agreed. "This frock I've altered for'ye ort to last a spell."

"I shore do thank'ye, Vi—Ma," Tillie smiled. "I needed a frock in the worst way. I was gettin ready to wear my dark Sunday'un for everyday."

Grandpa John and the boys had gone up on West Mountain with one of the steers and a sled to cut firewood, and did not get back until late in the afternoon. Will came home an hour later, dragging his slumped shadow up Stud Branch like a crow with a broken wing. Vi watched him approach, through a crack in the front door, and watched him pass, moving toward the woodpile, and she knew how his interview with Old Man Harrison had turned out. She knew and she was not surprised. Her disappointment was only a mild pain because, after only two days, she was learning to accept disappointments as the way of life here in the hills.

Will came into the house, leaving the boys chopping wood, and slumped down in a chair by the fire, his battered hat yanked low over his eyes. Alvira sat near the fireplace on the kitchen side churning milk. She stole a glance at Will's set face and looked back at the churn, raising and lowering the churn dasher with a regular rhythm.

Tillie sat at the other end of the hearth playing with the baby. "What'd he say, Pa?" she asked, finally. "I reckon it didn't go too good, the way you're actin."

Will threw up his head and stared around him. He looked at Tillie as though just locating her voice. "The old bastard wouldn't talk about sellin. Said the timber'd grow back for his boys. Goddamn, I reckon it means another generation of robbin the earth of its trees and saplins."

"Well, the old rascal!" Tillie fussed.

Anna looked up from her foot. She sat on the edge of her bed picking at her toenails. "I'd a-threatened him if he didn't sell," she snapped. "I'd a-threatened to set his woods on far."

"You'd a-done your business and fell back in hit, too," Will retorted. "I'm a law-abidin man, less I'm done wrong. Old Lake ain't never done me wrong, sept by accident."

In the narrow world of the poor, Vi understood that small calamities accumulated like aches in an aging man. The Wards sloughed off their disappointment at Lake Harrison's refusal to sell the land as casually as they froze in cold weather or got wet when it rained. Below the surface it was one more tiny grain to add to the peck of frustrations accumulating in the craw of each; frustrations which, along with labor and hardship, humped shoulders and chiseled lines of bitterness just below the surface of the quick grin. But by itself, old Harrison's rejection was hardly worth more than a few oaths. It was not taken quite so lightly by Alvira. After her first casual shrug, the old sense of entrapment rushed in on her with no end in sight.

On Tuesday, Will Ward came stamping into the house cursing and beating his battered black hat against his right thigh. "Goddamn the luck to hell!" he stormed. "Looks like when bad things start comin at a feller, they come like a goddamn landslide. I ain't got no more chance a-makin ends meet than a one-legged man at a ass-kickin contest."

Alvira turned from the cooking table, brows arched. This was her introduction to Will's capacity for bitterness, for vituperation, for eloquent blasphemy. She watched him stamp over to the fireplace and take down the huge muzzle-loading musket from its pegs above the mantel. He whirled back, checked the priming cap beneath the hammer, then stamped back toward the door.

"What on earth ails'ye?" she demanded. "What you fixin to shoot at?"

"My goddamn shoat!" he growled, stopping to stare at her with accusing eyes. "My goddamn best shoat is down in his hindquarters. Can't lift his ass off the ground."

"Well, what on earth caused it?" Vi asked, not really expecting a sane answer.

"How in hell do I know what caused it?" Will raged. "I ain't no shoat doctor. But I'd be willin to bet he done it to git ebem for havin his nuts cut out. The bastard deserves to be shot for doin me that a-way, good as I fed him." He was thoughtful for a moment. "Either that, or that damned Hill Anderson cut him wrong, when he was trimmin him back yander."

"Now, Will, you know a pore old hog cain't help it if he's cripple," Vi argued. "It's probably got some manner of paralysis."

"Well, he won't have none in about five minutes. I'm gonna put a Minnie ball in his head and cure him of all his ailments."

Vi doubted if Will had ever seen such a thing as a Minié ball. She followed him through the back door and up the slope toward the pasture. "It's a pity to waste him, and him this far along," she muttered to his denim-armored back.

The hog sat on his haunches, resting on his front feet, surveying the hog lot, which had suddenly become too large for him to cope with. Will poked him in the rump with the barrel of the musket. The hog grunted casually, apparently not in pain, and dragged himself forward a foot or two through the muck.

Will raised the musket, reared back the hammer, and aimed at the hog's head. "Damn your lazy soul, I'll larn'ye to set down on the job," he grumbled.

Alvira watched him close his left eye and squint along the barrel. "Will!" she called suddenly. "Will, wait a minute!"

Will Ward opened his left eye and slowly unwound as though he himself had been cocked instead of the gun. He turned his head to face her. "Yeah?"

"If I'll feed'im, will you give him to me, Will? I can feed him by holdin the slopbucket under his snout. I'll sell him when he's killed, and take the money and buy us a cookstove. You wouldn't begrudge me wantin to buy a cookstove, would'ye, Will?"

"I despise to see a lazy-assed hawg pampered that a-way," Will argued.

"It wouldn't be pamperin, Will. The pore creature can't use his back legs. You wouldn't have to worry with him, I garntee'ye. I'd do all the feedin and tendin to'im."

Will lowered the stock of the musket and gazed out across the valley. "Awright," he muttered finally. "It's your job. If the bastard eats all winter and gits big as Greely Milton and then decides to die on'ye, don't blame me." He turned away and slouched off down the slope.

And that was how Alvira created her first money-making job on Stud Branch. And job it was. During the very first meal, her arms almost dropped off before the crippled shoat could finish the slop in the battered bucket she held beneath his head. But there were so many other jobs, toil was so ceaseless, that feeding the hog was just one task, only a little more tiring than most of the others.

Vi had her first dealings with the Catletts that same afternoon, when Matt came carrying an empty snuff glass to borrow salt. "I hear tell you're Will's new wife," she grinned at Vi with snuff-blackened teeth. "I thought I'd come a-borryin some salt, seein we ain't had none for more'n a week."

"How-do," Vi greeted civilly. She did not like the woman's slovenly looks. "Won't you take a chair and set a spell?"

"When she borries salt," Anna said from her bed, "she means give it to her. She wouldn't pay it back no more'n she'd fly."

"Why, shore I wouldn't," Matt swore, her eyes flared wide. "Anybidy knows hit's bad look to pay back borried salt."

"Then why didn't you ast me to give it to'ye?" Vi asked.

Matt looked offended. "What you think I am, a low-down beggar?"

"I can't loan'ye no salt," Vi said. "I'm real sorry."

Matt Catlett narrowed her eyes, almost offended. "Why not?" she demanded. "I'd loan you salt if I ever had any or if you wanted to borrie hit."

"Cause where I come from, it's bad luck to loan salt," Vi explained.

Matt's forehead furrowed in puzzlement. "I can onderstan how hit can be bad look to pay salt back," she muttered, "but hit don't make no sense to me to be bad look to loan hit."

"Luck's a funny matter," Vi said. "It works different ways for different parts of the country."

Matt shook her head. "That shore is a quare kind of way of doin things. I reckon I'll git back up on the hill. I mortally love turnips with a tad of salt added."

Will did not come to Alvira again until Wednesday night, and it was a blessed relief to her that he waited until all the children were asleep. She accepted him as patiently as she could, feeling duty a little greater than that first time. But there was none of the inner warmth she had imagined she would share in a marriage, and the feeling of capture persisted in spite of her effort not to think about it. Although Will was as considerate as he knew how to be, Alvira soon realized that he was little concerned as to how she received him, so from that day forward she put it out of her mind.

Thursday morning, when Alvira went to call Grandpa John to breakfast, she saw his living quarters for the first time. The front half of the smokehouse was partitioned off from the rear area with a slab wall. A rough door, now closed, gave entrance to the room beyond. A grey shaft of morning light projected through the open outside door behind her. She stood in the narrow walkway between shelves on which lay slabs of pork covered with salt, slabs almost formless in the gloom. The room was colder, damper than the January dawn, and she shuddered at dankness, at the sensation of dampness rather than any actual discomfort.

She approached the middle door and stopped, knocking. After a silence, she raised her fist again.

"That you, Vi?" Grandpa John called from beyond the panel.

"Yeah," Alvira called back, "breakfast is about ready."

"I'm nigh dressed," the oldish voice came back. "Pull the latch and come in."

Vi groped, found the rawhide thong dangling from a hole in the door, and tugged it. The latch clicked up beyond the panel and the door swung inward. She stared about her at the narrow little world of order. The floor was rough planking, as were the walls, and an iron stove near the far wall was a black little monstrosity. But the rest of the furnishings were different. Grandpa John, trousers on over long underwear, sat on the edge of a narrow bed made of gleaming red maple. A kerosene lamp burned on a beautiful little walnut center table near the bed. Close to her was a throne-like rocker, also maple, and beside it sat a split-bottomed chair, apparently white oak. Alvira knew little about furniture other than its usefulness, but she stared at the few furnishings of the room, sensing more than realizing the art that had gone into their creation, the loving care with which they had been wrought. They were, she realized, made for their appearance as much as for their usefulness.

She looked back to her right. Near the wall sat a workbench with tools arranged carefully on a notched board. A bucksaw hung from a peg on the wall. Three wooden planes sat in their slots on the table. Beside them were a groove plane, a tongue plane, three wood chisels, in addition to several sizes of augers, and wooden T-bars with which to turn them. A wooden vise was attached to either end of the bench, and planed boards, half prepared for some new project, were stacked against the wall.

"Mornin, Grandpa," Vi said. "How'd you know it was me?"

"Cause the gals don't knock. They jest yank the latch up, shove open the door, and yell to come or starve."

Alvira laughed. "You've got a nice place here. If you had more room, I'd feel like movin in and runnin'ye out."

Old John grinned, his red lips rolling back his white beard. "You like it, eh?"

"The furniture's beautiful. Where–where'd you get it?"

The old man stood up, adjusting his rope suspenders. "Me!" he said, laughing. "I done hit."

She looked at the furniture again, each piece in turn, then looked back at the old man. She looked at the gnarled left hand, then at the stiff appendage which was his right arm, clamped against his rib cage. "You?" she said. "You made this—these beautiful things?"

He held up his left arm and flexed his hooked fingers in front of him. "I done hit," he repeated. "I done hit with one hand. I made the stuff in the house in there, but hit's not as purty as this. I got Lazy Susans and cupboard-safes and center tables and cheers scattered all over these hills I been a-makin for over forty year." He frowned. "All held together with tongue and groove and pegs. Most of'em as good as the day I finished'em." His eyes were bright as he stood before her.

"I do declare," Alvira sighed, "it's might near the purtiest work I ever seen done in furniture."

"Thank'ye," Grandpa John said, sadly. "I thank'ye for them kind words. Will don't think I'm wuth a cuss cause I lost my parcel of land, but I got me a idee my furniture'll be around a long time ater me and Will's gone and this land's growd up in pines and briers."

"I got an idee you may be right," Vi smiled. She turned away. "Come on in to breakfast now."

That afternoon Alvira walked down the Ridge Road to Cousin Bill's house. She decided she had to write her mother and father, could not put it off any longer. And there was not a scrap of writing paper in the place, let alone an envelope. She doubted if there was pen or pencil to write with, although she had seen writing in the big Bible on the center table.

Rosa Ward met her at what was actually the front door, although it faced East Ridge, away from the Big Road. "Why, Vi! how dare you!" Rosa laughed. "Comin to see me first. I was aimin to come up and visit you tomorr."

"This ain't exactly a visit," Vi said. "I'm not here a week, and I've already come a-borryin."

"Well, come in, Vi. Do come in." She stood aside and let Alvira enter the hallway. "You're welcome to anything I've got. Anything at all."

They turned right, through a door into the "settin room." Vi looked about her. The walls were neatly ceiled with knotty pine. A fire burned in a neat brick fireplace in front of her, warming the entire room. Several rockers and ladder-backed chairs were arranged about the fireplace, and a tall spool-bed stood in one corner with a trundle-bed beneath its skirts. Over the mantel was a painting—a man and woman praying in a grain field over a basket, a fork plunged into the ground beside the man, a barrow behind the woman.

"Have a seat, Vi." Rosa motioned to one of the rockers, which had a blue-checked pad at the back and in the seat.

Vi let herself down into the chair and watched Rosa arrange her prim little seat in another. Rocking quietly, Vi studied the painting above the mantel. Somehow they looked familiar to her. The man, especially, reminded her of someone she knew, but she put it out of her mind.

"Well, Vi," Rosa said cheerfully, rocking slowly, "how do you like married life?"

Vi looked at her and opened her mouth to answer. But she remained silent for half a minute. She could not answer lightly, and she could not lie. Neither could she confide in this kind, simple neighbor enough to explain her entrapment—even if she could have explained it. She doubted that she could, because she could not think it through clearly to her own satisfaction.

"Ah-h-h—" she smiled gently, "all right, I reckon. It's a whole lot different from the way it was before."

Rosa Ward stopped rocking suddenly and leaned toward her, her face serious, her eyes narrowed. "Vi, you're not over seventeen or eighteen, are you?"

Vi stopped rocking with such abruptness that the chairback struck her head. Disorganized, she stammered, "Sebemteen! I'll be eighteen, come March the tenth."

Rosa leaned forward and placed a fragile little hand on Vi's knee. "Honey, did Will Ward bring that mare and buggy down there and fool you into marryin him?"

Alvira looked away from the shrewd bright eyes, from the face pinched with concentration. She looked back at the field hands in the painting above the mantel. "I'd just as soon not talk about it," she said softly.

Rosa leaned back in her rocker and folded her arms beneath her bosom, rocking slowly. Her face relaxed, her eyes opened wider. "Of course not, dear. I was only concerned for you. What's done is done. There's no turnin back from marriage, I don't reckon. But you just remember, one of the things God put me here for is to help you all I possibly can."

"I thank'ye," Vi said, meeting her eyes. "I thank'ye with all my heart."

Rosa rocked for several seconds, studying the fire eating away at the oak logs. "Will was wrong in foolin you," she said to the fire. "But he's not a bad man. He means a whole heap better'n he's able to do. He's as honest as the day is long, and he's a hard worker. He's a slave to his work, but like a slave, he needs a master. Maybe you can help him plan. He's got a black temper like a one-eyed rattlesnake. But most of it comes from the trap he was borned in. If he could just one time break out of that trap at the head of Stud Branch, he might calm down some."

Vi listened to Rosa, nodding while she talked. Vi had arrived at about the same conclusions, but not in the same terms. She wondered how someone like herself could direct a bullheaded Will Ward. She wondered what would happen to him if he really did break out of the trap at the head of Stud Branch. She wondered if forty-two years of it was not enough to set him in his ways, like a mule that only knows how to pull a cane mill—around and around. After all, it was more than half an average lifetime. She started shaking her head in doubt, then remembered where she was. She looked quickly at Rosa.

"I can make out with Will good enough," she said. "By one way or another, I can make out with him. I think he's a little hateful because he feels bad about bringin me here. But I believe more than that, he wants to make up to me. No, it ain't Will that troubles me."

"It's them young folk," Rosa announced. "Three of them older'n you are. Not Tillie. She's decent. It's that Annie and the boys."

"Yes," Vi nodded. "Annie's got a mean streak in her. She started out bad and she's goin to get worse, I'm afraid."

"And the boys? Have they objected to'ye?" Rosa rocked quietly, waiting.

"Not yet," Vi said. "They run about a heap and ain't been home much yet. But there's signs. When I ask Van to do somethin, he looks at Dan and grins and says, 'Yes, Maw.' But he's done what I said to so far—little as it is. I'm afraid he'll cause Dan to make up his mind to get smart with me."

Rosa rocked for a few moments, her brow furrowed. "You've sure got you a job cut out for'ye," she mused. "Your own younguns'll be comin along before you can say scat. You've sure got a rough row to hoe for a girl your age. I wisht I could ease it for'ye. With all my heart I wisht I could."

They talked on for a while, small talk about neighbors and about the country around Stud Branch. Alvira told Rosa a little about her background, about her job folding the *Hornet* and about her stay at the Watson house, the best part of it. When she started to leave, she remembered to ask for a sheet of paper and an envelope so she could write her parents. Rosa did more. She insisted on giving Vi half a tablet and several envelopes, forcing her to take them.

"I'll take them," Vi agreed, on the porch. "But I'll pay'ye back. I'll buy me some soon. Maybe I can pull some mullen leaves or dig some pokeberry roots later on and sell'em."

"If it would make'ye happier," Rosa agreed, "you do that. Meantime, you go ahead and use what I give'ye and don't fret about it."

Alvira left the neat little woman on the porch of her orderly house surrounded by fruit trees. She trudged across the field toward East Ridge, heading for Stud Branch and the west end of Coottown—just outside Coottown, Will would insist. And for some reason the visit had not made her any happier, though she felt even closer to Rosa Ward now, thought of her more than ever as a mother. Her head was low in thought as she paced the stepping stones across Ward Branch. Somehow, the visit had depressed her, but she did not know why.

When she entered the forest covering the north end of East Ridge, again that fear of bears and wild Indians caused her heart to beat faster. The winter woods were quiet, except for the scurrying of a squirrel through the dry leaves. She kept glancing out of the sides of her eyes at the larger trees she passed, half expecting some creature to leap suddenly from behind one of them. The squirrel had disappeared, carrying away its noise like a plundered nut, and the forest was quiet again. Some distance away, through the branches, a last oak leaf fluttered downward, rasping from twig to twig. She started to hum.

She glimpsed the man, to her left, as he stepped from behind a huge poplar bole. She screamed, whirling in that direction, hands raised to shove. Grandpa John stepped backward, his red lips pursed through his white beard, his rheumy eyes wide.

"I didn't aim to scare'ye, Vi," he called. "Don't yell. I ain't aimin to hurt'ye."

"Lord ha'mercy!" Vi laughed. "You scart me near-bout out of my wits. What on earth are you a-doin slippin around up here in the woods like a wild Indian?"

The old man shuffled his battered shoes in the leaves and looked down, grinning. "Tillie said you'd gone to Bill's place. I wanted to show'ye somethin, so I come up here and set down behind that tree watchin a squirrel. I reckon I dozed off."

"Well, I declare! What in this world did you want to show me up here?" She approached him, climbing the low embankment.

"Come along and I'll show'ye somethin inter-restin," old John said.

He turned away and shuffled out through the decaying leaves. Alvira followed him, watching his stooped shoulders in the baggy black coat, watching his legs bend to either side, as though his knees were off-center, watching his good left arm, long and overdeveloped, swing loosely as though attached by a single tendon. She shook her head and felt a surge of tenderness for him because he was poor and because he was old. Because he was poor and old and had enough feeling to know the misfortune he lived with. Silently watching his mincing gait, she shuddered. Secretly, she felt her own hard biceps, felt the stretch of her long legs, and tried to imagine herself old and stooped. She tried to imagine her arms scrawny, her breasts sagging with age, her legs aching with the rheumatism of time, but she could not. Her imagination could not bridge the gap between the strength in her erect figure and what it would become. It was too far in the future, the far, dim future. There was too much labor ahead to bother with dread now.

Grandpa John stopped by a long, wide mound, around which larger trees clustered as though reluctant to advance (the same mound Will had pointed out when he led her back home Saturday). It was fleeced with shrubbery, huckleberry bushes, and briers. Vi stood, feet planted wide apart, and stared at the formation. It had a weird familiarity, like some place she had visited in a dream.

"They used to be a house a-standin on this spot," old John said, staring away through the trees toward the Bushy Mountains, dimly seen through the leafless branches. "You wouldn't hardly know it now, but a big house stood here over a hundred year—a hundred and twenty-odd, to be truthful."

"No," Vi said, shaking her head as she looked over the giant grave mound covered with shrubbery. "No, I wouldn't hardly know it. It looks just like a little flat hill in the middle of the woods all growd over. Looks like a place where the Indians might a-buried a whole passel of their dead, like over at Indian Grave Gap."

"Well, it was a house here," old John mused, not looking at her. "My great-grandpa settled here way back yander when they wasn't a livin white man for many a mile, sept one near what's now Northboro. Dan'l Boone used to stop by and stay the night. Great-grandpa brought him a big deef Scotsman with him, and they worked more'n a year and built a big two-story log house. Right in the middle of the woods, they built hit. Then he went back to the Virginny coast where his womern was waitin and married her that trip, and she bore my grandpa, John Thomas Ward, in less'n eight months. She was a English womern of some means, and she follered him over to Virginny. Down in that low country around the Tweed River, they come from."

"That was a long spell ago," Vi said, distantly. "A body wouldn't never know it, lookin at this spot now."

Old John turned his back on the distant mountains and faced her. "My great-grandpa laid claim to a whole passel of land around here, miles stead of acres. He lived a good life, and my grandpa, John Thomas Ward, lived good. He let some folks settle on his land and tend it and give him part of what they raised. Fields too scattered and hilly to make slaves wuthwhile, like over on the Yadkin. Grandpa didn't believe in slaves, nohow."

"That's a heap of land," Vi mused. "Looks like it'd take a lot of workers to tend it."

"It was mostly woods," old John replied. "Anyways, the onliest one of grandpa's younguns to live was my pa. Pa was a good manager too—so good he didn't git married tell he was fifty. He fixed the big house up and filled it with furniture and cleared the woods back from around it. He was well-off, and folks looked up to him. Called him Square Ward. Me and my brother and two sisters was borned after he was fifty-two, and we lived with him tell he was old as Methuselem, and we lived good. We lived fancy. I got married and lived in the Big House with my wife and fust youngun. Will thinks he recollects it, but he don't. He couldn't. Hit burnt jest before his time. He was borned in that old house he still lives in."

Alvira climbed the slope and waded through the huckleberry bushes to one end. She set her foot on a single field stone half buried beneath lichen, dead leaves, and grass. "I reckon this here rock come from one of the chimbleys," she called down to him.

John Ward shuffled through the bushes and stopped close to her. "Yep, they was two big chimbleys and eight farplaces. Two upstairs and two down, to each chimbley." The old man cleared his throat and looked upward at the blue sky, through the bare oak limbs. His face was thoughtful and sad. "Anyways, the Big House burnt down, and Pa built that sorry place Will lives in up on Stud Branch. When he was ninety-four, he rid his hoss acrosst his land two ways and blazed trees with a ax and divided it into four quarter-sections, for his four younguns. I didn't have no look, so I lost my section."

"Grandpa!" Vi said softly. "Grandpa John."

The fourth John Ward lowered his face and looked at her. His eyes gleamed with moisture. "Yes, daughter?" he muttered.

"Why did you bring me out here and show me this place?"

she asked. "Why did you tell me all this for?"

"Cause I left my two boys nothin," he said. "Cause Will punishes hisself day in and day out rememberin things he couldn't possibly remember. Cause he's worked like a mule all his life tryin to buy back the land I lost, and after all these years, he's only got back about five acres. Cause he's too bull-headed and blind to see the cleared land's run down and gone to seed." The old man paused. "Jest cause we live where we do, the way we do, I didn't want you to think Will was a Catlett that jest happened to be called Ward."

"I don't," Vi said. "I didn't have no idee Will was some kind of a Catlett. I knowd that straight off."

They walked back to the road together and headed back up the ridge. "It seems like a long time for a house to stand," Alvira said, "not to be nothin left but a low mound of dirt."

"And one rock from a chimbley," old John reminded her. He made it sound so important that Vi laughed, her voice rising high and clear, piercing the silent forest around them.

As they were descending the spur of the ridge opposite Coot-town, Alvira stared at the weathered shacks perched along the slope of Fox Mountain. "How did they happen to put down roots there?" she asked the old man. "I bet they don't own a scrap of that land."

"Grandpa let a feller named Catlett live there and tend the land up here," John Ward said. "He had a whole passel of younguns by his wife and his wife's sister. He slept betwixt'em. Some of the boys married and built around their pa, and the gals brooded or got married and brooded. They spread out like rabbits. Nobidy ever thought to run'em off any more'n you would wild critters. I ain't got no idee who's akin to who and how much, and I doubt if most of them do. Hit would take the feller that writ the Begots in the Bible to straighten out who begot who."

Vi laughed at him, and John Ward looked at her and grinned. His rheumy grey eyes shone with pleasure. "If you can laugh now and again and sleep sound," he said, "you'll make out in the long run."

"They're happy hours," Vi agreed, "them I spend a-sleepin."

5

SHE SCRIBBLED THE LETTER CAREFULLY with the scrap of pencil, pausing every now and then, point in mouth, to choose the right word. The problem was to tell them the truth and not worry them at the same time. She found it a hard letter to write.

Rowdy Branch, N.C.

Dere Mama and Papa,

Moren likly youve done and heerd from Ma Watson I gone and got maried. It happen Jan. 6. I maried a man name of Will Ward. Youall moren likly have seen him. He is the singin techer come to Ready River church house onct or twict for to run singins. We live in a big log house with plenty room. Will is a farmur and lives on his own land. Wills first wife died and he got some chilren by her. We git on good with one a nuther. Don't worrie bout me. I am makin out good enuff. Hopin to see youall some time befor long.

yours trulie

Vi

She addressed the envelope and asked Anna to walk with her across West Mountain and show her the short cut to Doc Ellis's store, where the post office was. Anna was sitting before the fire, her legs spread wide, her skirt above her knees, so that her naked thighs were exposed to the heat.

"I jest don't see how I can make that long walk," she complained. "My feet bother me a lot of late. I can't hardly walk about the place here to git my work done."

Tillie, who was washing the breakfast dishes in a rusty tin pan, turned from the table on which it sat. "It's not her feet that's botherin'er," she said. "It's her lazy butt. She shows signs of wearin it out settin on it, before she gets to be twenty."

Anna leaped to her feet and turned on Tillie, her dark eyes flashing, her face contorted. "At least I'm jest usin mine to set on!" she yelled, saliva forming at the corners of her mouth. "That's more'n some folks can say."

Tillie turned from the dishpan, her limp hands in front of her dripping dishwater onto the floor. Her expression was frozen between anger and some emotion she fought to control. "What does them words mean, Annie?"

Anna Ward slumped, her defiance receding. She dropped back into the chair and straddled her legs toward the warm fire. "Nothin," she grumbled. "I jest don't feel up to trudgin acrosst that damned mountain, the way my feet hurt."

Alvira shifted closer and looked down at her. "Supposin I told'ye to, young lady?" she demanded quietly. "Supposin I told'ye you had to go?"

Anna leaned forward and rested her elbows on her bare knees, cradling her chin in her hands. She laughed. "Did you see Pa tryin to make your old crippled shoat get up and walk? Less'n you want to tote me acrosst the mountain, you'd best leave me settin here warmin my straddle."

Vi stared down at her, debating within herself. She felt like grabbing her by her head of tangled hair and rattling her brains around like a pea in a gourd. A showdown had to come sooner or later, but it would probably turn out better with Will around. He and the boys were up in Fox Hollow with a sled hauling pine knots for kindling and would not be back before the middle of the afternoon. Yes, she decided, she would be better off to wait until Will was close by.

Before she could turn away, backing down, Tillie said, "Let her set there and singe her tailfeathers, Ma. Her time's a-comin sooner or later. Soon's I get through here, we'll put the baby to sleep, and then I'll walk'ye over to the store."

"All right," Vi agreed, moving away toward her bed. "I'm not up to no fussin and fightin today, nohow."

It was a long, steep climb up the slope of West Mountain. At the crest they sat down on a log to rest. Vi leaned back against a black-gum tree, her bosom rising and falling fast, and stared across the valley toward the winter haze along the eastern horizon, beyond Mount Hope Church. Below her, Will Ward's house—her house—was an ordinary box, orderly in shape and in relation to the smokehouse and crib. The fuzzy disorder of poverty and dirt was obliterated by distance. The setting looked almost tranquil from up here, when she dissociated herself from it. Even the shacks of Coottown did not look like ragged scabs on the flank of Fox Mountain, but more like angular little bird-houses (martin boxes, Will would say) waiting to be elevated on poles.

"It looks sort of peaceable from way up here," Tillie said, aloud, "like it was way off yander, some'ers."

"Yes, it does," Vi nodded. But she was thinking of Doc Watson and his misery. Already the agony of his long dying was fading out of her mind. She was remembering clearly only the good times she shared with Lucinda Watson.

"Tillie, tell me somethin," Vi said out of a long silence. She did not look at her, but stared out across the valley below. "I've got a curiosity about somethin."

Tillie looked at her, apparently startled. "What?" she called, half in fright, her round moon face alert. "I mean what did'ye have in mind?" she asked, more controlled.

"Grandpa John went up on West Mountain with the boys to

cut wood Monday without no argument. I noticed this mornin, when Dan laughed and asked him wasn't he comin with them up Fox Holler to haul pine knots, the pore old feller looked like he'd been hit. His lips trembled, and he turned around and went back in his place in the smokehouse and didn't come back out all mornin long."

"That Dan!" Tillie spat. "That infernal Dan! Sometimes I think he's as bad as Annie."

"What did he say to trouble the old man?"

Tillie was thoughtful for some time, staring off down through the winter woods. Her fat young body slumped forward, her full belly forcing her legs slightly apart. "That holler where West Mountain and Fox come together," she said thoughtfully, "that's Fox Holler. Grandpa killed a man some'ers up in there onct. And he ain't been back in there for more'n thirty year."

Alvira stared at her, brows arched. "Killed a man? Grandpa John? Why, he don't look like he could hurt a fly."

"Well, he did," Tillie said, looking back at Vi with pale-blue eyes. "But it was legal-like. Back durin the Silver War, Grandpa had to stay at home on account of his arm. A Yankee soldier tried to take one of Great-grandpa's hosses. Grandpa was compelled to shoot him cause hosses was hard to come by late in the war, when it happened."

"I do declare!" Vi said. "I never would a-thought it."

"It's troubled the old feller some," Tillie explained. "He went back to the spot after about ten year and tried to find the Yankee's grave and couldn't. Then he wouldn't go back no more and ain't been back in all that time, I don't reckon. You couldn't drag him back in there nowadays. Dan knows that. That's why he's not got no business joshin the pore old feller."

"Well, that's the strangest thing!" Vi said. "I wonder if he'd talk to a body about it."

Tillie turned on her and grasped her knee, clutching it. "Don't you mention it to him," she ordered. Then she relaxed her grip and patted Vi's leg. "I mean, he mentions it now and agin. But if anybidy else brings it up, he gets upset. It troubles him more of late than Pa and the other'ns at home knows or cares about. He ain't went to church in five or six year, and he don't read the big Bible like he used to. Somehow, I think it's all connected up with that Yank he killed when he wasn't more'n twenty or twenty-one."

"Them was strange times up in around the hill country," Alvira said quietly. "Some folks sacrificed everthing to go fight, when they wouldn't a-got any more if the South had come out on top. Then there was folks like my grandpa, William Matlock. He wouldn't have no part of fightin and wouldn't pay somebody to go in his place and got shot down like a dog by a bunch of trash callin theirselves the Home Guard. Somehow, I think he died as brave as any of the others cause he died standin up against what he thought was a foolhardy war. Pore Grandma was totin my pa inside her when they throwd Grandpa's dead carcass on her porch like he was a dead snake or somethin."

"Them days was too far ago for me to figure," Tillie said. "I don't think about them hardly. Pa still hates Yankees and Abe Lincoln. But me—it's bad enough puttin up with these times we've got to live through nowadays."

"I reckon that was a wise sayin," Vi smiled, standing up. "Come on and let's go, before our butts grow to this here old log."

Bessie Ellis was waiting on a dry little husk of a lady in a snuff-colored bonnet when Alvira and Tillie entered the store. Bessie's huge body filled the aisle between the counter and the shelves along the wall, her ample bosom projecting out over the counter. She grinned and nodded to the newcomers, than turned back to her customer, setting her sweet snuff in front of her. The little old lady fumbled with the dirty handkerchief, her hooked brown talons so calloused she could hardly flex the tips. Finally the knot was loose, and she counted out five tarnished pennies for the small box. She could not wait, but tore off the lid, seized her lower lip in a pinch with her left hand, and stretched it, forming an elastic spoon. She dumped half the box's contents onto the pink surface. This done, she snapped her lid back on the box in a brown cloud and hobbled from the store, her lip thrust forward.

"Probly not eat a bite today," Bessie observed. "Dyin for that lip snuff. How's the new wife gettin on?" She nodded to Alvira. "I see she's fixed you a new frock a-ready, Tillie."

"Ah-h-h! I'm gettin on fine, I reckon," Vi said. She glanced at Tillie, who had turned away, looking down at the old dress Vi had altered for her. "One of Tillie's old dresses. I let it out so's it would fit her better."

"I hadn't seen it lately," Bessie Ellis nodded. "But I noticed Tillie was gettin a mite heavy of late. You'd better watch it or you'll be as big as me, Tillie, and you not married yet."

Tillie attempted to smile and fumbled with her fingers. "It's my new ma's cookin, I reckon. If I get too big, I'll jest have to marry Greely Milton and raise a fambly of ellyphunts."

"You must have gained fast," Bessie went on. "Seein as your new ma's been with'ye less than a week. What could I do for you folks today?"

"First off, I got a letter to mail," Vi told her, laying the envelope and two pennies on the counter.

"Here no time a-tall and already mailin letters," Bessie said. "To Mister and Mizries Henry Matlock, Ready River, N.C.," she spelled out. "Your ma and pa, I take it? A young bride ort not to forget her bringing-up. A girl that remembers to write her ma and pa in less than a week after gettin married is bound to have a heap of good in'er." She grinned, indicating that she meant well by the compliment.

Alvira did not answer because she could not figure out the right words to Bessie's observation about young brides and life. She watched the huge woman fumble in a drawer, come out with a two-cent stamp, lick it, and stick it at an angle on the right-hand corner of the envelope. It bothered Vi. If she had been doing it, she would have put the stamp on straight, the way it was supposed to go. Bessie took a rubber stamp, beat it against an ink pad, then raised her fist high in the air, paused, and came down like a hickory maul, striking the small red target precisely with a thud.

"There you are!" she grinned at Vi, her sparse black mustache catching the light through a dirty glass window. "Now it's officially sealed." She squinted at it. "Rowdy Branch, N.C.," she announced. "Now it's in the government's hands."

"Sounds right to me," Vi agreed, wondering what she was expected to say. "Sounds like that ort to carry it clean to Jerusalem."

"What could I sell you folks today?" Bessie Ellis asked. "Did you just want to mail a letter and that's all?"

"We're not out of anything," Vi apologized. "I did want to ask you about the sort of roots and yerbs you take in."

"Well, if you'll foller me, I'll show'ye where I store it at, and we can talk. Tillie, will you kindly keep the store till I take your new ma upstairs a minute. Get'ye a stick of that horehound candy there in the showcase."

They skirted the potbellied stove, and Bessie grunted her way up the stairs at the rear of the store, Vi following. As she watched the big buttocks shift with each step, Vi had a sudden dread that the storekeeper would miss a step and come tumbling backward to bury her beneath a human landslide. She breathed in quiet relief when they finally reached the top. Vi looked around her. She was in a vast, dark loft, which covered the whole area of the store except for the stairwell. The A-structure of the gabled roof formed the only ceiling. The sun knifed through an occasional crack between the vertical siding or lighted up a red pine knot enough to illuminate the place dimly. Here and there about the floor were piles and lumps of some dark substance Vi could not identify. The air was hot and dry.

"The most common thing I take in," Bessie said, "is pokeberry roots and mullen leaves. They're the easiest to find. Then I take in white-pine bark—that's the inside part, not the rough outer bark. Of course I take in gensing, starroot, and any of the rare yerbs. But them are harder to come by. Then, of course, they bring a heap more money, too."

"Well," Vi murmured, staring about her at the shadowy piles, "I wanted to find out about it. A body's got to have a little money, and I thought I'd better start figurin how to make some."

Bessie Ellis stood in front of her, a huge shadow blotting out half of one wall. "Generally speakin, I've found they're two kinds of folks that come in my store," she observed to the dark emptiness around her, "them that's willin to work for what little they get and them that's willin to do without."

"You go down first," Alvira suggested. "You know the steps better'n me."

She felt better following the giant woman down the creaking stairs, but Bessie Ellis walked as surefooted as a girl.

Later, as Vi and Tillie climbed single file up the slope of West Mountain, Tillie asked suddenly, "Did you see the way she stamped Ruddy Branch on that pore stamp?"

"How could I miss seein?" Vi laughed. "It shook the whole store."

"That's the way she pulls teeth," Tillie said.

Alvira stopped, and Tillie halted, holding on to a sapling, facing her. "What do you mean by that?" Vi demanded.

"Bessie's the onliest tooth-puller hereabouts," Tillie laughed. "She pulls a tooth like she was yankin a tree up by the roots. But I garntee one thing. Ever tooth she takes a-holt of comes out."

Vi caressed her jaw thoughtfully. "I'll have to recollect to take care of my teeth," she said. "Why, big as she is, she's liable to yank a body inside out."

Tillie fell down on her back and rolled in the dry leaves, laughing hysterically. "Wouldn't that be a sight for sore eyes?" she gasped. "Bessie tryin to turn a bidy right-side out again, usin them big hands of her'n? Why, I bet she'd get the liver where the head's s'posed to be."

"Get up and stop actin a fool," Vi smiled. "If anybody was watchin, they'd think'ye had the hydriephoby."

On Saturday, Alvira had been married only one week, and it already seemed as though it had been a month. She had made some adjustment to the diet of sauerkraut, dried apples, dried beans, potatoes, pork, and molasses—a seven-day-a-week fare with little variation. She was becoming inured to the early-morning cold before the fire was blazing, the lumpy straw bedtick swaying across wooden slats, the continuing round of labor from dawn till after nightfall, and the inconvenience of crouching in the bushes like a wild animal to relieve herself.

But the one thing she could not adjust to, could not accept in the miserable routine, was the almost silent conflict between Tillie and herself on one side and Anna on the other. Nor could she accept much longer the quiet disrespect of the boys. So far, nothing serious had happened, but she had a feeling like she had had once when she cocked a shotgun and closed her eyes, bracing against pulling the trigger. She did not like to shoot a gun, and she disliked a row even more.

On Tuesday, Dan came striding down the slope with Van just as Vi finished milking. Suddenly, she decided to feed the crippled hog while she was up near the lot, to save herself a second trip lugging the slopbucket up the slope. Van said something quietly as they passed, and Dan roared with laughter.

"Dan!" Vi called after them.

The two huge young men stopped and turned, faces serious.

"Dan," Vi said, "I wisht you'd go to the house and fetch me the slopbucket back up here."

"I wisht I had wings like a buzzard," Dan grinned. "What do you wish, Van?"

"I wisht our new maw would feed me the same way she feeds that old hawg," Van laughed. "I'd git fat, too."

"You're welcome to all the slop you can hold," Vi snapped, "providin you'll get down on'ye hands and knees in the hog lot where'ye belong."

The laugh slipped from Van's square, bearded face, and his eyes narrowed as he thought over her remark.

"As for you, young feller"—she yanked a limb off a wild plum bush—"don't think you're too big for me to switch'ye." She set the milk bucket down and advanced on him, hand drawn back to strike.

"Don't! Don't!" Dan begged in mock fear, hands raised to ward off the blow. "I'm goin, Ma. Please don't whoop me, Ma. I'll run all the way there and all the way back."

Vi stopped, dropping the switch. "All right, just so's you know who to mind. When I say I *wisht* you'd do somethin, it's just the peaceable way of tellin'ye what to do."

She stood near the pail of milk and watched them stride off

down the hill, shoulder to shoulder, big as a team of oxen on their hind legs. She watched Dan turn his head and say something to Van and watched Van throw back his head and shout his laughter across the sunless valley.

"I bet they could pull a thirteen Oliver-Chill turnin plow," she thought. "I bet the two of'em could pull a plow." Then her mood changed, suddenly, and she slumped downward, hunkering beside the bucket. "I'm gonna have trouble with them. Sooner or later I'm bound to."

It was not much later that she decided when her trouble would be. She watched Van stamp into the house, watched Dan stalk on around the smokehouse and head toward the branch, where he had a rabbit trap set. She climbed wearily to her feet, picked up the pail, and plodded down the path to the house. Not speaking to Van, who sat slumped by the fire, she gave the milk to Tillie to skim, picked up the slopbucket, and lugged it back up the slope to the hog lot.

She held the bucket beneath the shoat's snout, resting the bottom on the ground, and watched him swill it down. The weight of the animal's head against the rim of the bucket pulled at her arm and at her shoulders, tugging at her back until it ached. It seemed to take twice as long for the hog to eat as it usually did. When the slop was all gone, she kicked its greedy head out of the bucket and plodded back toward the house.

As Vi came even with the woodpile behind the smokehouse, she noticed Will and Dan stooping to load their arms with wood for the fireplace. She dropped the slopbucket and approached them, stopping finally, feet apart.

"Will Ward!" she said, "when you married me and brung me up here in these woods, did you aim for me to take care of these big old yearlins of your'n and do ever lick of work all by myself?"

Will stood erect, a four-foot piece of oak limb clutched in his right hand. He stared at her. "What manner of damnfool question is that?" he demanded.

"I just ast Dan here to fetch me the slopbucket up to the hog lot so's I wouldn't have to traipse all the way down here twice. He sassed me, then said he would bring the bucket, but went on out to the branch and didn't come about me."

Will turned on Dan. "Is that so?"

Dan's face clouded, and he looked at the ground, shuffling his feet. He towered half a head above Will and outweighed him by thirty pounds. "Well," he grumbled, "I thought—"

"You thought hell!" Will roared.

He came around with a swipe of the stick, taking no time to raise it, and struck Dan across the back of his right thigh. Dan collapsed and rolled onto his back, drawing up his legs and throwing up his hands as a shield. In one stride Will had reached him, towered over him, the stick drawn back, his face working in fury.

"Don't kill me, Pap, for God's sake!" Dan yelled.

"You don't have to cripple him, Will," Vi called, moving closer to him.

"Goddamn you to hell!" Will Ward stormed. "When I said respect your new ma, I meant *respect* her. Do what she asts'ye to, goddamn hit, I don't care if it's eat a cowpile."

"But Pa," Dan pleaded, "she's only a young gal—"

"Young hell and damnation!" Will came down with the stick, and Dan caught it on his right foot, deflecting it. "If she's old enough to sleep with me, she's old enough to be your ma. Now don't give me no more bellyachin."

Will snatched up a backlog, tossed it onto his shoulders, and stamped toward the house with it. Alvira watched Dan gather in his arms and legs, test them, then wheel slowly like a giant half-crippled beetle onto his all fours and struggle to his feet. He stooped and began to fill his arms with firewood.

"I didn't aim for him to cripple'ye," she said to his arched back.

"Where I made my mistake," he grumbled, standing erect, "was bein in his reach when you told him. Besides, I thank'ye, he didn't cripple me."

He turned away and hobbled toward the house, favoring his right foot. Vi was compelled to smile after him, in spite of herself.

When Alvira awoke on Monday morning to a damp, chilling cabin, it was pouring rain outside. It rained for three days and nights, sending Stud Branch out of its banks, muddying the well, and making a mucky, stinking morass of the milking area in the pasture and of the hog lot. Will half-soled shoes most of the first day while Van and Dan played Fox-and-Geese with corn grains on a cardboard chart Grandpa John had marked off thirty years before. Alvira and Tillie shelled dried beans, with Anna helping them between trips to the bed to rest her aching feet. Grandpa John was busy on some new piece of furniture in the shop where he lived, and Vi saw him only at mealtimes. The baby scurried about the fireplace and about their chairs, chasing a red ear of corn. Every now and then he would capture it and sit up, grinning at them with his four teeth.

The first day it rained was not too bad. They managed to get through it and go to bed with only a few tempers flaring out of control. On Tuesday, Will and Van lugged in a washtub full of corn ears, and they all gathered around it, shelling corn for the mill. But they were through in three hours, with nothing left to do other than housework for Alvira and Tillie, labor which went on in spite of flood or fire or earthquake. Vi, and Tillie by implication, gave up on Anna and let her lie on the bed and brood. They were better off with her out of the way.

When Vi went to her toilet, through the dripping bushes, beneath dripping limbs, Will's soggy denim jacket spread over her and her white flesh shuddering with goose pimples, she began to appreciate how complete her misery could be. When she waded into the sloppy muck to milk, when she tried to find a firm island in the swampy hog lot where she could stand and feed the cripple animal, tears filled her eyes without her realizing it, and she thought of Lucinda Watson's warm kitchen, dry toilet, and comfortable bed. She did not think of the old doctor. Creature of a new misery, she wanted to remember only the comforts left behind, and this made her chores in the rain more depressing than ever.

Wednesday morning, Alvira dreaded to lift her head from her pillow. But she could already hear the downpour, even before she threw back the heavy quilts and sat up in bed. Will already had the fire going in the fireplace, but the wall of warmth had not yet advanced past the dining table. She shuddered, her teeth chattering, as she pulled on her dress, then worked her way into her faded purple sweater without unraveling still more the holes in it. Sniffing the moldy dampness, she picked up her shoes and stockings and hurried to the fireplace across a rough floor as cold as slabs of frozen granite.

"Hit's rainin out there like a cow pissin on a flat rock," Will grumbled. "I reckon hit'll flood hell if it keeps this up another day."

Vi sat down and began to pull on her stockings. "That would take a heap of rain," she answered, not thinking.

Will glowered at her as though she had disputed his word. "Well, that ain't hardly a heavy fog that's a-pourin down out there."

Vi shut up because she could see the conversation was leading nowhere except to foolish argument. It had been raining, it was still raining, and it looked as though it would keep on raining for quite a while—and she accepted it because there was nothing she could do about it. She leaned forward and started lacing up her shoes, her hair gleaming blackly in the firelight.

The rain slackened for a while around ten o'clock, and Will left, muttering that he was going to the store after tobacco. Van and Dan left a little later, saying nothing. Thirty minutes afterward, the bottom fell out of the sky. The rain came down in streams, splashing onto the roof and gushing against the walls and shutters. Vi, peeling potatoes beside the fireplace, cocked her head to listen, then shuddered. For a fleeting moment she felt that the dismal rain pelted her grave instead of the black roof overhead.

Tillie burst into the house through the front door, slammed it shut, and hung her dripping coat on a peg in the wall. "It's rainin pitchforks out there," she complained. "A bidy can't pee without gettin drownded." She hurried over to the fireplace, turned her back to it, and hoisted her skirt to warm her legs and naked buttocks in a manner as native to the hills, Vi had learned, as cracklin bread and fried pigs' feet. She shuddered. "Lordy, but that heat feels good to my poor tail," she sighed. "I wisht Pa would at least build a lean-to for us womernfolk to squat underneath of."

Anna sat on the edge of her bed, listlessly turning through a catalogue by the light seeping through the window shutters. She looked up and laughed. "Is your ittle bitty rump gettin too precious to get wet with a tad of rain?"

"Aw, shet up your nasty mouth!" Tillie snapped. "Anything I got is more precious than all you put together."

Anna laughed again, tossing her tangled mane of hair. "How about your ittle bitty ole maidenhead, sis? *Was* it precious too?"

Tillie dropped her dresstail and charged toward Anna, her face twisted in anger. She stopped ten feet short of her. "What do you mean by them words, Annie Ward?"

"What do you reckon I mean?" Anna grinned. "Don't you reckon I can see your belly pokin out furder ever day?"

Alvira had turned to watch them. She put down her knife and pan and stood up. "Them's dangerous words you're a-floutin," she called to Anna. "You'd better be careful of your tongue, young lady, less'n you know what you're talkin about."

Tillie still stood between Alvira and Anna, her feet spread. All Vi could see was her back, as still as a fence post.

"I ort to know," Anna snapped. "She used to be as regular as the new moon. She ain't fixed rags for a period in more'n five months now."

One moment Tillie was still standing there, her back to Vi, as still as a fence post. The next, she struck. She came down on Anna like a chicken hawk. She clutched her by the hair of her head, yanked her from the bed, and fell on top of her on the floor. Anna screamed, writhed on her back, fought back, spitting and hissing and scratching, like a half-angry, half-frightened cat.

"You bitch!" Tillie screamed, pounding her head against the floor by her hair. "You nosy bitch, why don't you tend to your business? I'll kill you, kill you, kill you! I'll beat your dirty brains out! I'll kill you, kill you!"

Anna drummed her heels against the floor, trying to unseat Tillie, who sat astraddle of her belly. Her naked legs thrashed and twisted as she tried to turn her body. But Tillie would not yield. She continued pounding Anna's black head against the floor, her fingers in her hair. Alvira, in the few seconds the fight lasted, hesitated, then rushed to where the two women struggled between the two beds. She saw the black fire in Anna's eyes change from anger to fear to desperation.

Stooping, Alvira seized Tillie's right arm and tugged at her, but it was wasted effort. Weeping now, raging, gnashing her teeth, Tillie pounded, pounded Anna's black head against the cabin floor. Vi tore at her arm. Her hands slipped and she fell backward onto her back. Tillie now held Anna's hair in her left hand, beating her in the face with her right fist.

"You bitch!" she wept. "You big-mouthed bitch! I'll beat your ugly face to a pulp."

Alvira struggled to her knees, walked on them close to Tillie. She stared at the girl's face. It worked with insane fury, fury and agony. She was beyond the reach of reason. "Let up, Tillie!" she shouted. Vi caught her full in the face with an open-handed slap that turned her head to one side. Tillie stopped and blinked her eyes. She shook her head. She stared at Vi. She looked down at Anna, who watched her, transfixed, afraid to break the spell. Eyes flared wide, Tillie climbed slowly to her feet. She looked dispassionately down at her sister, naked from her hips down. Four red and white streaks spread across Tillie's cheek. Vi placed her arm about her shoulders and led her toward the fireplace. She walked stiffly, the expression on her face fixed, her eyes straight ahead.

"Now, what's this foolishness she's talkin about?" Vi demanded. "What's she gone and made up them lies for?"

Tillie shuddered. Alvira's arm quaked as a shudder began at Tillie's feet and swept upward. Her shoulders quaked beneath Vi's arm. She raised her cupped hands slowly and clamped them to her face, digging her nails into her cheeks. Whirling, she stumbled toward the back door, tore it open, and slammed it after her. Vi followed, fumbled with the door, finally got it open. Tillie had disappeared in the rain. Slamming the door, she hurried across to the front door and opened it. Tillie was nowhere in sight.

Alvira closed the door and turned wearily back into the silent house. The baby sat near the fireplace playing with a spoon, unconcerned with the problems of those around him. Vi glanced at him, then walked toward Anna, who sat on her bed caressing her bruised head.

"Now, what's this all about, Tillie not havin no period lately?" she demanded.

"I've spoke my piece," Anna muttered. "You heard all I got to say on the matter."

"You'll say more when Will gets back. I'll garntee that much."

"Then jest hold'ye tater and listen at what I tell him."

"You're gettin too big for your britches, if you wore any britches," Vi said. "Your say-so don't hold no water with me. I don't any more believe pore old Tillie's bigged than I believe you're worth shootin."

She turned around and sauntered back to the fireplace, head lowered. Leaning her right forearm against the mantel, she stared thoughtfully down at the red and blue flames. There was a sick fear in her throat salting her taste. Tillie was large. Her stomach did protrude unnaturally for a girl no older than she was. Her nerves were strung too high for her nature. But Vi denied to herself any possibility of Tillie being pregnant. Anna? More than likely, but Tillie, hardly. She just did not fit the type at all. Below such reasoning, however, Vi was afraid to learn the truth. Anna's charge was too rash even for her to have made without cause. And there was another thing she had learned in the few years she had lived—it is often the good and innocent souls like Tillie that lightning strikes first.

Suddenly a new dread curdled the saliva in her throat, and she turned back to the fire. Knowing Will no longer than she had, she could well imagine what his reactions would be to the fight between Anna and Tillie. It would be bad enough if Tillie proved she was innocent, especially for Anna. But if it turned out that Tillie was pregnant, God help them all! She tried to think of some way to avoid telling him, knowing full well there was no way.

She steeled herself to wait for Will's return, and the cold winter rain soughed about the cabin.

6

The rain slacked off around four, and Will came in just at nightfall, his denim jacket and overalls wet as the plumage of a half-drowned crow. Vi had supper on the table waiting for him. She fed the baby at the table, waiting for Will to sit down before serving herself. Anna lay on her back on the bed staring upward. Tillie had not returned, and Vi had put off going for Grandpa John, though she had called him twice from the back porch.

Will slapped his battered hat against the wall, catching it over a peg. Moving stiffly, as though his joints had rusted in the rain, he began to strip off the wet jacket and shirt, letting his overalls drop around his ankles. He hung the two garments on another peg, near the fire, and kicked out of his overalls, hanging them up also. The back and shoulders and leg fronts of his underwear were soaked, clinging to his hard frame. He shuffled closer to the fire, still wearing the heavy brogans. With the darker clothing off, standing there in the grey balbriggan longhandles, he reminded Vi of the crow she had thought about a few moments before, after it had been plucked bare of feathers.

"Goddamn rain," Will muttered to the fire, "if a feller throwd his head up to sneeze, he'd drown before he could duck back down again."

Wisps of steam began to curl up from his underwear. He lowered his head before the flames and extended gnarled hands like some Stone Age fire worshiper. His bald head gleamed whitely. Vi watched him close his eyes and heard him sigh in comfort as he adjusted his loins.

"I got supper a-waitin for'ye," Vi called softly.

"Don't you reckon I can see you got supper a-waitin?" Will said grumpily. "I got to dry out a little tad. Can't you see I'm wetter'n a drowned duck's ass at the bottom of a millpond?"

"It'll be here when you're ready."

After a while, he took his other pair of overalls, faded and patched, from a wall peg and put them on. He plodded over to the table and sat down.

"Still got to feed them damn steers," he grumbled. "I'd bout as soon go to hell with my back broke."

"I done fed the steers for'ye," Vi said, serving herself some potatoes.

He looked at her suspiciously. "I never heard tell of such a thing before this," he growled. "What's gonna happen?"

"I didn't have no way of knowin when you was comin back," Vi explained. "Pore critters was a-lowin to eat."

Will dipped into his plate and began to cram food into his mouth, through with feeding the steers. When he was halfway through his third helping, he threw up his head suddenly. "Where's Pa?" he demanded. "And Till, where's she? That no-count Annie moping on her bed again? Them goddamn, run-about boys might jest as well leave home for good."

"I called Grandpa John twict from the back porch," she said. "I got no idee where Tillie went to."

He stared at her. "That's quare. She ain't never done like this before. When did she leave?"

Alvira swiveled her chair away from the table and set the baby on the floor. "Will, I got a important matter to tell'ye, and I want you to listen and not blow up till I'm done."

His white brow furrowed. "What in God's name you beatin around the bush about?"

"Tillie and Annie had a fight today, and Tillie run off some'ers when I stopped'em."

"What'd she run off for?" Will demanded. "She's not afraid of that no-count Annie."

Vi looked away from him at the anemic white potatoes in the bowl. "Annie accused Tillie of bein bigged," she murmured. "Tillie whooped her."

"Why, godamighty! she ort to a-beat her brains out!" Will swore. He laughed. "What chance has pore Tillie had to git big?"

"Will," Vi said. "Will, listen a minute."

Will shut up, the laugh slipping away. "Well?"

"Tillie didn't say she wasn't big. She flew all to pieces. She went runnin out of here cryin like her pore heart would break."

Will Ward stared at her, his face blank. Vi watched comprehension take hold and possess him, warp the lines of his face gradually, like sunlight breaking through a cloud—except the result here was darkness. She started when he leaped erect, kicking over his chair. She could see his narrow grey eyes light up as he remembered little things, disconnected, concerning Tillie.

"It ain't so!" he yelled. "Goddamn hit to hell, hit ain't so!"

And Vi, looking at his twisted face, knew it was so. In some unreasonable way that would make no sense till the truth was known, Tillie had got herself pregnant. She looked away, at the cold potatoes.

Anna had sat up on the side of the bed, watching Will. He turned his head and saw her. Fists clinched by sides, he pounded across the floor toward her. Anna contracted into a dark wad of fabric, black tangled hair, and white legs. She scurried crab-like backward across the bed and lodged her back in the corner between the wall and the headboard.

"Pa!" she yelled. "Pa, it wasn't my fault. I didn't tell'er to git herself knocked up."

Will staggered to a halt, even with the foot of the bed. Vi could see him sway in indecision. His dirty-white underwear across his stooped shoulders looked snow-white against the dark at the end of the cabin. He whirled in his tracks, pointed his finger at Vi.

"If she's big, I'll kill her!" he roared. "Goddamn her soul, I'll kill her. I don't care what her excuse is. I ain't no goddamn Catlett trash to granddaddy a passel of bastards. And by God, I ain't aimin to put up with hit."

"Now you calm yourself down, Will," Vi warned. "You know good and well you're bound to listen at her. You know you're duty-bound to hear her out."

"I ain't duty-bound to nothin," Will roared. "I ain't duty-bound to a goddamn thing except breathin and paying my taxes and votin Democrat."

The back door swung inward, slammed, and Grandpa John intruded on their sudden quiet. "I was standin jest outside the door, Will," the old man stated, "and I heerd what you said."

"What the hell do I care?" Will growled. "Matt Catlett could a-heard if she'd been a mind to tune up her years."

"This here's a foolish stand you're a-fixin to take toward pore Tillie," the old man pleaded. "Hit's foolish and hit's not fair to her."

"What do'ye want me to do?" Will yelled. He shuffled closer to the white-bearded old man, moving in an arc, and Grandpa John stepped backward, toward the closed door. "Do'ye want me to stick a blue ribbern on her ass cause it worked like it was s'posed to?"

"I want you to lissen at her," old John argued. "I want you to heer her side. Then I'll garntee you won't be mad at her no more. You'll be mad at the guilty party."

Will glowered at his father. Alvira watched the cold light in his grey eyes fade. Watched the gleam of reason reassert itself. But his chin remained outthrust, and his white, wrinkled forehead reminded her of nothing so much as a chiseled flint rock. He sauntered over to the fireplace, stood before it, feet wide-set, and stared down at the licking flames. For over two minutes he stood like that, while the conflict inside the dimly lit cabin remained in balance. Finally he turned.

"Where's the gal now?" he asked, with more control.

"She's out in my place," old John said. "She's out there on my bed a-weepin her pore heart away."

"Well, don't stand there all night. Go fetch her here and let her say her say."

Grandpa John pivoted, yanked the door open, and closed it behind him. He returned shortly, pushing Tillie in front of him. They stood in file, the stooped old man almost concealed by the large girl, who faced Will Ward, only a faceless shadow between her and the flames. Tillie's dark, tangled hair fell about her shoulders and about her lowered face. Tears wet her cheeks, and her hands opened and closed by her hips, opened and closed like the gills of a stranded fish. Her eyes appeared to be focused on the shadow that reared up to judge her.

"It—it wasn't my fault—" Her voice caught on a sob and slanted away to silence.

Will Ward did not speak. Vi got up from the table and crossed to Tillie. She placed a hand on the older girl's shoulder. "Now you just calm down, Tillie, honey," she murmured. "We know it couldn't be your fault. Now you jest slack up on your cryin and tell us calm-like how it happened."

Tillie looked into the face of her stepmother, the child-woman face with the wisdom of compassion staring back out of blue eyes. She looked, and again Vi felt a shudder almost lost deep within the frightened girl. She shuddered that once, and the plump flesh stilled, like a pond surface when the wind drops suddenly. She did not look back at the shadow against the firelight.

"It was that mean old Hill Anderson," she explained softly to Vi, but her voice carried to every niche of the silent cabin. "Pa sent me to fetch him to cut that shoat that's cripple. He was at the barn. He caught me in the cuttin-room and held me. I fit him. Oh, God, how I fit him back. And he couldn't make no headway. He was bad off. He was worse'n a old goat. He had my frock up to my waist, but I had my legs wound round one another, and he couldn't break my holt. And then he threatened Pa. He said he'd fix it so's Pa would lose his little tad of land.

He said he'd get with Old Man Harrison and they'd take it away from Pa. I knowd Pa couldn't stand that, and I knowd he'd manage to steal it somehow. I knowd if Pa lost his little tad of land, it'd finish him up. I couldn't bear to see Pa go through that, so I give in. I thought maybe somethin wouldn't happen after jest one time. But he's a sneakin hound. He waylayed me two more times in the woods. The last time was in July. I couldn't endure watchin Pa lose his little tad of land. It's his lifeblood, might nigh. I jest couldn't endure—"

Her voice broke, her hands flew to her face, and she whirled, burying her face against Vi. The plump, warm flesh began to quake again, shuddering from head to foot, but no sound escaped the open mouth biting into Vi's shoulder.

The cabin was quiet. Grandpa John hung across an invisible wire, good arm dangling. Anna sat coiled in her corner staring sullenly at nothing. The baby was sprawled beneath the table, asleep. And somewhere inside the dark shadow against the firelight, Vi knew that Will Ward absorbed what he had heard and adjusted to it. A spark snapped suddenly in the fireplace, loud as a rifle shot. The front log collapsed and fell, dumping the burning wood into a red heap. The flames leaped high, with new fuel, and a ruby light gushed across the front area of the house. Will Ward had whirled, on guard. Relaxing just as suddenly, he turned back.

One massive shadow quivered against the wall beyond Vi and Tillie, who still stood embraced. Old John was lost in it.

"Git your things off and git some rest," Will said firmly, not calling Tillie by name. "You're bound to be tard. We'll talk this matter out tomorr."

Hearing him, Vi understood that the few words were Will's concession to reason, to sympathy for his daughter and her plight—as much concession as Tillie Ward would ever get in this world. And Vi understood further that the meager response did not result from any cruelty in Will as an individual, but resulted from the very nature of his stock and way of life. And as Tillie softened against her like a relaxing hand, Vi sensed that Tillie also understood and accepted the compromise.

Alvira floated in a half stupor through the long night and heard—or felt or sensed—Will pacing the cabin floor, pacing back and forth, backward and forward on naked feet, a quilt draped about his head and shoulders. His footfalls drummed on her awareness with the persistence and rhythm of a cat's padded paws, as she fought to escape into sleep. Far away, beyond the reach of her understanding, she heard Van and Dan come in and gather in hushed conference with Will. She tossed up her black head and squinted through salty lids and then floated back into her stupor. In her brief glance, she had seen them hunkered on the hearth in an arc about the coals. They were muttering and grunting, their voices low and guttural, their hands flickering, slicing, stabbing their own silent language as old as man. When she thought about it later, she remembered that the huge fireplace had reminded her of the rocky mouth of a cave opening on outer darkness, against which the three men and the dying fire were projected.

Toward dawn the two boys climbed the ladder to their pallet, and Will quieted down. Vi slipped into sleep, feeling somehow more secure. She awoke suddenly to a quiet cabin. Sunlight knifed through the cracks of the window shutters. She reared up in bed and stared about her. Tillie, Anna, and the baby still slept in the bed nearby. She cocked her head. The boys were quiet in the loft above, and Will was nowhere about. She climbed from bed, slipped on her shoes, and hurried across the cabin. The fire had died down. She piled wood on it and soon had it blazing again.

Working swiftly, she had breakfast on the table before she called the girls. They came to the table, Tillie carrying the baby, and sat down. Grandpa John came in rubbing his eyes and unfolded into his chair. Everyone was quiet, apparently remembering the night before. Vi called the boys but got no answer. They ate in silence, mostly, and Alvira kept wondering how it got so late before she woke up, and where Will had got to. She wished Will had some kind of clock so she could tell what time it was.

Vi was almost through eating when she stopped suddenly, a bite halfway to her mouth. She went stiff. She lowered the fork to her plate, remembering the fireplace in the night like the rocky mouth of a cave against which the three men were outlined as they muttered and growled. Shoving back her chair, she got to her feet and crossed the cabin. She climbed halfway up the ladder and peeped into the loft. The covers of the pallet were thrown back. The boys were gone. She backed slowly down the ladder, a rung at a time, her head high in thought.

She walked back to the fireplace, feeling the eyes of Grandpa John and the girls watching her. Leaning her right forearm against the mantel, Vi pressed her forehead against it, staring at the flames. Something was wrong. Somewhere there was a clue, but she could not quite grasp it. Then she threw up her head, staring. The big musket was missing from its pegs above the mantel.

She spun toward the table. "Grandpa!" she called, "Will and the boys has gone for Hill Anderson."

The old man dropped his fork into his plate. Tillie gasped, whirled. Anna did not miss a bite. "How'ye know that?" Grandpa John asked.

"When the boys came in last night, they talked a spell in front of the fireplace. The boys is not upstairs. Will's musket is missin from its pegs."

"God help us," the old man sighed. "I'd a-never thought he was that addled."

"They left about sunrise," Anna muttered through a mouth half full of food. "I knowd when they left."

"Why didn't you wake somebody?" Vi demanded.

"Cause it wasn't none of my business, that's why." She poked another forkful into her mouth.

Vi turned away, ran to the wall beside the front door, and snatched her coat from its peg. She worked her hands into the sleeves, past torn linings, tore open the door and slammed it after her. She headed down Stud Branch at a half run, her shoes sinking into the soggy path. Muddy water swirled down the flooded branch. Raindrops sparkled by the millions on dead grassblades and weeds as far as she could see. Beneath the bright sun, they almost blinded her, forcing her to squint ahead of her splashing feet.

She slowed suddenly. She heard them before she saw them.

She heard their roaring laughter, their shouted remarks before she passed the loop of alders and saw them dancing around the spring. Will Ward held his musket by the barrel, the stock on the ground, and stamped around it, shouting through gasps of laughter. Van dipped water from the spring with the gourd and threw it into the air, and they all crouched gleefully as it rained back on them in cold globules and sheets. Dan stamped the soggy meadow with his right foot, howling his mirth, splattering gobs of mud all over himself, Will, and Van. Vi stopped staring at the strange ceremony.

"Did'ye see his face?" Will Ward yelled. "Did'ye see his face when I tuck his nuttin knife and tar of tartar can and bent over him? Great godamighty! he'd druther lose his brains than his balls."

Vi came on up to them and halted again, hands on hips. "Will!" she called. "Will Ward!"

They did not seem to hear her. Van dipped another gourdful of water and slung it upward. A blob of cold water, falling back, struck Vi on her neck, ran down her spine, chilling her.

She waited till she caught all three of them at the bottom of an instant's silence. "Will!" she shouted at the top of her voice.

Will Ward straightened up and squinted at her as though she were a stranger. Van stopped and placed the gourd back on the rock where it belonged. Dan stopped stamping and stood erect, feet planted in the middle of the shallow mudpuddle he had tramped out in the grass.

"What manner of monkeyshine are you fools a-cuttin, out here in the middle of the broad-open daylight?" Vi demanded.

"We jest had a little visit with Hill Anderson," Will said, "and it turned out a whole heap different from what we aimed to do when we set out for his place."

"Yeah, a whole hell of a heap different," Van said, then threw back his head and opened his red mouth to the sun as he roared with new laughter.

"We was a-aimin to trim him," Dan said, "but the slick bastard laid there on his back lookin at us acrosst his big, naked paunch and clean talked us out of it."

"Will somebody stop talkin in riddles long enough to straighten me out on what happened?" Vi said.

Will stopped laughing and leaned on the antique musket, thoughful, as he gathered his words. Then he told her what happened at Hill Anderson's place, as he told Grandpa John and the girls later, and as he repeated it, with more and more elaboration, for years afterward—but never to anyone outside the family. What had happened to Tillie was a disgrace he could not allow anyone else to know. Although Tillie was not at fault, had even sacrificed herself for him, is was nonetheless a disgrace. But nothing could keep him from telling and re-telling his own folks what happened to Hill Anderson. All he needed was an audience of one.

"I come down the road to the barn about the time he was a-feedin his stock," Will told Vi. "I got him to talkin in the driveway. Then Van and Dan slipped out of the field pines on the side of the ridge and come up behind him. Van had the musket. You ort to a-seen Hill's face when he turned around and seen them two big yearlins behind him and this here big old musket.

" 'What you fellers up to?' he ast. His face turned as white as whey, all sept them two little red horns.

" 'You sonofabitch,' I say, 'you raped my gal and bigged her, and we're aimin to fix'ye up so's you won't harm no more womernfolk.'

"Well, sir, he denied it up one side and down the t'other, but we marched him into the cuttin-room. Dan shoved him back'ards on his back acrosst some sacks of cottonmeal and yanked his britches down. Van poked the barrel of the musket agin his head, and he laid there quiet-like, but he was tremblin like a dog a-shittin peach seeds on shingles. I got his big trimmin knife off of a shelf and a can of tar of tartar to disinfect the cut, and he danged nigh kicked the bucket.

" 'Will! You-all ain't shore-nuff aimin to cut me, are'ye? Not *shore-nuff?*'

" 'Shore-nuff as hell's hot, I aim to,' I say, and I kneeled down and reched for his ballocks.

"Well, sir, he busted out bawlin like a little bitty gal-chile. 'Please don't nut me, Will,' he pled, 'and I'll do anything'ye say. Anything! Jest anything!' he begged.

" 'You ain't got nothin I can use,' I say to him, 'nothin but these big fat fambly jools of your'n.'

"When I grabbed a fistful of his sack and teched the knife blade to hit, he yelped tell you could a-heard him clean to Goshen. Then I got right quiet and thoughtful, but I give him a squeeze that made his eyeballs roll like marvels.

" 'If you don't do this, I'll fix it so's you can git your pa's land back, Will, most of it,' he begged. 'I swear to God, I'll fix it so's you can git ever scrap of the land he held back, from your place clean to the Big Road.'

"Well, sir, that stopped me. I stopped and got thoughtful-like. 'How can you arrange that,' I say, 'and me without no cash handy?'

" 'It's easy,' he says real fast, like he was hurtin to git it out. 'I'll sell you two mules on credit. I'll talk Old Man Harrison out of sellin'ye the land on time and let you work it out over the years, haulin lumber and tanbark for'im.'

"Well, that stopped me cold. I turned his cods a-loose, and he sighed like a whore a-leavin church. What he said made good sense straight off.

" 'Go ahead and nut him, Pa,' Dan says. 'He's jest a-trickin 'ye.'

" 'How bout Tillie?' I ask. 'I ain't aimin to have her a-droppin no bastards at my house so's folks can pint their finger at me. And I can't afford to send her off nowheres.'

"Old Hill Anderson set up and yanked up his britches. 'I got a aint that lives at Reynolds,' he says, fast like water runnin downhill. 'I'll send her there and pay her keep tell the youngun's borned and she can go to work.'

"Well, I thought that over, and I stood up. 'Hit's a bargain, Hill,' I say. 'But you jest recollect this. Them's my balls you got, totin around now. If you back out on me, I'll fetch my boys back up here and collect'em, jest as shore as Hell's dry.'

"He jumped up and fastened his belt, happy as a toadfrog in

a fly factory. 'Oh, I swear. You can count on it,' he says. 'You jest wait and see. The land's as good as your'n.'

"And that's what happened at Hill Anderson's place," Will Ward laughed. "And now I'm aimin to have my land after all, it looks like."

Vi shook her head sadly. "And pore old Tillie pays the cost."

Will looked at her, his face hard. "That was already done," he argued. "It was jest a matter of tradin for Hill Anderson's fambly jools. It was way yander past havin anything to do with Tillie. Tillie was already tuck care of. Her bed was made long time ago."

7

WILL BORROWED COUSIN BILL'S BUGGY and hauled Tillie to Coleman's Ford the next week. She embraced Vi briefly when she was leaving but said nothing. Anna had gone off somewhere to hide after she learned when Tillie was leaving. Tillie held the baby close and cried over it for half a minute, then give it back to Alvira and turned away, climbing into the buggy. She waved to Grandpa John and the two boys, who squatted at the woodpile, watching her. Van and Dan threw up their hands casually. Old John struggled to his feet and hobbled to the smokehouse, disappearing inside.

"I'll see you-all," Tillie called.

"Take care of yourself," Vi called back.

She watched as Will drove off, carrying Tillie out of the yard forever. He put her on the train at Coleman's Ford, he told Vi later, and gave her the ten dollars Hill Anderson had sent as the first installment on his sixth or seventh or eighth child out of wedlock. There was no sure way of knowing how many Tillie's would make. In that manner, Tillie Ward left Stud Branch, wearing the clothes on her back and carrying her few other belongings wadded in the bottom of a flour sack. Alvira and Will talked about it when he got back, in the afternoon. She dreaded to think about doing without Tillie. It would make her life harder to bear.

"They was a time," Will growled, "when a Ward wouldn't a-lost a good hand to a prick like Hill Anderson."

Will went to see Old Man Harrison the day after Tillie left, and found that Hill had kept his word, at least up to a point. Harrison was willing to sell the land between his eastern boundary, along Tadpole Branch, and Cousin Bill's western boundary, along the Ridge Road—but not all the way to the Big Road, on the south, as Hill had promised. Greer, Harrison's youngest son, the old man explained (and Will repeated it that night at the supper table) was planning to build him a house on the south spur of West Mountain, overlooking the Big Road. Will Ward's southern boundary would have to end on a straight line three hundred yards short of the Big Road.

"Well, damn that Hill Anderson!" Van exploded, mouth half full of corn bread. "That's jest one ball's worth of land. Let's go back, Pap, and cut one of'em out."

Will Ward was thoughtful. "Nope," he said, finally. "Nope, the way I see it, Hill tried to keep his word. He wouldn't chance makin me mad. No, I'll jest have to settle for what I can git. That section along the road's mostly red clay and rock. Washed out bad, too. Nope, he can keep his nuts for my part of the bargain, but he'd better not cross me no furder."

"How about the mules, Pap?" Dan asked. "Did he say when'ye can git your new mules?"

Will leaned back, belched, and crammed his horny hands inside his overalls, adjusting his loins. He looked at the ceiling, using the silence to goad their curiosity. Watching him, Vi understood what he was up to. She was beginning to understand him, to see through him, but he would never know it. It would not do to let him know she saw through him. She did not belong to him yet, inside. Her flesh was his, but inside, she still kept at arm's length and could not move closer, even if she wanted to. Sometimes she despaired of ever being close to him.

"I'm aimin to take the steers tomorr," he said, as though he had invented stock trading. "Hill's takin them for loggin steers on a pair of buck mules. Harrison gits the steers. I'll fetch the mules back with me and start haulin next week."

Toab and Fred, two big red mules, became a part of the Ward landscape, and with them came a second-hand wagon on which Will would haul lumber and tanbark. The steers had been allowed to run free in the pasture when not at work. Will and the boys quickly threw up a stable for the two mules. Although it was made of slabs and scrap lumber, it protected the animals from the worst weather. And more important, it satisfied Will Ward's need to have something resembling a barn. In his estimation, no man who was worth a pinch of salt in a windstorm would allow his mules to stamp around in the pasture in the snow and sleet and rain.

Watching him covertly, some time after he had acquired the mules, Vi analyzed the difference in the way he walked, the way he worked, in his attitude toward his narrow world. In the chilly twilight, he whistled loudly about the shabby barn, although he had just spent fourteen hours at hard labor. Harnessing the mules in the cold gloom of dawn, he sang "Bringing in the Sheaves," and his lusty voice carried across the valley and echoed back from the hollow between West and Fox mountains. Vi could imagine the Catletts aroused, turning on their rickety beds or on their ragged pallets and cursing Will Ward's big mouth. He seemed to walk more erect, pulling back at the heavy lumps that tugged at his groins.

He's forty-two, she thought. Almost forty-two. All his life, he's been pushin logs uphill and watchin them roll back. Now that he's got decent tools to work with, for a change, I hope his luck holds out awhile.

"I'm plumb sorry I didn't git that land all the way to the Big Road," Will swore loudly, one night at supper, his face washed by the pale light of the kerosene lamp. "I'd a-built me a house where that looky sonofabitch Greer's gonna build his'n, and I could a-seen everthing pass by. But goddamn, a man can't have everthing he wants in this world, don't make no difference how hard he works at it or deserves it. But I can still build the house

I planned on the side of East Ridge. And by God, I'm aimin to start haulin lumber there and stackin it, jest as soon as I can talk it over with old Harrison."

Watching his proud, grinning face, his flint-white bald dome crowned with an arc of whispy auburn hair flecked with grey, Vi could gauge the change taking place within his mind. He was adjusting rapidly to his new possessions. He had worked hard for them, had earned them, and—by God—deserved them. His memory was already by-passing knowledge of Tillie's predicament and the precious nuggets Hill Anderson had bartered for the progress of Will Ward.

Through the rest of January, February, and March, Will hauled daily except Sundays, Van and Dan alternating as his helper. A portion of the money earned went automatically to pay on the land and on the mules and wagon. But enough cash came in so that Will, for the first time, had a little extra to spend. He bought new overalls for himself and the boys, and cloth for a red dress for Anna. He bought Alvira a new ready-made coat and material for a blue dress, but when Vi hinted at a sewing machine to make the things with, that was "a hoss of a different color."

"What the hell you think I am, a banker?" Will growled. "Jest cause a little tad of money's a-comin in, don't think I can stock this house like some goddamn Yadkin River mansion."

So Vi was compelled to carry the cloth to Cousin Bill's house and make the dresses on Rosa's machine. But she was a seamstress born, and the garments turned out well. In fact, they were the "purtiest goddamn frocks seen around Holkirk Church in a coon's age," according to Will, who ordinarily doled out blood as quick as a compliment. Even Anna was humbled by the gift from her father and the care Vi had put into making it, a humility which lasted more than three days.

In mid-March, they butchered the crippled hog and sold it. Minus the deformed hams, it came to eight dollars and thirty-three cents. Vi tied the cash in a handkerchief and hoarded it until she could add enough for some kind of cookstove.

One evening Will drove into the yard singing at the top of his voice and unloaded several long, wide planks, leaning them upright against the eaves of the smokehouse. Vi, passing by with the empty slopbucket, paused to stare. Will and old John were in an animated conference near the mules' heads, and strain as she might, she could not overhear what was said. She knew better than to interrupt because she knew Will Ward did not hold with mixing men's business with women's business. It was a part of his raising.

But the plans were no secret, at least for long. Grandpa John worked busily for a week with saw, plane, tonguer, and groover. Vi watched the new wagon-bed take shape in slow stages, as the old man's good left hand worked its art on the formless wood. His Lazy Susans and cupboards and center tables were made with more care and more skill than any two-handed artisan could have wrought or would have wrought, lacking the incentive of handicap; therefore the wagon-bed was a masterpiece of its kind. The green paint Will brought back from Northboro added the finishing touch to near perfection.

And so it came to pass that John William Ward, for the first time in forty-two years, drove his own team hitched to his own wagon, riding in his own wagon-bed, and hauled his family to Holkirk Church on the third Sunday in March. True, he did not have a fancy spring seat, as Cousin Bill had, but—by God—split-bottomed chairs were "way yander hell and gone better settin" than any wooden seat, springs or no springs. He sat on the left, next to the brake line, Alvira on his right holding the baby. Anna sat in her chair behind them, stiff and proud in her red dress. They drove into the church grounds early, in order that Will might find a place for his wagon as close to the front steps as possible so as many people as possible would notice or could notice his new wagon-bed and team and wagon. Vi did not need any book-learning to figure out why he came early and why he stopped the wagon where he did.

And the church-goers did notice it. They gathered around it after the meeting was over, pleased with its construction, happy for Will Ward and his new possessions and his pride in owning them. Vi watched them examine it, heads aslant, and touch it like happy children, laughing with Will, happy that he was happy, without envying one who had worked hard enough to deserve it. And another stage of her education was past, the growing understanding of the hill folk and their outlook on life.

And with her growing knowledge came a growing affection for them. But she included Will Ward as only one of the many, a member of the folk group. Her acceptance of him as her mate had little to do with Will Ward as an individual. When he came to her, deep in the silent nights, she still put him out of her mind as an individual, as Will Ward, one specific man. It was easy in the darkness. However, there was no bitterness in her attitude. She had rejected bitterness months ago, after walking her first mile, and then walking back.

On the way home that Sunday, out of a happy silence, Will tossed up his head and squinted at Vi. "Did you notice how pleased Preacher May looked when he seen my wagon-bed up clost?" he asked.

"Yeah," Vi nodded, although she had paid no attention to the preacher. "Yeah, he looked like he thought it was about the purtiest wagon-bed he ever set eyes on."

Will was thoughtful again, a half smile on his lips. "You know, by God—by gracious—I think I'll ast him for dinner one of these here Sundays. Been aimin to for some time and never got around to it. I could buy a chicken off of Cousin Bill." He wheeled on her, accusingly. "Can you cook chicken and dumplins?"

Vi laughed. "I can make the softest, tenderest dumplins you ever set teeth in. Looks like you already forgot eatin'em down at the Watson place."

Will looked back at the mules' swaying rumps. "Damn if I didn't forget. That seems like a long time ago. Seems like you and me been married longer than I was to Bell."

Although Vi could have taken the remark wrong, she knew it was a compliment of sorts and accepted it as such. What he had meant, she decided, was that he had adjusted to her and had found her acceptable as a good wife. Coming from Will, she suspected it was praise as high as she would ever hear in this world.

"It don't look to me like folks would have to wait for a preacher to have chicken and dumplins," Anna complained behind them. "I can't see where preachers earn chicken and dumplins more'n anybidy else."

"The trouble with you is you listen at Old Scratch a-whisperin under your bed," Will growled. "You don't look up at the face of Godamighty in the clouds and hear his voice in the thunderstorm and harken unto him."

"I shore don't," Anna giggled. "When a thunderstorm hits, I crawl under the bed with Old Scratch."

Will turned in his chair, frowning. "We'll have no belittlin of God in my wagon, young lady," he barked. "Or I'll put'ye out to walk. He's liable to strike my new wagon-bed out of a clear sky, you talkin like that."

"It ain't likely in March," Anna said, before lapsing into sullen silence.

Anna was much better at helping with the housework after Tillie left than she had been before. She was intelligent and reasonable enough to understand that routine work had to be done and that Alvira could not possibly do it all. With little grumbling she pitched in and did the jobs Vi alotted her, tasks like changing the baby, making the beds, and washing the dishes. Vi was certain that one of the reasons she co-operated so well was to prevent Will from becoming involved and thus ending up with more work than Vi would insist on. From early February to early April she did well enough so that Vi had little or no complaint, though she was not as efficient as Tillie had been, and never would be.

Around the end of March, Vi received a postal card from her father telling her that he and her mother were coming for a visit on the following Saturday and would stay until Monday. Vi was both excited and perturbed. She carried scrub dirt from the S-curve in the Big Road below Lake Harrison's house and scrubbed the cabin floor. She also scoured the pots and pans and the skillet and did what little she could to improve the appearance of the Ward household. But after half a day of hard work, she gave up, defeated.

She might have saved her time and energy. Henry and Amanda Matlock rode into the yard Saturday afternoon, in Cousin Bill's buggy, grim-faced, already prepared in part for what they would see. Henry Matlock stepped down from the buggy and embraced Vi briefly, dark eyes staring across her head, from the cabin to the other buildings. Her mother covered her face with her hands, refusing to move from her seat. Will Ward watched them balefully from the stable on the slope above. Cousin Bill seemed to find interest in a passing cloud. Vi's breasts felt like two hard, ingrown weights dragging her inside herself.

Henry Matlock, tall and lean as a rawhide whip, patted her on the back with gnarled hand, then climbed back into the buggy. He motioned back the way they had come. Vi stood wide-eyed, tears seeping over her lids, and watched them ride back up the spur of East Ridge. She inhaled with a catch in her throat, then swallowed it.

"If I'd a-knowd they wasn't goin to stay for supper," she muttered, turning away, "I wouldn't a-gone to all that trouble cleanin the place up."

In early April, spring switched overnight from lingering, blustery March to the blue-eyed skies and fluffy puff clouds of premature May. Barefoot weather hurried northward, leaping the Bushy Mountains, spanning hills and dales with seven-league strides, to leave giant footprints filled with puddles of violets. As the weather warmed, Anna's energy waned, until she reached the point by mid-May where she had been before Tillie left, lying around, arguing, doing little or nothing to help. During corn-planting time in April, she had watched the baby and had helped at mealtime while Vi went out and dropped seed corn.

Between planting and hauling lumber, Will Ward did not have enough time to know or care about what went on around the house. He was up before dawn and busy until after nightfall working hard, but singing or whistling as he worked. The long hours, the humping, measuring-worm pace of his progress had so far failed to impress on him that decades could pass before he began to emerge from beneath his mountain of debt. But he had his land, part of the old Ward holdings, and what else could a human being long for in this world?

One day in April, Anna went over West Mountain to the post office for mail, but forgot to give Vi the letter from Tillie for almost a week. Alvira was so angry with her she almost boxed her ears, but held back, realizing that a slap would end in a fight, and she had no desire to lower herself to that level if she could avoid it.

"Why didn't you just save it till Christmastime?" Vi snapped.

The address scribbled on the envelope was in hard pencil and almost illegible. The letter itself, on rough tablet paper, was no easier to read. Vi took it out in the sunshine where she could see it better. It was brief and simple.

> Deer ma and folks—
> The babie come on Marsh twelft. Its doin fine. Its a bigun. Didnt have no trouble hadlie a tall. Miz Baker is good to us. She is goin to keep babie, and I goin in seegrit factorie real soon. Rite me sometime if you got time. I wisht I could see youall.
>
> yours trulie,
> Tilly

Vi sat down on the porch and stared out across the green valley. "I do declare!" she mused. "That is the strangest thing."

"What did she say?" Anna asked from the doorway. She did not sound interested.

"She had her baby March the twelfth," Vi said, distantly. "Called the baby *it* and didn't say where it was a boy or girl."

"Up in these parts," Anna said, "we ain't that fancy. A youngun is *it* tell its about a year old. What difference does it make?"

That night at supper, when Vi told Will about the letter, Will stopped chewing and stared at her. "Goddamn, that's quare!" he growled. "Looks like she could a-let its onliest grandpa know where it was a boy or gal."

Anna laughed. "That do make you a grandpa, don't it, Pa?"

Will glowered at her. "You find somethin funny about me bein a grandpa?"

"I was jest thinkin," she said, "when Vi—when Ma—has her first youngun—and it's bound to happen—you'll be a new grandpa and a new pa, and Grandpa John will be grandpa to one of'em and great-grandpa to the other'n. Your youngun'll be younger'n Tillie's, and yit it'll be Tillie's youngun's aint or uncle."

Will stared at her, blinking owlishly. Vi could see he was trying to follow Anna's reasoning and was momentarily befuddled. She saw the shallow smile on Grandpa John's lips as he watched Will. Van and Dan were too busy eating to listen.

"If you'd use your noggin for workin as good as you do for figurin out damnfool kinfolk riddles," he grumbled, "Vi wouldn't have to do her work and your'n too."

Anna tossed her black mane, a reaction which to her meant, perhaps, kiss my ass, but she knew better than to answer because she was well inside Will Ward's reach.

In May, Will's hauling fell off considerably while the Wards plowed and hoed the thirty acres of upland corn. It was a family affair. Even Anna was made to stumble down fresh green corn rows in the hot sunshine while chopping at the cloddy hillside. The baby was left alone to play on a pallet at the end of the rows. Vi, Anna, and one of the boys hoed while Will and the other boy plowed the corn, each cultivator pulled by one mule. From the very first, Vi noticed the attitude Will had toward working the corn, and she made a remark about it. But she never made the same mistake again.

She learned that Will hoed the corn three times and plowed it five, regardless of the condition of each field. She had assumed the object was to eliminate weeds and briers until the corn grew tall enough so there was no danger of it being choked out. Some of the fields were, she discovered, much more weedy, more ready to produce briers than others. One small field was as clean as the clay yard. But Will did not choose between them. The clean field was hoed three times just as the weedy fields were, and if he did not find hoe marks around every hill of corn, he raised holy hell with the offender. His pa and his grandpa had—by God—hoed corn three times and plowed it five, even without gooseneck hoes, and there was no other "earthful" way to do it. But there was more to it than this, Vi decided. She decided, after thinking about it from time to time, that working the corn in this manner was a sort of ceremony as well as a method of cultivation. God created the earth to grow corn on, in addition to a few other incidental plants. It was a known fact that corn grew and produced with the precise amount of hoeings and plowings. What would happen to the corn without this ritual was not a known fact. Ergo, by God: Corn had to be hoed three times and plowed five in spite of hell or high water—or lumber piled up in old Harrison's yards higher than a mountain's rump waiting to be hauled to the train at Coleman's Ford.

"Will," Vi said one morning, "that little field down there on the side of East Ridge below where you aim to build your house is not too weedy. Looks like all a body would need to do is go over it onct or twict and chop out the few weeds. They ain't a dozen in the whole field. Nettles and mollypop vines is all."

"Jesus Christ almighty!" Will blazed. He yanked off his black hat and slapped it against a plow handle in amazement and disgust. "Who ever heard tell of a bidy choppin out weeds and not hoein corn? Hoein means saftenin the dirt up around the cornstalk and diggin fresh dirt up around it. Godamighty, womern! Corn's got to be hoed three times. That's the way God aimed for it to be done clean back to Eden, and I ain't a human bein to piss up his works. I'd end up with enough nubbins to reach from here to Cubie."

Vi opened her mouth to argue, glanced at his bald, flint-hard head, studied his grey eyes and set face. Then she turned away. "Just like talkin back at a rock wall," she muttered as she walked away, carrying her hoe on her shoulder.

One day late in May, Alvira carried a bag of dried pokeberry roots over the mountains to Doc Ellis's store. She was trying to add to the hog money whenever she could find time so she could buy some kind of cookstove, but it was growing painfully slow. It was a task to stoop over the skillet and pans before the hot fireplace, especially now that warm weather had arrived. After a long day's work hoeing corn and after milking and her other chores, kneeling before the fireplace added the final agony to a backbreaking day. She felt almost as though she wore a yoke on which was piled half the burdens of the farm, and had to heave it aloft each day she arose from bed.

Bessie Ellis was dusting shelves with a feather duster when Vi walked in, stooped with her awkward load. Letting it swing carefully to the floor, Vi straightened up and leaned backward against her cramped back. "Whew-w!" she sighed, "I know how a mule feels totin corn to the mill."

"Well, howdy, Vi," Bessie Ellis greeted. "You still tryin to get enough money together to buy a cookstove?"

"Yes, I am," Vi nodded. "And I'll keep a-tryin to till I get one. After that, I reckon it'll be somethin else. Maybe a sewin machine."

"It's a shame Will Ward can't take care of household articles," Bessie observed, "seein as how he's haulin regular when he's not farmin."

"Will's got land sickness," Vi answered. "Ain't nothin from now on gonna come ahead of buyin that land or takin care of the team that makes payin for it likely."

"By the way," Bessie said in a different tone, looking at her feather duster, "a letter come through the post office from Tillie lately. How come she up and left home so all of a sudden?"

Vi was caught off guard. "Why, why—" she stuttered, examining her calloused hands. "Why, she got a chance to go to work down at Reynolds. Lots of folks from up in around here are goin down there to work in the backer factory."

Bessie looked straight at her. "I never would a-picked Tillie for the goin kind. I would a-bet that hateful Annie would a-left home way yander before Tillie left."

"Well," Vi mused aloud, "folks don't always turn out just zactly like you figure they will ever time."

Bessie turned her back on her, dusting the tops of some snuff glasses. "It's a quare thing to me," she said over her shoulder, "that *you*'re not big yet. I would a-bet Will Ward would have you big in a week."

Vi looked at her feet. She licked her lips. She figured in the first place it was none of Bessie Ellis's business nor anyone else's whether she was with child or not. In the second place, it was not the sort of thing she could discuss freely with just anybody.

"I don't know how you know where I'm big or not," she finally said, firmly. "I jest been married four months. Most usually a woman don't hardly show in four months."

"Well, in your case," Bessie said, "there's nothin to show yet. Things like that get around."

When she thought about it later, Vi recalled that Bessie had not just casually asked about Tillie, and she wondered if it was the storekeeper's way of hinting at a connection between having babies and Tillie leaving. It could have been her sly way of telling Vi that she knew why Tillie left home. Vi thought of mentioning the conversation to Will, then decided not to for fear that he would raise some kind of hell.

But the remarks did start her thinking about herself for a change. Up until that time she had been too busy or too preoccupied to think about the possibility of pregnancy. Although she knew it had to come sooner or later, so far she had not worried about it. But for some reason, after the talk with Bessie, she started checking herself, started listening to herself, as though by listening she could hear the first impact of conception, although she had only a vague idea as to what caused it. And behind her dread was the old feeling of capture. She understood without admitting it that pregnancy would be one more shackle holding her to Will Ward—a knowledge that refused to concede that there was little hope of escape anyway.

During the cultivating season in May and June, Anna had been kept too busy between corn rows to do much revolting. The exhausting work drained most of the resentment out of her during the week, leaving only Sundays for any kind of freedom. And she began to make the most of them sometime late in May, by refusing to go to church with Will and Alvira. Actually, it was a matter of declining rather than refusing because neither parent insisted that Anna go with them.

What worried Vi was not that she did not go to church. It was her running around, her disappearances until late in the evenings. Will did not pay much attention to it at first. So long as she was up bright and early Monday mornings with a hoe in her hands, he was not especially concerned with what she did on Sundays. But Vi was concerned because she could see trouble sneaking up Stud Branch like a hungry fox.

One Sunday evening around eight-thirty, Vi was carrying a bucket of water from the well when Anna came striding up the path along the branch, her red dress almost black in the moonless gloom. She and Vi intercepted each other just short of the front yard. Anna staggered to a halt and threw up an arm, startled.

"Who is it?" she called. "You scart me half to death."

"It's me," Vi said. She set the bucket down. "I want to talk to you a minute."

"Talk!" Anna said gaily. "Talk! Talk! Talk! I'm all years—Maw."

"Where you runnin around to all day long Sundays till a way in the nighttime?" Vi paused. "It don't look good, a girl your age. And it can't bring you to no good end."

"A whistlin womern and a crowin hen always comes to some bad end," Anna chanted. She began to whistle.

"Where do you go?" Vi insisted, moving closer in the gloom. Anna was a darker outline against the dark silhouette of East Ridge. "Who are you foolin around with?"

"It ain't no Catlett," Anna laughed. "Now don't you think I'm a nice gal?"

"It's got to stop!" Vi snapped. "This here traipsin around till all hours is got to stop. You'll just bring trouble down on our heads."

Anna leaned toward her, thrust her face close to Vi's. "You try and stop me—moth-er dear!"

Alvira swung at her with an open hand. Anna was quick. She leaped back, ducked around Vi, and ran toward the house, gobs of laughter flung like clots of dung back over her shoulder.

Alvira stood there in the darkness trembling with anger. But she was too practical to stay angry long. She picked up the bucket and hurried across the yard, climbed the steps, and entered the cabin. Late as it was for him, Will still sat by the table scanning a songbook, a tunefork clutched in his right hand. Anna was sitting on her bed taking off her shoes. Vi carried the water to the cooking table and set it down. She turned, glanced toward Anna, and opened her mouth to tell Will what had happened outside. Then she changed her mind. If he was not concerned, why should she shoulder this burden too? She walked to the front door and leaned against the doorjamb, staring off down through the darkness, watching the fireflies—lightning bugs—winking in the night like fallen stars.

They began to eat out of the garden in May—the large garden Vi had insisted on, robbing Will of a quarter acre of good corn land. First it was young spring onions, followed by spring onions cut up with leaf lettuce, hot pork grease poured over them. A little later it was garden peas. Vi made a white sauce with flour, in which they were cooked with dumplings, and Will ate over a quart. The only reason he stopped was because the bowl containing the peas was sopped clean with a bread crust. Another spring specialty of Vi's was wild "sallet." She picked dandelion leaves, plantain leaves, cress—called creesie by Vi—and pokeberry leaves, and boiled them together until tender, then fried the "sallet" in pork grease long enough to add flavor. Will wondered why the hell Bell had never thought of that.

After corn was laid by in June, Will returned to hauling, through the heat of late June and the blazing days of July and

August. Van and Dan helped him, sometimes alternating, sometimes both going along on the same trip. And during this period, with no field work to demand her time, Anna began to slip off during weekdays and stay gone for hours. Actually, it was not a matter of slipping so much as walking brazenly away when Vi's back was turned. They had a violent argument about it in early August, and Vi stopped just short of taking her by the hair and shaking her until her nose bled. She reported the trouble to Will, but he only threatened Anna from across the cabin. He was too weary from hauling and too full of his toilsome job to worry about Anna's behavior. He did not need her in the fields at the moment, and beyond that, his concern dwindled out.

One Friday in late August, Vi started over the mountain to Ellis's store to buy some sugar. When she sat down on top of the mountain to rest, she discovered she had left back at the house the handkerchief in which her money was tied. She turned around and made her way back down the steep slope, rather than ask Bessie Ellis to charge it.

She had left Anna at home with the baby and intended to try to call her from near the base of the mountain and ask her to meet her with the money. She remembered that Grandpa John had gone with Will to pick out some plank for a cupboard he planned to make. As she came down through the thin fringe of trees along the bottom of the slope, she could glimpse the house through the foliage, and saw that the back door had been closed.

"Plague-gone her!" Vi muttered. "She's gone and run off some'ers and tuck that pore chile with her. Shorely she wouldn't leave it there all by itself."

She crossed the small cornfield below the garden, passed the smokehouse, and stepped up on the narrow back porch. She stopped, listening. She had caught a peculiar sound from somewhere, but it was not repeated. She relaxed, crossed to the back door, pulled the latch thong, and pushed the door open on silent leather hinges.

The first thing she saw was the baby, who stood holding on to a chair near the fireplace and staring toward the back of the cabin, a look of wonderment wrinkling his infant face. The next thing she heard was the sound, much louder. She stepped past the door and stopped, staring, her mouth dropping open in shock.

Anna lay on her back on the hard cabin floor, her dress up around her waist. She was being pounded frantically by a black-haired man whose dirty overalls were lumped about his brogans. Neither of them was aware of anything but each other, so lost were they in their fornication. Anna's eyes were open, her eyeballs rolled back showing almost all white. Saliva drooled from her gaping mouth. Her fingers were a cat's claws against the back of the man's dirty blue shirt. Only her face, her hands, and her long white legs were in view.

Vi's first sensation was one of disgust, followed by reaction without plan. She seized a nearby chair and swung it above her head. Just as the man was dropping in a frantic thrust, she struck him in the hairy white rump with the heavy weapon. The momentum of the blow added to his own, drove the man down with cruel force. He yelled in pain and surprise. Anna yelled too, kicking high with her knees.

The man whirled to a seated position, yanked at his overalls, staring up at Vi, who was swinging the chair again. He yelled in fear, swiveled to his knees, and ran toward the door on them, covering the ten feet like a legless midget before he remembered he had two good feet. He lurched upward as Vi's chair missed, and charged from the cabin, his windmilling arms trying to work his galluses over his shoulders. Vi stared after Tom Dugan as he disappeared from view.

Her pause was only momentary. She dropped the chair and snatched up the broom leaning against the wall, a bundle of tight-bound broomsage. Vi turned back toward Anna, who had whirled onto her hands and knees, her frock still up around her waist. She scurried toward the back of the cabin on all fours, but she was too slow. The broom whistled through the air as it fell. It caught her across the rump with a dull *whack*.

"Ow-w-w!" Anna yelled. "Stop that, you crazy fool!"

"You strumpet!" Vi stormed. "You low-lifed bitch. Right in the house we live in."

She raised the broom again. Anna increased her stride, but her knee caught on the hem of her dress, and she plunged forward onto her nose. It started to bleed. *Whack!* The broom struck her again on her red and white buttocks.

"The nerve!" Vi yelled. "The brass!"

"Damn you!" Anna screamed. "Don't you swarp me in the ass again with that prickly old broom. It's my business what I was a-doin. It's my property." She had whirled back and now faced Alvira, standing on her knees.

Swarp! The broom caught her across the side of the head. "You'll peddle your *property* some'ers else besides where I sleep at," Vi raged.

Anna fell forward and threw her arms about Vi's legs. Vi collapsed but landed sitting down. Dishes rattled on the table. The baby began to cry. Anna reached for Vi's face with bared fingernails.

Vi's motions were purely instinctive. She reached forward, caught Anna by her hair, and yanked with all her power. Anna screamed. Her claws retracted, and her limp fingers clutched at her head in an effort to ease the pain along her scalp. Vi worked Anna onto her back, straddled her, on her knees, and pounded her head against the floor. One side of Anna's face was bloody from her crushed nose.

"Stop! Stop! Please stop!" Anna wailed. "I give up! I give up! You done and won, goddamnit to hell. You wanna bash my brains out along with all my blood?"

Vi released her and climbed to her feet. Anna sat up, wiping her nose on the back of her hand. Vi looked down at her, her breasts rising and falling, rising and falling.

"What you reckon Will's gonna say about you and Tom Dugan?" she asked softly. "He mortally despises that rascal, anyways."

Anna threw up her head, her eyes white in horror. "You ain't aimin to tell him?"

"I'm bound to. You know that."

"You lookin for'ards to gettin me killed?"

"It's my bounden duty," Vi said. "I ain't got no other choice."

"After how he tuck Tillie's mess," Anna groaned, "he'll purely brain me."

"You should a-figured on that before you spread yourself out for Tom Dugan," Vi said. "Will specially can't stand that devil. You shore got a appetite for trash. He's no better'n a Catlett."

"Well, he's not a Catlett," Anna grumbled.

"How many times does that make with him?" Vi demanded.

Anna looked up at her through her bloody, tangled hair, amazement on her face. "How far you think I can count?" she demanded. "I jest went through the fifth grade."

Vi shook her head. It was more than she could understand. "And pore Tillie, she got knocked up after just three times with that scoundrel. It's a quare world we're a-livin in."

Anna uncoiled to her feet and staggered to her bed. The blood from her nose had slowed to congealed crimson blobs. She lay on her back and stared upward, a dazed look in her eyes.

"I'm goin back across the mountain to the store," Vi said. "You'd better wash that mess off your face. You'd better think up a good tale to tell Will."

Anna did not answer. Vi crossed to her bed, took the money handkerchief from beneath her pillow, and turned to leave. The baby, having forgotten what had frightened him, was playing in front of the fireplace with two spools Rosa Ward had given him.

"And you'd better take care of this baby, too," Vi called back over her shoulder.

Cousin Bill and Rosa were at the store when Vi got there. She and Rosa had a long talk, much longer than Vi had intended to stay. It was after sundown when she came down out of the woods and approached the house. She stopped short of the back yard, staring. Matt Catlett sat on the back porch rolling the spools to the baby.

"Where on earth is Annie?" Vi called, before she even reached the packed-clay yard. Before Matt turned her head, Vi felt the old lurch of apprehension.

Matt turned, grinning, exposing her rotting snags. "She gimme a dime to keep the youngun tell you got back," she explained. "She packed her rags in a flour sack and lit out. Said she was gonna leave this here Coottown porehouse before her legs growd together."

"I reckon she's a way past that danger," Vi mused. She paused. "Well, you can go back up on the hill now. I sure do dread to have to tell Will. He'll cuss a blue streak."

And Will did curse a blue streak, but by then it was too dark to see the color. And it did not change anything. Beneath his anger, Will seemed relieved that Anna was gone. That was how Vi figured it, listening to the undertone of his oaths. Now he would not have to confront her with this terrible sin she had committed against the name of Ward. Besides, she did not earn her salt anyway.

8

SUMMER PASSED. Fall rode in astride the cool breezes. Will Ward slacked hauling long enough to pull corn, shuck it, and store it in the narrow corncrib. After that, he began to haul again. He reminded Alvira of a busy ant hurrying backward and forward from food supply to ant hole, dreading winter, except when he came in at night, after feeding the mules. By that time of day he looked like nothing so much as what he was—an aging, exhausted man aching for rest and sleep. She thought about him while squatting by the fireplace on a cold winter night cooking supper for him and the boys. It was January 10, 1907; she suddenly remembered she had been married over a year—a year and four days, and she had just remembered. She shook her head, staring at the coals piled on top of the skillet. It seemed as though it had been forever and a day since she slipped out of Lucinda Watson's house that long-ago chilly dawn.

In June of that year, two remarkable events happened in the life of Alvira Matlock Ward. Early in the month, Will took the money she had saved from the crippled hog and the bit she had added to it, contributed a little more from his hauling, and brought home from Northboro a new cookstove. It could have been fitted, minus its legs and pipe, into the oven of Lucinda Watson's range, but to Vi it was a real blessing. Only two stove-lids, where the cooking could be done, covered the narrow fire-box, although there was space to the right where pans of food could be kept warm. There was a miserly little oven a few inches wider than a breadpan. A stovepipe rose out of the back, then elbowed through a hole Will cut in the closed shutters back of the cooking table. To Vi, the huge range she had cooked on at the Watson place was little more than a dream, something she had imagined from out of a starved girlhood. The squat little cookstove was a reality, a beautiful black help-mate that would get her up off her knees and onto her feet, the way a human being was supposed to cook.

The second thing that happened was not so obvious at first. Late in the month Vi began to suspect that she was with child. She was not surprised. What was surprising was that it had taken so long. By the middle of July she had confirmed it to her own satisfaction, but said nothing to Will for the time being. She figured Will was too busy to look at his own child, even if it were already born and she led it up to him and introduced them—unless, of course, it was born big enough to hoe or plow. She felt easier, now that the waiting, the listening to the inner workings of herself were over. Now she did not have to half dread pregnancy the way she watched sideways a black thunderhead shouldering skyward to the west when her washing was still outside undried.

It was over and done with, the waiting. Now the baby had to be born just as rain had to fall, and she was bound and compelled to be the best mother she possibly could. But she could look up and see the blue dome of the sky settling closer above her, see the walls of the horizon closing in. She felt, deep down in her crimson bloodstream and in the fibers of her flesh, that God had already made up his mind she was to stay on in Stud Branch Valley and bear fruit, that he had made up his mind long, long ago.

In August, she crossed over West Mountain to buy coffee at

Ellis's store. As she was leaving, she turned from the door. "You reckon the Doc's out at the house?" she asked, as though it were an afterthought.

Bessie turned away from Doll Dugan and grinned at her. "You planning on breakin the news to Doc that you're spectin?"

Vi went stiff, her eyes narrowing. "How come you're jumpin at conclusions like that? I don't look no more big than Doll there does." She looked down at her flat stomach to prove it.

"Cause it's high time you was big," Bessie said. "Ain't no shame in a married woman gettin with child. I done got two boys growd up and livin at Northboro."

Doll Dugan turned, her bright auburn hair turning maroon in the sunlight slanting through the dirty west windows. She laughed, her pretty face without dread. "If you're a-comparin yourself to me, Vi," she said, "you're a-makin a mistake. I'm as knocked up right now as a bitch rabbit in a brier patch."

Vi stared at her. "You mean you stand there and admit—"

"That I'm gonna have me a youngun?" Doll grinned. "Why not. All that goes up has got to come back down in one shape, form, or fashion. I got to hurry up to ketch up to my sis."

Vi turned away from her, toward Bessie. "Did you say that Doc was out at home?"

"You can take a chance and look, Vi," Bessie said. "I hope you don't have no trouble totin it and birthin it."

Doc Ellis was at home. He seemed to know what was on Alvira's mind the moment he saw her face. He checked the width of her hips and listened to her heart, but she had a feeling he did it just to make her feel easier. Finally he sat down in a chair and faced her.

"You're a healthy, sturdy woman, Vi," Doc Ellis said. "You've got nice hips and a nice pelvis. Barring unforeseen trouble, you ought not to have no trouble at all bearin your first child."

Vi looked at her feet. "It sure is worryin me, Doc, not knowin much about it. I wasn't allowed around when my brothers and sisters was borned. I got a deep-down need to get ready for it. What ort I to do first?"

"You get you some clean white rags together, Vi," Doc Ellis

said. "Boil them just before your layin-in and dry them and pack them away in a boiled pillowcase. That's about all you can do, I guess."

"Doc," Vi said. She met his eyes. "Doc, I got a favor to ask."

"Yes, Vi," Doc Ellis nodded, "you just name it."

"Will you be sure and be there? I've got a fear of bein there without good help. I couldn't stand that."

Doc Ellis, who had stood up, leaned down from his slender height and placed a hand on her shoulder. His eyes twinkled through the silver-framed spectacles. "Vi, I'll be there in spite of hell or high water. I promise you that nobody but me'll deliver your firstborn."

Alvira's steps were lighter as she returned back over the mountain.

That evening while Vi was milking, over her head in twilight, Will came stamping up, a dark mass with slumped shoulders and dangling arms. From where she squatted, he reminded Vi of a small, distorted thunderhead bobbing along close to the ground.

"Well, by God!" Will growled, "looks like I'm the last'un in the community to be told I'm gonna be a daddy."

Alvira stopped milking, her hands swinging onto the cow's limp udders. The cow turned her head, paused in her cud-chewing, and focused her long ears forward to identify the growl. "What're you a-gettin at?" Vi asked.

"I stopped at Ellis's store on the way down from Stoney Fork while ago," he went on, "and Bessie Newspaper tells me that you're big. That's a hell of a way for a feller to larn it."

Vi began to milk again, the white streams crossing lances as they jetted into the pail. "I never told her no sech a thing," she said. "She jumped at her own conclusions as usual."

"Well, what in hell made the old busybidy do a thing like that for?" He took off his dark hat and scratched his flint-white head in the gloom.

"Cause I ast her was the Doc out at his house."

"What in hell did you want to see him for?" Will leaned toward her, staring, as though looking for some raw wound in her head. "You wasn't a-bleedin or nothin, was you?"

"Cause I thought I might be big," Vi said.

Will jammed his hat back on his head. "Well, goddamn, stop beatin around the bush. Are you big or ain't you?"

Vi paused again and changed her squatting position to ease the cramp in the calf of her right leg. "I reckon I am," she said. "Leastways Doc thinks so."

Will turned and stamped away. "Another mouth to feed," he muttered. "Then there'll be a nother'un and a nother'un, and hit'll be doomsday before they're big enough to tote a hoe to the cornfield."

Alvira watched him retreat like a cloud rained out, still flashing and rumbling but no longer dangerous. She shook her head. "If it was to be another Messiah," she thought, "he'd not rest till he got it old enough to hoe corn."

In September, Will started hauling lumber for his new house. He brought a couple of loads a week down from one of Old Man Harrison's sawmills and stacked them on the side of East Ridge near where he had picked his house spot. In the meantime, he had changed his plans concerning the spring at the foot of West Mountain. Reacting to Alvira's complaint that it was too far to lug water, he started a well near where the north end of the house would stand. He did little work on it himself, however. Van and Dan alternated at digging, depending on which was helping Will haul at a given time. With no supervision, the boys made slow progress. At the end of six months they had dug a shaft four and a half feet in diameter and eight feet deep.

One Saturday, while Vi stood by the well, Will came stamping up and watched Dan shovel dirt into the square box attached to rope and pully. Will squinted downward, spat tobacco juice to one side, and wiped his mouth with the back of his hand.

"Well, it'll be a God's blessin if we don't have to go a hundred foot to strike water," he swore.

Dan, looking for some excuse to pause, stopped and stared upward. "Why so, Paw?" he asked.

"Cause, by God, it'll be a hundred month before we get a drink out of it," Will said, then turned and shuffled back to the wagon on the slope above.

Vi thought about telling him that a hundred months was only a little over eight years, but she changed her mind. Will had already made his point and was through with the subject. A foot and an eighth per month was too damned slow and that was that.

When Will started moving dirt, Vi led Mal, the baby, down Stud Branch to watch. Will worked a one-mule scoop, Van and Dan standing by with mattock and shovel. The scoop was shaped something like a huge, square-lipped spade with two wooden handles extending backward. A flat steel bail was attached just forward of the center on each side, and the singletree was attached to the center of this bail. Will seized the wooden handles, lifted them, and edged the sharp lip of the scoop into the earth. When the mule tugged forward at his command, the edge of the scoop bit deeper into the ground. When the scoop was full, Will shoved down on the handles, and the scoop was dragged forward to the embankment. Here, it was dumped down the hill, when Will lifted the handles and the back of the scoop flipped forward, turning upside down.

Only about a half yard of dirt at a time could be moved in this manner, and long months passed before a sizeable step was cut in the red clay of the ridge slope. When Vi shook her head at the slow progress and wondered how many months it would be before the house was built, she had no idea how long it really would be before they could move from the log house at the head of Stud Branch.

By November, Vi's stomach had begun to swell noticeably, and when she stopped to listen, she could almost trace the outline of the fetus growing within her. At least she felt she could. Sometimes during the past month, she had awakened during the still, hovering night with the feeling that something amazing was about to happen or had just happened and she had missed it. She had the crazy idea that Gabriel was about to appear before her and read an announcement to her out of a golden book. She grinned upward into the darkness because she had enough sense to know that would never happen on Stud Branch. But it was something of great importance, and she wondered if she should awake Will as a witness.

Then it came again. Her heart leaped and surged wildly, and a tenderness swelled in her throat almost like a sob. Something had kicked her suddenly in the stomach from inside. Not something—somebody. Her child. She had a living being alive now inside her, feeding on her life, and somehow she felt the child knew her and the kick was a signal that he or she was glad that Vi was his or her mother, and wouldn't it be nice when they finally met face to face? Quietly, Vi crawled across Will Ward's curled legs, working her way to the floor. She found her shoes, slipped them on, slipped on her coat, and went outside, beneath the October stars.

She stood a long time in the sharp air staring about her at the starry sky, where no moon was. Her heart drummed inside her a tempo she almost recognized. Finally, she could control herself no longer. She walked to the back of the smokehouse, picked up a rock, and tapped on the wall near where Grandpa John's head would be, inside the house. After a brief wait, she dropped the rock and circled to the door, knocking softly on it. She stood there so long staring at the sky that she had forgotten where she was, only that it was chilly.

The smokehouse door was yanked suddenly inward, and Grandpa John hobbled into the yard, holding up his pants over his underwear. He peered at Alvira, blinking into the gloom. "What on earth ails'ye, this time of night, Vi, a-bangin on my wall that a-way."

Suddenly Vi felt foolish and hesitant. But she knew she had to tell him. Any other explanation would make no sense to the old man. "I was just waked up a while ago," she said, yearning for him to understand. "My youngun just kicked with life and waked me up."

Grandpa John stared at her as though she had changed suddenly before his eyes. She felt like she had a square head, maybe, or two noses. "I just had to tell somebody," Vi went on. "I just couldn't keep it to myself till daylight, and I knowd Will wouldn't want to be waked up."

Old John's face softened, and his eyes squinted, trying to see her better. He reached forward with his good left hand and patted her on her belly, through the coat. "That's good news, daughter," he said gently. "Hit makes you a real mother now. Go on back to bed and git some rest and take care of my grandchile."

Vi dropped her hands and placed them on his, then turned away and slipped back into the house. Will, in the same position she had left him, snored loudly. The baby, alone in the bed Tillie and Anna had shared, lay uncovered on his stomach. She tiptoed to him, covered him up, and returned her coat to its peg. Then she crept back beneath the covers. The place she had left warm was now cool. She lay on her back for a long time unable to sleep, concentrating on her womb, but the baby did not signal again that night.

In January of 1908 Alvira Matlock Ward began to prepare for her firstborn, due in March. She was like a mother cat on her last day before bearing a litter, a cat which paced restlessly until it selected a spot, then circled and stamped, as its ancestors had fifty thousand years before, packing down the jungle grass to give its new kittens room. She paced. She boiled white rags and sheets, and stuffed them away into a clean pillowslip. Then in February, she took them out, washed them, and packed them all over again. She paced the cabin floor, measuring her distended stomach with her spanning hand and grunting when the child kicked impatiently to be done with the waiting.

Her water broke during the night of March 9th, and Will sent Dan for Doc Ellis around dawn of the tenth. Doc Ellis arrived around seven. There were no complications. The pain was surprising but bearable. The baby was a big, brawny boy weighing about nine pounds, with lungs to match. Alvira refused to let him live one day as an unidentified *it* and plucked his name from somewhere deep inside her mind, not realizing it was Dr. Watson's middle name. Lynn Ward, male, was born to Alvira Matlock Ward and John William Ward at high noon on March 10,

1908. Will did not insist that he have John as a part of his name and thus become John Ward VI.

The date seemed of unusual importance to Vi, as though some historical event were commemorated by the birth of Lynn Ward. It was not until a week later that she recalled March 10th was her own birthday, her twentieth. She felt relieved then, believing the child had an important future of some kind. Somehow it seemed that her first child's birth on her own birthday was arranged by some cosmic power. She did not think beyond that, and kept the idea to herself. But she felt better than she would have had he arrived on some less auspicious day.

The baby grew rapidly and showed signs almost at once of being tall, rather than the stocky giants Van and Dan were and Mal, now going on four, would probably become. Vi's breasts were large and full, with more rich milk than the child could absorb at first. Vi was compelled to milk herself occasionally to relieve the pressure, but after three months, young Lynn Ward was consuming everything he could reach. He would turn loose of his nipple and stare up at her with large, gold-flecked eyes as though he wanted to speak and was trying to tell her he could understand if she would just use the right words. Then when she tried baby talk on him, he would clench his fists and grin and shake all over as though he thought she were some kind of fool for speaking gibberish. It puzzled Alvira. Try as she might, she never could come up with a word he did not scoff at with red, toothless gums.

After the corn was laid by in June of that year, Will Ward began to haul field rocks to the new house spot, when he could find time from his regular hauling. He pulled the extra hand out of the well, now—and forever to remain—only fourteen feet deep, and put him to collecting the rocks and piling them at intervals along the side of East Ridge. They were to be stacked into pylons to support the heavy house sills when they were laid. Alvira persuaded him to dig into the old Ward-house mound to see if he could find a few stones he could use in the new chimney. Will wanted to leave the house grave untouched. He said it had been robbed enough by the goddamn Catletts, but he did find four or five rocks, after Vi had insisted that it was only fitting and proper that they be put back to work, being as they were handed down, so to speak, from his great-great-grandpa.

It was about this time that Van and Dan started running around again, staying out until all hours and sometimes not coming in for as long as two days. Will was compelled to haul alone at these times, loading and unloading by himself. He would get in late at night, so tired he would not bother to speak, and Vi did not care to test him, even though it meant sympathizing with him. When the two boys (men now) did come in, Will would pelt them with curses, but they rattled off Van and Dan's denim armor like sand off a turtle's shell.

One Friday in August, Will took young Mal with him on a short haul, dropping Vi and the baby off at Ellis's store. Van and Dan were hell and gone somewhere, over the mountain. When Vi entered the store, she found Bessie alone. She sat in a ladder-backed rocker, fanning herself with a cardboard fan which advertised Bruton Snuff and rocking her huge body sluggishly. Sweat oozed out of her forehead and glinted like dew on her silken black mustache.

"Howdy, Bessie," Vi said, shifting the baby on her hip. "How you makin out today?"

"Whew-w-w!" Bessie sighed, closing her eyes, "if you're astin for the truth, I'm as weak as swamp water. This heat has purely cooked all the starch out of me and I'm limber as a dishrag."

"It do be a hot day," Vi agreed, taking the split-bottomed chair Bessie motioned toward with her fan. "I feel sorter like a baked rabbit myself."

"If it don't rain soon," Bessie allowed, rocking and fanning, "the whole world's gonna dry up like snuff and blow away."

"It's a blessin the corn's done and past its growin season," Vi added, pulling out her left breast and stuffing the nipple into Lynn's gaping maw, "or we'd have nothin left but a passel of nubbins for our slavin."

Bessie rocked for a few minutes in silence, eyes closed, belly quaking slightly. Then she studied Vi through slitted lids, as though they were too heavy to open in the heat. "Wasn't that Will just passed about the time you come in?" she asked, her words projected now, no longer broadcast without direction.

"Yes, it was." Vi looked down at the baby, who released her nipple and gritted red gums at her. She placed the nipple back into his mouth. "Me and the baby rid this far with him. He was goin to haul sills to use on the new house."

Bessie rocked again, eyes closed, fan fluttering like the exhausted wing of a wounded moth. After a few moments her lids cracked open again, revealing a dark gleam. "Wasn't anybody with him but that youngun, Mal, was they?"

Alvira looked up sharply. "No, they wasn't. The big boys was off some'ers when we got ready to leave."

Bessie rocked on, covering this portion of her journey through life in short arcs. "Vi, what do you know about Lem Dyer?" she asked with her eyes closed.

Vi stared at her. Although Bessie's eyes were still closed, her round face still, the tone of her voice had changed so completely that Vi was startled. Then she thought about the question. "I don't know much about him. He stopped onct at Albert Essex's house while I was there. Seemed like a good-lookin, friendly sort of feller." She paused, her eyes narrowed. "I did hear tell that he makes likker some."

Bessie Ellis laughed, her voice sharp, her lap full of belly bobbing like a ball dropped into water. "Heard tell!" she said. "Makin *some* likker! Boy, if that's not prayin for a hoss and leadin home a squirrel!"

Vi's blue eyes squinted. She could not unravel Bessie's riddle. "What are you a-gettin at?"

"Why, it's a known fact from Hog Elk Creek to way past Northboro that Lem Dyer makes more likker and better likker than anybody else in Wilton County—and that's right up there with world champions." Bessie lifted her left hand and smote her left knee for emphasis, or smote at it. She missed her target and let her arm drop to her side.

"Well," Vi said, shifting the baby to her other breast, "that's inter-restin news, but I don't see what it's got to do with the price of eggs in Chinie."

"Lem's grandpa worked out a recipe for likker," Bessie explained, rocking in slow spasms, like a toy wound up long ago and almost wound down. "Can't nobody match it, the Doc says. Folks have heard tell of it as far away as Richmond, Virginny. Lem's grandpa passed his secret recipe on to Lem's pa, and his pa passed it on to him, and now he's the expert."

Bessie rocked slowly, pausing at the end of each arc, then turning back. Vi watched her for a signal to speak, but saw none. She decided the storekeeper would give her a hint when it was her time to say, "Well, I do declare!" or "I do know!" because she did not have any idea what Bessie was leading up to. It was not like her to lay groundwork for a question or an observation. She usually got straight to the point, the way she pulled a tooth.

"The Dyers used to live and do their stillin up on Hog Elk Creek," the storekeeper went on. "For some reason, Lem left up there and moved back in yander on the north side of Fox Mountain. About eight months ago, it was." She paused and looked at Vi through slitted lids.

Alvira squinted at her, waiting. "Well, I do declare!" she finally said. "I wonder what he moved for."

Rock, rock, rock went Bessie's chair. Back, forward, back bobbed her belly in her lap. "Doc has rode over about his place several times a-callin on the sick," she said. "Doc don't miss much with his eyes, but he don't say a whole lot about what he sees except to me."

The baby released her nipple and closed his eyes, then swung a clinched fist at her breast as though it had offended him by gorging his tight little gut to the bursting point. Alvira tugged outward on her dress, then buttoned it. She studied Bessie, her brow furrowed. "Just what did Doc see over about Lem Dyer's place that's got to do with me that you can't come right out with like pullin a sore tooth and be done with it?"

Bessie laughed, her belly quaking from the center outward. She opened her eyes. "Vi, you just won't do!" she grinned. "Most folks you can beat around the bush with till you lay the foundation for your news. But you're bound and compelled to have the chestnut without pullin off the burr."

"Are you aimin to tell me," Vi asked, "or just keep a-rockin till all your words settle in the bottom of your feet and you can't get'em up?" She smiled to show she was not impatient.

Bessie's face became stern. "I heard tell Will was cussin cause the boys ain't been helpin him haul lately," she said, looking straight at Vi. "They have been seen layin around Lem Dyer's place, and Dan was seen with a bag of corn on his shoulders a-headin into the woods up Sourwood Branch."

Alvira felt the old familiar lurch of dread. "Well, I swear!" she swore. "They ort to be skinned alive, both of'em. Somebody ort to turn that Lem Dyer in."

"Somebody is liable to get shot for their trouble," Bessie said. "Lem shot one feller over on Hog Elk Creek for just that. Couldn't nobody prove it though, if they'd tried much."

Vi sat up straight in her chair, jarring the baby's eyes open briefly. "How come decent folks like you and Doc put up with outlaws like that?"

"You're obliged to understand how folks feel up in here about stillin," Bessie argued. "I'm from low country, just like you are. And down in there it's looked down on. Up here in the hills they've been doin it far back as they've been here. Some famblies like the Dyers never done anything else. They're proud of their produce like Will's proud of a good corn crop. It's just a state law, I mean against makin likker, and the county sheriff and deputies don't fight it much. They like the people's vote too much. Men like Doc and Will Ward wouldn't still in a thousand years, just because it's against the law. But they don't preach no sermon against them that do make it. It's been around too long."

She stopped, gasping for breath, her word supply exhausted for the time being. Alvira studied about it for a minute, staring past Bessie Ellis's sweating face, not seeing her. "Well," she said, "I don't reckon it's any hangin crime, but I'd be willin to bet Will's not gonna take kindly to the idea of the boys messin with stillin."

Bessie grinned. "Nope. I'd be willin to bet he'll cuss one of them blue streaks he's noted for."

Will and Mal came by an hour later and picked Vi and the baby up. She rode on the load of sills beside him, holding the baby, hanging her feet off the front end of the load, young Mal between her and her husband. They rode in silence for a while, up over the ridge beyond the store and down the other side, toward where Old Man Harrison's house sat, to the left of the road. Will hunched forward, elbows on knees, staring moodily at the mules' swaying rumps. Young Mal held the whip, a four-foot shaft with a leather thong attached to its end, and fished with it down behind the doubletree.

"I heard somethin at the store that ain't likely to set well with'ye," Vi finally said, looking straight ahead.

Will was silent for a long time, as the wagon rattled and bounced down the road. Finally he spat a stream of tobacco juice to the left and wiped his mouth with his hand. "If it come from Bessie Ellis, it couldn't be nothin but bad," he grumbled. "She's got a goddamn patent on all the bad news that ever happens around here or gets told."

"I reckon they's a premium on good news around here." Vi was silent briefly.

"Well, what in hell did Miz Newspaper say that's so bad?"

Vi glanced at him, licked her lips. The wagon jostled over a rock, clicking her teeth together. "She said Van and Dan has been seen messin around with Lem Dyer, carryin bags up Sourwood Branch and stuff like that."

Will turned and stared at her. "Well, what in hell does she mean by that?"

"She means," Vi said precisely, "that your two oldest boys is takin up stillin with the head likker-maker in all Wilton County and probly the world."

Will sat up straight, staring straight ahead. "Well, I do be doubled goddamn! That's where them hellions has been layin off at. Helpin that outlaw to still. No goddamn younguns of mine is goin to bring the law down on my head. I don't give a goddamn cat's ass if he's eighty year old and bigger'n West Mountain." He went on from there to curse precisely and scientifically all of Van's and Dan's shortcomings, and he cursed all the way home. As Bessie had predicted, he cursed a blue streak.

And unfortunately for them, Van and Dan were waiting when the wagon rolled into the yard. Will had not unloaded the sills at the house spot because it was late, and he needed help to move the big beams. He placed his left hand on the end of the load and his right on Toab's rump, climbing stiffly to the ground. He turned and helped Mal down, then took the baby so Vi could climb down as best she could. Van and Dan shuffled up behind him.

"Why didn't you tell us you was goin after that load?" Van asked. "We'd a-hope you."

Will turned and glowered at him from his huge feet, slowly upward past his massive shoulders to his massive head. "How in hell and damnation did'ye spect me to git word to'ye?" he growled. "By revenooers?"

Van's eyes flared open, then narrowed. He turned and glanced at Dan. Dan looked down at his bare feet, scuffling them against the ground. "I got no idee what you're a-talkin about," Van mumbled.

"You know damn good and well what I'm a-talkin about," Will retorted gruffly. He sounded to Vi like he was about cussed out, like he hardly had enough breath saved up to make further cussing worthwhile. "You and Dan have been seen helpin Lem Dyer around his stillin, now ain't that the damned truth?"

Will Ward watched Van, holding him squirming on the prongs of his cold grey stare like a gigged frog. Van turned his head and looked at Dan, but Dan had suddenly discovered he had ten dirty toes. Van focused on Will's black hat. "Well, we did help a little tad, totin meal and sech like. Wasn't no harm done."

"Harm my ass! If the high sheriff or a passel of his debdies took a notion to raid his stills, you and Dan would be put in jail same as if'ye owned the goddamn still. And I don't take to no damn jailbirds roostin in my fambly."

"Aw, hell, Paw," Van argued, "they's good money in stillin. Lem Dyer makes the best damn likker in Wilton County. If a feller could jest larn how he does it the way he does it, he could make his own—"

"Is that what you got in mind?" Will demanded. "You figurin to start stillin on'ye own—you and Dan, here?"

Van turned and looked at Dan. Dan squinted and began to whittle on a stick. His face retreated beyond the tilted top of his head, thatched with black hair. "Well, it was way back in the back part of my mind," Van admitted. "I got no clear plans, precisely."

"Well, I got this to say," Will said gruffly. "I ain't havin no goddamn stillers livin in my house. You stay with me, and you stay the hell away from Lem Dyer. I can't whoop'ye, neither one of'ye. But by God, you try keepin this up, and I aim to shoot'ye. I'll git my musket and blow a hole in'ye big enough to poke my fist in. You want to fart around with Lem Dyer, and you can move the hell out'n my house. That's all I'm aimin to say on the matter."

He turned and began to unhitch the mules from the wagon. Vi walked toward the house with baby Lynn, Mal tagging at her heels. Van and Dan turned and faced each other, looking at the ground, apparently waiting to talk after Will had led the mules away.

When the Wards sat down to breakfast the next morning, Van did not show up. Dan said he got up and left before dawn, and he sullenly argued that he did not know where Van had gone. But Van came back a week later while Will was away, and picked up his extra overalls. He told Vi he had married a widow who owned a rich farm over on the Yadkin River, and intended to raise corn for Lem Dyer's stills.

Later, when Vi told Will, he scratched his flint-white head and squinted at the sun, then said, "Well, hell, I don't reckon they's a law agin raisin corn."

9

In April of 1910, Will Ward worked carefully, laying off furrows and placing corn grains tenderly into the moist womb of earth, where they would sprout and out of which they would grow tall and green. He watched Vi and Dan carefully to see that they followed the ancient ritual which he called "corn plantin." The job had to be right. There was only one way it would be done. It would be done when the moon was right and the earth was ripe and the weather favorable.

Other seeds that he planted more casually in the same month, with less ritual and no concern for favorable signs, began to sprout immediately in the warm womb of Alvira Ward. However, the corn was up and green before anyone was aware of this secret known only to Vi's young flesh.

After corn planting, and between loads of lumber, Will, Dan, and Grandpa John began to lay the sills for the new house. Pillars were built by stacking the field rocks carefully so that they would hold together without mortar. The heavy timbers were eased into place under Grandpa John's supervision, and by early August the foundation was complete, ready for the frame. That was as far as the work progressed for a long time thereafter. One reason for this was a sudden flurry of hauling lumber, demanded of Will by Old Man Harrison. This labor was followed almost at once by harvest time, when the corn had to be pulled, shucked, and stored in the corncrib.

Before the corn was half pulled, late in September, Dan left the house one morning for the "business bushes" along Stud Branch and did not return. Will waited in the yard with the team and wagon. He yelled for Dan several times, then stamped out to the branch to see "if, by God, he's done his business and fell back in hit." But Dan had disappeared. Will yelled, cursed, and threatened, but got no response. Dan had finally left home too, and Vi, standing on the front porch, had a feeling it would be many a day before they saw hair or hide of him again. She left young Mal and the baby with Grandpa John and went off to the fields, tugging at the dry corn until her hands chapped and cracked open, caking her fingers with blood.

On January 6, 1911, just after midnight—while drinking water was still turned to blood, while the mules and cattle were down on their knees in their cold stalls praying to God—Vi came to the end of a short labor, and a daughter was born. There had been no complications, and the baby was a ten-pound mass of appetite. Alvira named her Vern. At this birth, Mal was a husky seven and Lynn almost three. Will, weary and stooped from hauling alone, wrestling with his hernias, and puttering around the new house foundation, was almost forty-seven. And Vi was not yet twenty-two.

Alvira Matlock Ward, mother of two, was far from being the tall, hopeful yet worried seventeen-year-old girl who had ridden up the Ridge Road with Will Ward in January of 1906, five years before. She had developed the broader hips of a mother, and had gained weight in her thighs and arms. Her shoulders were stooped ever so slightly from the long days stretching out ahead of her. The birth of Vern weighed a little more heavily on her mind, but in spite of this, she sometimes toyed with the delusion that this was all a dream, that there was no such person as Will Ward, that she would wake up some morning in Lucinda Watson's warm bed, rested and free. Vi was by far too much of a realist to become irrational about such dreaming. It was only along the ragged edge of her thinking that she still denied her relationship to Will.

About this time, a letter came from Tillie—Tillie Miller, now —with the news that she had been married about two years, that she had a new baby, and that Anna had run off to Carson County with some kind of a drummer. Vi wrote back, telling her about Van marrying and Dan going to live with him. She did not mention their stilling connections.

In early summer, after the corn was planted, Will hired Albert Essex to help him raise the frame of the house on East Ridge. Afterwards, they covered the roof with the dried oak shingles Will had split the winter before with the same froe his grandfather had used. The frame stood for almost a year above the rough plank flooring, holding up the roof, with only the skeleton of two-by-fours in between. Rain, snow, and hail pelted the roof and darkened the floor, while Will Ward's more pressing duties drove him away from the luxury of house building. It was not until late in 1912 that he finally got around to adding the weatherboarding. The narrow glass windows were added at the same time, and doors went up almost immediately afterward, doors with latches and doorknobs, by God, and not "them goddamn Coottown wooden latches with leather thongs."

One day in November, Vi, carrying the baby with Lynn tagging behind, walked down the branch to see how the work was going. She had lived in the single-room cabin so long now, she felt like a turtle trapped in its ugly shell. She despaired of ever moving into the new house—or rather, she did not trouble her mind any longer with impatience to move. *Despair* was a word she had discarded a long time ago, because she found no use for it on Stud Branch. While living here, she learned not to dwell on problems other than those she could reach out and grasp and perhaps (or perhaps not) remedy. But she had to admit that a lot of water had flowed down the branch since the day Will had promised her the house, back in 1906. Almost seven years, it had been. She saw no point in impatience now.

A few more months were a drop in the bucket to the seven weary years they had already waited.

Will and Mal were busy in the middle room, ceiling it. Vi came around between the house and the slope, stepped up on the back porch, and entered the narrow cubicle that was to be her kitchen. Lynn ran on into the next room, where his father was hammering and muttering. Vi looked around her. A small eight-paned window faced the rising slope of the ridge, and a second window faced the door. The back of the chimney rose along the wall to her left, with a flue-hole for the stove-pipe high up. In her mind, she furnished the room: the stove on her left, back to the chimney; the cooking table in the far corner to her right; the small cupboard—or safe, as Will called it—in the near corner to her right; and the round table occupying the center of the room. That arrangement would leave only three or four feet between the Lazy Susan and the stove on one side, the cooking table and cupboard on the other. She remembered Lucinda Watson's spacious kitchen and sighed almost audibly. Even the cabin had more room to move about in than this room could ever have.

Will stopped hammering when Vi entered and looked around curiously. He had finished ceiling the room except for one wall and was two-thirds done with it. Although the room was a third larger than the kitchen, it was far too small for a bedroom and sitting room combined. Vi looked about her, feeling easier than she had a few moments before. The fireplace in the wall next to the kitchen was small, but ceiled as the room was, it promised to be comfortable, at least more comfortable than the drafty cabin. Across from the fireplace, facing down the slope, a narrow window admitted the grey fall daylight. A second window, to her right, faced north. A doorway, minus door, led into the third room, to her left.

Will dropped his hammer, grinning tiredly. "Come to see how our new house was a-buildin, huh?" he asked. "I'm ceilin this here room first. We can move in fore long, and I can take my time ceilin the kitchen and Big House."

Vi thought about saying, "Like sebem years, maybe?" But she

let the opportunity pass. She would not punish him by reminding him of what he lived with, deep down, and could not change—the knowledge that time was flowing, flowing seaward twice as fast as he could swim, that he had started late, that he would always be behind, years behind, even if he worked till doomsday. Instead, she said, pointing, "You call that other room in there the Big House?"

"Yep," he nodded. "Come on and I'll show it to'ye," he added, like she had not seen it a dozen times from ribbed frame to finish.

Mal took Lynn aside and began to explain how you ceiled a room, fitting tongue into groove and driving square nails at the base of the tongue. Will shuffled across the floor, and Vi followed him through the doorway, shifting the baby from hip to breast. She would look again and not rob Will of his chance to talk, to explain plans she already knew by heart, to straighten up for a few minutes and adjust his hernias beneath vice-like trusses. She would listen and nod at the right time and perhaps ask a question or two that would prolong his rest, before he returned to the hammer and saw.

The room was large, larger than the other two together. Lighted by only one small window, directly opposite the doorway through which they had entered, the Big House was gloomy as a barn stall and somehow reminded Vi of one. Rough plank lay on top of the rafters, creating a storage loft above. Only the thin weatherboarding protected the room—against which the rough two-by-fours stood out in stark, rugged columns—from outside weather. A closed door near the wall where Vi stood gave admittance to the back porch and the uphill slope. A second door, across from it, faced the downhill side of the house.

"What I aim to do is this," Will swore, squaring his shoulders. "I aim to have me a hallway here sooner or later like Cousin Bill's got. I'll build another wall a little furder in the room with another door leadin into the Big House through it. I aim to have me a glass door, one of these days, yander facin downhill, maybe on the uphill side too."

"Wouldn't it take up a awful lot of useful space to put in a hallway?" Vi asked. "Looks to me like the Big House the way it is now can stand the extry room way yander more'n a useless hallway."

"Useless hallway!" Will exploded. "A hallway ain't useless. Good Godamighty, womern! A bidy can't have no manner of fancy house without a hallway and glass door, the way Cousin Bill's got."

Alvira shrugged further argument aside. It was not as though the hallway would be built next week or next year. She had the feeling they would use the Big House for many a day before any partition ever rose up to create a fancy hall. "What it needs more right now," she said, "is another winder. It's as dark as a barn stall in here."

"This here room is for sleepin in mostly," Will argued. "What does a bidy need light for a-tall if he's fixin to sleep?"

"A body might want to read sometime," Vi said, not thinking, "if they was anything to read."

Will started to answer, took off his hat and scratched his head, then gave up and went back to work. Vi left the house, trailed by Lynn, as warty as a toad from blocks he had crammed into his pockets.

One Friday evening two weeks later, Alvira was washing the dishes while Will spelled in harsh whispers the words from a songbook, pausing now and then to hum the melody. The baby and the two boys were long ago in bed, and Grandpa John was in his quarters. Will leaned forward as close as he could to get to the kerosene lamp on the round table, his brass-rimmed spectacles perched on the high bridge of his nose. His white forehead was wrinkled with concentration as though the letters were heavy boulders he tried to wrestle into line.

"E,M,B—" he spelled in a loud whisper, "Amb—" he tried it for size, dropped it, and began again. "Imb—" He shut up, muttering impatiently. "E,M,B,L,E,M," he spelled again. He looked across his glasses at Vi. "What in hell do *e,m,b,l,e,m* spell?" he demanded.

Vi threw up her head, listened, as though waiting for his words to make a second circuit of the room. "I would say it spells *em-blum,*" she explained.

"Em-blum?" Will tasted the word on his tongue. "Em-blum. What in the hell is a em-blum?"

"Why, it's a—a sort of a badge," Vi said. "Like you pin it on your overhall bib for other folks to look at."

Will glowered at her back as she dipped her hands back into the greasy dishwater. His eyes were narrowed thoughtfully. "How in hell could a bidy wear *sufferin* and *shame* on his overhall bib? He could have a hole in his head and that's sufferin, and he could have his pecker danglin out, and that's shame. But you couldn't git them right on a badge on no overhall bib."

Vi turned and looked at him. He had a puzzled look on his face as if she had missed his point. "Em-blum of sufferin and shame is just a manner of speakin," she explained.

"Hit's a hell of a manner of speakin," Will argued. "If singin is s'posed to lead folks on the straight and narrer to the Promised Land, then, by God, they ort to be writ in words most folks can catch holt of. Em-blum, my ass! If the song feller meant badge, then the bastard ort to a-writ *badge,* and not had me spellin out loud all night."

There came a loud banging on the front door. Vi whirled from the dishpan, dripping water on the floor. Will turned in his chair, rolling the songbook into a weapon. He glanced toward his bed, where the ax was already in place for the night, beneath it and in easy reach from above. The banging came again. Vi took a half step toward it, drying her hands on her apron. Will braced his hands on his thighs and unfolded upward. Before either of them could move farther, the door burst inward, and a young woman stumbled into the room. She staggered to a halt, staring about her.

She was a tall, skinny woman, except for her protruding belly, big with child. Her black hair was tangled about her shoulders, her face bruised and bleeding. Her dress was ripped down one side, exposing the ragged petticoat beneath. She wore no coat, not even a sweater, as protection against the cold night air, which had followed her into the room in a frigid blast.

Her eyes were wide and tearless and filled with anguish. Her heavy breasts were heaved high and sank rhythmically as she fought for breath.

"Are—are you Will Ward?" she panted, staring at Will. "You must be Will Ward. Please don't send me away too. Please don't, Mr. Ward." She turned her eyes on Vi to enlist her aid.

"Hell, yes! I'm Will Ward. But who in the world are you and what ails'ye, bustin in my house like the devil was ater'ye?" He hurried past her and slammed the door shut, then turned back.

The woman turned to face him, then back to look at Alvira. Will circled her like an alert gamecock until he was close to Vi, with the woman between them and the door.

"Who are'ye," Vi echoed. "What's troublin'ye, sending you out on a cold night like this, half naked?"

"My name—name's Deller," the woman panted. "Was Deller Prophett. Married that devil Tom Dugan six or sebem months back. I'm Deller Dugan now, you might say."

Will turned and met Vi's stare, and she caught what he was thinking. "So this is that sonofabitch's womern?" Will had on his mind. "She shore has stuck clost at home for us not to never seen her before."

"Well, what's eatin'ye, Deller?" Will demanded. "You liable to git shot, bustin into folks's house all of a sudden like a wild Injun."

"Don't turn me out," she pleaded, moving two uncertain steps closer to Will. "Please take me in. He'll kill me for shore."

"You're welcome in this here house," Will growled. "Nobidy's aimin to turn'ye out in the cold. Who's aimin to kill'ye?"

"That Tom!" she moaned, wringing her hands. "He come in drunk and beat me half to death. I run out in the dark and got away. Them sisters wouldn't help, and Pink was gone. Tom's a pure devil when he's drunk."

"He's a pure devil when he ain't drunk," Will said. "You set down in this here cheer and calm down and tell us what'ye want done."

She followed dully as he led her to a chair in front of the fireplace and pushed her down into it. Vi threw more wood on the coals. The fire blazed up, spreading a wave of heat across the three. Vi stepped back farther into the room. The woman's face was more composed now, her eyes normal. She shuddered as the heat enveloped her. Will dropped into a chair close to her.

"Now, what was you fixin to tell us about that hellion?" he asked, as gently as he knew how.

"He tried to kill me, I reckon," Della Dugan moaned. "He swore he would. I could see it in his eyes. I run and run. I went to Mr. Essex, and he said Tom was liable to burn his house down. I went to Mr. Bill Ward's next. He said he was real sorry, but he couldn't get mixed up with Tom Dugan. Said he had too much to lose. Then when I started to leave, he called me back and told me to come see you. Said if anybidy could help me, you could. Said if anybidy would help, you would."

Vi watched the change pass over Will's face, watched his grey eyes chill and his jaw muscles bulge, watched his thick lips draw taut as stretched wire. "Cousin Bill wouldn't take'ye in?" he demanded.

"Said he dassent," the woman muttered. "Said he wanted to ever so bad, but Tom Dugan was liable to burn his barn or slit open his stock."

"It's so," Will nodded. "He might a-done that. Sonofabitch tried to borry money from his granny, up on Stoney Fork, and when she didn't have it, he ripped her onliest cow open with his pocket knife. She run off and drug her guts on the ground tell she dropped dead."

"He's mean—mean!" Della Dugan swore. "How come me to to marry up with a varment like that?"

Will turned and stared at the blazing fire. Vi watched him. Light from the flames washed his face with crimson splotches. The wisps of hair on each side of his bald head stood up, curved, and his shadow against the far wall was a huge black head with horns. The black head shifted to round as Will faced the woman. "Have you got any folks?" he asked softly, his voice no longer harsh.

"Yeah. My folks live over on Bushy Mountains. Pa raises apples mostly. But it's over thirty mile from here, the way the road runs. I'd never make it before Tom cotch up to me."

Vi stood near the end of the fireplace watching Will. He sat straighter in his chair, his shoulders back. His face was calm now, his chin outthrust. He turned his head and looked at her. "Vi," he said, "go git Pa and have him to put his clothes on and come in here."

Vi left the house. Outside, a sliver of a moon sat above East Ridge in a clear sky. The forest gleamed like snow in the moonlight, and Vi shuddered, as much from seeing the frost as from feeling the cold, dry air engulfing her. The old man woke almost at once, but he was five minutes getting to the door. That was one of the ways she could tell that age was catching up with him, that and his moods. He was not as pleasant nowadays as he had been when she had first arrived on Stud Branch. Some days he was depressed, and others, he was downright hateful.

He thrust his head through the crack between the door and the jamb. "Yeah?" he fussed, "what you wakin me up this time of mornin fur?"

"It's not mornin, Grandpa," Vi said. "It's no more'n nine o'clock. Will wants to see you bad in the house. Somethin mighty important has come up."

"Well, what the devil is more important than sleepin?" he grumbled.

"He said for you to get your clothes on and come in the house," she explained. "You'll find out when you get there."

He turned away, muttering, and Vi re-entered the cabin. She stopped, past the slammed door, watching. Will had extinguished the lamp and only the flickering flames in the fireplace lighted the room. The huge antique musket now leaned against the wall near the stove. Will and Della Dugan were carrying firewood and piling it against the front door. Vi started to protest, but shut up. She did not know what she could truly protect against. She could not think of any course Will could take other than the one he had obviously chosen. In the half minute he had taken to make up his mind before he sent her for Grandpa John, his brain had shaped his plans and had set like cement, and she knew nothing she could say or Grandpa John could say, or any force of nature or man could exert would change Will's mind. She had often despised his stubbornness—

she called it muleheadedness—but a strange tenderness toward him swept over her suddenly and was gone, a feeling alien to her, and she stared at him, trying to see, in his lined face and bald head, more than a tired, aging man.

She did not speak, but crossed the room and moved to the back of the cabin. The boys were sound asleep in the bed Tillie and Anna had once used. The baby girl slept peacefully in the cradle Grandpa John had made for her. Vi turned back when the door opened, slammed behind old John. He hobbled toward the fireplace, craning and squinting like an ancient bird plagued with cataracts.

"What you-all doin flittin around in here in the pitch dark?" he grumbled.

Will stopped with a backlog in his arms. He set the flat end on the floor and straightened up, facing old John. "This here is Tom Dugan's wife," he said.

Grandpa John turned and squinted at the woman near the door. "Good gracious, I must be a-goin blind," he complained. "I thought she was your shadder. What's she doin here?"

"That bastard Tom tried to kill her," Will said. "Wouldn't nobidy else take her in. We're bound to take care of her and git her to her folks cause they's nobidy else on God's green earth to do it."

The old man peered at the woman, craning his neck from side to side. "That Tom's liable to burn us out," he complained.

"He'll have to deal with me first," Will said. "You'd better sleep in here tonight, jest in case. You can crowd down in front of the boys and git a little sleep, I reckon."

Alvira lay, fully clothed, covered with a quilt, and stared at the overhead rafters, lost in gloom where the firelight did not reach. The strange woman, Della Dugan, lay quietly beside her breathing evenly. Vi could not tell whether she slept or was awake, but felt her awake and alert beneath the quilts, every nerve strung tight and leading to her ears. Across from her, Grandpa John snored loudly, peacefully, as though the world would never end, as though he were not old and worn out, as though no danger existed far or near outside the cabin. The fire had burned down to a flicker in the fireplace, and Will did not replenish it. The room was filled with hulking, shifting shadows floating in gloom.

Vi heard Will move again and turned her head to look. He paced across the floor from the back door to the window beside the front door, carrying the heavy musket in his right hand. He carried it easily, swinging the long barrel to his left hand, as though it were a small-caliber rifle instead of an ancient antebellum muzzleloader long ago bored out to project a charge of shot (as though it had not already killed Joe Milton by accident when a member of the deputies mistook him for Ligh Church, the outlaw; as though Joe had not bled to death, his head on Aunt Nancy Ward's lap). Will carried it with authority, with the authority reflecting skill and familiarity, despite the fact that it almost kicked him over every time he shot it, as it had the time he shot one of Hill Anderson's stray bulls with a rolled meat skin and sent him bellowing down the branch and for two miles beyond Bare Creek before he slowed to a walk. Vi watched him lean forward and place his eye to the crack in the shutter, squinting out into the moonlit night.

Two thirds of the night had gone already, inching slowly by with the pace of the moon, westward above the silent valley. Vi knew the moon must be close to the mountains now. She knew there would be a short period of darkness before dawn seeped in from the east. And she could tell from Will's increased restlessness that he was thinking the same thing. The gap of darkness would be a safe time for an Indian to strike, but it was hard for her to imagine Tom Dugan going to that much trouble, cold as it was outside. She thought about calling to Will and telling him what she thought, then changed her mind. He was far away from her, from all of them in the cabin, trapped in a duty he was compelled to carry out to his own satisfaction.

Will turned back from the window and crossed to the fireplace. He stopped in front of it, the gun diagonally across his chest, his bulk dark and massive, like the other shadows in the room. Vi could not tell whether he faced her or the fireplace. All she could see was his mass and the silhouette of the huge gun. For a strange moment she felt the prickle of chill along her spine.

She felt she was not Alvira Matlock Ward but somebody else—a frightened woman from a far-off land, and that she lay and watched the first John Ward in his log house alone in a vast wilderness, miles west of Mulberry Fields, the closest settlement. A moment later the impression was gone, and she grimaced at her girlish imagination. It was hard to imagine Tom Dugan as a stalwart Indian of other days.

At the crack of dawn, Vi got up and started breakfast. Will left the house with the musket and was back in the yard in twenty minutes with the mules and wagon (he had fed the mules earlier). By the time he entered the house, Grandpa John was up, but the children were still asleep. Like deaf-mutes, they gathered around the table and sat down, even Della Dugan finding her chair and taking it with only a nod. They ate in silence, hurriedly, feeling the pressure of haste, gulping hot coffee, sopping biscuits in gravy. Will finished first, leaned back and belched, wiping his mouth with his hand.

"We'd better git the younguns up," he said, not looking at Vi. "We'd better all go. I'd better not leave you-all here by yourselves."

"I ain't aimin to shake my old bones all to pieces from here to the Bushy Mountains and back," Grandpa John mumbled. "Tom Dugan can cut my throat from year to year, and I won't make that trip."

"It looks like to me it'd be better for me and the younguns and Grandpa to stay here," Vi said, trying not to argue. "Tom Dugan is sneakin as a polecat. He'd never dast to come here in broad open daylight and harm anybody. If he found everybody gone, he might harm the place then."

Will Ward was thoughtful, his white forehead pinched into a frown. Vi could see stubbornness setting in. Then the forehead smoothed out. "I reckon you're right," he nodded. "I'll go by Albert Essex's and ast him can he help out enough to go git Dan and let him come and stay tell I git back."

"That would be a good idee," Vi agreed. She paused. Suddenly she stiffened as a thought struck her. Della Dugan spun toward Will, her eyes wide with last night's fear. She opened her mouth to speak, but Vi was ahead of her. "You've got to drive plumb by the Dugan house on the way to the Bushy Mountains."

"I done thought of that," Will said. "I got everthing planned out. If it don't work, I'll jest have to blow that sonofabitch's head off, I reckon. He needs it worse'n medicine."

When they were ready to go, Vi carried quilts outside and made a pallet in the wagon bed. Della Dugan stretched out on the pallet, and they covered her with another quilt, leaving only her face exposed. Then Will drove alongside a fodder stack and covered the quilts with a layer of fodder bundles. Alvira studied the load the wagon carried and breathed easier. Anyone who did not know better could not have guessed that a woman lay beneath the small mound of feed. When Will placed the musket on the floor of the bed in easy reach, Vi felt he would make it safely to the mountains and back.

Vi waited nervously all morning, one eye on the boys, but Dan did not show up. Early in the afternoon, Albert Essex rode by on his mule and stopped for only a few minutes. Vi was at the well when he reined to a stop close by.

"Howdy, Albert," Vi greeted. "Light and rest a spell."

"No, thank'ye, Vi," he said brusquely. He stared across her head toward the Bushy Mountains, in the distance beyond the valley rim. "I couldn't find Dan nor Van, neither. I rid all over creation. They was both off some'ers with Lem Dyer, folks said. I done my deadlevel best to find'em."

Vi felt a sharp dread and gazed toward the woods along the base of West Mountain. "Well, I guess his best is all a body can do," she said.

"Well, I got to be gettin back down the branch," Albert said. "I don't know nothin else I could a-done."

"Thank'ye, Albert," Vi said. "You-all come and see us."

"You-all come," Albert nodded, and kicked his mule in the ribs.

They rocked off down the branch, like a huge rocking horse on hidden rockers. Vi watched them go, feeling a bitter taste in her throat. Albert Essex had been a stranger with a familiar face.

Late in the afternoon, Cousin Bill came, walking up the branch with his head down. He did not say much. He sat by the fire and watched it. He held the baby for a while and bounced her on his knee. He talked solemnly to the two boys about squirrels and coons, and the time he saw Barr hanged at Northboro and thirty people fainted dead as doornails. Cousin Bill and Grandpa John eyed each other like hawks across the supper table, hardly saying a word. When Will drove by the house around nine o'clock, Cousin Bill left by the front door. Vi watched him plod off down Stud Branch in the moonlight, a silver ghost moving across a silver landscape. She turned back, slammed the door, and started warming supper for her husband.

Will did not come in until the mules were watered, stabled, and fed. He plodded across the floor and placed the musket back on its pegs, above the mantel—or fireboard, as he called it. He turned back, looked closely at Vi, as though searching for a wound. His face was drawn from fatigue. His shoulders slumped. The strength that had wound him erect the night before had run down during the tedious journey to the mountains and back, leaving a tired and hungry man, forty-eight years old, with eighty years of labor yoked about his neck.

He ate quietly, seeming too tired to gulp his food as he usually did. He did not ask about Dan. Once or twice Vi started to tell him about Albert Essex and Cousin Bill, but changed her mind. She had no words she knew how to use that would help him understand. It was better to let it dwindle out and die—as much as it would ever die, in the back of everyone's memory.

Once Will looked up and said, "We didn't see hide nor hair of the bastard. The whole household was still asleep when we passed the Dugan place. I got Deller up, a few miles yander side of Bare Creek, and she rid all the rest of the way in plain sight."

Vi nodded, leaving it there. They went to bed then. She lay awake for hours while he slept the sleep of exhaustion beside her. She lay and puzzled far into the night. She tried to figure Will Ward out, the man she had married seven years before. She thought of many things he had said and things he had done. Once or twice she approached the margin of understanding him, and her young body sang with the knowledge. Then it would fade and she would slip back into the old wonder. She slept with a man she lived with every day. She had lived with him for years, had mated with him in the silent night, when he was only bulk and energy, and had borne him two children. Yet she did not quite know him, did not quite understand him. The thing he had done for a strange woman had helped, had brought the knowledge closer, but not close enough. Who was Will Ward? The answer eluded her, hovering just beyond her understanding. Someday she would know; she was bound to know. It did not seem right, living a whole lifetime with a man who puzzled her.

The Della Dugan affair was not settled until three weeks later. It was never settled, really, because Vi was certain Tom Dugan would bear a grudge against Will for his part in Della's flight until the day he died. But the subject never came up again between Will and Tom. Mal came rushing into the house one morning, his eyes wide with excitement, gasping for breath. He grabbed Vi's arm, staring into her face, trying to talk.

"Tom—" he pointed. "Tom Dugan—Pa—Pa, he—they—"

Vi was suddenly frightened. "What happened?" she cried. "Where's your pa? Is he all right?"

"Pa's at the new house a-workin," Mal gasped. "He's all right—nothin wrong with my pa."

"Then what happened?" Vi demanded, her voice calming down. "What about Tom Dugan?"

"Pa and me was a-workin on the new smokehouse," Mal panted. "We heerd a noise and turned. Tom was slippin up on Pa with his knife open. Pa didn't even jump. He jist picked up a piece of two-by-four and he say, 'You come on, Tom Dugan, if you want your goddamn head bashed in. I'm ready to end the matter right here and now. You jist step up clost with your frog-sticker open, and I'll fix your clock for good, you low-down bastard.' "

"What did Tom do?" Vi asked softly. "Did he try to fight?"

"Naw," Mal said, calmer now. "He shet up his knife and put it in his pocket and grinned and say, 'I was jist a-fixin to scare'ye a little tad, Will.' And Pa say, 'I don't scare none too easy, Tom Dugan. Now you drag your ass off'n my land before I do mankind a favor and brain'ye jist for bein ugly.' Well, sir, Tom Dugan backed off and stomped off down the hill cussin to hisself, and that's all they was to it." Young Mal hushed, waiting for Vi to answer.

"All they was to it," Vi echoed. She tried to think it out, but gave up. When she turned back to her work, she felt easier. She felt that some problem had been solved for the time being. And when Will came home at noon, laughing and bragging about scaring the shit out of Tom Dugan, she listened to what he said because she figured he really had scared Tom Dugan half to death, and it was Will's nature to brag about what he had done. Anyway, it was all right with her.

The Wards moved into the new house in March of 1913. It was far from being the mansion Will had dreamed of and had promised Vi seven years and two months earlier. But she did not complain. She reckoned beggars could not be choosers. Abe Catlett, a working Catlett around forty, helped Will move, Abe had made arrangements to move into the log cabin for twenty-five dollars a year or the equivalent in work. Grandpa John refused to move, and they left him in his quarters in the back of the smokehouse. Abe Catlett's wife promised to cook him a meal whenever Mal did not carry him something from Vi's kitchen or when he did not walk down the branch to eat with the Wards.

While they were moving, the old man sat in the back yard and stared up the hollow, where West Mountain converged with Fox Mountain. He did not seem concerned that they were leaving or whether he ever ate again or not. Vi stood on the back porch feeling the warmth of promised summer, and watched him. "Old age is a-winnin out," she muttered. "He's jest a-sittin there makin a bargain with death, and he's goin to go and meet him. He's about ready to give up."

Will bought some new furniture for the new house. He bought three iron bedsteads, the rods forming the headboards and footboards joined together by huge metal fists. He bought a second-hand dresser from somewhere—a faded mahogany chest with four drawers and a cracked mirror standing three feet high above it. Two of the new beds went in the room where the fireplace was. The third one and Will's wooden bed from the cabin were moved into the Big House with the dresser and the center table, which held the Bible. There was plenty of room for another bed or other furniture in that room, but there was none to add.

The kitchen was as Vi had imagined it, crammed so full she could hardly move around the Lazy Susan table. But it was better than the log house, at least some better. She was not sitting in the edge of Coottown eternally. And she could raise her some chickens, perhaps turkeys, now. The first morning she woke up and looked about her at the neatly ceiled room, she felt almost happy. The feeling was days wearing off.

The first year in the new house passed rapidly for Alvira Ward. By the second spring, she had over fifteen laying hens and worked at building her flock larger. Will was working almost night and day in the fields, and hauling. From Bessie Ellis, Vi learned that Van and Dan were prospering in their stilling business with Lem Dyer, although the sheriff had been compelled to destroy one of their largest stills when he happened up on it. Anna had married the drummer, Tillie's last letter had said, and Tillie was expecting another baby. A letter from Vi's father in March of 1914, postmarked "Reynolds," caught Vi by surprise. Her parents had sold out and moved to Reynolds, and both of them were working in a tobacco factory there. It was about this time that Vi decided another child was growing inside her.

Around the first of April that spring, Mal returned home from taking Grandpa John some food, and gathered the big family Bible in his arms, taking it from the center table in the Big House. He had tiptoed to the front door, hugging it awkwardly, when Vi came in from the kitchen and caught him. Mal wheeled, drooped the huge book onto the foot of the nearest bed, and sat down on the floor, picking at his toenails and humming to himself.

"Where on earth was you a-slippin off to with that Bible?" Vi asked.

Mal looked up, his square face twisted into a puzzled frown.

"What Bible was that you was a-speakin of, Ma?" he asked in surprise.

"The biggest Bible in the house," she said. "The old Ward fambly Bible. The one you just had your arm wropped around and was tiptoeing out the door with. *That* Bible right there."

Mal looked around, saw the Bible on the bed through the iron footboard. He pointed at it. "You mean that Bible right there?"

"Yes. I mean that Bible right there. Now, where was you a-goin totin it to?"

Mal stood up, his face wistful. "To tell'ye the truth, Ma," he said, "I was takin it to Grandpa. He told me to slip it out and not let nobidy know about it. Said he wanted to read a spell in it one more time."

"Pore old feller," Vi mused. She stared through the doorway, off down the hillside. "He ain't read in a Bible nor gone to meetin since he was a young man. I wonder why does he want it now."

"I don't know, Ma," Mal said. "But he looked mighty sad. Looked like he might cry if I didn't fetch it."

"I tell'ye what," Vi said. She moved to the head of the bed and took a pillowcase from a pillow. "I'll put it in here. That'll keep it clean, and you can tote it better. Take care and don't drop it, specially crossin the branch. And don't tell'im I helped you."

"I'll take care, Ma," Mal grinned. "I sure will. And I know Grandpa's gonna be glad to get it."

One morning a few days later, Mal took old John some food but returned to the house, running, twenty minutes later. His face was dark with worry when he found Vi in the garden. "Ma," he panted, "Ma, he ain't there. Grandpa's gone."

She rested her hoe and turned on him. "Gone?" she echoed. "Gone where?"

"Miz Catlett said he left early this mornin. Said he went off up that holler where West Mountain and Fox come together, follerin the branch. Said she hadn't seen hair nor hide of him since."

Vi frowned in puzzlement. She felt a sudden chill in the April sunshine. "He wouldn't go up that holler," she argued, more with herself than with Mal. "He ain't been up that holler since—for years and years."

"Well, he's gone up it now," Mal said. "And he's liable not to never come back if somebidy don't hurry."

"You stay here with Lynn and Vern," she ordered, leaning her hoe against the paling fence. "They're playin in the yard. I'll go see can I find out what he's up to."

Lou Catlett waylayed Vi in the back yard in front of the smokehouse, her swarm of offspring, four sets of twins, surrounding them both, clammering like chickens when a hawk flies over. Lou was an ageless brooder, her belly drawn tight with a new litter, thrust forward against the frail fabric of her cotton dress. Snuff and saliva discolored the corners of her mouth.

"Howdy, Vi," she grinned. "I was spectin'ye. He went right up that holler thar—" She pointed. "Early this mawnin, and I ain't seed hair nor hide of'im sinct. I called to him, but he wouldn't stop. Jest kept a-goin like he was led by a rope. Been actin quare for more'n a week, like his mind was way off some'ers. I'd a-gone lookin for'im but couldn't leave my younguns to theirselves."

"Thank'ye, Lou." Vi smiled and nodded. "I'll go find him. He's just probably gone for a walk up in them trees there."

"A man his age is a-beggin for trouble when he goes off like that in the deep woods by hisself." Lou was sad now. She wiped at one eye.

"That's a fact," Vi agreed.

She waded waist-deep through the black- and tow-haired twins, and headed on up the slope toward the hollow. The trees closed in around her and met over her head. She walked beneath a mottled green canopy through which green light seeped. The forest hushed when she entered it, looking her over, testing her, but gradually let go, accepting her as she became a part of it, tiptoeing from tree to tree along the rippling branch. A bird began to chirrup again, high up in a hickory. A sapsucker scurried up a dead chestnut trunk. A male squirrel chased a female along a limb, concerned with nothing but the warm promise beneath the flirting grey tail just ahead.

Vi stopped and listened. The forest sounds encircled her and spread out around her, rippling off into the distance. The woods were cool and seemed to stretch away to the end of of the world, to the end of time. She felt strangely at peace, despite the nature of her search, but only briefly. She had a duty to perform and no time for dreaming beneath green trees. She crept on up the floor of the hollow, searching the slopes on either side with squinting eyes.

Grandpa John was not as hard to find as she had feared. He sat near the bottom of the slope on the West Mountain side, his back against a giant black oak. His bare head was leaned back against the trunk and his eyes were open. His wispy white beard stirred, though Vi could feel no breeze. From where she stood, it looked to her as though he could see the far-off edge of the forest, wherever it was. She walked up close and stared down at him.

"Grandpa!" she said softly. "Grandpa John!" Her quiet voice seemed to rumble out through the trees in an avalanche of sound. She started to speak his name again, then tasted the strange words on her lips, strange because they no longer belonged to anyone. Then she muttered, "John Witherspoon Ward, borned—" She tried to remember the date she had seen in the big Bible, but she had forgotten. "Died—" She stood, thinking. "Died April the sixth, nineteen hundred and fourteen. God be with him."

She stooped, reached out, hesitated, finally touched his old face. It was still warm—warm as the cool woods. Working carefully, she moved him. He was as light as last year's locust husk. She stretched him out on his back against the slope on the decaying leaves, his feet together, hands crossed on breast. She found two round pebbles, closed his eyes, and placed them on the lids. They were not coins, but they would have to do. She closed his mouth. Then she turned away and hurried back down the hollow, eager to be out of the cool woods and back beneath the hot sun.

She managed to slip inside the smokehouse without Lou Catlett seeing her. The big Bible lay open on the neatly made cot. She bent over it, stooping, and squinted at the white paper dimly washed by light seeping through knotholes and cracks in the slab sides. It was turned to the half-filled blanks for recording family genealogy. She ran her finger down the list, reading softly:

"John MacDonald Ward—Born March 4, 1740
Died April 6, 1803

John Thomas Ward—Born July 20, 1767
Died December 13, 1839

John Baylus Ward—Born August 13, 1789
Died November 4, 1893

John Witherspoon Ward—"

Vi leaned closer, squinting.

"—Born March 4, 1844
Died—" She filled in vocally, "April 6, 1914."

She paused, then read the next line.

"John William Ward—Born May 5, 1865
Died—"

The record stopped there, as though Time had paused to dip his pen in ink. She wondered fleetingly which of her own promised children would be recorded on the next line as the sixth John Ward. Obviously, there had been no design in naming the sons, no respect for primogeniture. A scribbled message in the margin caught her attention, writing that had no business cluttering up the solemn record of a family tree. She spelled the words out slowly, the way Will spelled out words of a new song. "Kindley burie me wher youall find me. I thank you. Amen," she read carefully. Then she read it again to be sure she understood the message.

Carrying the Bible in her arms, she made her way back down Stud Branch. When she reached the house on the hillside, she sent Mal after Cousin Bill. He drove up to the woodshed in his buggy a little later, Mal beside him. Vi climbed the path to where he sat looking down at her, his face set for bad news.

"Grandpa John's passed away," she said. "Went up that holler he don't like and leaned back against a oak tree and died. Would you kindly go fetch Will? He's gone to the sawmill at Stoney Fork for a load of lumber."

She watched tears well into Cousin Bill's eyes as he stared at her, through her, perhaps seeing the dark hollow in the woods and an old man dead against a tree, except she knew he was no longer against a tree but laid out in a fitting and proper manner, even if only squirrels and birds attended his wake. Cousin Bill did not speak to her. She watched him back the mare in a half circle and head out toward the Big Road.

Will rode up in Cousin Bill's buggy an hour later, the mare panting for breath. He did not tell her, but Vi knew Cousin Bill was coming on behind with the mules and wagon. She met him at the woodshed. Will's face was troubled, but to Vi it looked more like dread than grief. He let himself down stiffly from the buggy and walked up to Alvira, staring at her, waiting for her, waiting for her to confirm what he already knew.

"He's dead, like Cousin Bill told'ye," she said. "Up the holler against a tree. I laid him out as best I could before he got stiff. Come on to the house with me. I got somethin you're bound to see."

He followed her past Lynn and the baby, playing with a frog in the back yard, past Mal, who stood in the kitchen door and stared at them with understanding and with silent grief, on into the Big House. The Bible was lying open on the center table near the single window. She leaned over it. "Here's the last words he ever writ before he died," she said. Then she read the message to Will.

Will Ward stepped back, clutching at his forehead. "Why, he must a-been crazy as a bedbug," he stammered.

"I don't think so," Vi argued. "I think he knowd exactly what he wanted."

"But why?" Will protested, his face warped in puzzlement.

"Why in God's name would a sensible man want to be buried way off in the woods like a wild animal, stead of a neat, clean graveyard?"

"Maybe they was somebody in them woods he needed to go back to," she said thoughtfully. "Maybe he needed to go back to that Yankee soldier he shot and buried up there that time."

"It looks to me like, from where I stand, that that Yankee soldier has done got ebem with him in the long run, finally at last," Will said.

"You can't go back on his wish," Vi went on. "You're bound to honor his last will, sech as it is. And we got to move fast if we bury him today. He must a-meant not to bring him out of the woods."

"Yeah," Will nodded. "We're bound to go along with what he wanted. That was all he had left in creation, that woosh and his few cabinet tools. I reckon I wouldn't be much of a man if I went agin him, if I don't bury him like he said to, jest to please my own mind."

When Cousin Bill arrived with the wagon, Will drove it on up to the old cabin, and had Abe Catlett build a rough coffin from the plank, using Grandpa John's tools. It was a crude box, which John Ward would have split up for kindling, but functional. There was no problem preparing the old man further because he had dressed up in all the decent clothes he owned before he had gone up the hollow. They worked fast because the sun was leaning in favor of West Mountain, where twilight already lurked below the thick foliage. Albert Essex and Abe Catlett had dug a shallow grave, cutting down through green roots, which bled sap into the dark, moist earth, and had hollowed out a space large enough for the ugly casket.

Cousin Bill read from a battered little Bible while the mourners stood by the raw wound in the earth and stared out through the shadowy trees in puzzlement. It was a small, silent congregation. Besides Cousin Bill and Will, there were Alvira, Rosa, Doc Ellis, Albert Essex, and Abe Catlett, a reluctant sexton. The Harrisons had not come, despite their close kinship. Van and Dan could not be found. No one else had been asked, even told, of John Witherspoon Ward's death and funeral, although anyone would have been welcome to attend. Vi, hearing the sound of Cousin Bill's voice, understood why others, including the Catlett clan, had not come, the few who must have learned of the funeral. This was not the kind of burying the hillfolk were used to, and they wanted no truck with it. There was something akin to the devil's doings about burying an old man way off in the dark woods by himself. An angry God could have little dealings with such unholy goings-on.

Cousin Bill read in a monotone that drowned out the forest sounds, "What profit hath a man of all his labor which he taketh under the sun? One generation passeth away, and another generation cometh: but the earth abideth for ever. The sun also ariseth, and the sun goeth down, and hasteth to his place where he arose."

Vi only half listened, her mind far away, as he read, "For what hath man of all his labor, and of the vexation of his heart, wherein he hath labored under the sun? For all his days are sorrows, and his travail grief; yea, his heart taketh not rest in the night."

And he read, "For that which befalleth the sons of man befalleth beasts; even one thing befalleth them: as the one dieth, so dieth the other." For a moment Vi's attention drifted. She shook her head, listening. "Wherefore I perceive that there is nothing better, than that a man should rejoice in his own works; for that is his portion: for who shall bring him to see what shall be after him?" Cousin Bill stopped and stood silent for half a minute.

And then he read, "As he came forth of his mother's womb, naked shall he return to go as he came, and shall take nothing of his labor, which he may carry away in his hand."

And he read, "For the living know that they shall die: but the dead know not any thing, neither have they any more reward; for the memory of them is forgotten. Also their love, and their hatred, and their envy, is now perished; neither have they any more a portion for ever in any thing that is done under the sun. Go thy way, eat thy bread with joy, and drink thy wine with a merry heart; for God now accepteth thy works." His voice faded, then came back strong. "Whatsoever thy hand findeth to do, do it with thy might; for there is no work, nor device, nor knowledge, nor wisdom, in the grave, whither thou goest."

Cousin Bill's voice dropped lower, tiring. "In the days when the keepers of the house shall tremble, and the strong men shall bow themselves, and the grinders cease because they are few, and those that look out of the windows be darkened, and the doors shall be shut in the streets, when the sound of the grinding is low, and he shall rise up at the voice of the bird, and all the daughters of music shall be brought low; and when they shall be afraid of that which is high, and fears shall be in the way, and the almond tree shall flourish, and the grasshopper shall be a burden . . . or the golden bowl be broken, or the pitcher be broken at the fountain or the wheel broken at the cistern. Then shall the dust return to the earth as it was: and the spirit shall return unto God who gave it. Amen."

The little train of mourners filed slowly down the hollow, leaving Abe Catlett to race with gloom, filling the shallow grave. Vi peered out through the trees spreading out around her, and she thought of Grandpa John stumbling away among the shadowy trunks till the end of time, pursuing the shadow of the Yankee soldier he had killed. Suddenly December was heavy in the forest air. She shuddered. They filed out of the hollow and onto the bare hills beneath an April sky. They were still in shadows because the sun had crossed over West Mountain, but the air here was warm.

Vi looked upward and breathed deeply. The sky was dark blue and empty except for three puffball clouds arranged in a triangular formation and scudding eastward. Then she looked down at the red clay field and remembered milking time and supper to cook and a dozen other jobs waiting for her to finish before she could sleep again, and she shifted to the back of her mind further thought of an old, bearded face and a grave in the cool forest.

10

Venna Ward was born July 20, one of the hottest days Vi could remember. She labored for a while in the hot, stifling room, sweat pouring from her bloated body, and was rewarded in the end with a shrill yell of protest, following Doc Ellis's slap on moist red rump. Venna Ward came into the world kicking and yelling back. Her eyes were emerald green the day she was born, her hair a sandy brown, and her long nails clawed gashes in Vi's bloated breast the first time she nursed.

Will Ward leaned over and looked at her. "She's gonna be a heller," he grinned. "She's startin off like a wildcat. Got some of Annie's spunk and vinegar in her."

"She'll never be another Annie," Vi muttered. "I'll see to that."

"I think she was meant to be a boy," Doc Ellis laughed. "Only trouble is she's got the wrong equip-ment."

Vi looked up from her pillow in protest. "She's a purty little girl," she snapped. "She don't no more look like a boy than Vern does."

"I was just joshin, Vi," Doc Ellis laughed. "You got a fine little gal baby there. You just be careful she don't chew your bosom off."

The baby was never satisfied with either breast. She would

gulp at one a few minutes, almost drowning in the rich milk, then go groping and nuzzling for the other with blind, gaping muzzle. Only moments there, and she would switch back to the first, then search for a third one in between, or above or below. When she decided she had a choice between only two, she would drop back to the first one she started with and shove at it with her face like a hungry calf until Vi spanked her lightly; then she turned loose to argue with an infant yell.

"Little bugger," Vi grinned at her. "If I had ten tits like a collie, you'd be tryin to find the leventh."

The next year passed with only routine toil to break the everlasting monotony which was Alvira Matlock Ward's life—or what would have been monotonous, had it not been for her young family. One event did occur which jarred her briefly out of the rut of tedious hours and days and months. Young Lynn decided to go on another journey, this time in search of the Big Sea. By the summer of 1915, Mal was a big, burly eleven-year-old and Lynn was seven. Mal had turned out to be entirely different from the older boys. He was quiet, soft-spoken, and obedient. Vi was certain he loved her as much as though she were his real mother, and she showed no partiality between him and Lynn except that required by a difference in ages.

Lynn had long ago struck off in a different direction from the size and shape taken by the three boys in Will's first family. He was tall for his age—taller than Van, Dan, or Mal had been even at nine—with broad shoulders and narrow hips. Where Bell Ward's boys had had dull black hair, Lynn's was a glossy black, an Indian black, parted in the middle and falling away on either side as shaggy as a pony's mane. His eyes were blue with flecks of gold in them, and his face was aquiline, with Vi's prominent cheekbones, and a nose thinner than Will's.

Vi glanced at him occasionally, noticing his handsome face, his lithe physique, and felt an inner satisfaction that her first-born would be a handsome man, an intelligent man, but she feared he would be a man with itching feet. From the time Lynn was four, Vi had a silent understanding with Mal that he would report when his half-brother disappeared for any length of time.

He had already wandered off to Cousin Bill's house, up to Abe Catlett's, and once had walked halfway to Holkirk Church before Doc Ellis met him, talked him into riding double, and had brought him home on horseback.

On this particular day in steaming August, Vi sent Mal to the spring at the foot of West Mountain for a bucket of water, and Lynn tagged along as Mal's second shadow. Mal returned some twenty minutes later, brought the water into the kitchen, where Vi was preparing the noon meal, then disappeared back outside. Vi thought no more about either of them until dinner was on the table and she had set four-year-old Vern at her place, dipped food into her plate, and was ready to sit down with Venna and stop her fussing for food. She stepped to the kitchen door and called Mal, who lay on the porch messing with a rock sling. He crammed the weapon of string and leather into his pocket and leaped up, his face lighting up at the prospect of food.

"Where's Lynn?" Vi asked, when he was almost to the door, "Go fetch him."

Mal staggered to a halt and stared up at her, his face at first blank, then dark with understanding. "I left him at the spring," he muttered. "He was tryin to catch a spring lizard to feed a crawfish he's got penned up out at the branch."

"Well, go get him," Vi ordered. "And hurry. Dinner'll be cold d'rectly." She turned back and sat down at the table, holding on to the squirming Venna until she could get some food in her plate.

Vi had not taken more than three or four bites before Mal charged back into the kitchen, his bare feet pounding the floor and rattling the dishes on the table-waiter. "He ain't there, Ma!" he panted, his eyes wide with dread. "Lynn has run off some'ers again."

Vi was more annoyed than concerned. She placed Venna on the floor, checked on Vern, then walked out into the white sunshine. Circling the house, she stood in the back yard facing down the hill. She shaded her eyes, squinting, but no Lynn was in sight. She traced the branch with her eyes until it disappeared at the bend near the Big Road. There was no movement on her side of the bank growth.

"Lynn!" she yelled through cupped hands. "Oh-h-h, Lyn-n-n!" Her voice bounded across the narrow valley and echoed back from West Mountain, then echoed and re-echoed like ripples dying away from a pebble cast into a pond. She stood silent and listened. There was no response.

Her heart began to pound, the blood to surge in her temples. Lynn was a good eater. He did not like to wander far from the table this close to mealtime. He should have been in hearing distance but was not. She turned, almost stumbling over Mal, who stood close behind her.

"You know better'n to let him out of your sight," she snapped. "Now go take care of the girls. See that they eat. I'll try and go find him. You reckon a leven-year-old yearlin boy can do that?"

Mal turned away, his head down, and Vi was immediately sorry she had talked so rough. She started to call to him, then decided to hurry after Lynn, wherever he was. She turned back and almost ran down the hill toward the branch, tearing her dress on the pasture fence when she crawled between the strands. He was not at the footlog across the branch, the area where he usually played. She stood in the meadow beyond, trying to turn in two directions at once, upstream and down. She made up her mind with no reasoning behind it, and headed down the branch.

She trotted down the path parallel to the branch, moving in close when it veered so far away she could not see below the bank. But she reached the Big Road without seeing any sign of him. She stood in the dusty road, confused, torn between the need to return and look after the little girls and the need to go on looking for Lynn. But she wasted little time in indecision. After a moment she crossed the new bridge over the branch and continued southward, following the left bank.

The Dugan house came in sight around the bend ahead, and she slowed her pace, almost out of breath. Doubts were beginning to cloud her thinking. She wondered if he had not gone upstream to Abe Catlett's or perhaps headed across the mountain toward Holkirk Church again or to Doc Ellis's store. The more she thought about it, the slower she walked, though not forgetting to glance at intervals below the banks of the meandering stream. But when she decided, suddenly, to go as far as Bare Creek before turning back, she speeded up her pace again. She passed between the stream and the Dugan house, and thought about checking with them. The shutters of the back windows were open and smoke was spiraling out of the stone flue. But if the boy had followed the streambed, they could not have seen him. And she always felt nervous around two women who bore bastards so shamelessly, as though they were peach trees in full bloom for all creation to look at. She continued onward, and approached Bare Creek a few moments later, feeling exhausted and a little frantic.

She reached the creek road and turned left, following it to the fork, where the branch road converged with it. She stood for a moment at the intersection, burdened with a choice of three narrow, dusty roads to choose from, yet knowing it had to be the one back up the branch, back to the house, where the younger children needed her. She stood and she pivoted first one way, then another. She shaded her eyes and stared down the road along Bare Creek, and then she squinted as someone came into view around a distant curve, walking slowly. No, it was two somebodies, a tall and a short one. No, it was a man and a child. Then she recognized Lynn, and air gushed into her lungs with an intake of relief. She wanted to break his neck with her bare hands and then hug him half to death.

Feet bare, Pink Dugan approached her, tall, redheaded, and shy, carrying a fishing pole in one hand and leading Lynn with the other. He reminded Vi of Jesus on the back of Bruton Snuff fans. Lynn was staring, trying to read her face like Will watched thunderheads when corn had to be worked. She could see he was in doubt as to what her weather would be, and she kept her face stern to trouble him.

"I reckon this here's the young feller you's a-lookin for," Pink Dugan grinned.

"Whoever his pa was," Vi thought in a flash, "he's a different breed from them other Dugans. In spite of his beard and shaggy hair, he's a nice-lookin feller. I don't any more believe he sleeps with his sisters like that Tom than nothin." But she said aloud, "Thank'ye, Pink. He's the very critter I'm a-huntin. Where did you tree him, anyway?"

"I was fishin down the creek there a ways, and he come along wadin up to his knees." Pink grinned again. "Said he was aimin to foller the creek to the Yadkin, and the Yadkin clean to the Big Sea."

"I didn't mean to, Ma," Lynn broke in, solemnly. "I was just a-goin as far as where Pink was a-fishin at, and then I was gonna turn back, if he didn't bring me back hisself like this."

Pink Dugan laughed, white teeth flashing through his red beard. "How'd you know I was a-fishin down there when I didn't know I was goin to myself tell a hour back?"

Lynn looked up at him, puzzled. "Cause last time I rid by there w‘th Pa on the wagon, you was a-fishin there."

Pink looked at Vi, his brow furrowed. She bit back a smile and took Lynn's hand, yanking him close beside her. "You just wait, young man!" she threatened. "When I get you home, I aim to wear you out with a switch."

She did not whip him, though. She was too glad to have found him and too relieved that Mal had taken good care of Vern and the baby. He had even wrestled Venna into the cradle and rocked her to sleep, something she had been unable to do lately. She gave Lynn a good talking to and let it go at that, wondering how long it would last.

In the fall of that year, her parents sent her money, and Vi took the children to visit them for three days at Reynolds. Mal went along to stay with Tillie, who would not know him, Vi reasoned, any more than she would some eleven-year-old boy from England. But she did not have the heart to leave him behind. They rode with Will on a load of lumber as far as Coleman's Ford, and he put them on the train there.

The ride down the river, the stop in Northboro, then the journey on to Reynolds was an adventure that kept the children gawking through the windows at the trees and houses rushing by at up to forty-five miles an hour. Vern sat quietly as always, mouth open in amazement at the changing landscape. Mal and Lynn tried to shout each other down. Venna was concerned with more immediate things. She wanted to see where the doors led to at either end of the rocking car, and Vi had to fuss with her the whole way.

When Henry Matlock met her at the station, Vi thought he looked more than ever like an aging Indian. He was still tall and sinewy, though his black hair was greying high up on the sides and his face was lined. Her mother looked like the same Dutch housewife, a little older, a little more pink-cheeked, a little better fed than that terrible day when she had visited them briefly at Stud Branch. Her father greeted her solemnly, patting her on the back with an arm about her. Her mother embraced Vi, her eyes filling. Vi swallowed the lump in her throat, and smiled to see them. But they were almost strangers. Too many years of toil had come between her and girlhood, between her and her parents. She felt almost as old as they were, almost as though she could set them down and teach them lessons about problems they had never heard tell of. But she had not come for that, and she tried to act like a daughter coming home for a visit, although it was a home she had never seen.

Henry Matlock looked her up and down, his dark face grim. "You're lookin—strong, daughter," he said, and turned away.

Amanda Matlock studied Vi's face. That seemed to be as far as she dared look, for the time being. "I hope your new house is a heap more livable than the other'n," she said.

"It is," Vi nodded, shifting the baby on her hip. "It's a heap more satisfyin than the log one. Can we go now and get these restless younguns settled down?"

Henry Matlock herded them into a trolley, and they went rattling and clanging toward the northern edge of town, out of an ocean of raw-tobacco odor, toward where clean air blew. Vi stared at the cars sitting along the street or scooting back and forth like black waterbugs. She had not dreamed there were so many in the whole world. Lynn was fascinated. He watched them wide-eyed, as though they were something from another world. The trolley track ended near her parents' house.

The Matlocks lived in a white bungalow with a hipped roof far enough out so that they had a garden and a small field of corn. The dead stalks were standing with the fodder hanging like burnt strips of paper in tattered banners. The tobacco odor reached here only when the wind-tide was high.

Vi's mother and father, both working, lived like royalty compared to the life they had led near Northboro, compared to the life Vi herself led from day to day. They had beds with springs and mattresses, and a gas range, and an icebox to keep things cold, like milk and butter. Henry Matlock had not been idle since Vi married. Two new children, a boy and a girl, had been added to the six she had left at home, when she had last visited, late in 1905. The two oldest boys, Zeb and Carl, were married and had moved to Cannonville, where they worked in the towel mill. Jessica was now nineteen and housekeeper for the Matlock family. All the children were shy strangers except the youngest ones, Roy, eight, and Emma, six. Roy took Lynn over immediately and gave him a tour of the grounds. Emma started a campaign trying to treat Venna like a baby doll, but Venna fought back until her young aunt gave up and turned to Vern.

Tillie and her husband came by late in the afternoon and picked Mal up. She was glad to see Vi, apparently, but seemed another stranger Vi had met once on a lonely road and had nodded to. Her husband was a tall, quiet man who hardly said more than the necessary "How-do." Tillie told Vi that a housekeeper looked after their children and that they had come directly from the tobacco factory after quitting time. Somehow, after seeing her, Vi felt very sad. She felt happy that Tillie had turned out so well, yet she felt sad. When Tillie had ridden away from Stud Branch that time, it was just as though she had ridden off to die. This young woman was just somebody named Tillie she did not know.

When she looked back at the visit, even years later, Vi could remember many things about it. But the lasting memory concerned the photograph. On Saturday, Henry Matlock took her and the children downtown to a photographer and had a picture made. Later, he sent them an expensive framed copy, oval with a convex glass cover. It hung on the wall of the Big House year after year, recalling to her mind that one brief escape from the drudgery of the farm.

Vi, dressed in navy blue with a white collar, sat stiffly in a chair holding the baby on her lap. Her black hair was parted in the middle and pulled tightly back to a bun, out of the picture. Her cheeks were hollow, causing her cheekbones to stand out more prominently. Her mouth was straight and unsmiling. There was a sadness in her face the photographer had recorded for all time, and she looked ten years older than a young mother of twenty-seven.

Venna was dressed in a long white dress and stared about her like a sparrow. Vern stood on Vi's left, her long hair in two plaits down her shoulders. Her face was solemn and thoughtful. Lynn, dressed in the new suit Grandpa Matlock had given him, stood on Vi's left. His hair, neatly cut, was parted in the middle. His eyes were focused on the camera, as though he would stand there for centuries trying to figure out how the contraption worked. Will Ward said later he thought Vi looked too damned thin in the face. He was afraid some sonofabitch would think she had not been getting enough to eat. Besides, he liked his women with enough meat on their bones to cast a good shadow.

On Monday, they rode the train back to Coleman's Ford, and Will picked them up with the empty wagon. He had to haul one layer of plank back to Stud Branch, creating a platform large enough to hold them all, but apparently he was happy enough to have Vi back running the house that he was willing to put up with this wasted labor. When she entered the crowded kitchen later, Vi looked about her and sighed. The air rushed in so fast it choked her, and she had to blink back unexpected tears.

Lynn started school that fall, walking the three miles to Allen's Shop School. Will thought Lynn should wait another year, but Vi would not hear tell of any such delay. She did not argue. She walked the three miles with the two boys and got them started. Mal was already in the fourth grade and doing well. She was not certain Lynn would be a good student, not certain he would even stay in school for the few necessary hours each day. But he surprised her. He made good grades from the beginning, the best grades in the first grade, or primer, as it was called.

By late October, Alvira was certain she was carrying another child, but she had no trouble, no illness from conception on. When she mentioned it to Will, he did not bat an eye. "God-amighty!" he growled, "if this keeps up, I'll have to knock a wall out and add on a barn full of stalls."

"They's not but one way to stop'em from comin," Vi said. "And they ain't a man in all creation that would pay that price."

Will opened his mouth and reached for an answer, but there was none. She could tell he knew there was none. He moved away, talking about something else. "Gonna kill hogs next week," he said, "if this cold spell hangs on."

May 2, 1916, Alvira Matlock Ward, twenty-eight, had her first glimpse of real tragedy. Her fourth child, a third daughter, was born with a double cleft lip. Will hardly said a word, hardly realized the magnitude of the child's tragedy. But Vi had known a young woman who was "harelipped," and her heart broke a little and remained broken. Holding the quiet, content infant close in her arms, alone, she had broken down and wept for the first time since girlhood. But once the grief was out of her system, she did not yield to it again. The child had no problem nursing, and Vi settled down to do with her the best she could, to make her life as normal as possible. By nature, she was like Vern, quiet and easy to please, just the opposite of the squealing, scratching Venna.

She named the baby Ora. Where she got such a name she did not know. It came to her one night when she could not sleep, and she decided that was meant to be her name. The next morning at breakfast she said, "Will, I aim to name this'un Ora."

Will stopped with a forkful of eggs halfway to his face, mouth wide open. Then he closed his mouth. "Is that some manner of Bible name I ain't never heard tell of?"

"No," she said, "it ain't no Bible name, I don't reckon."

"Well, where in hell did you git sech a name at?" He stared at her. "It sounds plime blank like some manner of salve from Sears, Roebuck's catalogue."

"Well, it ain't no salve," Vi argued. "It was give to me out of the thin air last night when I couldn't sleep hardly."

"Well, if you ast me, I'd say to give hit back." He started to eat again, and that ended the matter. The baby was named Ora.

That summer, as always, crops were planted, corn was plowed and hoed dutifully as in other years and all the years that followed. When the corn was laid by, Will started hauling again from Stoney Fork to Stud Branch, where he spent the night, then up at five o'clock and on the hard, jolting road to Northboro (after the Big Fresh), twenty miles away. He would spend the night there, sleeping on a quilt beneath his wagon, then return home the following day. These long hauls netted him a few dollars each, and during the nights he was away, Vi was left alone with the children, spread in age from Ora, months old, to Mal, only twelve.

That summer Greer Harrison built his house by the Big Road, on the spur of West Mountain, built a huge barn up the branch where Will had talked of building his, and erected a fancy outhouse out over Stud Branch. Greer moved his new, pregnant wife into the white house early in July. And that summer Will wore out his first team of mules, Toab and Fred, and traded them for a pair of black colt mules named Beck and George. Beck was female. The mule trade meant far more to Will Ward than news filtering into the hills of a big war going on across the Big Waters.

During the night of July 14, 1916, it started to rain. Vi woke in darkness and blinked in amazement at the roar of the downpour without thunder or lightning. She went back to sleep, but when she awoke at dawn, the rain was even harder than at first. It rained for over thirty hours, so loud against the shingle roof that the Wards had to raise their voices when they talked. Will paced the floor in amazement, half afraid, Vi could see. Never in his memory or the memory of his father had there been such a rain in Wilton County. It was unnatural. It was an act of God. Stud Branch was a raging river, over the meadow, the spring, reaching far up the slope toward the house. When Vi and Will stood on the front porch and listened, after the rain slackened, they could hear the roar of the Yadkin River, like wind in high pines, more than four miles away.

When the rain stopped, Stud Branch fell fast, but the river continued to roar like distant surf. Vi left the girls with Reba Harrison, Greer's wife, and walked with Will, the two boys, and Greer across Soapstone Mountain to see the river. They stood on the front porch of Anson Silver's house, where a crowd had already gathered, and gazed out across a rushing ocean of muddy water. The Yadkin River lapped at the edge of the slope just below the edge of the porch and stretched away to a distant shoreline of hills.

"Jesus Christ!" Will Ward breathed, "hit must be fifty foot from the medder to the top of that water."

"Lookee there!" somebody yelled. "There goes a lumberhack with a old hen walkin around on it like she was cock of the walk."

"And yander goes another house," Anson Silver called.

Pink Dugan raised his banjo and began to pluck, singing softly:

"Down the roarin river
Come a lumberhack,
And on it a old hen
Walked for'ard and back,
In them days when that Great Fresh come down."

This was the tenth stanza Pink had made up while standing there. Vi thought she recognized the tune. She thought Pink was trying to follow a song he already knew called "The Sinking of the *Titanic.*" But Pink's tune was a little different. Hearing him, a stanza of the *Titanic* song ran through her head.

"Husbans and wives
And little chilren
Lost their lives
It was sad when that great ship went down."

News and rumors were carried from house to house during the weeks that followed. Vi heard that houses and other buildings were washed away, many people were drowned, as well as stock and fowl. The railroad from Northboro into Carson County, including the branch line up Hog Elk Creek to lumber country, was washed away to the last crosstie. The lumberyard at Coleman's Ford went, too. Landslides along the slopes of the Bushy Mountains carried away houses and barns to destruction, leaving dark scars visible from Stud Branch. But Will Ward's house and buildings had been safe, on high ground. The only lasting effect concerned his hauling. From that day forward, Will had to make the long haul all the way to Northboro, a good twenty miles from Stud Branch, the way the winding road ran.

Sometimes Lynn sat on the front porch beating time on the bottom of a bucket or pan while Pink Dugan played on his banjo and sang "The Great Nineteen Sixteen Fresh," a flood God sent to punish Wilton County. Few of the hillfolk other than Vi ever learned of the hurricane that struck the coast of South Carolina and broke up over the mountains, spilling its floods over the hills and valleys. If anyone had told Will Ward about it, he would have frowned and asked, "Who in hell ever heard tell of any sech of a thing as a hurry-cane?"

Will let up from his hauling that fall only long enough to harvest the corn, and as usual, Vi worked in the fields until her hands chapped and cracked, opening raw wounds in old callouses. The next year passed routinely, filled with labor and long hours which were as much a part of life as breathing, and were accepted as normally. March, 1918, arrived, blustering but bright, and Vi looked forward to spring, as she always did, as a release from the cramped, cold little house.

One morning during the first week in March, Will got up before dawn, stretched his rheumatic muscles into line, adjusted his hernias, broke wind six times, and left with a load of lumber for Northboro. Vi remained up after he had left, and prepared breakfast for the children an hour later. After milking, she got Mal and Lynn ready and sent them off to school, then prepared to skim the milk. She had just finished, when there came a loud knock on the kitchen door. She circled the round table, opened the door, then stiffened, on guard. Tom Dugan stood on the porch slouched against a post, hands in pockets.

"Howdy, Miz Ward," he said through his perpetual scowl.

Vi hesitated, wondering whether to shove the door and latch it. "What do you want here?" she demanded.

"You still knockin folks around with cheers like up at the old place?" he grinned.

"If needs be," Vi said. "And I just might stoop to usin axes on heads, stead of the other end. What do you want, Tom Dugan?"

"You don't have to be so on-neighborly. I brung you Will's cradle back. Pink borried hit late last summer and didn't recollect to fetch hit back tell now."

"Where's it at?" Vi looked about the porch and yard. "I don't see no cradle."

"Hit's there by the end of the house yander." He pointed toward the end of the kitchen, out of sight from where he stood. "Pink said much obliged."

He turned his back on her, stepped off the porch, and walked away toward the stables, where the path led down the hill. Vi paced to the end of the porch, stepped into the yard, and looked at the cradle. It consisted of a long, almost straight scythe blade attached to a longer handle, with several thin wooden fingers parallel to the blade and set about four inches apart. The tool was in good condition except that the outside finger had been broken off ten inches from its base.

Vi whirled. "Tom Dugan!" she called.

Tom stopped and turned. "Yeah?"

"Who broke this finger off this here wheat cradle?"

"I done hit. Hung hit over the bobwar fence down this side of Greer Harrison's barn. Why?"

She strode toward him. "Cause you'll have to pay for it, that's why."

He threw back his dark head, spurting out laughter like vomit. "Who's aimin to make me? You?"

Vi was close in front of him now. "I figure Will can, maybe."

"That old broke-down hauler?" He laughed again.

Vi was suddenly furious, raging, blindly furious; more angry than all the times before in her whole life. "You listen here. That old hauler's got more manhood in his little finger than you got in your whole carcass, you low-down trash. You ain't fit to break bread with no Catlett that ever drawed breath."

A March cloud scudded across the sun, dropping its shadow on Tom Dugan's face. When the cloud moved on, the shadow was still there. He closed the ten feet between himself and Vi with a scurry of broganed feet. His open palm caught her in the face. Her head rocked back. Then he was through. He stepped back, amazed.

Anger pounded inside Vi's chest. Her face burned from the blow. "You just wait till Will comes home," she said, almost gently. "He won't take kindly to this, Tom Dugan."

Tom laughed, but it was far back in his mouth and too high for a good laugh. It sounded far away. "He'll have to ride a long and crooked road to find me, when he gits back," he scoffed. "Give him a few days, and he'll git over hit." He whirled and struck off down across the field at an angle that would bring him to the path leading down Stud Branch.

Alvira nursed her hurt like an aching tooth all that day and the next. She did not mention it to the boys because that could serve no purpose. She heard Will "whoa!" the mules to a stop at the woodshed around eight o'clock that night, and met him down in front of the stables. As he led the mules down the steep path in the moonlight, he seemed to walk without his knees bending, and his shoulders were slumped, thrusting his head forward. He did not see Vi at first, in the shadow of the building, and began to unharness George. She watched him closely. He moved awkwardly, like a drunk man. She heard him sigh or groan, it was hard to tell the difference, as he lugged the harness and collar to the side of the log stable and hung them on a peg.

She started to turn away and slip back to the house, when he saw her. "Vi?" he called, alert. "Vi, is that you?"

She turned back. "Yeah. Yeah, it's me."

"Is anything the matter?"

"Well, not now, they ain't."

He plodded closer to her, leaned forward and peered at her from beneath the brim of the battered hat. "What the hell you a-talkin about, Vi?"

"Well, I may as well tell'ye now as later. That Tom Dugan brought the cradle back Pink borried. He broke a finger out of it a-crossin Greer Harrison's fence."

"Well, hell, I can't worry bout that tonight," He sighed. "I'm so damned tard I couldn't fart without a dose of sodie." He turned back and started unharnessing Beck.

"When I told him he'd have to pay for it," Vi said, "he slapped me in the face. Near about took my head off."

Will whirled back, staring at her. "That low-down sonofabitch dared lay a hand on you?"

"He slapped me hard as he could," Vi said.

"Well, by God! I'll jest have to go and find him and beat his goddamn ass."

"I got supper waitin," Vi said. "Why don't you come on to the house and go tomorr?"

"It's got to be done tonight," Will growled. "If a feller can't take care of his own womern, he's a damn pore man."

"He said you wouldn't find him," she argued. "Said you'd have to ride a long, crooked road to find him."

"You know what that means?" He dragged himself awkwardly onto the mare mule's bare back. "It means he's a-hidin out up at his granny's place on Stoney Fork. Put George up for me, will'ye? And feed'im."

"Why don't you just wait till mornin, Will?" she pleaded. "It's over ten mile up there, follerin that crooked road."

"They's some things a feller can't put off till tomorr," he said wearily. "Besides, that bastard's been doggin my heels like bad luck since as far back as I can recollect." He reined the mule around, and she plodded up the path toward the Ridge Road, Will Ward on her back, slumped forward like a man riding blindly into a windmill.

Watching him go, Vi felt a sudden surge of tenderness. It was no longer pity. It was something much deeper than pity. It was an emotion unfamiliar to her. She turned the mule into his stable and fed him, then started back to the house. Halfway out the path, she stopped and stared upward at the blue sky. The moon was close above, close as a golden pear, and the scudding clouds she could have batted down with a broom, it seemed like. But the sky was high. Looking at it, she could tell it reached out forever, in unending blue. There was plenty of room to move around beneath it.

She kept a small fire in the fireplace and sat up, waiting for Will, a quilt draped about her. She put his food in pans and set them close by the fire to keep them warm. She was wide awake. She could not have slept to save her soul. But when he finally shuffled in, hours later, he was too tired to eat much. He picked at the potatoes and kraut and ate a few pieces of sliced sidemeat and some corn bread. Then he struggled out of his overalls and shoes like a creature shedding its skin.

"The sonofabitch was at his granny's, asleep," he said finally. "I called him out. He come up to me grinnin and bullshittin and holdin out his hand to shake. I never said nairy a word. I stood there holdin Beck's lead strop in my left hand tell he got clost enough to reach. Then I let him have it on the jaw with my right fist. Damn nigh tore his head off. He fell back-'ards and laid still. I got back on Beck and rid off and left him a-layin there in the dirt."

He turned away, tottered to the bed, and collapsed across it, pulling the covers up over himself. Vi glanced at the new clock on the mantel. It was almost two o'clock. She undressed slowly and crawled past him. He was asleep, snoring evenly. She lay there on her back beside him for hour after hour, unable to sleep. That strange feeling still plagued her. She could not identify it. She reached out and ran her hand along his hard back beneath the covers. She felt his arms, hard as river rock even in repose. His strong, astringent body odor was as familiar as his remembered face, with its stubborn jaw and ice-grey eyes.

Toward dawn, he stirred and turned toward her, and she took him into her arms. She received him with joy, understanding the emotion she had thought was new. And for the first time Alvira Matlock knew Will Ward.

Part Five

TIME IS

JOHN MATLOCK WARD

Yes, such as it was, this had been his world, in the beginning, and John Ward was amazed to discover that he had never really escaped it, that he would live on Stud Branch, as Will Ward had, all the days of his life.

He stared south. The blue Bushy Mountains still lay there against the sky, a barrier between this valley and the real world. Hill Anderson's house—craphouse gothic, Doc Ellis had called it—was no longer there. His wife had burned it and Hill and herself years ago, after Hill had made arrangements to bring one of Doll Dugan's girls in to live with them. Half a chimney stood there like a truncated phallus against the mountain and sky. John dropped his gaze to the rusty tin roof of Greer Harrison's house, what had been Greer Harrison's house. The gold-plated lightning rods were gone. After Reba had died of a stroke running for the safety of the house to escape a small thunderstorm, Greer had had the rods torn down and hauled away for junk. He had married again but lived only a few years after Reba's death.

John thought briefly of other histories his mother had told him. Someone had killed Tom Dugan with a river rock. Lem

Dyer had become rich during the Prohibition era, with a fleet of Ford V-8's hauling north, but had not escaped entirely. An old man, he now lived with his son, successful in real estate, on a shady street in Northboro behind bastard Doric-Ionic columns, and boasted to his grandchildren that he, like some of his neighbors, had once spent time in a federal pen (anyone who had served in a state prison for bootlegging was of a lower caste).

John cocked his head. From far away, over the thickets to his right, came the whine of a saw blade and the throb of a tractor—one of Ben Dugan's sawmills, his mother had said when they parked on the ridge above the house, cutting the timber Will Ward had once owned. Alvin Harrison hauled for him, driving one of Ben's trucks. Walter Harrison had hauled for a while, until he was killed in a wreck. One of Albert Essex's boys lived in the faded Harrison house beside the Big Road, down which Time no longer rattled in a lumber wagon, but zoomed in sleek, fast cars.

Sissy Catlett had joined the WACs during the war, and had never come back to the hills. Jake and Matt could not give up the old shack any more than a turtle could give up its shell, Vi Ward had told him, and they still lived in it. Their six sons had all married and extended Coottown for a half mile along Fox Mountain—except it was no longer Coottown. It was Catlett Town, with more TV antennas per capita than any other village in Wilton County.

Cousin Bill and Rosa had died years ago. Doc Ellis and Bessie were dead. Doll Dugan had died in childbirth at fifty-two. John tried to remember others. His mind went blank for a moment, like a screen when the film breaks.

Black and white patterns picked up again. He traced the Big Road, now paved, some of its worst curves eliminated. He remembered the neat bungalows here and there along its course. He recalled the covey of unshaven young men hunkered down beside the road, near where Allen's Shop School had stood. They had looked up from their whittling as his car slowed, thirty minutes before, as he had searched their impassive faces for something familiar. One of them had spat a jet of tobacco juice to one side, then grinned at him. Although his face had not been familiar, the gathering, the familiar Sunday afternoon conference of silence, had stirred briefly the growing unrest deep within John.

In his mind, he traced the Big Road on past Bart Harrison's old place, down Anderson Ridge across the S-curve no longer there, past Greer Harrison's house, across the end of East Ridge, back past Albert Essex's place (Albert, still as straight as the ramrod of his ancient hog rifle), on past Cousin Bill's well-kept place, past Otto Milton's son's poultry farm, past Mount Hope High School, past the graveyard where John William Ward rested beside Bell, his first wife, past the neat little brick church house to where the road slanted into the new highway which ran from Northboro over the mountains into Tennessee—a highway as straight as one of Will Ward's furrows, a highway over which John could cover the distance between Mount Hope Church and Northboro in fifteen minutes; twenty minutes from Stud Branch to Northboro, past Will Ward's grave.

Kelly stood up and shuffled closer to the edge of the embankment. His white shoes stumbled over a stick. John went stiff. Ann minced toward him on her tiptoes, lifting her high heels above the grass. John saw in a flash a scrawny John Ward, skinning a cat in the Juneapple tree. He saw barked knees and stumped toes, turtle-headed with a white-rag collar. He remembered bee stings and cut fingers, stone bruises and sprained ankles.

"Let him alone!" he said shortly to his wife. "He can't get hurt here. Not much, anyway."

Ann stopped, frowning in puzzlement, then moved over to the porch and braced her hand against a post. Alvira Ward watched the boy anxiously. Kelly squatted again and started teasing a bug with the feather.

John looked away from him, over the rolling hillside. The wilderness was coming back. There was almost no sign that Will Ward had ever labored here, except for the decaying house. And even it was not long for this world without repairs. The black shingles were curling up, letting the weather in. A few years, and the walls would cave in, or some tramp would burn it down. Then the trees and shrubbery would own everything again, the way it had been in the beginning. No sign Will Ward had been here except for the locust-shell house.

His eyes wandered to the woods, off to the right, where the cowpens had stood. A white-oak tree caught his attention, a deformed tree. It grew up about six feet, then curved at right angles for ten feet, before the top gradually curved upward again, the trunk about six inches in diameter. John smiled thoughtfully. There was a sign! That had been the sapling Will Ward had bent over to sit on while relieving himself. It would be around for a long time, its broken back proving that Will Ward had once sat there. Cousin Bill had been right, John thought. John Witherspoon Ward's furniture had become coveted antiques. The Lazy Susan the family had grown up around was the proud possession and tourist showpiece of a motel in the western part of the state.

But Will Ward had left other signs, not on the landscape. There were Van's children and grandchildren. Van had died, a respected farmer, during the war. Dan, his bootlegging years behind him, had died and left a large family. Anna had died barren and alone. Tillie and Mal were still living, with children and grandchildren.

After a few wasted years of guitar playing, Lynn had worked his way up from truck driver to superintendent of a huge construction company which built highways. Now he owned his own earth-moving business, and Jack worked with him. Vern and her husband, on factory wages, were sending their children through college. Venna's son was a teacher in a state college, her daughter a college-trained secretary. Ora owned a beauty salon in one of the state's larger cities. Jim, a pilot, was a major in the Air Force. And Tad, the youngest, who had been born after the Wards moved to Carson County—when Vi was forty-two and Will, sixty-six—was now an attorney in Rionel.

That left only John Matlock Ward, who had fled, year after year, all that Stud Branch represented, until it had finally caught up with him today. He thought briefly about that frustrating climb upward to this moment, but his mind persisted in coming back to Will Ward. As he stared down across the fallow hillside, John remembered three lines of a poem he had once written about his father:

> He plowed at six, he said: at sixty-six
> He plowed his own and every farm he could
> And would have tilled the world with hands enough.

John Ward's eyes narrowed thoughtfully when he recalled his father's funeral. The young choir sang "We Shall Gather at the River" so sluggishly he half expected the old man to sit up and raise hell with such a half-assed tempo. Just after nightfall of a Good Friday, Will Ward—stroke-smitten—had followed a phantom plow into the darkling forest until he collided with a tree, and then, with only Vi Ward attending, had died grudgingly, arguing with the sky that the earth was too hard to harrow.

The last time John saw his father alive was when he took Ann by home soon after their marriage as he was being transferred to Lowry Field, near Denver. The old man sat by the cookstove pressing his clasped hands over a calcified nodule of his liver projecting upward past the base of his sternum. The ice in his grey eyes was melting now, seeping over his lids.

"Godamighty, boy!" the old man said, looking Ann up and down, "she ain't no bigger'n a piss ant. She won't last a hour in a cornfield."

That was the time John had mentioned that he should not have left him loading hay that time, with a storm coming up. Will had frowned. "Did you do that?" he asked. "Hell, that ain't no different from what Van and Dan and Lynn done. They all left me, too."

His answer had not satisfied John then, but now, here in front of this relic of a house, John Ward felt suddenly at peace, as though awaking after a long sleep. After they left, in a few minutes, he intended to stop briefly at Mount Hope Church. He would stand beside Will Ward's grave. Perhaps he would tell the silence there, "Here's that high, tall, rawboned boy bout the size of a man, run away from Bussley Bungs day after tomorr. Now where's that pint of pigeon milk churned by the scratch of a duck?"

There would be no answer, of course, but if there could, it would be a boisterous, "What the hell you a-talkin about, you danged idjet?"

Even if Will could meet him there, that was perhaps all they would say, all they would need to say. John had known as much all along, just as he knew there was nothing that needed to be said to his mother, who stood only a few feet away from him.

John Ward looked back quickly at Kelly, squatting close to the edge of the bank, where he still played with the red feather. John felt a resurgence of that irrational fear for his son. Kelly stood up—and suddenly he was gone, heels over head, arms floundering. Ann screamed and stumbled toward the bank on wobbling heels. Alvira Ward hobbled across the yard, her wasted arms reaching. John Ward dashed for the edge of the bank, then stopped. Kelly lay at the bottom of the slope. His arms and legs treaded the air like the limbs of a topsy-turvy turtle, and his mouth was wide in yowling despair.

John hesitated, then thrust out his arm to stop Ann's awkward charge. "Let him alone," he said. "He's not hurt much. Just scared."

"How do you know he didn't break an arm or a leg?" Ann argued, crowding against his arm. "Or crack his head on a rock?"

"Do you think his arms and legs look broken? Do you see any rock?"

He left her and waded through the weeds, down the bank. He bent over John Kelly Ward and took hold of his arm. The boy stopped crying and stared up at him through his tears, the feather still clutched in one fist. Suddenly an echo ricocheted out of time across John's memory, as echoes used to bound back from West Mountain. He tensed and tilted his head to listen. But it did not come again. He remembered it though. It was still there in his brain, leaving a burning track. Kelly started whimpering again.

"Get up off your ass and stop crying," John Matlock Ward

said, so low only the child could hear him. "If you're hurt, that spot won't ever bruise again."

The child hushed and stared up at him, a puzzled frown on his face. John dropped to one knee and carefully disentangled the Jerusalem-oak weeds and briers from about him. "Now get up, boy," he said. "That's all the help you'll get this time."

He turned away and ascended the bank. When he reached his wife and mother and looked back, the boy was climbing the slope after him, and he had forgotten to cry.

About the Author

JOHN FOSTER WEST was born in 1918 near Champion Post Office (Wilkes County) in the foothills of western North Carolina. After the family land was sold, young West, as the son of a tenant farmer, attended eight public schools, graduating from Morganton (N.C.) High School. When not busy at hard labor, his interests ranged from writing to football and track. He edited the Mars Hill Junior College newspaper, played in the first football game he ever saw, and was never defeated in the mile and two-mile run.

After three years in the Air Force he resumed his studies at the University of North Carolina, where he received an A.B. in Journalism in 1947 and an M.A. in English in 1949. While there, he helped found the *Carolina Quarterly*. His stories and poems have appeared in several periodicals, and a book of his poems was published in 1951. Mr. West taught English and creative writing at Elon College (N.C.) from 1949 to 1958, and since at Old Dominion College, Norfolk, Virginia, where he resides with his wife and three children.